For Bruce, Lily and Izzy
Thank you for humouring my many obsessions and providing my life
with an endless stream of joy and drama.

Echoes of the Past

Lyndsey Jeminson

Life by Charlotte Brontë

Life, believe, is not a dream
So dark as sages say;
Oft a little morning rain
Foretells a pleasant day.
Sometimes there are clouds of gloom,
But these are transient all;
If the shower will make the roses bloom,
O why lament its fall?
Rapidly, merrily,
Life's sunny hours flit by,
Gratefully, cheerily
Enjoy them as they fly!
What though Death at times steps in,
And calls our Best away?
What though sorrow seems to win,
O'er hope, a heavy sway?
Yet Hope again elastic springs,
Unconquered, though she fell;
Still buoyant are her golden wings,
Still strong to bear us well.
Manfully, fearlessly,
The day of trial bear,
For gloriously, victoriously,
Can courage quell despair!

Prologue

On the eve of her seventy-fifth birthday, Eva studied her reflection in the gilded mirror sitting atop her Queen Anne dressing table. She was a striking looking woman; time had been kind to her in that respect. Her silver hair was as thick and luxuriant as the day she had married. The lines on her face told a story; of love and wild abandon, of happiness and hope, and of a deeply heart-breaking tragedy that had come bitterly close to ruining her.

She smiled with a sadness in her heart for the love she had lost, and a glint in her eye for a future she could never have anticipated. She thought back to the naive young girl she had been, swept up in a romance so intense she could never have imagined anything hindering it. As she ran the brush through her hair, she remembered fondly the elegant mother-of-pearl hair comb she'd worn on her wedding day. An heirloom from her great-grandmother, the comb had been passed down through the generations. Now it was coming back, full circle, bringing with it a new sense of joy.

Lottie 2019

'Lottie, are you even listening to me?'

Rosie's words echoed in the depths of my mind, but my hearing had been engulfed by my other senses. Goosebumps danced on my skin as I locked eyes with the dark-haired beauty perched on a high stool at the bar. Dressed in denim and a leather jacket, his hair curled softly at the ends, skimming his collar. His eyes were cavernous, and I was stirred by his presence. He was definitely not my usual type. There was no question he was good looking in the traditional sense but that wasn't what had captivated my attention. There was an explicit feeling of intimacy as our eyes foraged for the familiar, and our stare held for several long seconds before he broke contact, a frown appearing on his face as he looked away quickly.

'What are you looking at?' Rosie asked as she turned her head to try and locate the reason for my sudden distraction. My chest burned; a rosy glow flushed my neck, and the warm blush spread to my cheeks. Embarrassed at being caught gawking, I shook my head to try and dismiss my discomfort.

'Nothing, just that guy at the bar. He kinda seems familiar.'

'Ooh, Mr Dark and Broody?' Rosie tilted her head to one side taking him in, not at all concerned about hiding the fact that she was blatantly staring at the guy. 'He's definitely not someone you'd forget in a hurry, although, he's not your usual nerdy type.'

'Geez Rose, make it obvious we're talking about him why don't you?' I nudged her arm, prompting her to turn back around.

'Okay,' Rosie laughed, 'but you literally haven't taken your eyes off him!'

Rosie tried to steer me back to the conversation with talk about her birthday, but my eyes were fervently drawn back towards the bar.

'Lots! What's with you tonight? I can see you watching him.' Rosie screwed her face up, obviously intrigued by a side of me she hadn't seen before. 'I mean, as much as it kind of excites me a little bit to see you fawning over a real flesh and blood guy instead of some nineteenth century fictional hero, tonight's supposed to be all about me!' Rosie dismissed the guy and clapped her hands excitedly.

She was like a little girl sometimes, the way she got overexcited about everything. I often wondered how we were so close; we were the literal definition of opposites attracting. We'd met on the first day of kindergarten. My reserved nature had led me happily to the quiet corner to look at picture books, but Rosie's effervescence bubbled over, infecting everyone in her presence, and she'd persuaded me to join in with her dress up game. Rosie had been fiercely loyal from that day on.

She loved to dance and perform on stage, whereas even the idea of people watching me was enough to bring me out in hives. As a teenager I spent most of my time in the ocean or laid on the beach with a book. Open water swimming at a national level kept me busy for several years; now it was just something I did without thinking, the foundation of my daily routine.

'So, your birthday finally arrived Rose. Are you feeling twenty-two?' I asked her, trying to focus our attention back to the birthday celebrations and away from my newfound muse. Rosie laughed at my not-so-subtle attempt to bring her idol, Taylor Swift into the conversation.

'It feels so old, but I swear we're still twelve years old,' Rosie groaned. 'Can you believe we're about to graduate?'

'I know, scary hey? I still have no idea what I'm doing with my life.'

I had an undergrad degree in English Literature and was about to graduate with a Master of Teaching but had serious doubts about my ability to teach a class of fifteen-year-olds. I longed to be as prolific a writer as some of the greats I'd studied, but I'd opted for security and chosen teaching, a reputable career with stability. My greatest literary loves were the Brontë Sisters, and I would love to study them further, but I figured I needed to jump into the twenty-first century at some point.

'You're still gonna travel after graduation though, right?' Rosie asked.

'Yeah, definitely. Still not sure where though, I don't think Contiki specialise in nineteenth century literary tours of the UK.' I grinned at Rosie's dramatic eye roll.

'The sad thing is, you're not even joking,' Rosie shook her head in disbelief.

My eyes began to drift back towards the bar and Rosie slapped my hand to deflect my attention, but not before I caught his eyes on me again. I turned back to Rosie, once again feeling sheepish for being caught.

Her face was incredulous.

'I actually can't think of a time when you've shown even the slightest interest in a guy before,' Rosie laughed.

She was right, I was never interested in the guys at school. I even took my brother's best friend to my end of school ball. They'd been mates for years and Ben was like another brother. As far as adult relationships went, I'd made a huge mistake with a guy a couple of years ago and I'd sworn off relationships ever since.

'I know. I think the whole Josh incident put me off for life. I think I'll just become an epic writer and live alone with my cats in a shack on the beach.'

A waitress interrupted us with our food, and I felt grateful for the temporary pause in our conversation. As she put the plates in front of us, Rosie downed her vodka and soda and held up her glass.

'Can we get two more please?' she asked, smiling at the waitress.

'Sure, I'll be right back.'

I used Rosie's distraction to sneak another glance in the direction of the bar, but my stomach dropped when I realised he'd gone. I internally berated myself for acting so pitiful over a guy I'd never met. My reaction was extreme, and I struggled to make sense of it. Rosie caught my bewildered expression and was speechless for the first time in her life.

'Don't look at me like that,' I whispered. 'I don't know what's with me tonight! I'm behaving like a certain thirteen-year-old at a Justin Bieber concert!' Rosie rolled her eyes in horror.

'Well, maybe not quite that bad,' I laughed at the look of shame on Rosie's face, remembering the days when nothing and no one could come between her and her love of Justin. We were still laughing when the next round of drinks arrived, and the intensity of my fixation was tempered.

As I scraped the last spoonful of pasta sauce from my bowl, Rosie surprised me with the direction of her question.

'Could you imagine having a kid now? At our age I mean.'

I gulped my drink too fast, and the fizz bubbled from my nose. Rosie snorted at my reaction.

'I'm not pregnant or anything!' Rosie quickly confirmed.

'Oh! That didn't even enter my head. I thought you were talking about me!' I was confused at just where this conversation was going.

'You? Where would you get that idea from? I'm pretty sure you took human bio at some point in school and therefore would have an idea where babies come from!'

My mind flashed back to Dark and Broody at the bar and my cheeks inflamed. Rosie laughed when she figured out where my mind had gone.

'Easy tiger, I wasn't talking about your new love interest, I was just thinking about my mum. She was our age when I started Kindy. It gives me a whole new level of respect for her. I can't imagine having a kid now and not screwing it up, but she was amazing. I mean look how fantastic I turned out!'

I shook my head and laughed at Rosie's self-assured arrogance, but I admit, I was pretty much in awe of Gina too. She'd been a great mum to Rosie, much the same as my own mum had to me, but there was a stark contrast in their ages. My mum was over forty when I was born so there's nearly twenty-five years between her and Gina. My mum was now in her mid-sixties, taking things easy but Gina had embarked on a whole new life once Rosie graduated high school becoming an emergency foster carer.

'I know what you mean, I wouldn't have a clue where to start with a kid. I wouldn't mind getting down and dirty with some leather and denim though,' I teased.

It was Rosie's turn to choke on her drink, shocked by my salacious comment.

'Who are you and what have you done with my friend?'

'I'm only kidding, I just wanted to see your face!'

But I wasn't sure I was joking. The guy had definitely had an impact on me. I'd never had such a visceral reaction to a guy like that before. My thoughts drifted back to his eyes, the way he seemed to penetrate my core. My stomach fluttered at the fantasy of something happening between us.

We left the bar in high spirits and made our way to the club to meet Rosie's friends. Most of them were in Rosie's Theatre Studies course and were all a bit wild. I'd been out with them a few times, but Rosie knew not to invite me too often because she knew I preferred less rowdy occasions. There was no way she would allow me to miss her birthday celebrations though, and they were a good crowd to hang out with in small doses.

Waiting in line outside the club, Rosie began pondering over the guy in the bar and how she could hook me up with him.

'Rosie, stop, I don't need you to find guys for me.' I shocked myself with the force behind my words, but the things he'd made me feel from across the bar had thrown me, and I needed to unpack that in my own head first. I could tell she was upset by my outburst, and she quickly dropped the subject and turned her attention to her phone, messaging her friends to see if they were inside yet.

As we approached the front of the line, I regretted my harsh tone and felt guilty for the tension between us.

'Hey, I'm sorry Rose,' I told her, not wanting to spoil her birthday. 'He just threw me that's all, you know what I'm like when I'm not in control.'

'Sure,' Rosie agreed, 'I'm sorry too.' She leaned in for a quick hug to let me know there were no hard feelings. 'But remember who your best friend is when you eventually lose control with him.'

I laughed at her tenacity, gently pushing her towards the doorman asking for our ID's.

Rosie soon found her friends inside and quickly introduced me to the few I hadn't met. Rosie's good friend Oli got the party started, as always, ordering a round of shots for everyone. Several shots later and I was happily dancing with Oli and a couple of girls when Rosie grabbed my arm and pulled me away.

'Lottie, check your phone,' Rosie shouted in my ear. I frowned at her and pulled my phone from my purse. 'I got a message from your mum, she's been trying to call you,' Rosie explained. Eighteen missed calls from my mum. Shit. My heart raced and I immediately began to sober up.

'I'm just gonna go outside and call,' I yelled over the noise of the music.

'I'll come with you.'

'No, you stay with your friends. It's probably nothing, I'll let you know.'

I stumbled out of the club onto the bustling street. The air outside was warm for early spring but there was a cool breeze drifting from the ocean. I could barely get my thumbs to work scrolling through my phone for my mum's number.

'Oh Lottie!' Mum cried answering on the first ring.

'Mum, what's wrong?'

Between the sobs, I only managed to pick up odd words, but I obtained enough information to plan my next move. I dialled another number from my contacts.

'Lottie?' I breathed a sigh of relief when he answered.

'Oh Ben, thank God. Where are you?'

'I'm at The Bank with some of the guys. Tom was supposed to be meeting us here, but I can't get hold of him. What's wrong?' Ben replied.

'He's been in an accident Ben. I need to get to the hospital right now.' Tears flooded my cheeks as my throat constricted and I trapped a sob.

'Fuck. Where are you? I'll come and get you.'

'Thanks Ben. I'm on the strip.' I looked around and noticed I'd been walking aimlessly while I'd been talking. 'I'm outside the Mexican.'

I could hear Ben talking in the background, saying something to his friends. 'Stay right there Lots, I'm on my way.'

Luckily, he wasn't too far away. In fact, he was at the same bar Rosie and I were at earlier. I allowed my mind to drift back to the guy from earlier in an effort to distract myself from the pain that lay in waiting.

Dad. Tom. Accident. Bad. Those were the words I'd heard Mum say, followed by the name of the local hospital. I looked up to see Ben's car pull up at the kerb and a guy jumped out of the passenger seat, holding the door open for me. Fuck. It was him, the guy from the bar. Shock and concern emanated from his face simultaneously as he appeared to put two and two together and realised who I was. I was confused as to why he was with Ben, I thought I knew all their friends. Maybe that was why he seemed so familiar, but I'm sure I'd have remembered if I'd met him before. I blinked my thoughts away, bringing me back to the present.

I slid into the seat, and he closed the door behind me, climbing into the back behind us. Ben reached out to me and gave my hand a squeeze as I frowned and nodded towards the back seat, a thousand unspoken questions in my eyes.

'Oh, this is Beau, he's good mates with Tom. He was with us when you called. Beau, this is Lottie.' Ben introduced us as he put the car in gear and sped off towards the hospital.

The atmosphere in the car was tense; I was worried about what scenario I was about to be faced with, all while feeling the intensity of meeting Beau in the flesh. As Ben concentrated on driving, Beau's eyes seared the back of my head.

Ben dropped me off outside the emergency department and told Beau to go with me.

'I'll come and find you as soon as I've parked the car,' Ben shouted through the window.

I shivered; my flimsy top not suited to the drop in temperature. Beau took off his leather jacket and laid it gently round my shoulders. The weight and scent brought me a strange sense of comfort. I ducked under his arm as he held the door open for me, and my eyes quickly scanned the room. There was no sign of Mum, so I gave my name to a man at the desk. I explained the situation, and the moment I told him my dad and brother's names, his face told me everything I needed to know. I fought to keep my composure. The nurse told us to take a seat and the faint brush of Beau's fingers on the small of my back gently guided me to a nearby chair. The outside door opened shortly after and Ben rushed in, his eyes searching frantically. Beau waved him over and he took a seat next to me, his arm instinctively resting around my shoulders to bring whatever comfort he could to his best friend's sister. Ben and I had always been close but never anything more than friends. We had a brief flirtation at my school ball, but it ended up feeling too weird for both of us.

'Lottie?' A nurse appeared in front of us. I was suddenly alert and on my feet.

'Come on love, your mum's waiting for you.' She spoke in that voice typically reserved for toddlers and relatives of the dead, soft but cajoling.

The two guys followed along behind us, both mute as I fired questions at the nurse trying to find out what had happened.

'Let's just get you to your mum and I'll explain everything.'

Before the four of us even reached the relatives room, I could hear Mum wailing. I stopped dead in my tracks and my hand instinctively searched out Ben for support. But it was Beau who reached out first and squeezed my fingers, drawing me towards him.

'We'll be right here. You go and see your mum,' he whispered softly in my ear, filling me with a resolve to follow the nurse inside. When he released me, I kept my head down, not daring to look at him, conscious of spending such an intimate moment with a complete stranger.

Inside the room, the full reality of the situation hit me head on. My mother, Anna; the matriarch, the foundation of our family, the rock that had given us all strength for so many years had been reduced to a ravaged shadow. Her arms hung limp by her sides as her head tipped back against the wall. The piercing mewl emanating from somewhere deep within her was like that of a distressed cat.

'Mum?' I spoke warily, not really wanting to hear what she had to say, but knowing it was inevitable. 'Tell me.'

It took Mum a moment to register that I was there, and when she did, she simply closed her eyes and slid down the wall, dropping her head into her hands, her shoulders heaving with the pain.

My eyes quickly darted to the nurse.

'They couldn't save them love.' Her voice was kind and gentle. 'I'm so sorry, they didn't make it.'

My stomach lurched and the vodka from the abandoned birthday celebrations was forcefully expelled, the nurse catching the remnants with a bowl. She handed me some paper towel to clean up my face and pulled up a chair for me while she set about cleaning the floor. Once she was done, she opened the door and motioned for the two guys to come inside.

Ben and Beau hovered in the doorway, watching the scene play out before them, a look of alarm on their faces.

They were ignorant of the severity of the situation and my eyes filled with tears at the thought of telling them. I managed to catch a breath as I was saved from that particularly horrifying task by the nurse, who addressed them herself.

'Lottie's dad and brother were involved in a road traffic accident this evening. Unfortunately, it's the worst possible outcome. Tom was killed on impact. His father suffered a heart attack and passed away a short time after arriving here. I'm so very sorry.' She patted Ben's arm as she left the room to allow us to try and grasp the situation together.

Ben stared at her in horror. I watched as he processed the news. Tom, his best friend, was dead. Beau's eyes filled with tears as his hand firmly gripped Ben's shoulder, and Ben turned to see his own horror mirrored on my face. He sank to his knees in front of me, and taking my hands in his, he rested his forehead against mine, our tears merging as they flowed freely down our cheeks.

Stifled by the closeness, the cloying atmosphere in the tiny room overwhelmed me. I pushed Ben away and bolted from the room, running for the closest exit. My lungs struggled with each breath until I reached the main doors and gulped the air outside. In that moment of quiet, I reflected on the last hour and knew that my entire life had changed forever.

Eva 1962

Eva was excited for her first meeting. She'd noticed the typed flyer pinned to the notice board in the church hall and couldn't wait to be a part of the group. Her love of the Brontë Sisters ran deep. Whether it was her proximity to their lives, growing up in the same village the three young writers had called home, or just her passion for books in general, she wasn't sure exactly where it had stemmed from, certainly not from her parents. As much as they had indulged her love of reading, they certainly hadn't shared her interest. She loved them both of course, but their views were conservative, Victorian even. Their ideas and values were poles apart. Eva grabbed life with both hands, she was a romantic with a passion for change. She had big ideas and a vision for life that went way beyond the four walls of her parents' dreary home. Their frugal ways meant Eva had always been dressed in homemade clothes and her life experiences were limited. Reading was an acceptable pastime and Eva had grown to realise her parents' reason for indulging her passion for books, especially classic literature, was to keep her under their control and away from all the popular culture other young people were enjoying.

Eva lived vicariously through her books, experiencing life in the only way she knew how. As much as Eva loved the Brontës novels, it was their poetry that truly captivated her, and she couldn't wait to talk about them in length with likeminded people. Applying the finishing touches to her outfit, she tightened the belt around her lemon-coloured dress, accentuating her tiny waist. Red pumps finished off her sunny look and gave her a spring in her step. Skipping down the narrow staircase, her hands trailing the gold art deco patterned walls that failed to disguise the bumpy walls of the early Victorian terrace, Eva's face shined with a light that emanated from within her. She always looked for the best in people and situations; that's how she'd managed to stay positive against the adversity of life with her joyless parents.

Making her way through the back lane towards the church hall where the group was meeting, she darted between the potholes, her ponytail swinging behind her. The spring weather had been unusually balmy for that time of year and the midday sun scorched her pale skin. Rounding the corner at the end of the lane, she arrived at the church hall and let herself in through the back door. A flutter in her belly caused her to stop and collect her thoughts. She breathed deeply. Polished wood and a trace of damp assaulted her senses. In the far corner there was a table set up with tea and coffee. A large steel urn was heating water, a floral-patterned sugar bowl with mismatched teacups were set out neatly in a row. Eva wasn't sure how many people would be attending but she was slightly disappointed there seemed to be no one else here. A door opened and an older lady shuffled in, her gnarled hand clutching a walking stick. She smiled at Eva and eagerly introduced herself.

'Hello love, I'm Edna. Are you here for the Brontë group?'

'Yes, I am. I'm Eva. Are there many coming do you know?'

'I wasn't sure if anyone would turn up to be honest with you. It might just be you and me,' Edna chuckled.' Let's grab a cuppa, shall we? I'll put some biscuits out.'

Eva moved towards the table in the corner and began to pour herself a cup of instant coffee. It wasn't often she got to drink coffee; her parents refused to buy it, preferring instead a pot of Yorkshire Tea. She added long-life milk and two sugars to reduce the bitterness and stepped back to allow Edna to arrange a plate of Grandma Wilds biscuits.

'Would you like me to pour you a tea or coffee Edna?' Eva asked politely.

'That'd be lovely. A nice cup of tea thanks love. Milk, one sugar.'

As Eva busied herself at the table, Edna began to move a few chairs into a circle. The door to the hall opened and a few more people joined them. An elderly gentleman led the charge. He was an eccentric looking fellow, wearing a tweed jacket and matching cap paired with mustard-coloured corduroys. An old-fashioned pocket watch finished the outfit, and a monocle hung on a silver chain around his neck. The man tipped his hat towards Eva and introduced himself as Bert. Behind him, a timid lady smiled shyly. She shuffled quickly towards the beverage table and made herself busy.

Eva stepped away from the table with the two cups, and as she did so she came face to face with the final arrival. Eva's butterflies returned and she felt a rush of excitement climb her neck and explode like fireworks on her cheeks. Embarrassed by her outward appreciation of the intriguing man stood before her, she simply nodded and walked quickly towards the circle of chairs, seating herself next to Edna. Eva couldn't help but steal a glance at the young man, the only member of the group even remotely close to her age group. She wasn't sure she could handle herself in close proximity. She'd had no experience with boys and had certainly not felt anything physical before.

Eva watched as the timid lady, who would later introduce herself as Emily, handed the young man a cup and set about adding milk to her own. The two walked over to the circle, the man immediately making a beeline for the empty seat next to Eva. He smiled at everyone and introduced himself as Charles. Edna began the meeting with a little speech about her love of the Brontës and her hopes for the group.

'I just want to meet people who love their work, who still get excited by reading it. And I'm very happy we have some young people here too. I often feel the classics are becoming forgotten and I think it's a real shame. Does anyone have any thoughts on how they'd like to proceed?' she asked, not waiting for a reply. 'I was thinking maybe we could concentrate on one particular novel or poem each meeting. Maybe all think of some questions we'd like to ask of the others? How does that sound?'

Murmurs of approval circulated the group and Edna continued.

'So today then, why don't we each say our favourite work and a little bit about why, and what it is that brought us here today. Who wants to go first?' she asked excitedly.

Charles immediately raised his hand and began talking.

'I'm a schoolteacher so I know how reluctant people are to go first,' he explained. 'Right then, my favourite is by Anne. The Tennant of Wildfell Hall was the first of the Brontës books I read and has always remained my favourite. I have a penchant for tenacious women and Helen Graham was probably my first love.'

Eva was startled by the words coming from Charles's mouth and found herself hanging on his every word as he talked ardently about women's rights and how his favourite book opened his eyes to the multitude of injustices in the world. Eva wasn't the only one affected by his speech; Charles managed to render them all silent as he drew to a close. Worried he'd gone too far, he appeared to look to Eva for reassurance. She stumbled over her words, barely managing to respond in broken sentence.

'I … well…gosh. That was…that was so passionate,' Eva blushed.

Bert cleared his throat and began to discuss his favourite book, followed by Emily and Edna. Eva was up last and unlike the others discussing The Professor, Jane Eyre and Wuthering Heights, she talked about her favourite poem.

'The poem Life by Charlotte Brontë is like a bible to me. It has taught me so much about how to live life to the fullest and absorb everything. My parents are quite old fashioned in their outlook and they often don't understand me, but this poem has allowed me not to feel disenchantment with my life but to embrace my own passions. The only aspiration they have for me is to marry a sensible man with a secure job, and I've taught myself to understand their reasons but to also challenge them. I will only marry for love and my husband will be a man of integrity, someone who will share my passions and dreams regardless of his background or how much money he makes.' Eva's impassioned speech received a fervent round of applause from Charles.

'I feel embarrassed to admit I haven't actually read any of their poetry, but I will make sure I do. It sounds like a wonderful poem Eva. Do you have a copy I could perhaps borrow?' Charles asked.

Eva reached in her bag and pulled out her dog-eared anthology, handing it to Charles.

'Thank you, I promise to take good care of it.'

Eva smiled at him, heat flaring in her throat. After the group agreed on the agenda for the next meeting, to read The Tenant of Wildfell Hall and discuss its merits and faults, the eclectic bunch washed their cups and returned them to the table. After saying goodbye to them all, Eva made her way out of the back of the hall the way she'd come in, and out into the lane. With a smile she raised her head towards the sky and let the sunshine beat down on her face. Breaking her reverie, a familiar voice called her name.

'Eva!'

She turned to see Charles rushing through the door and into the lane after her. He paused, unsure of what to say next.

'Is everything okay?' Eva asked, playing dumb to his obvious advances. The chemistry between them in the meeting had been difficult to miss; their close proximity in the hall had felt like a furnace and she wondered if the others could feel it too.

'Yes, I … I wondered if you'd like to go for a walk. Or maybe get an ice cream? It's a nice day for it.'

'I'd like that.' Eva smiled at his shyness, a stark contrast to the confidence he'd portrayed in the meeting.

Charles led Eva down the lane and out into the park beyond. Eva loved this time of year; the flower beds were awash with colour, bees buzzing around them in a frenzy. Walking slowly down the path towards the ice-cream van's regular spot, Eva and Charles chatted genially. Although there was a little under four years between them, and Charles was a high school teacher, they found they were evenly matched on many levels. They had much in common, from their backgrounds to their interests. Both came from strict homes where nothing was fun or challenging. There were no discussions or debates about life, and no day trips to the seaside or picnics in the woods. Life was quiet and still for both Charles and Eva, and both were yearning for more.

'So, what job do you do now Eva?' Charles asked.

'I'm waitressing at the cafe at the top of Main Street. It's a job but I can't say it inspires me. There must be more than this.' Eva said with an undertone of melancholy.

Charles smiled at her. 'What is it that would inspire you, Eva?'

Eva's face lit up and she pondered over his question for a moment.

'I want to live,' she said with fervour. 'I have no care for finances or material things. I want to write poetry, ride a bicycle in the rain, visit the seaside and stuff my face with candy floss. I want to experience real love; the kind that is full of passion and all consuming.' Eva stopped and realised what she'd said to this complete stranger. 'I'm sorry, I got a little carried away.' The heat rose from her chest and coloured her face with the palest pink hue. 'I just don't want to be my mother; stuck in a loveless marriage cooking the same miserable food day in and day out, and ironing shirts for a man with no soul.'

Charles stopped walking and reached out for Eva's elbow, gently turning her to face him.

'Don't ever apologise for sharing your thoughts and feelings Eva. I want to get to know you, not whom your parents or anyone else wants you to be.' Charles made her feel something she'd never experienced before; a feeling of worth, that she had something important to say. He listened intently to everything she was saying, and by the time they reached the ice-cream van, she felt quite sure she was in love with him.

She was kidding herself, of course. Who was she to know what love was? This was her first experience with a man, let alone one who paid attention to the details. A man who was interested in her thoughts and opinions, not just her face and her homemaking skills. The thought of spending more time with Charles filled her with anticipation.

'What would you like Eva?'

'Can I have a 99 please?' she asked politely.

'Of course,' he replied. 'Two 99's please,' he said to the ice-cream man.

Charles handed a cone to Eva and gently placed his free hand at the small of her back, leading her towards a bench. Eva shivered, even though the sun cast a warmth over them both.

Eva lapped up her ice cream with pure delight. Treats like this weren't something she had often. Even though she was now working, her money wasn't her own. She was made to hand her pay packet over to her mother every Friday and her mother would hand her a small amount back for pocket money. She hated how she was made to feel like a child.

Charles watched on, captivated by the pleasure on Eva's face, then reached out and wiped the excess ice-cream from the end of her nose. Eva was mortified and Charles chuckled at her embarrassment.

'Don't be embarrassed Eva, I think you're wonderful.' Although she could feel her skin begin to glow once again, Eva was buoyed by Charles's words.

Charles and Eva finished their ice-creams in comfortable silence. Eva began to worry that their day was coming to an end, and she wouldn't see him until the next Bronte meeting.

'What are you doing tomorrow?' Charles asked as they meandered back up the path towards the church hall.

'Nothing special,' Eva said, hopeful that her plans were about to change.

'Let's go to the seaside. We'll catch the train, eat fish and chips on the beach and stuff our faces with candy floss,' Charles said, mimicking Eva's earlier wishes.

Eva laughed. 'Can we really?'

'Of course, we can do anything we like,' Charles said with absolute surety.

'I would have to ask my mother,' Eva frowned, feeling once again like a little girl.

'Then let's go ask her now.'

Eva was shocked at his persistence but was so desperate to go, she had no mind to disagree.

Eva's eagerness to get home was endearing to Charles. She was vivacious yet innocent, spirited with a hint of naivety. Charles thought her an enigma. One he truly wanted to know better.

Letting them both through the gate into the tiny back yard, Eva looked up to see her mother in the kitchen window. Eva waved brightly but her mother only returned a frown.

She rolled her eyes as she climbed the stone steps to the back door, hesitating briefly before pushing the door open.

Peeking her head around the door she said, 'Mother, I have someone I'd like you to meet.' She invited Charles to come inside and made formal introductions.

'It's very nice to meet you Mrs…oh, I apologise, I don't even know your last name.' Charles blushed and looked at Eva for confirmation.

'Sorry Charles, it's Thompson. My mother is Winifred Thompson.' Charles reached out a hand and offered it to Winifred who took it and smiled. Eva hadn't seen her mother smile often and wondered if she was thinking Charles might be marriage material.

'Sit down Charles, would you like some tea?' Eva's mother was practically gushing over him, not in the slightest way portraying the miserable and sour woman Eva had described.

While Eva's mother made tea, Charles and Eva sat down at the table in the tiny kitchen, Charles smiling at Eva to try and put her at ease.

Winifred brought out the best china teapot with matching cups and saucers, setting them down on the lace tablecloth. She opened a packet of digestive biscuits and arranged a few on a plate, offering them to Charles. Taking one, he balanced it on his saucer and took a sip of the tea Eva had poured him.

Eva was beguiled by his easy nature and the way he had naturally won over her mother.

'So, Charles, what do you do for a living?' Eva rolled her eyes, internally berating her mother's question, quite sure she was weighing up if he was good enough for her.

'I'm a schoolteacher at the Boys Grammar School,' Charles told her. Winifred clapped her hands and Eva was bewildered by her mother's strange behaviour.

'That's wonderful, and a very reputable career. What is it that you teach?' Winifred asked.

'English Literature,' Charles replied. He began to sense Eva's uneasiness and decided not to elaborate.

'Mrs Thompson, I'd like to take Eva to the seaside tomorrow. We'll take the train and I'll have her home before dark. Would that be okay with you?' Charles kept it very formal because although Mrs Thompson seemed quite friendly to him, he trusted Eva's own perspective and he didn't want to overstep, giving her reason to throw a spanner in the works. Winifred looked at Eva with a questioning frown. She wondered just how long she had known this young man.

'Yes, I think that will be acceptable Charles. Eva could make up a picnic to take.'

'Oh no, that won't be necessary, we'll have fish and chips for lunch.' Charles wanted to treat Eva not have her slaving away in the kitchen for him. He wanted to take her out, to show her a fun time, away from her drab existence.

'Very well then,' Winifred agreed, a little irked by his rebuke.

'Well, thank you for the tea Mrs Thompson,' Charles said politely. And to Eva he said, 'I'll pick you up tomorrow morning at eight.'

Eva nodded gratefully and showed Charles to the door.

Lottie 2019

The heat was stifling for early spring. My feet shifted uncomfortably, and my jaw clenched until my muscles hurt. Consumed by the need to breathe, I clawed at my throat desperate for the air to surge my lungs. Pressure built inside my head, and I needed a release. Surrounded by hordes of people, I'd never felt so alone. My skin was clammy, the little breath I managed to inhale was shallow and I could feel the colour drain from my face. The noise suddenly left me in deafening silence and my vision turned black.

I'm jolted from my anxiety by a loud bang. Terror blankets me as my lungs still scramble for air. The noise is deafening. I'm no longer sure of where I am; a sense of pain still surrounds me but not in the same way. This is physical. Liquid is trickling down my leg, and as I move my hand to touch it, a sharp pain shoots down my arm. The pain consumes me, and I feel my body begin to shiver and shake. I have no control over my body. I know instinctively that I need to move but that seems beyond my capability. I half open my eyes but all I can see are flashing lights, so I quickly close them again. The noise fades away and I can hear a familiar sound. A muted sniffle, and then,

'Mama.'

It's a word I recognise, and it calms my mind instantly. I focus on that one word until the other feelings begin to fade.

I came to with a jolt. My mum's face hovered above me; the grief clearly visible. She was so close I could count the lines around her eyes. I hadn't realised how much she'd aged of late, or had that just crept up over the past week? There were dark circles under her eyes, the life in them all but gone. Her skin was grey, her lips blending into the ashen hue. We'd barely spoken all week, only to confirm arrangements. Neither one of us had mentioned the accident, nor had we mentioned Dad or Tom by name.

Everyone around us began to move slowly towards the doors of the crematorium, leaving us alone.

'Mum? What happened?' I asked, noticing I was on the floor, and my elbow was grazed. Mum looked dazed, like she wasn't quite sure herself what had happened.

'Why am I on the floor?' I glared at Mum as I pushed myself up, not sure whether I was embarrassed or angry.

'I think you fainted; it was probably the heat. Come on, let's get you up.' Mum held out her hand to me, looking around, seemingly more concerned about who was watching.

'You go on inside Mum, I'll be there in a minute.' I needed a minute to gather my thoughts. I distinctly remembered blood trickling down my leg, and an excruciating pain in my arm. But on examination, there was no blood, just the small graze on my elbow. My heart pounded heavily, and my chest constricted as I watched her disappear into the crowd.

Standing alone, a sense of unease built up inside. I wasn't sure how I could face the hordes of people that had come to pay their last respects and I was beginning to regret my hasty decision to send Mum away.

'Hey, Lots.' I turned to see Rosie make her way towards me and I breathed a sigh of relief. I could feel the tension lift, relieved that Rosie wasn't acting weird towards me. As Rosie approached, she looked around, her eyebrows raised in suspicion.

'I've never seen so many people, have they just come for the free food afterwards?'

Laughter bubbled up inside me. I could always count on Rosie to lighten the mood, but a sudden onset of guilt sobered me up quickly.

'Hey, you are allowed to laugh you know,' Rosie said, pulling me in for a hug.

I smiled at my best friend, thankful that she was here with me. I'd only seen her once since the night of her birthday; she'd been consumed with guilt that she hadn't followed up with me that night after I'd left the club and I'd had to go through the most difficult time of my life without her.

As the crowd died down and the last stragglers were dragging their feet, Rosie linked her arm through mine and guided me towards the door. My hands trembled as I reached up to wipe away a stray tear. It seemed only seconds ago I'd been laughing, but the stark reality of the situation had thrown its heavy cloud over me once again and the next hour of my life disappeared into a vast emptiness.

As Rosie led me back outside after the service, I felt numb. It was like someone had flipped a switch and turned me off. I knew the crematorium was full, but I couldn't remember a single face in the crowd.

The key struggled in the lock as though it knew how I was feeling. It was a door I didn't want to open. The one that led us into the rest of our lives. A life where Mum and I were our only family, the two of us alone in the world with only each other to count on. I watched silently as Mum disappeared into her bedroom without a word. The door closed behind her, and I realised I was wrong; I had no one. For the first time in my life, I was truly alone. All those times growing up wishing my parents would just leave me alone came rushing back to haunt me. I blamed myself; this was all my fault. My wish had been granted. The guilt was too much to think about. My knees buckled and a dark void rose up to swallow me.

Breaking through the darkness, I feel a sense of panic. I'm not sure where I am but my senses are heightened, and I can taste fear. I try to stand up, but something seems to be pushing me back. There's a gentle hum coming from behind me. A lullaby plays softly; a calming antidote to the chaos surrounding me. I tell myself to go with it and let the gentle sound lull me back to sleep. But sleep doesn't come.

'Open the fucking door bitch.'

'Lottie!' I could hear Mum's voice shouting at me. I forced my eyes open to see her hovering over me again. My heart pounded in my chest and my limbs trembled uncontrollably.

'Mum?'

There was no response.

'Mum? What happened?' I repeated.

Her face was vacant as she stared down at me. The air chilled around us and the hairs on my arms bristled. My head hurt and the terror I felt just a few moments ago was still real. She remained deadpan.

'Mum!' I yelled.

'You were calling out, were you dreaming?' Her words were slurred.

'It felt so real.' I told her about the lullaby. I couldn't place it but I knew it from somewhere.

Mum stiffened. 'It was just a dream Lottie. Forget about it. And get up off the floor.' She dismissed me with her clipped tone and retreated to her room leaving me sat on the cold tile. I watched her go, my eyes locked on her bedroom door. I could hear her sniffling as I tried to process what had happened. Twice now I'd blacked out, and each time my subconscious mind had taken me to the same place. A place so tangible the fear palpated my body, and my anxiety intensified with my mum's harsh reaction.

I woke early the next morning, my mind bleary from a dreamful sleep. A pair of emerald green eyes, vibrant yet sorrowful, had seared through me as though imploring me to remember. They were familiar yet I couldn't place them. The image faded as I began to wake fully, and I dragged myself out of bed feeling lethargic and in need of comfort. I crept out of my room and gently opened Tom's bedroom door. Standing in the doorway I breathed in Tom's scent as I looked around the room at all his football trophies and posters on his walls. He'd moved out the previous year, but Mum couldn't bring herself to clear his room. His smell lingered and it brought me the solace I craved. I just wanted to snuggle under his covers and pretend he was at home in the flat he'd shared with Ben, but when I reached to pull the blanket back, I realised Mum was asleep in his bed. I tried to creep back out, but she woke up startled.

'Tom?' she asked hopefully, her voice so choked that it all but broke my heart.

'No Mum, it's me, Lottie.' I walked over to the bed and sat down.

Mum's expression shifted; a dark cloud heavy in her eyes. I witnessed the exact moment that she remembered Tom was gone. I knew how she felt, it was something I experienced every morning. The first few seconds everything is normal, then the memory comes, and the grieving process starts all over again.

'Have you been in here all night Mum?' I asked her.

She shook her head, 'I couldn't sleep. I can still feel him in here.'

We were both wary of each other, neither sure of what to say so I went with changing the subject.

'Do you want some coffee?'

She gave a brief nod, her eyes not once meeting mine. I made coffee and toast for both of us, and she quietly slipped into the kitchen and took hers back to her bedroom without saying a word. I was hovering between anger and sadness. I knew she was hurting; I couldn't imagine what it must be like to lose a child, but I'd lost my dad and my brother, and I was grieving too. I sat outside on our old couch, sipping on my steaming black coffee and I let the tears flow, not even bothering to stifle the sobs.

I stayed outside while the sun came up, holding on to a glimmer of hope that Mum might have joined me when she'd finished her breakfast. As my optimism faded, I decided there was only one way to get me out of my funk. I hadn't been for a swim since before the accident and it had long been my go-to stress reliever. Before I could talk myself out of it, I threw on some bathers and stuffed a change of clothes in my swim bag.

I pulled up at the car park next to the beach and dumped my bag and towel on the sand, running into the cold water before I could think too much about it. I dived under the waves, coming up for air before turning and swimming parallel to the beach. The cool temperature of the water snatched my breath and I gasped for air until I found a steady rhythm. I focused on my stroke and my breathing to calm my thoughts and when I felt like I'd gone far enough, I turned and headed back, my body slick in the water.

I'd been a swimmer for as long as I could remember. Some of my earliest memories were in the pool, but open water had always been my draw. I loved the freedom of it, not bound by lane ropes and turns. I glanced quickly towards the beach to see if I'd reached my starting point. There was a lone figure sitting on the sand watching me, right next to my bright orange bag. I couldn't make out who it was from that distance, but heat scorched my body despite the frigidity of the water. I stopped swimming and stood up, pulling my goggles off and wringing out my hair before striding through the shallow water towards my towel. As I got closer, I recognised the guy on the beach. It was him. I didn't want to stare but I felt powerless to turn away. I waited for him to speak but he remained silent. I would've expected to feel awkward, but I didn't. His presence was comforting, exactly what I needed. I grabbed my towel from the top of my bag and wrapped it around my shoulders, dropping to a sitting position on the sand.

'It's Beau, right?' I asked him. My voice felt unsteady after the long silence. He seemed surprised that I knew his name.

'Yeah, you remember?'

'From the hospital, I...' My voice choked and I was unable to finish my sentence. I never wanted to relive that night.

He nodded in reply and his eyes never left mine. They were awash with emotion as though he had inside knowledge of my thoughts. The atmosphere between us was palpable and I felt it sucking up every breath of air, squeezing my throat. I blinked to break the connection and looked down at the sand flowing between my fingertips. I wanted to ask him why he was here but as if he could read my mind, he answered before I could ask.

'I was just out for a ride, and I saw Tom's car in the car park. It hit me in the gut. I figured it must be you down here.' His voice was so quiet it was barely a whisper, and as I took in what he was saying I realised I'd hopped in Tom's car without thinking. I'd left the keys in my room a few days ago when Ben had dropped it off.

'I'm sorry,' I told him. 'Did you know Tom well?'

'Yeah, we met through Ben, and we became quite close this year.'

My mind went into overdrive trying to remember a time when Tom had mentioned Beau, but nothing came to mind. It's definitely not a name I would've forgotten. And if I'd met him before, I would've remembered those eyes.

Silence fell upon us once again and there was still no awkwardness. I felt so comfortable, something that, other than family, I'd only ever felt with Rosie.

'You want to get out of here?' he asked, nodding to the shiny black motorbike in the car park. My curiosity peaked and a rush of adrenaline gorged me. I'm not sure whether it was the thought of riding on a motorbike or the fact that I'd be sitting so close to Beau.

'Sure,' I said, trying to act calm. 'I'll just go change out of these wet bathers.' I swung my bag casually over my shoulder, gripping my towel around me, and headed to the changing rooms. When I came back out, Beau was leaning against the rail with a spare helmet in his hand.

I balked at the scene before me and was suddenly wary of his motives.

'You carry a spare helmet? Do you pick up grieving girls often?' He'd done nothing to make me think that, so I wasn't sure why I was accusing him. I guess with my mum's recent behaviour I didn't know who I could trust.

Beau's face clouded over, and he stepped back. His face twisted in torment as though my words had really hurt him. I was ashamed of myself for questioning his motive.

'It belongs to my foster brother; he rides with me sometimes. I've never taken a girl for a ride.' His tone was matter of fact, clearly pissed about what I said but he handed me the helmet as though telling me the subject was closed, so I respected his wishes and pulled the helmet over my head.

The engine rumbled to life between my legs and Beau turned round to check I was ready. I nodded once and the bike roared as we pulled out of the carpark. I had no idea where we were heading but the thrill I felt ignited every nerve ending, and I hoped he was taking me somewhere far away.

As we roared down the freeway, the bushland passed by in a blur. The speed was exhilarating; I felt so reckless but safe at the same time. If Rosie could've seen me, she would've been shocked, but maybe a little proud too. I'd always been the quiet girl, the straight A student, dedicated swimmer and all-round achiever. Rosie had tried to drag me out of my comfort zone for years. She thought once I left school, I'd let myself go more but to be honest, it just made me uncomfortable. I always hated big crowds and would much rather have dinner with a couple of friends than go clubbing. I'm definitely not the girl who gets on the back of a motorbike with a random stranger. I had no idea what made me do it, but I'd never felt so at home. It felt like a defining moment in my life.

My entire life had always been set out before me and I'd always known that I was one of the lucky ones. I was cognisant of the fact that life had been easy for me. I had a stable, happy family life, a good education and little to no stress. But as much as I knew I was lucky; I don't think I'd ever truly understood the hardships other people suffered. I didn't feel so lucky anymore. My entire life had shattered, and I had no idea how to rebuild it. My mum was barely speaking to me and when she did her words seemed to drip with contempt. It felt as though she'd died along with them and left in her place was a shadow of who she'd been. I'd planned to move out after graduation, but now I didn't even know if I'd graduate. Luckily, I had no exams this semester, but I still had assignments to finish. My own reality began to overwhelm me, and I could no longer prevent my tears from falling.

I gripped tighter round Beau's waist and he slowed the bike, glancing over his shoulder to check on me. I nodded to let him know I was okay, but he took the next exit off the freeway following some back roads towards the coast. He pulled to a stop at a quiet spot overlooking the beach. Flicking the stand down, he climbed off the bike and offered me his hand. I climbed off quickly and removed my helmet, the full extent of my tears showing all over my face. Without questions, Beau wrapped his arms around me and drew me to his chest. He didn't need to say a word; my thoughts began to erase themselves with the sound of his heartbeat humming against my cheek. At that moment I was exactly where I needed to be.

We wandered down the steep path to the beach, a southern breeze chilled the air, and I pulled my jacket closed. A couple of beachgoers were throwing balls for their dogs to fetch. They darted in and out of the ocean, barking at the waves. I got caught up watching them, feeling jealous of their simple lives. Dropping to the sand, I hugged my knees to my chest and fixed my eyes on the steady roll of the waves. The monotony of the ocean had always brought me peace. Mesmerised by the therapeutic power of the water, I didn't notice Beau had sat down next to me until he leaned towards me, our arms touching, his pinky finger grazing mine. The warmth he radiated spread through my body, and I turned to see him looking at me. He spoke few words but the depth in his eyes and the rousing caress of his fingertip permeated me more than any words possibly could. I felt more at peace than I had in over a week, and I finally felt like I could say something without having to choke back sobs.

'It's so hard to be at home without them.' My voice was little more than a whisper. 'There's just a huge hole in my world.' His fingers entwined with mine.

'I know,' he murmured so quietly I could barely hear him, but the power of those words reached right inside me, tearing at my heart. Beau had his own story of grief; it was evident in everything he wasn't saying. I watched him closely, not wanting to pry but hoping he would feel comfortable enough to share. His silence filled the air between us and just as I thought he was going to break it, he untangled his fingers from mine and I feared the moment was lost. He drew his knees up and hugged them, mirroring my position. His breath became shallow and I began to worry he was having a panic attack, so I assured him he needn't tell me anything. Whatever happened to him was obviously still raw.

Then he began to speak.

'My mum and little sister were murdered. I was twelve.' His revelation floored me.

'Shit, Beau. That must've... Beau, I'm so sorry, I don't know what to say.' I knew from recent experience that there was nothing I could say that would even remotely make him feel better.

'You don't need to say anything. I just want you to know that I do understand what you're going through. I may not say much, but I'm here if you need me. Please know that.' His eyes never left mine. 'That's only the second time in my life I've spoken those words out loud.'

'Thank you, it means a lot.'

When Beau dropped me back at my car I stood and watched him ride away, suddenly regretting all the things I hadn't said. I wished I'd told him about the dreams I'd been having, how I felt so alone, and how my mum could barely even look at me. I felt like he would've understood.

Driving my car didn't come close to giving me the same thrill as riding on the back of Beau's motorbike so I turned the music up until the sound was distorted and rolled the windows down. It wasn't the same, but it was the best I could do. I didn't feel like going home, it just felt too sad. Silence echoed through the house and sucked the life out of me. I sang at the top of my voice, with no idea where I was heading, only realising my destination when I found myself parked on Rosie's driveway. Rosie's car wasn't there so I flicked the car into reverse and started back down the driveway until I spotted Gina on the front porch waving at me to come back.

'Hi Lottie, how're you doing?' she said affectionately as she came down the front porch steps, her arms open for a hug.

'I'm fine,' I replied, knowing Gina could see straight through me.

'It's okay to not be fine Lottie. Grieving takes time and everyone handles it differently.' She released me from the hug and gently touched my cheek as my eyes began filling up again. I tried to talk but the lump caught in my throat and nothing but a whimper came out. I tried again.

'It's Mum,' I said. 'She's not talking to me. She can barely look at me. She just stays in her room all day. It's like she blames me for still being here. Like the wrong kid died.'

'Oh Lottie, don't blame yourself. She's just hurting. She'll come around, try and be patient.'

'But I'm hurting too Gina, she doesn't seem to care about that. I'm her child too and I didn't die.'

Gina wrapped me up in her arms and held me until the tears stopped. 'Come inside, I'll make us some coffee.'

I've always loved Gina's house. It's one of those houses that feels homely as soon as you walk in. It's only small but with Rosie being an only child, there's always been a spare room for the kids Gina and Brad have fostered. The thought took me straight to Beau. He'd said he had a foster brother, so I began to wonder if he'd been put in foster care after his mum died. I tried to recall if he'd mentioned his dad, but my mind came up blank. I pondered all the possible scenarios and they all left me feeling uneasy.

I sat in the window seat while Gina made coffee. It had always been my favourite place to sit, and once Gina had finished making coffee she came and joined me. We chatted about everyday life, which was a welcome relief and Rosie was surprised to see us when she got home. She made herself a hot chocolate and joined me as Gina squeezed my hand and left.

We hung out for a while, but I didn't seem to be able to involve myself in her gossip. I knew she was just trying to take my mind off things but all I could think about was Beau. And that, in itself, was weird. I'd never been one to obsess over a guy before. When I first saw him at the bar, I felt an instant pull, but it had grown rapidly into so much more than that. We'd barely spoken and yet I felt like he could already see me on a deeper level than anyone else. Of course, Rosie and I had been close for a long time but sometimes it felt like we were on different planets, orbiting around each other, never truly connecting.

'Lots, are you okay?' My mind had been drifting for so long I had no idea what Rosie was saying.

'Yeah, I'm fine; just not really in the mood you know? I'm sorry.'

'It's okay Lots, I understand. You can talk to me about it - I am capable of listening you know.'

I laughed and threw a pillow at her.

'I dunno, it's difficult to get a word in sometimes.' I tried to lighten my mood, but I just wasn't feeling it. 'I think I'm gonna go. I probably should try talking to Mum.'

I gave Rosie a hug and she held on a little longer than usual. I knew she felt my pain and she wanted to help, but I felt like I had to guide her and reassure her that she was saying the right thing and it was just exhausting.

When I opened the front door, the house was quiet, and I noticed Mum's bedroom door was still closed. I knocked gently and opened the door a crack to see if she was awake. I heard her groan.

'Leave me alone.' She sounded half asleep so I contemplated doing what she said for a split second, but decided I needed to make more of an effort. Someone needed to be the grown up and make some decisions.

'Mum, you need to get up, this isn't good for you. You still have a daughter in case you haven't noticed.' The sarcasm wasn't intended but I needed to provoke her into communicating somehow.

'I said leave me alone,' her tone was more assertive. 'Can you not understand that?'

I fought back tears, but I didn't even feel upset anymore; I was angry. I didn't understand how she could treat me like this. I needed to vent but I didn't feel like I had anyone to vent to. I've never had a lot of people in my life, but I've never felt lonely. I've always enjoyed my own company — reading or swimming but in that moment, I wanted to climb out of my own skin and get as far away as possible.

I tried searching Beau on social media, but he was nowhere to be found. I found that a little strange at first but then as I thought about the person I'd got to know through the tiny window he'd opened, I understood perfectly why I wouldn't find him. I crept into Tom's room and found his phone in the bag of stuff from the hospital. Once it was powered up, I searched his contacts but still had no luck. For someone who said he was friends with my brother, there was no sign of Beau anywhere in Tom's life. I didn't doubt their friendship, but it was starting to frustrate me not knowing how to contact him.

I laid on my bed feeling sorry for myself, and when I could feel my eyes grow heavy, I gave in to sleep.

I awaken to someone banging on the door. When I open my eyes, I realise it's not morning yet; the room is shrouded in darkness. Terrified, I lie still. The idea of opening the door feels like I would be inviting the devil inside. The banging stops and there's silence. My breath is audible, and my body is visibly shaking. I think maybe he's gone but deep inside me I know he's still there, pacing. The silence is deafening. I hold my breath. A tap on the window sets my nerves on edge and a whimper escapes my lips.

I woke with a start, my eyes searching frantically to lock on something I recognised. I scooted backwards up the bed until I reached the headboard, my knees tight to my chest. My heart was pounding so hard my chest felt like it was under siege, and my skin prickled, sending shivers right through my body. I pulled the covers up around me, not daring to close my eyes again. I glanced quickly at the clock. It was 5am. I'd slept over fifteen hours.

Eva 1962

On Sunday morning, Eva woke early, tripping over herself to get ready for her date. She picked out her favourite sundress and sandals, taking time with her hair and make-up. She stood back to admire herself in the mirror on her old wardrobe door. Happy with her reflection, she felt excited for the day ahead. Her mother was already up and cooking when Eva made her way downstairs for breakfast. Her father sat at the table with the morning paper and a pot of tea.

'Morning!' Eva said brightly, as she did every morning, trying to start each day with a burst of positivity. There was a grunt from her father as he slurped his tea. Eva wasn't going to let anyone ruin her mood today. Winifred passed Eva a plate with several rounds of buttered toast.

'Put this on the table and sit down Eva. The eggs are almost ready.'

Eva did as she was asked and helped herself to a cup of tea from the pot. Her father glanced at her and looked her over, no doubt deciding if her clothes were suitable for her date.

After finishing up her eggs and brushing her teeth, Eva heard a knock on the back door. She raced down the stairs to try and get there before her parents, but her father was one step ahead.

'Good morning, Mr Thompson.' Eva's heart began to race at the sound of Charles's voice. 'I'm Charles, I'm here to pick up Eva.'

'Mmm,' her father said, frowning, as Eva appeared behind him at the door.

'Morning Eva,' Charles said, beaming when he saw her. 'Are you ready to go? We don't want to miss the train.'

'Yes, I'm ready.' Eva grabbed her cardigan and purse and said goodbye to her parents before ushering Charles backwards out of the house.

'Hi,' she said when they were out of earshot, relieved all the formalities were over and they could finally be themselves again. Their time in the park yesterday had been so much more relaxed than being in the house with her parents, she couldn't wait to get Charles to herself again.

'Hi yourself,' Charles said smiling at her. He looked so handsome in shorts and a checked shirt with his sleeves rolled up to his elbows. He was wearing aviator sunglasses pushed up on his head and he felt so far removed from anyone Eva had previously known, yet she felt a connection to him like no other.

They chatted amiably as they reached the station, and Charles bought return tickets for both of them. Eva thanked him as they climbed aboard the train and found a couple of seats. She sat in a backward facing window seat and as the train began to move, she turned to Charles and beamed at him. Her excitement about the day ahead bubbled over and she chattered incessantly. Charles had been insistent yesterday that she be herself so she hoped her vibrant, bubbly nature would be enticing and wouldn't put him off.

Charles was enamoured with Eva's effervescence. He loved her free spirit, her thoughts and opinions, and wondered how on earth it hadn't been drained from her in that dreary household. When the train eventually rolled into the station in Morecambe, the two of them were excited for what the day held.

Eva was bursting to see the sea for the first time, and she wasn't disappointed when she saw the waves rolling on the shore. She took Charles's hand and ran down the steps onto the sand. Quickly removing her sandals, she danced on the soft sand, feeling the grains between her toes. Charles twirled her around and danced with her, feeling more alive than he'd ever felt in his life. She was magical, and he never wanted to let her go.

'Let's get our feet wet,' Eva said, taking off down the beach towards the water, the full skirt of her sundress flowing out behind her. Charles chased after her, delighted by her sense of fun. Eva dropped her sandals on the sand and splashed into the cold water. Charles kicked his shoes off, tugging off his socks as he went. Following her into the sea, he splashed water at her, gently at first to gauge her reaction, and when she quickly joined in, he became braver. Within minutes, they were soaking wet, and Eva began to shiver. Charles wrapped his arms around her waist from behind.

'Come on, let's go lie on the sand and dry off before we catch a cold,' he whispered softly in her ear. They picked up their shoes and carried them further up the beach so as not to get caught out by the tide. Eva dropped on to the sand, laughing at their antics and Charles sat down next to her, leaning back on his elbows, eyes closed, feeling more than content with the way the day was going so far.

They'd been there a while and were almost dry when Eva rolled onto her side and propped herself up on one elbow, her face close to Charles.

She couldn't tell if his eyes were open through his sunglasses, so she touched her hand gently to his chest to see if he was awake. His breath stilled at her touch.

'Have you had many girlfriends?' Eva enquired curiously.

Charles jolted himself to a sitting position, and Eva followed suit.

'Why do you ask?' he said, a little more formally than his usual relaxed self.

'Just curious,' Eva replied, trying not to make a big deal out of it.

'A couple, but nothing serious.' Charles removed his sunglasses so he could see her more clearly, squinting in the bright sun. 'I've never met anyone quite like you before.'

Eva blushed, thinking she'd never met anyone quite like him either.

'But you've, well, you know…' Eva pressed on wanting to know his history so she would know what she was getting into.

Charles laughed. 'Eva Thompson, are you asking me about my sex life?'

'Maybe,' Eva said sheepishly.

Charles shifted his position on the sand then so that he could face her properly. 'Yes, I've had sex, but only with one person. We were together for six months, but it didn't work out. How about you?'

Eva looked shocked at his question. 'I've never even been on a date before, when would I have possibly had sex?'

'I didn't want to assume,' Charles told her. 'You seem to surprise me at every turn.'

'Do I?' Eva was intrigued.

'I love your spirit; you have such a sense of fun. I wonder where it comes from. Your parents and your upbringing really don't seem conducive to producing someone like you.'

Eva laughed at his bluntness about her parents. 'I told you they were dull.'

'Come on, let's go explore some more before lunch,' Charles said grabbing Eva's hands to pull her up.

Eva's dress felt almost dry as she smoothed her hands over the creases. They climbed the steps back up to the promenade but before going any further, Charles turned to Eva and said,

'I don't think I've told you how beautiful you look.' He leaned forward and chastely kissed her mouth. Eva felt her heart ignite and feeling emboldened, reached out a hand to guide Charles's lips back to hers. Charles couldn't believe this seemingly naive young girl from a miserable family who brightened up his life in every way and was far from shy in showing him what she wanted. He loved her independence and forward nature, never frightened to give her opinions or ask questions. She was quickly beginning to mean more to him than he'd expected and was taken aback by the feelings her kisses had stirred.

Meandering aimlessly along the promenade, Eva and Charles chatted easily, learning about each other and their dreams for the future. Eva was intrigued by Charles's background; growing up in a similar household to hers, with no space to grow, he had developed his own sense of style and outlook on life, contradictory to that of his parents. He had moved out of home and rented himself a tiny bedsit as soon as he was making his own money. Eva's imagination grew wild at the prospect of a relationship with this wildly independent, thoughtful and considerate man. She knew if things were to work out between them as she hoped they would, that she would have the opportunity to pursue her dreams and surpass her parents' expectations of her. Even if they married and had children, she knew he would value her opinions and encourage her thoughts and creativity. She felt in the short time they'd known each other, a kindred spirit, someone who she would always believe in.

'Eva?' Charles interrupted her thoughts.

'Sorry, I was away with the fairies,' she laughed.

'Tell me what you're thinking.' Charles was always interested in her thoughts. She felt a little embarrassed to tell him where her mind had gone but she could tell his feelings for her were growing in much the same way and so felt confident to share her thoughts.

'I was thinking about us and where this is going,' she mused. 'You have a beautiful soul. Stop me if I'm getting ahead of myself, or my judgement is clouded by the fictional romance novels I love, but I am developing feelings for you.'

Charles, still astonished by her confidence for someone so young, was rendered silent by her honesty. Eva's cheeks blushed, thinking she might have overstepped but was quickly appeased when a fervent glance from Charles released a kaleidoscope of butterflies in her belly. Charles reached his fingers to her cheek, brushing several strands of stray hair from her face, tucking it behind her ear.

'I'm falling for you too Eva,' he whispered and sent her into a spin as his mouth found hers in a feverish assault. Right there, on the promenade, Eva's innocence vanished as his passionate kisses led her to want more. She pulled back, aware of their conspicuous position, and needing the intensity of their tryst to die down until they were in a more private situation.

'Are you okay? Did I go too far?' Charles asked with concern in his voice. The last thing he wanted was to push Eva too far. He would go at her pace.

'Not at all,' Eva replied breathlessly. 'But what happens next is definitely not for public consumption.' Charles stared longingly at her; his eyes tinged with ardent desire. He had never wanted anything more in his life than to get this beautiful young woman alone and the fact that she was the one steering the course only heightened his want.

'Right,' Charles said, 'let's take this down a notch and go have some fun.' Eva smiled at Charles's attempt to compose himself and grabbed his hand, brazenly claiming him as her own.

Charles bought ride tickets at the Pleasure Park, and he wasn't in the least surprised at Eva's daring spirit and eagerness to ride the rollercoasters. They strolled along eating candy floss, competing against each other on the arcade games. Charles stood back and watched Eva effortlessly toss balls into a hoop to win herself a giant teddy bear. She hugged it with glee as the young man running the attraction handed it over.

'I've never won anything before,' Eva said, thrilled with her prize.

'I have no doubt it won't be the last thing you win Eva. You have an exciting life ahead of you. I only hope I'll be lucky enough to share in your successes,' Charles told her with unprecedented pride.

Eva turned to him, her ego full. 'That's a lovely thing to say, Charles.' She leaned towards him on her tiptoes and brushed her lips to his, electricity tingling between them. It was a chaste kiss but with deep implications.

Their time at the Pleasure Park came to a natural end when they had exhausted all the rides and spent far too much of Charles's money on the arcade games. Eva insisted on buying lunch for the two of them, and Charles accepted politely, knowing even in this early stage of their relationship that Eva was independent and would always want to contribute equally.

They took their fish and chips wrapped in newspaper and a bottle of Dandelion and Burdock to the beach. Renting a couple of striped deck chairs, they sat close together, devouring the fresh fish coated in a crispy batter, and the chunky chips smothered in salt and vinegar. The pleasure on Eva's face was breathtaking to Charles and he watched in wonder as she vigorously licked the grease from each finger. After swigging the fizzy pop, she burped loudly in a manner that she would have been severely reprimanded for by her parents, but Charles laughed loudly, thoroughly pleased with her willingness to be herself and not conform to her parents' standard of acceptable behaviours.

'Excuse me,' Eva said shocked by her own outburst, 'not very ladylike.'

'Who says?' asked Charles seriously. 'Who dictates what is or isn't ladylike? And why would you want to conform to those standards anyway? I love your unique sense of self Eva. Don't ever let anyone squash that from you.'

Eva smiled, already resigned to the fact that she was in love with this man. He had opened up a whole new world for her outside of the novels she read. And not one of her romantic heroines had prepared her for the onslaught of contrasting feelings she was now experiencing. These feelings swirled in her head and touched her heart in a way she'd never even dreamed could be possible.

The two of them sat in their deck chairs, quietly enjoying the sunshine on their faces, holding hands while watching other beachgoers. Eva's creativity came to life as she started making up stories about the people they saw. Charles laughed at some of the elaborate backgrounds she created but encouraged her to continue.

'What story would you give us?' he asked, curious as to how she saw them.

'Oh, we would be two young lovers having a clandestine affair. I'm married to a much older man; his power and greed is repulsive to me, but I had no choice but to marry him when he got me pregnant at the age of sixteen, promising me the world.' Charles looked at her in surprise, wondering if that was a fear she had. She continued, 'I'm swept off my feet by you, a beautiful and compassionate waiter at a fancy political function. I'm only there to look good on the arm of my husband. You catch my eye immediately and we discuss your promising career as an international bestselling author, and we decide to run away together.'

'And the baby?' Charles asked, amused.

'Of course, we bring him with us,' Eva replied, holding up the giant teddy bear.

They both laughed at her wild imagination before Charles switched gears and took on a more serious note.

'Do you want kids?' he asked, knowing it would be a struggle to resign himself to a life without children.

'Of course,' Eva said as Charles breathed a sigh of relief. 'Once I'm in a position to provide them with the kind of life I never had. How about you?'

'Oh, definitely.'

'Why do you ask?' Eva asked curiously. She felt his demeanour change slightly and wondered what was going on in his head.

'Just your story, it sounded like you feared being trapped by children,' Charles said.

'I think trapped in a loveless marriage is more in keeping with the image I was going for,' Eva explained. 'I've watched my parents express absolutely no love for each other and I just can't think of anything worse than feeling trapped by that, let alone bringing a child into that kind of life.'

Charles squeezed Eva's hand, giving support but urging her to continue.

'I've had a miserable upbringing Charles. I'm only grateful for the fact that I was introduced to literature at a young age. It has been my escape. I've lived so many adventures through my books, but I don't want my children to grow up only knowing life through their imagination. I want them to experience that life is an adventure, because in all honesty books don't come close in comparison to the real thing.' She turned to Charles then. 'There is no book in the world that has prepared me for the feelings I'm having right now, or the adventure you've brought to my life in just two days. I know this might sound crazy to you, and you probably think I'm just a romantic fool, or unacceptably forward. But Charles, the truth is, I think I'm in love with you.'

Charles was dumbfounded by Eva's declaration and his words lodged in his throat. He felt the same, there was no doubt in his mind, but he needed to collect himself and process the speed in which these feelings had built, so his only reply was a kiss to her forehead.

As they left the beach, Charles carrying the teddy bear under one arm, Eva wondered if she'd gone too far too soon. What did she know about love anyway? Her experience was limited to romance novels. But surely she didn't need fictional characters to substantiate her feelings. No, she knew her own mind. Charles wanted her honesty, and she couldn't deny how she felt, but his reaction wasn't what she had expected. Their whole day so far had quickly built up to this point, and she was so sure he felt the same. She glanced at him and saw a subdued expression, his cheeks pale.

Her heart sank at the prospect she might have ruined things between them. They wandered along the beachfront until they came to the pier. Without a word spoken they headed through the arcade at the entrance and walked out along the pier. Charles ushered Eva towards the railing and looking down at the Irish Sea sloshing beneath them, Eva gained the courage to ask if she'd said too much.

'I'm not going to apologise for how I feel Charles, but I hope I haven't ruined things for us. I know we've only known each other a very short time but what I feel is real to me. I appreciate the fact that you might not feel the same, and I don't expect anything from you, other than to know where I stand.' Eva's tone was kind and thoughtful even though her words were forthright and honest. Charles, continually blown away by her candid words, felt like she was the more experienced of the pair. The quiet walk that had ensued after Eva's declaration had given him plenty of time to process their situation but still, he felt at a loss for words.

'Eva, my sweet Eva,' Charles breathed while he fought with himself for something to say. Eva was beginning to look less sad and more angry.

'Charles, what's wrong? Just spit it out for goodness' sake.'

'I'm scared Eva,' he admitted. 'I'm scared of the depth of our feelings after only two days. I'm in love with you too, don't doubt that for a second. While you were winning this teddy bear, I was figuring out where we would get married!'

Eva's expression turned quickly from irritation to joy to one of pure shock.

'You want to marry me?' her voice quivered.

'Absolutely! Eva, you are the most beautiful and beguiling woman I have ever met. This is it for me. But I'm still scared. You're so young and inexperienced. You said yourself you've never had a boyfriend before; how do I know you won't meet someone else who is more deserving of you.' This was not like Charles. Eva didn't profess to know him thoroughly, but she had a good idea of him by now. He didn't strike her as lacking in confidence, or someone to hold back on what he wanted. She wondered where this was coming from.

'Charles, what's really going on? Be honest. You can't really be concerned about my lack of experience.'

Charles breathed deeply. 'Eva, I want to give you the world. Or give you the freedom to explore the world for yourself. And I know you've had an upbringing that's been less than perfect, but I don't want to come between you and your parents.'

'What on earth makes you think you would do that?' Eva asked incredulously.

'I fear they won't like me once they get to know me Eva, I'm not sure I would live up to their ideal standards of a husband. And if I'm honest, I wouldn't want to.'

'What about the life I want for me? Isn't that what you keep telling me is more important?' Eva's voice was raised, her tone getting angrier by the second.

'Of course it is,' Charles was struggling to get his point across, 'it counts for everything. Don't get me wrong Eva, I want you to live the life you want to live, and I am committed to being there alongside you every step of the way. But I'm also scared that you'll come to resent me if your relationship with your parents breaks down because of me.'

'Charles, sweetheart, I have no relationship with my parents. I have had to fight against them every day of my life so as not to disappear down their miserable hole. I will always choose happiness. I will always choose joy. You have opened my eyes to a whole life of adventure. If you'll allow me, I will always choose you.'

'Eva…' Charles was speechless. He would thank his lucky stars every day of his life that he walked into that book group and met this wonderful young lady. He leaned in to kiss her, their love on display for everyone on the pier.

The ride home on the train gave them a chance to unwind and relax in each other's company. Eva rested her head on Charles's shoulder and smiled to herself, thankful for their day together. She dreaded going home to her miserable reality but tried not to think about that as she watched the scenic countryside pass by out of the window.

'When will I see you again?' Charles asked, breaking her reverie.

Eva thought about her roster at the cafe. 'I work weekdays until 3pm and every second Saturday. Apart from that I have no life.'

Charles chuckled. 'How about I make tea for you on Tuesday evening? I can cook us up some chops?'

'You cook?' Eva asked, not really surprised by the revelation.

'I'm not too bad,' Charles replied.

'Then I would love that. Although, I'm not sure my parents would allow me to come to your flat alone. Maybe I'll tell them we're going out to eat,' Eva pondered. She didn't want anything to get in the way of their date.

'I understand. How about I pick you up at six?'

Eva smiled in answer, already feeling giddy for their date. The mere thought of being alone with him in private brought a warmth to her cheeks.

They arrived home before dark as promised, and Charles was invited in to join Eva and her parents for tea. He accepted graciously as he eyed the bubbling pot of stew and dumplings on the stove.

When her mother spied the giant teddy bear, she began chastising Eva for her frivolous spending. Charles could immediately sense Eva's embarrassment for being spoken to like that in front of him so cut into the conversation.

'Mrs Thompson, it was me who paid for the fair ground tickets. Eva's ball skills were excellent, and she won the bear easily. It really didn't cost much, and besides, seeing the joy on her face when she won was worth every penny.'

Charles smiled at Eva, and her mother turned to the cupboard to get out the plates, humiliated by the direction of the conversation.

Eva suppressed a giggle at Charles's condescending tone and fell in love with him a little bit more for putting her mother in her place.

Lottie 2019

It was no use trying to get back to sleep, all my years of swimming had dictated my wake-up time and even though I hadn't swum with a club for several years, I was still programmed to wake before sunrise. That's the main reason I could usually be found at the beach before breakfast; not because I made a conscious decision to go, but because I didn't know any different. It was in my blood.

So that was where I found myself at 6am, trudging across the sand with my bag over my shoulder. Stripping down to my bathers was always painful so early in the day, no matter the weather, so I made it quick. There was no hanging around—I ran into the water and dived under a wave, temporarily losing my breath.

I swam for a long time, trying to process my latest dream. My dreams had never been so realistic before, they were always so surreal; about abstract things that made no sense. But the dreams I'd had lately made complete sense to me; not in a way that I understood, but in a way I could identify. The surroundings were so familiar to me, and even though I couldn't explain it, the dreams were somehow relatable.

Finishing up my swim I kept my body submerged in water trying to build courage to make the freezing dash up the beach to my towel. As I was treading water, I caught the welcome sight of Beau straddling his bike in the car park. Feeling a sudden and intense flood of heat, I caught a wave and body surfed to the shore. I carefully wrapped my towel around me for maximum warmth and made my way towards him, wondering if his presence was purely accidental or whether he deliberately sought me out.

'Hey,' I said as I reached the car park.

'You are one crazy woman,' he laughed. 'It must be freezing in there, go get dressed before you turn blue.'

Smiling to myself I ducked into the changing rooms for a quick shower. I dressed quickly and wrapped my hair into a messy bun. Checking my reflection in the crazed mirror, I noticed it wasn't even in the middle of my head, but I was too eager to get back outside to correct it. I chastised myself quietly for being so caught up in this guy, but somehow managed to justify my reasons at the same time.

He was leaning against the rail taking in the sounds of the ocean, and for a second, I stopped and stared at his profile. He was definitely not my type. That stereotypical chiselled jaw look had never been my thing. I'd always been attracted to the quirky and I started to question whether that was a reflection on me when he turned and caught me watching him.

'Hey, that was quick.' His smile was genuine, and it threw me off guard a little. I'd always expected guys that looked like him to be self-absorbed, and I anticipated him saying something arrogant about me

41

watching him. Again, I questioned my own bias.

'Can't stay under that shower too long, it's colder than out there,' I nodded my head towards the ocean and pulled my jacket around me for extra warmth. 'So, what are you doing down here so early?'

He looked a little flustered at my direct question and I suddenly regretted asking. All his confidence seemed to disappear, and his eyes searched for anywhere to look other than at me.

'I just wanted to check you were okay and I don't have your number. I took a guess that you might be here. You seem like a routine kind of person.'

I wasn't sure whether that was meant as a compliment or not so I didn't answer. I moved closer and leaned on the rail next to him. We stayed like that a while, just watching the waves crash. The awkwardness quickly lifted, and we were back to a comfortable silence.

'Have you had breakfast?' His question surprised me.

'Not yet,' my stomach growled at the thought of food and we both laughed.

'I'm guessing you're hungry. Come on, I'll take you for breakfast.'

I felt a sudden rush of anticipation about riding behind him again; my arms wrapped tight round his waist. The city was beginning to wake up, the traffic building to a steady crawl so I didn't get the same rush as I did the last time. I had no idea where we were going but it wasn't long before we pulled up beside a cafe overlooking the river.

'This okay?' Beau asked as he removed his helmet.

'Sure,' I told him looking around.

We sat outside under a patio heater, and I ordered Eggs Benedict and a coffee. The coffees arrived quickly and I was grateful for the caffeine hit.

'You don't say much,' I mused, trying to figure out his motive for being here.

He shrugged, 'I'm not big on small talk.'

'Yeah, I can see that, me neither.'

He seemed surprised but didn't say anything in return.

'Why did you bring me here Beau?' His forehead wrinkled with confusion. 'I mean, not here specifically, just in general. Why did you come looking for me this morning?' I clarified.

Beau's frown deepened; his eyebrows knit closer together.

'Are you angry with me?' he asked, concerned.

'What? No! I'm just confused. You bring me out here, buy me breakfast but don't seem to have much to say to me,' I sighed, 'I guess I'm just trying to understand what's happening here.'

'I'm sorry. I just thought you might want someone to talk to. Someone that understands. I'm a good listener and I completely get what you're going through. I just…I'm not good at the trivial stuff and you make me nervous.'

I laughed at his honesty. 'Good, at least it's not just me that's nervous.'

We smiled at each other shyly as our breakfast arrived, allowing me a reprieve and a chance to think of something to say. I hadn't realised how hungry I was and probably made myself look greedy, but I cleaned my plate in no time. I caught Beau staring at me in surprise, so I picked up my coffee mug and cradled it with both hands, eager to avoid his gaze.

Beau cleared his throat, and I waited expectantly for him to say something. I didn't really care much what he said, I just wanted him to talk. His presence, and the underlying sense of support calmed me, but I knew his words would resonate. I was about to dive in and start the conversation myself when my phone rang. I checked the screen and saw my mum's name. I quickly cancelled the call and put the phone face down on the table.

'Is something wrong?' Beau asked, concerned.

'No,' I shook my head. 'Just my mum, it's not important.

'You could've answered. She's probably worried about you.'

'I doubt it, she barely notices I exist anymore. It's like she died too.'

Beau reached out unexpectedly and touched my arm.

'I'm sure that's not true, she's just grieving.'

I shrugged in reply.

'She's your mum, give her time. You both need to grieve in your own way.' Beau began to talk more, he seemed much more comfortable, so I put myself out there too and asked him a personal question.

'Is that what happened with your dad when your mum and sister died? Did you feel like there was no one there for you?' I asked cautiously but his hand immediately jerked back from my arm as though scalded. His face turned frigid.

'I'm sorry, did I say something wrong?' I didn't want him to shut down on me again.

'It's not the same.' His eyes were downcast. 'I literally had no one, at least your mum's there.' His voice wavered between anger and raw emotion. He was silent for a minute, but I felt like he might say more so I stayed quiet.

'He killed them.' He delivered the blow in barely more than a whisper. My thoughts swirled like a kaleidoscope. Was he talking about his dad? My eyes met his and I could see them begin to shimmer, tears pooling in the corners but not yet ready to spill over.

He gathered his thoughts.

'My dad murdered them. He set fire to the house while they were both asleep in bed. He assumed I was there too, but I'd had a last-minute invitation to a sleepover and mum hadn't told him. He was an addict. Alcohol, gambling, you name it. He was up to his neck in debt and planned to claim on the insurance. He thought that if his family were in the house, it would look less like arson, and he'd get away with it.'

I was stunned by his confession. That was the most he'd said to me, and it wasn't something I knew how to follow.

'Beau...I...' I shook my head unable to continue. I detected a hint of relief ghost his face, but his distress was evident in his eyes.

I wasn't sure when it happened, but I realised we were holding hands across the table. We were two people alone in our shared grief.

My drive home was filled with thoughts of Beau and the things he'd told me. I couldn't wrap my head around the trauma that would cause to a twelve-year-old boy. It's been difficult enough at twenty-two and no one was murdered here. As I thought about Beau and the past few weeks, my mind wandered back to my dreams. They'd been intense lately and I began to worry that they meant something; like maybe they weren't dreams at all but some kind of repressed memory. My mind started to conjure up all sorts of possibilities and by the time I pulled up in the driveway I'd convinced myself I'd had a past life.

'Mum?' I called as I took my key from the lock and shut the front door behind me. Her bedroom door was slightly ajar, so I pushed it gently to find an unmade and empty bed.

'Mum?' I shouted louder. At least she was out of bed, I figured that was a good sign but there was still no answer.

The house was silent, and I thought maybe she'd finally gone out. But then I heard sniffling coming from Tom's room. She was curled up on his bed, his favourite hoodie muffling her sobs. My heart ached seeing her like that, but I was at a loss as to how to help her.

'Mum?' I tried again but her glazed eyes stared right through me as though I was a ghost. A shiver racked my body at the thought, and I felt a cool sweat sheen my skin. That was exactly how I felt; ghostlike. Even in my dreams I felt as though I was hovering over a life that wasn't mine. I turned to leave, angry at her for leaving me to deal with this alone and annoyed at myself for being selfish.

My phone buzzed and a quick glance at the screen confirmed it was Rosie. I automatically pressed accept and then regretted it instantly. Rosie was way too chirpy for my current mood. She babbled on excitedly, only occasional words sinking in. There was an awkward pause and I realised she'd asked me a question.

'Lottie, are you even listening?' She sounded pissed off.

'Sorry Rosie, I'm really not good right now. I'll call you later.' I pressed end call without waiting for her reply. I knew she'd be upset with me, but I didn't have the energy to deal with her. Anger rose within me to a point where I was so filled with rage, I didn't even recognise myself. I threw my phone at the wall, which relieved absolutely none of my frustration, so I stormed into my bedroom and kicked the door shut, pulling at my bookcase until books and trinkets were tossed to the floor and the bookcase tipped hesitantly before smashing against my bed frame, wood splintering and breaking apart. I sank to the floor beside my bed, my fists hammered on the hardwood in a rhythmic pattern as I tried to bring some kind of order to my thoughts.

'Lottie! What the hell are you doing?' Mum came charging through the door, her hair wild and her face incandescent with rage.

At least I was no longer a ghost, but a sudden onset of shame made me feel like a spoiled brat throwing a tantrum to get attention. I glared at her as if I couldn't care less that she was even there, when deep down I was craving the attention.

'Lottie, why are you behaving like this? Can't you see that I'm grieving?'

I stared at her incredulously.

'Oh, and I'm not?' My tone was harsh, but I didn't care. I didn't care about anything anymore, I just wanted something to take the pain away. Once again, she abandoned the conversation, not able to give me even a tiny shred of hope to cling to.

The pain and sadness eventually took over. Overwhelmed and exhausted, I curled up on my rug, and as my breathing slowed, a heavy force pulled at my eyelids.

Inside the locked bathroom I huddle on the floor, humming to myself, a peaceful lullaby trying to block out the thunderous noise. The door visibly shakes as his heavy fists try and beat it down.

'Unlock the door bitch.' I jump at the voice.

Emerald green eyes shimmer in the dim light. Tears pool and guilt floods my body. Gentle arms encompass me, a feeling of warmth and comfort. The familiar sensation brings solace.

My face felt clammy when my consciousness returned. My shaking fingers found my cheek and I quickly pulled back from the wet touch. Had I been crying in my sleep? I wasn't sure what was real anymore, and I felt sure I was losing it. I had no idea how long I'd been passed out for.

I crawled over to where my phone had landed in my rage and was relieved to see it only had a small scratch on the front. Seeing the face light up with a string of messages, it was obvious I was out of it for a while. Scrolling through I noticed most of them were from Rosie. I felt ashamed of my feelings towards her, but I just didn't have the energy to fix things. I stopped scrolling when I saw a message from Beau.

Hey, sorry I loaded all my shit on you. I've never shared that before. Thanks for not judging. Hope things with your mum improve xx

I was torn for a moment between texting back or calling but my decision was answered for me when Beau's number appeared on the screen. Not sure whether the sudden surge of nausea was from excitement or nerves, I answered quickly.

'Hey,' his voice was low and rasping and I felt instant calm, grounded somehow.

'Hey, I just got your message. Sorry I didn't reply sooner, I had a fight with mum.'

'Are you okay now?'

I shrugged and breathed heavily. There was a silence on the line, and I realised I needed to respond verbally.

'I don't know.' My voice cracked and I was aware of my emotions swelling as a lump formed in my throat.

'Come for a ride with me,' Beau whispered. 'There's a place I go when I need space to think.'

Slipping out of the house quietly to avoid another run in with mum, I pulled my denim jacket on as Beau's bike came into view, gliding to a stop in front of me. He signalled to the box for me to get the spare helmet and in minutes my reality was left behind and all I could feel was a warm buzz that I couldn't even bring myself to feel guilty about.

I had no idea where we were going, and I didn't really care. I wasn't even bothered about having a destination, I was happy to just float along in the warm breeze, adrenalin pumping through my veins making me feel like someone else.

I wasn't sure how long we'd been riding but we'd left the city behind and made our way through the winding roads up into the hills. Beau parked the bike at a lookout, and I took off my helmet, shaking my hair loose. I could see the city in the distance, the sweeping serpent of the river winding out to sea, ships bobbing on the horizon. Beau turned off the engine and kicked the stand down as he hopped off, holding the bike steady for me to do the same. He walked to the fence leaning his forearms on the splintered wood, taking in the stillness of the day. I removed my jacket and joined him, edging close to his side. He put his arm around me, squeezing me towards him.

We stood together in comfortable silence, and I was beginning to appreciate his lack of conversation. After what he'd told me that morning, I was reluctant to press him for more details. It would've taken so much courage to say those words, so he caught me by surprise when he started talking.

'I was completely alone afterwards,' he said. 'I had no one. My dad confessed soon after, I guess the guilt began to eat away at him. I had no other family, so I was taken into emergency foster care. I don't really remember much about the first place I went, I guess I've shut it out. I was only with them a couple of weeks until they found me somewhere more permanent,' Beau shrugged. 'Or as permanent as foster care can be.'

I tilted my head to take in his profile as he continued to focus his gaze straight ahead, or at the city, or the ships on the horizon. Or maybe he wasn't focused on anything outwardly, he seemed so far inside his own head that his eyes appeared glazed over. I watched him, my breath shaky, silently anticipating his next words.

'I was put with Kate after that. I've been with her ever since. Technically I haven't been in her care since I was eighteen, but she's been like a mum to me and the closest I have to family.'

'Wow, that's huge Beau. I'm so sorry you had to go through all that but I'm happy for you that things turned out the way they did.' I paused, contemplating whether I should ask the question that had been circulating my thoughts.

'Do you feel like you've become a different person because of your experience?' I asked, warily. 'I don't feel like myself anymore—I'm not sure how to describe it.'

Beau's jaw clenched tight, and he breathed out a loud puff of air. I worried I'd gone too far and was relieved when he answered.

'I don't see how you can go through such a life altering event and not be changed by it. For years afterwards I was angry with my dad. Kate helped me process my feelings, but it took a long time for the anger to subside and by then I was no longer the carefree kid I used to be.' He turned his head to look at me and his breath caressed my face.

'Don't fight your feelings Lottie, try and accept the changes and move forward. Don't try to be who you were because every experience you have changes you into the person you'll become. You can't hold on to the past. Kate taught me that.'

Our faces were so close, I felt vulnerable but surprisingly peaceful. I was shocked by how much Beau had opened up to me. He'd told me earlier that he didn't like small talk but when it came to deep and meaningful, he sure knew how to communicate.

'Thank you for sharing, it means a lot,' I whispered, our breath mingling.

He lifted his chin and rested it on the top of my head as he pulled me closer. He was beginning to stir feelings that I'd never felt before; something deep and solid, which scared me, but at the same time I trusted it completely. There was an understanding, like we recognised ourselves in each other.

'I wish I could stay here all day,' I said, my voice shattering the stillness. The feeling of calm up there was transcendent. I'd never been a particularly spiritual person but the sense of someone guiding my path in that moment was overwhelming. I'd lived my life as though by a rule book. I guess I'd been an easy child for my parents; never causing any hassle. I always did as I was told and never felt the need to rebel. The thought of that nauseated me now. The clear vision I'd had of my life, of where I was going had begun to blur. I'd always known the steps I needed to take to get me there, but I could no longer see them. A gravitational pull was dragging me down a different path, and I felt the need to allow it to take this new me wherever I needed to go.

Beau's lips gently brushed across my hair. I lifted my head from under his, my mouth almost grazing his, his warm breath like silk on my lips. I thought he was going to kiss me, but his mouth just lingered, hovering over mine, his dark eyes penetrating my thoughts. He turned his head and stepped back. Surprisingly I wasn't disappointed. I smiled at him, linking my fingers in his as we walked back to his bike.

Lottie 2019

I try to open my eyes, but it hurts so much. My forehead is throbbing, my temples pounding in a steady rhythm. I feel lightheaded as if I stood up too quickly but even without opening my eyes, I know I'm in my bed. I manage to open one eye, but the other feels glued shut. A searing pain shoots through my face from my eyes right down to my jaw. I trace my fingers tentatively across my face, feeling the swollen tissue. Fuck. It's bad.

I jolted awake. My breathing was heavy, and I opened my eyes to find Mum standing over me, worry lines criss-crossing her face.

'Lottie, you're dreaming again.' Despite the worry apparent on her face, her tone was harsh. 'It's disturbing seeing you like this, lashing out in your sleep.'

Her tone riled me, and I was on the offensive immediately.

'I can't help it, they won't stop. Every time I close my eyes, I'm terrified.'

Mum's face drained of colour. 'Is it the accident?'

I couldn't lie to her, but her absence of empathy told me she wasn't the right person to confide in right now.

'I'm not really sure what they're about, they just scare me that's all.'

'Get some help Lottie, I can't deal with this drama every time you fall asleep.' Her lack of compassion tipped me over the edge, and I could no longer hold back.

'You know what Mum? Maybe I can't deal with your drama either. You have no right to tell me what I should do when you're clearly not doing what's best for yourself. You haven't been there for me once since they died. I know I'm an adult but you're still my mother. I might as well have lost you too.' My words cut her deeply, the hurt was right there in her eyes. I'd never spoken to her with such venom before, even in the worst of my teenage years.

Shaking, I climbed out of my bed and shut myself in the bathroom. I looked in the mirror at my emotionally charged face and for the first time since the accident, I acknowledged the strength and possibility. The change in me was evident, and I knew it was time to take charge of my own life. I made up my mind to talk to Beau about my dreams. Even if he did no more than listen, I knew that just the act of sharing with him would bring me some clarity.

By the time I left the bathroom Mum was back in her room with the door closed so I quickly got dressed and flicked Beau a message.

Hey, I really need to talk. When are you free?

His reply was instant

Now? I'm at home, come over.

Beau sent me his address and ten minutes later I was pulling into the driveway of his unit. Stood at the front door, my hands felt clammy as I prepared to knock. I had no idea if he lived alone or with flat mates and I was suddenly nervous about seeing him.

I was obviously being irrational because as soon as he opened the door my nerves dissipated as he smiled warmly.

'Hey, come in,' he said stepping aside. 'Go straight through.'

The tiny hall opened into a light and airy room with floor to ceiling windows across the back. There was a tiny kitchenette along one side and the rest of the room was designed for both sitting and sleeping. Ikea furniture was dotted between a mix of antique styles and seventies retro. Brightly woven rugs covered the old timber floor and there were plants everywhere. The air was filled with lemongrass, the scent swirling from a huge candle in an earthy looking pot on the coffee table. The back wall was filled with books, and I was pretty sure I'd died and gone to heaven. I looked around taking it all in, throwing Beau a questioning look about his eclectic tastes.

'What?' he asked. 'Why so surprised?'

'Everything about you surprises me,' I said in a voice barely above a whisper.

Beau tipped his head to one side and studied me closely. The way we were standing just looking at each other with no words would usually make me uncomfortable but I wasn't, it was the most comfortable feeling in the world.

Beau broke the silence first.

'Coffee?'

'I'd love one.'

As he turned to the kitchen I spun around and devoured the bookshelves. I could feel Beau's eyes burning into the back of my head as I gently ran my fingers across the spines of the books. His eclectic taste didn't end with his furnishings, it extended to his choice of books too. There was everything on that shelf from Shakespeare and Tolstoy to Margaret Atwood and Eva Hartley. My hand stopped at a familiar sight, and a single bead of sweat trickled down my spine as an involuntary shiver passed over me.

"The Tennant of Wildfell Hall." I'd loved the Brontë sisters for as long as I could remember, and this book had always remained my favourite. I was stunned to find it there and as I pulled it carefully off the shelf and ran it lovingly through my hands, I sensed Beau's presence close behind me. I turned and searched his eyes for an explanation of his reading tastes, hoping above all else that he loved this book as much as I did.

'More surprises?' he asked me, a small grin forming a dimple that I hadn't noticed before.

'You never fail,' I told him.

He handed me my coffee and with the lightest touch on the small of my back ushered me towards the couch. Kicking off my shoes, I curled up with a cushion, my feet tucked under me.

'You read a lot?' he asked casually.

'All the time, I guess I'm a bit of a loner. Clubbing's not really my scene, I much prefer to curl up with a good book and a glass of wine.' I laughed at how I was describing myself. 'I'm a real catch!'

'You are to me.' His voice was barely audible, and I wasn't sure what to do with his words, so I looked awkwardly into my coffee. Beau sensed my unease immediately and pointed to the book that I hadn't realised I was still clutching.

'You like the Brontës?'

'They're my favourites, this one especially,' I gushed, holding up the cover. 'I majored in English Lit and the unit on the Brontës was just pure joy for me. My tutor was asking for my validation on everything she was saying by the end of the semester.'

Beau laughed at my enthusiasm, and I was grateful we had more in common than just death and tragedy.

'You wanted to talk?' he asked, turning the conversation serious.

Finally telling someone about my dreams gave me a huge sense of release. Beau watched me attentively as I filled him in on each of my dreams. I described them in vivid detail, and he never once interrupted or pushed me to continue when I stumbled. As I reached the end and finished telling him the dream I'd had that morning, a look I couldn't read properly briefly crossed his face. It disappeared as quickly as it arrived unsettling me slightly.

'I think you've got some really deep stuff going on there. Maybe you should talk to Kate.'

I stared at him confused. 'Your foster mum?'

'Yes, she's a psychologist. I really think she could help you. She dabbles in dream therapy, and she knows how to really dissect them and pull out the deeper meanings.'

'But aren't you a psychologist?' I asked, wondering why he couldn't help me.

'I'm almost there yes, but I think we have a conflict of interest here, don't you?'

'Do we?'

Beau reached forward, taking the coffee cup from my hand and putting it on the table. He shifted his position, edging closer to me.

'I'm pretty sure we do,' he said, his mouth close enough that his breath was tickling my lips. I reached my hand to the back of Beau's neck, my fingers stroking the soft dark curls, but I didn't pull him any closer, hoping he'd be the one to close the gap. His lips hovered over mine as if he knew that breaching that gap would take us to a place there would be no coming back from. Time stood still, and just when I felt my desire begin to mutate into nerves, his lips crashed into mine. His eyes still focused on mine, his tongue dipped tenderly between my lips, gently exploring. I let my mouth fall open, allowing him in, my tongue hesitantly caressing his. He shifted himself again, this time to free up a hand and his fingers skimmed my neck as his thumb brushed the corner of my mouth. Not once breaking eye contact, Beau's hand cupped my face affectionately as his tongue pushed deeper. He was right to hesitate before; there was no way back from that place.

'You're right,' I said breathlessly. 'Definite conflict here.'

He laughed again and I wondered if he laughed often. It wasn't something I'd seen him do a lot, but I guess he hadn't had much to laugh about with me.

'You should laugh more,' I told him. 'You look beautiful when you laugh.' I loved the way he took my compliment. He wasn't embarrassed, but neither did he verbally acknowledge it. He just accepted it with a small nod, as if he was processing what I said.

He took my hands in his, holding them both in his lap and looked at me earnestly.

'You'll like Kate, I promise. Why don't I speak to her for you and see if she could help?'

I nodded silently because I really did think I needed help. Beau was right when he suggested the dreams seemed deeper than just ordinary dreams. Sometimes I felt like I was right there in someone else's life. As I thought about the dreams again, my mind turned back to the reality I was facing. Not quite ready to go back there just yet, I pulled Beau towards me again, losing myself in him for a little while longer.

We finally had to come back up for air when we heard a knock at the door. Beau got up to answer it as I straightened myself and ran my fingers through my hair hoping to eliminate the 'just fucked' look that I was pretty sure was painted all over my face. Not that it went that far but it sure felt that way.

I heard a woman's voice and then Beau speaking in low tones before he returned with her behind him.

'Charlotte, this is Kate, my foster mum.'

Kate stepped forward immediately and extended her hand. I stood and did the same but sent a questioning glance to Beau as to why he'd called me Charlotte, it sounded so formal. I'd only ever called myself Lottie, although Tom had called me Charlie sometimes when we were younger. I think he did that whenever he was pissed at Mum, she never liked him calling me that.

'It's nice to meet you,' I said smiling at her. I felt nervous, maybe because I could feel her already analysing my body language.

'You too, Charlotte, I've heard a lot about you.'

'Please, call me Lottie,' I said as I glanced at Beau questioningly, surprised that he'd spoken to his foster mum about me.

Kate noticed the look we shared and laughed.

'Oh, not from Beau, he hasn't said a word.' She lowered her voice to an almost whisper, 'Tom spoke of you, I'm so very sorry for your loss.' She grasped both of my hands in hers. 'How are you holding up?'

'I'm doing okay. I didn't realise you knew Tom,' I told her, still surprised.

She cast a hurried glance at Beau, and his eyebrows knit together. I wondered if I was imagining the weird tension in the air. It felt like I was completely out of the loop.

'I got to know Tom quite well this year through Beau, we talked a lot.' Kate definitely appeared guarded, and my mind was set on high alert.

'Talked a lot as a friend of Beau's or in a professional sense?' I queried. 'Beau mentioned you're a psychologist.'

Kate looked a little sheepish as if she wished she'd held her tongue.

'A little of both. I'm sorry Charlotte, Lottie, I shouldn't have mentioned it.'

I turned to Beau. 'You knew about this?'

He stepped forward, concern laying heavily in his eyes, but I backed away not sure how to take all this. It's not like he had an obligation to tell me, but I still felt a little deceived. I felt like Tom had a whole other side to him that I never knew. Friends I had no idea existed, mental health issues he never talked to me about.

'But we were so close,' I said. 'Why didn't he tell me he was having problems?'

Kate stepped in as if to mediate. 'I think he just wanted to get things straight in his own head first. He talked of you often and I know he would've spoken to you about it had he not...' Her voice trailed off as if she couldn't bring herself to say the words.

I wished I could rewind the clock ten minutes to escape all this. I'd felt so happy on the couch with Beau. We were in a good place. Now I didn't know what to think. He looked at me longingly, awash with guilt for his part in my discomfort.

'Hey,' Beau stepped towards me again and this time I allowed him to take my hands in his. 'I'm sorry you're feeling this way but please don't let it affect the way you think of Tom. He was just very protective of you and didn't want you to feel burdened by his problems.'

I dropped my head as I felt tears well in my eyes. I didn't want to cry but there was nothing I could do to prevent them from spilling over. A sob escaped me, and Beau pulled me in to his chest, his arms instinctively wrapping around me. His closeness was like a blanket smothering all the bad. The comforting feeling allowed my breathing to calm.

Beau kissed my head and unwrapped himself.

'I really do think you should speak to Kate, even just once. If you don't get anything out of it then at least you would've tried.'

I nodded, my eyes casting a furtive glance towards Kate.

The morning sun is drifting through the window. I smile. A sudden clarity takes over and I feel a sense of peace for the first time in years. I know things are about to change. I can feel it coming. The gentle breeze squeezes through the small gap in the window and I breathe in its sweet aroma.

I'm pulled from my trance by the shatter of glass, raining down on me. Razor-sharp shards pierce my skin and terror looms over me.

Fear struck me as I woke, a sheen of sweat layered my skin. The dread was so real I called out for help. The words stuck in my throat and a hollow sounding whimper was emitted. Mum came running in, visibly panicked by my call.

'You're burning up Lottie,' she said resting the back of her hand on my forehead. 'What's going on?'

The lump in my throat that had seized my words grew rapidly when I saw kindness in mum's eyes for the first time in weeks.

'I don't know,' I managed to choke out, before tears streamed my face. 'They're so real Mum, the dreams. I feel like I'm right there inside my own head, and they feel so familiar to me, like memories.'

A sudden darkness crossed her face and the change in her was discernible. She quickly returned to the mother I'd come to know more recently, not the kind and loving one I remembered. I wanted my mum back.

'I think you should make an appointment to see the doctor, Mum,' I told her, nothing left to lose. 'You're too thin, you need to eat. I think you need some help to deal with your grief.'

She immediately stiffened. Her whole demeanour had changed and she backed away from my bed as though a blanket had just been thrown over her, dampening the tiny spark of light I'd seen when she'd first rushed into my room. Her eyes glazed over and the contempt she felt at my suggestion was clear. She turned her back and left me alone to deal with my sorrow.

My thoughts turned to Rosie. Maybe she was thinking the same about me. Maybe I shouldn't have been blaming Mum for something I've been equally guilty of. I was so sick of all the conflicting feelings; I just wanted normal for one day.

Pulling into Gina's driveway, and noting Rosie's car was absent I breathed a sigh of relief. Although it was Rosie I'd come to make amends with, I thought talking to her mum first might break the ice.

'Lottie! It's so good to see you!' Gina squealed as she opened the door and pulled me in for a big hug. 'Rosie's not here.' She tipped her head on one side suddenly questioning my reason for visiting.

'That's okay, I came to see her, but I'm open to coffee if you have time for a chat.' My voice was small and childlike, and I was angry with myself for sounding weak and pathetic.

'Never too busy for my daughter's favourite friend,' she said. 'Come on in.' I followed her inside, dripping with guilt.

'I'm not sure I deserve that title right now.' I felt sheepish.

'Nonsense, Lottie. It's a difficult time, that's all.'

Gina busied herself with coffee capsules, pouring her milk into the frother in silence. She threw the odd smile my way and I was suddenly nervous. Sliding a coffee mug towards me, Gina leant on her elbows on the bench opposite me as she waited for her milk steam.

'How are you Lottie?' she queried.

The concern in her voice tightened around my throat, panic overwhelming me. I tried to tell myself that it was only Gina. Gina who has been like a second mum to me my whole life. But the more I tried to compose myself the more agitated I felt.

I slammed the coffee cup down a little too hard, the dark liquid spilling over the sides, pooling on the cold granite.

'I'm sorry Gina,' I mumbled as I headed for the door.

I sat in the car, shaking too much to drive. I shouldn't have come here. I leaned my forehead against the steering wheel and tried to calm myself down. My mind was racing, trying to process all the thoughts swimming in my head. The dreams, Dad, Tom and his secrets, Beau and how he fit into my new life, Mum, Rosie. It was all too much to manage, and I just needed to get it all out of my head. I banged my head on the hard leather trim, an overwhelming sense of heartbreak suffocating me.

A knock on the window startled me from my brooding and I turned to see Gina's worried face as she opened the car door. Crouching down next to me, she pulled me into her arms, and I collapsed exhausted into her comfort.

'You don't have to carry all this alone Lottie. We're all here to help you through this.' Gina pulled back and lifted my chin so our eyes met. 'Let's go finish that coffee.'

I took a sip of coffee as I tried to unscramble my thoughts into something vaguely coherent. 'I don't even know where to start Gina, I can't think straight.'

'Start wherever feels comfortable Lottie. This isn't an essay, it's life, it doesn't need structure.' She rested her hand gently on mine and I felt the kind of concern I used to get from mum.

'I feel like I've lost my entire family. I feel so alone but I also can't deal with being around people. I've been a complete bitch to Rosie, and my mum hates me. I don't feel like I'm me anymore. There's a whole side of Tom's life I never knew about. He was seeing a psychologist and he never even told me. I didn't even know there was anything worrying him. We were so close, and I thought we shared everything, how could he keep it from me? I feel like my whole life was fake. I was always the good girl, the sensible one who worked hard and got good grades, but now it just feels like I had no control over my own life, as though I was doing it all for the sake of everyone else. I'm about to qualify as a teacher and now I'm questioning if I ever wanted that. I'm questioning everything, Gina. I feel like a completely different person, and everyone hates me.'

'Lottie, no one hates you. You're grieving, and so is your mum. Neither of you know how to deal with this, there's no right or wrong way to grieve. You have to take it one step at a time and learn to process your thoughts in a different way. Have you thought about seeing someone? Like a counsellor? It might help you process.'

'My friend Beau's mum's a psychologist. She's offered to help me,' I told her.

'Take her up on it Lottie. It'll help, trust me.'

I finished my coffee and got up to leave.

'Thanks Gina,' I said, giving her a quick hug.

'My door is always open, you know that. And don't worry about Rosie, she'll be here for you whenever you need her. I'll talk to her, tell her to give you some space.' I nodded, silently grateful for a breath of air that didn't cause me pain.

Eva 1962

Eva couldn't stop thinking about Charles over the next few days. Her boss at the cafe had even pulled her to one side to ask if everything was okay as she'd made several mistakes with orders and was unusually distracted. It surprised her that a man had sneaked his way under her skin so easily, but she was certainly enjoying the fact that he had. He was like no one she'd ever met before, not that there was anyone to compare with. The men she mixed with from within her parents' circle were all very traditional types, viewing women as someone to serve them in both the kitchen and the bedroom. Sitting on the back step of the cafe kitchen during her tea break, her thoughts turned to sex. She knew the men she had grown up around would be the types that only concerned themselves with their own pleasure; they would have no thought for their wives. At only eighteen her naivety was not lost on her. She'd overheard the women in her mother's knitting circle discussing their dislike of "relations in the bedroom," yet she'd read widely, secretly obtained books like DH Lawrence's Lady Chatterley's Lover, which had opened her eyes to a pleasure she began to dream of. She wanted to experience that kind of passion. Heat rose from her chest as she thought about the evening ahead, alone in Charles's flat. Her thoughts were interrupted when her boss called her back to work.

'Eva, we have customers waiting.'

'Sorry, I'm coming,' Eva said chirpily, smoothing down her apron. The next few hours were busy, and Eva managed to get through the rest of her shift without too much distraction, but when she clocked off at three o'clock, she practically skipped all the way home eager for her evening to begin.

She spent hours in the bathroom getting herself ready. Foregoing one of her mother's homemade dresses she pulled on her new pair of Lee Cooper jeans that were becoming fashionable with teenagers. Her mother had been horrified when she brought them home, after saving her money for weeks. They were fitted and showed off her curves, much to her mother's disgust. Eva dabbed on a touch of lipstick and unbraided her hair, shaking her head as her curls cascaded down her back. She checked herself in the mirror several times. She knew Charles was drawn to her intelligence and wild spirit, but she wanted him to find her sexy too and with this new look she radiated confidence.

Picking up her purse, she ventured downstairs, awaiting the disparaging remarks from her parents about the way she was dressed. As usual, they didn't disappoint. She wouldn't allow her father's brash words about looking like a whore or her mother's disapproving tone about inappropriate attire for a date with a respectable schoolteacher to ruin her mood. She chose to ignore her parents and sat quietly in the kitchen nervously tapping her fingers on the table, waiting for Charles to arrive. He was right on time but when Eva's mother answered the door with an apology for her daughter's clothing choices, the smile on Eva's face dropped and she felt close to tears.

'Well, I think she looks beautiful,' Charles stated as he stepped inside and took one look at Eva.

'Maybe the two of you should just stay and have tea with us instead of going out,' Mrs Thompson said obviously embarrassed by her own daughter.

Charles was personally affronted by Eva's mother's comments and was incensed on Eva's behalf.

'Thank you for the offer Mrs Thompson, but I have a table booked,' Charles said curtly, biting his tongue so as not to let his true feelings show and put Eva in an awkward position. 'Come on Eva, let's go.' He took her by the hand and led her through the back door into the lane.

Charles was seething, and stopped once they were out of sight of the kitchen window. 'I can't believe the way they treat you, Eva. It amazes me how you stay so positive.'

Eva's face saddened. 'I guess I'm used to it, I've had it all my life. I wake up every morning and tell myself I will have an extraordinary day despite the criticisms and put downs from my parents.'

'You inspire me,' Charles whispered and gently pressed his lips to hers. 'And you look stunning in those jeans.' His hand lightly skimmed the curve of her hip, his fingers lingering on her backside. Eva's mood instantly lifted and there was a skip in her step as they set off walking.

The butterflies in Eva's belly quivered as she waited on the doorstep for Charles to unlock the door. She glanced at him discretely and could see the nerves showing on his face. She wondered what he was nervous about. Was he worried he would take things too far? Was he worried things wouldn't go far enough? Or, like her, was he nervous about wanting everything to be perfect. Eva wanted to feel things she'd never felt before, she hoped for new experiences that would lead her to new discoveries about herself. She wanted him to kiss her in places that only she had touched. They'd spent the weekend getting to know each other's minds; their deepest thoughts and feelings. Now she wanted to get to know him in a physical sense, to explore every inch of his body and learn what he liked. She felt ready.

Charles led her inside his tiny space.

'Charles, I love it!' she exclaimed as she looked around, her eyes taking everything in. There was a tiny kitchenette, barely more than a few cupboards really. An oven and sink stood separately, and a small Formica table sat to one side. There was a double bed against the back wall, which made Eva's heart race, and a small bathroom separated by a curtain. The walls were filled with books, which Eva was immediately drawn to.

'Make yourself at home while I finish up cooking. I've prepared most of it so it shouldn't take long. Can I get you a glass of wine?'

Eva suddenly felt very grown up and nodded excitedly. Charles poured two glasses and handed one to her as she was exploring his eclectic taste in books. She noticed her worn copy of the anthology of poems she had lent him at the Brontë book club sitting on his bedside table and felt heartened to know he would've been sitting in bed reading it and thinking of her.

Eva smiled to herself as she leafed through his library of books. She blushed as she came across Lady Chatterley's Lover and felt emboldened. Picking the book from the shelf, she took it with her to the table and sat down, sipping on her wine, flicking through the pages.

Charles served up the chops and vegetables with mashed potatoes. Pouring gravy into a jug, he set the food on the table, his lip curling when he noticed the book in her hand.

'Have your read it?' he asked, curious to know how far her knowledge extended.

'One of my favourites,' she answered seductively. 'I was just looking through to see if you'd made any notes in the margins.'

Charles blushed fiercely, something she'd never seen before. 'I haven't. But I do have a good memory when it comes to literature. It is my job after all.' He was flirting with her, and Eva felt aroused by his comments. She took a swig of her wine to steady her nerves and Charles replenished her glass from the bottle.

'Let's eat before it gets cold. We've got plenty of time to relax afterwards,' Charles said.

They ate their meal chatting easily about the couple of days they'd spent apart. Charles regaled Eva with tales of his students, many of them not much younger than her.

'You seem so much older than the boys I teach,' he mused.

'Good,' Eva laughed, 'I would hate for you to see me as your student.'

'I don't have any dessert I'm afraid,' Charles apologised once they'd scraped their plates clean.

'Oh, I'm sure we can think of something.' Her tone became more sultry as her fingers drifted along his arm and over his bicep.

'Eva, what are you doing to me?' He was enamoured by her tenacity and as much as he thought they should slow down; he was excited to go at her speed.

Charles pushed his chair back and stood, taking Eva's hand as she joined him.

'I'm sorry, I only have an armchair, no settee. Do you mind sitting on my bed?' His heart raced at the thought of her on his bed and the seductive eyes she made at him at the mere mention of the word.

Eva kicked off her shoes and climbed on his bed, leaning herself back against the pillows. Charles stood, admiring her confidence, in awe of her beauty.

'Join me?' Eva whispered, holding out her hand to him. Charles climbed on the bed, tentatively hovering over her before crashing his mouth to hers. Eva pulled him down to rest the full weight of his body on hers, encouraged by his appetite for her. She writhed her body under him, feeling sensations that were new to her. His kisses became softer, more gentle as they settled into a steady rhythm. He stroked her cheek, tangling his fingers in her hair as his tongue delicately dipped into her mouth, tenderly stroking her tongue with his. Eva groaned at the exquisite sense of touch, causing Charles to pull back before things were over too soon.

'What's wrong?' Eva asked concerned.

'Absolutely nothing, I just need to collect myself. I don't want this to be over before we've even started. I want this to be special for you,' Charles told her.

'Charles, you have no idea how special this is for me. I love you so much.'

'I love you too,' Charles's voice was breathy as he sat back on his haunches to give himself a break. Eva didn't want to stop. Her fingers drifted across the bottom of his shirt, and she lifted it over his head to reveal his bare chest, defined muscles aplenty. She gasped at the beautiful skin, just a smattering of hair creeping downwards from his navel, blushing when she thought about where that trail led. Eva sat up, touching him, bringing her lips to drop tender kisses on the smooth canvas.

She began to undo the buttons on her blouse, her eyes never leaving Charles's face. His eyes grew at the sight of her naked breasts. She'd worn no bra because she couldn't bear for him to see her in the old washed-out bras she owned, and she didn't have the finances to purchase something sexier and age appropriate. Charles took her waist in his hands and pressed his mouth to her waiting nipples. Pushing her gently back against the pillows, he adjusted his position and with a silent question in his eyes, she nodded her consent as he unfastened her jeans and pulled them slowly down her legs. Naked expect for her underwear, Eva felt sexy and exposed before him. Her skin tingled at every touch as he worked his way down from her lips, kissing every inch of her skin. Eva's hand worked its way into her underwear, pushing them down as her eyes locked with Charles's.

His mouth touched all the places she had hoped it would, and when he had prepared her fully, he reached for protection and took her to a place she was sure she never wanted to return from. Nothing in the books she had read had ever prepared her for this. It was uncomfortable at first, but the tender way Charles touched and caressed her was the most sensational feeling. She thought afterwards about those women in her mother's knitting circle and how they were missing out on something so incredible. She felt sorry for the miserable lives they led and promised herself that she would never let herself experience that kind of life.

Charles and Eva laid side by side, naked and breathless, their little fingers the only part of them touching. Eva's skin was highly sensitive, and she wallowed in the pleasure.

'How do you feel?' Charles whispered.

'I don't have the words to answer that question,' Eva smiled and turned her head to face him. 'I never imagined it could be like that.'

'Neither did I,' Charles said honestly.

Eva turned her head to face him, perplexed by his answer. 'But it's not your first time.'

'Eva, it was definitely my first time like that. You are exquisite. Your wild spirit definitely carries through into the bedroom,' Charles laughed.

Eva was pleased at his reaction to her. She felt she was his equal in every way now, and never wanted this to end.

They turned their bodies to face each other, their eyes connecting deeply as they whispered made up stories of their future together.

Charles got up and poured more wine, bringing the glasses back to bed. They climbed under the covers to keep the chill off, and with one arm draped around her shoulder, Eva snuggled her head into the crook of his arm.

'I never want to leave,' Eva said dreamily.

'I don't want you to go,' Charles agreed, dropping a kiss on the top of her head. 'Imagine living together, we could do this whenever we wanted. We could spend lazy Sunday mornings making love and reading to each other. I would cook you bacon and eggs and feed them to you naked.'

Eva laughed at Charles's sudden affinity for nakedness and blushed at the things they could do if she had the freedom from her parents.

'I love you Charles,' she said simply, without expectation or stipulations. She just quite simply loved him.

'Marry me Eva,' Charles said.

Eva's reaction was not what Charles expected. She leapt out of bed, dragging the sheets with her to protect her modesty. She stood with her back to him for several minutes, looking out of the window. Charles grabbed a shirt to cover himself and sat anxiously waiting for Eva to say something. She didn't.

'Eva...' Charles ventured, 'I'm sorry, that's not the way I wanted that to go at all. I apologise for upsetting you. I know it seems hasty, but I don't want to spend another moment without you.'

Eva slowly turned to face him, her grin splitting her face from ear to ear.

'Are you serious?' Her voice wobbled but Charles was buoyed by her beaming smile.

'Of course I'm serious Eva,' Charles laughed.

'Charles...' she began, and promptly burst into tears. Charles was bewildered by the rollercoaster of emotions Eva was displaying and stood to wrap her in his arms.

As Eva's tears began to subside, Charles stepped back and held her at arm's length, his eyes searching hers longingly. Eva stilled, not sure what to do next but when Charles dropped his hands to hers and knelt before her, she gasped.

'Eva, I know this is ridiculously quick and we've hardly had any time to get to know each other but I feel like I've known you my whole life.' Eva smiled, knowing she felt the same.

Charles continued, 'I love you, and I know in my heart that what I'm feeling now is only going to grow stronger. I don't want a life without you in it; I don't want to wait another minute to begin this adventure with you. Marry me. Be my wife.'

Eva slowly knelt in front of Charles; her hands still clasped in his. She leaned in and gently kissed his lips.

'Is that a yes?' Charles's eyes sparkled in anticipation.

Eva nodded excitedly. 'Yes, it's a yes.'

Charles pulled her towards him, his arms wrapping around her so tightly, he never wanted to let her go.

Eva, still wrapped in only the bedsheet, perched on the edge of the bed, concern in her eyes.

'Charles, you'll have to ask my father first, you know, do it properly. I'm not sure how my parents will react, you've seen how they are.' She looked disheartened at the prospect.

Charles sat on the bed next to her, draping his arm around her shoulder.

'Don't worry Eva, I'll ask him soon. Until then it can be our little secret. I want to propose properly anyway, with a ring.'

Eva smiled, but struggled internally with the thought that her parents might put an end to this. She hated being controlled and had feared marriage for that very reason. The thought of being stuck with someone like her own father filled her with dread. But this felt so different. Charles was different. He was a dreamer like her. He didn't want ordinary, he wanted adventure and passion, and she knew that a life with him would be everything she wished for. Not only did he love her, he also respected her, and that would give her the freedom she'd craved. Freedom to choose her own path, her own future, with Charles by her side.

Charles interrupted her reverie. 'I'd better get you home my love. I don't want to do anything that puts me on the wrong side of your parents.' He kissed her forehead, then winked, adding, 'at least not before we're married anyway.'

Eva laughed, a booming, hearty sound.

'Never stop laughing Eva,' Charles said. 'It suits you.'

Eva blushed and smiled shyly. 'I'd better get dressed first,' she said. 'I don't think my parents would approve of me turning up in a bed sheet.'

'Definitely not!' Charles replied, standing and pulling Eva up with him, the bed sheet dropping to the ground. Charles was hungry for her; Eva could see it in his eyes. The intimacy they'd shared rose up between them and she couldn't find it in herself to take her eyes off him.

After what felt like an eternity, Charles broke the intoxicating silence between them.

'As much as it kills me Eva, we have to go.' Eva nodded. Charles planted a chaste kiss on her lips and whispered, 'We have the rest of our lives to love each other.'

The bus dropped them at the end of the lane that led to Eva's back door. They lingered over the last stretch of their journey, not wanting this perfect evening to end. The light was on at the back door and Eva could see her mother pacing in the kitchen window.

'I'm not late, am I?' Eva asked.

'Right on time, she's probably just overthinking.' Charles pulled Eva back into the shadows to kiss her properly once more before walking her up the steps to the back door. The door opened before they'd even set foot on the bottom step.

'There you are,' Eva's mum exclaimed. 'You've been a long time.'

Eva balked at the formality of her mother's stance, her hands resting delicately against her apron.

'Yes, the evening ran away from us. Your daughter is wonderful company, and very intelligent. It's a pleasure spending time with her,' Charles answered.

Eva tried to suppress a giggle at the conversation, reliving the evening's pleasure.

Both her mother and Charles glared at her for obviously different reasons.

Eva turned to Charles, quickly brushing a kiss to his cheek. 'Thank you for a lovely evening. I hope to see you again soon, good night,' she said ducking past her mother's suspicious frown.

'Good night Eva, good night Mrs Thompson,' Charles said, and turned to walk home, a grin on his face so wide his muscles ached.

Eva floated through the rest of the week, buoyed by her new romance. She felt happier than she could ever remember, and she knew Charles was the reason. Still, she was conflicted by her feelings. Her whole life she had fought against her parents' ideas of traditional roles and vowed to herself that she would never let a man determine her happiness or success. Yet here she was, smitten by the first man who had paid her any attention, jumping into marriage at the age of eighteen. She was wavering between the fact that she had fallen so completely in love with him in such a short time, and the fact that he was also her ticket to freedom. Trying to consolidate her head and her heart was taking up a lot of her waking thoughts, yet the contention she was feeling couldn't overshadow her high spirits.

Charles had a lot on at school and Eva was busy at the cafe, so their time together was limited. Eva arrived home from work after a busy Saturday, looking forward to her date with Charles. A friend from work had lent her a dress to wear, modelled on the latest Mary Quant style, and she couldn't wait to show it off on her date, knowing her parents would strongly disapprove. Charles was taking her out dancing, which was another new experience for her, and she was feeling excited as she pushed open the back door into the kitchen.

She was surprised to see Charles sitting at the table with her parents, drinking tea and looking glum. Eva glanced at her watch, and threw a questioning look at Charles wondering why he was so early.

'Hello Eva,' Charles said formally.

'What's going on?' Eva questioned, concerned.

After a short silence, it was Eva's father who spoke.

'Charles here came to ask for your hand in marriage.' There was no lightness in his voice at all and a feeling of dread draped itself over Eva. Her eyes darted quickly to Charles, and he gave a small shake of his head, his eyes downcast.

Eva tried to keep her voice from shaking. 'And what was your answer?'

Her father raised his voice. 'Well, obviously the answer was no Eva, what kind of ridiculous question is that? We don't know this man. All we know is he seems to be filling your head with fantasies. You've been behaving frivolously since you met him. I won't agree to this.'

'I know who he is. He's the man I love, and I will be marrying him. I'm eighteen years old, I don't need your permission,' Eva said defiantly.

Her father seethed at her audacity.

'Do not speak to me like that young lady. While you live under my roof, you will follow my rules.' Turning to Charles he said, 'I think it's time you left, you've done enough harm.'

'No!' Eva shouted. 'If he leaves then I'm going with him.'

'Eva, stop behaving like a petulant child,' her father shouted. 'I'm sure after seeing this behaviour Charles will be grateful I said no.'

Charles stood, his height towering over Eva's father.

'Mr Thompson, if you don't mind, I'd like to speak.' He looked at Eva, reassuring her with a smile. 'First of all, I'm not leaving unless I'm sure Eva is safe. And secondly, Eva is not a petulant child. She is an intelligent young woman who is speaking her mind and standing up for herself. I understand your concern that we haven't known each other very long and we would be happy to have a longer engagement than we'd planned if that would appease you.'

Eva interrupted, 'Charles, no. Don't give in to him.' Tears sprung from her eyes.

Charles rested his hand gently on Eva's arm. 'It's okay Eva,' he said gently, before continuing to speak to her father. 'If you're not happy with that, then I'm not sure what else I can do.' Charles's voice was calm, his manner was respectful, but his tone was unyielding.

'How dare you speak to me like that in my house?' Eva's father bellowed at Charles. 'You can get out, that's what you can do. And don't ever come back.'

Charles nodded respectfully before hugging Eva tight and whispering in her ear. 'I love you, Eva. Let things settle, have a think about what you really want. I'll be at home. Take as long as you need.'

'Charles no! I'm coming with you.'

'Please Eva, for me,' he replied quietly, gripping her hand to provide little comfort.

Charles walked slowly to the door and turned, addressing both Eva's mother and father. 'I wish you could see Eva's brilliance. I wish you would get to know her mind like I have, instead of berating her at every turn and putting her down. With a little support, she has such a bright future ahead of her, and I am determined to be right alongside her and watch her achieve her dreams.'

Eva's parents were rendered speechless. Eva smiled at Charles as he mouthed the words, I love you as he pulled the door closed.

Eva turned to her parents. 'You won't stop me from seeing him. I cannot wait to leave this miserable house and go out into this big wide world and really begin to live. Because this? This is not living. You have a miserable excuse for a marriage, I've been nothing but an inconvenience to you my whole life, and you,' Eva said looking at her mother, 'you let yourself be walked over and undermined by him constantly. I will not become you, and if I stay in this house much longer, I fear that's exactly what will happen.'

Without waiting for a reply, Eva stormed up the stairs to her bedroom. She perched on the edge of her bed, her hands trembling as the adrenalin coursed through her. She had never stood up to her parents before or spoken to them like that. She felt energised, ready for the next chapter in her life.

She cleaned herself up and put on her new dress, carefully zipping up the back. She was going out with Charles tonight whether her parents liked it or not. How would they stop her? She'd never known her father to get physical, his abuse was only ever channelled through words and control. Being shouted at didn't affect her anymore, she'd switched off to it years ago. Pulling on her only pair of heels and grabbing her purse, Eva made her way downstairs, ready for whatever was waiting for her.

When she reached the kitchen, she found her mother sitting at the table sniffling into a scrunched-up tissue. Catching Eva's eye, she wiped her face and sat upright, the archetypal British stiff upper lip.

'Where is he?' Eva asked, not bothering to question her mother's tears.

'He went to the pub. He needed a drink after that tirade.'

'And what about you?' Eva asked her mother.

'You're too young to understand Eva. Life isn't that simple. You've grown up with your head in fairy tales. Real life isn't like that.'

'Maybe, maybe not, but real doesn't have to mean this either,' Eva said, waving her arm between her and her mother. 'I want real love in my life. Love isn't about control, it's about mutual respect and supporting the other person in their dreams. That's what Charles is to me. He understands me like no-one else ever has. You just want me to marry someone respectable and become you.'

Eva's mother closed her eyes and took a breath. 'You're wrong Eva, you have no idea what I want.'

Eva stared at her mother waiting for her to elaborate but her mother kept silent. Eva wasn't sure what she had meant but wasn't about to get into it now.

'I'm going on my date with Charles. Don't try and stop me,' Eva told her mother, and turned on her heels.

Lottie 2019

While I was experiencing a tiny window of hope from Gina's words, I pulled Kate's card from my purse and dialled her number before anxiety had the chance to take over. She answered on the first ring, and I stumbled over my words.

'Erm, Kate?'

'Yes, who's this?'

'It's Lottie, we met the other day at Beau's.'

'Lottie, hello, how are you?' Her voice was warm and peaceful, and she put my mind at rest immediately.

'I…I'm not great to be honest.' I felt like I shouldn't say that, but Kate seemed unfazed by my honesty.

'What are you doing right now?' Kate asked.

'Nothing.'

'Come on over, I'll put some coffee on.'

After quickly typing her address into the Maps app on my phone, I hung up and drove straight to Kate's house. She answered the front door dressed in soft grey tracksuit pants and a navy-blue hoodie. Her hair was loosely twisted into a knot on top of her head with wispy tendrils softly framing her face. She wore no make-up and her smile lit up her whole face. I felt an immediate affinity with her that overwhelmed me. She had the same aura that Beau emanated, and I felt surprised that she wasn't his biological mother.

She reached out and gently touched my arm, ushering me inside as she held the door open. Kate smiled tenderly, the comforting scent of fabric conditioner drifted from her and caressed my senses. I felt a rush of affection and I stumbled, unable to articulate the emotion I was feeling but knowing it was something I'd been missing of late.

As we reached the kitchen, the smell of coffee instantly washed away the strange sensation and my senses returned to normal.

'That smells so good,' I told Kate.

'A little birdie may have mentioned that you have a caffeine addiction,' she laughed as she handed me the coffee. 'Black, I believe?'

'Perfect, thank you.' We stood together in silence but there was no feeling of awkwardness between us, just a kind of acceptance that I was right where I need to be.

Kate led me through to a large, airy room at the back of her house which was possibly the most comforting place I'd ever been in. It was cluttered with plants and candles, overflowing bookshelves filled the wall while the floor was littered with boho style woven rugs. There were two huge armchairs that looked like they would swallow me whole. The large bi-fold doors opened out into a quaint little courtyard, filled with flowers of every colour.

'Wow, this is stunning Kate. If I lived here, I'd never leave this room.'

Kate laughed. 'This is my office. I designed it to welcome my clients and make them comfortable, it's more conducive to my job than a stuffy office. Grab a seat.' She motioned towards one of the oversized armchairs.

I settled into one of the chairs and it was as welcoming as it looked. I tucked my feet underneath me, clutching my coffee cup in both hands. Kate sat opposite but the chairs were angled slightly so it didn't feel intimidating. It did feel a little surreal though.

'You know, if someone had told me six months ago that I'd be here now in this place I'd have laughed in their face,' I sighed. The contrast of my life before and after had become so real.

'What place are you referring to Lottie?' Kate asked. 'The physical place; talking to a therapist? Or the emotional place of grief?'

I studied her face. She was beautiful in an unconventional kind of way. A real earth mother type: nurturing and calming, and her voice soothed my thoughts into some kind of coherent structure.

'I guess I mean my whole life. I had it all planned. Graduation, travel, be happy. Write a Nobel winning work of art, you know the average stuff,' I laughed. I hadn't thought about my life in a positive way in a while. It all seemed futile. I mean, what's the point of it all?

'So, what's changed?' Kate asked, and I glared at her as if she had two heads. She obviously noticed the look of incredulity on my face and added, 'I don't mean in a physical sense Lottie. Obviously you've suffered a great tragedy. What I mean is, what's changed your plans? They played no part in the future plans you just mentioned, apart from being in your life in a supportive, family kind of way.' I couldn't believe what she was saying, and I opened my mouth to interrupt but she continued. 'I'm not saying this to upset you, I'm playing devil's advocate. The only thing stopping you from achieving these goals is you. It's not the death of your dad and Tom that we need to confront here, it's your thoughts and feelings towards it, and how you process and approach things going forward.'

I wasn't sure how to respond so I sat quietly, contemplating what she'd just said. After a long silence, Kate began to speak again. She asked a few questions to guide my thoughts but mostly encouraged me to ramble. She was easy to open up to and it felt good to speak to someone impartial.

'I think we should leave it there today Lottie, give yourself some time to process what we've talked about. My door is always open.'

'What about money? I mean, I'm not sure how much I can pay you.' I suddenly felt guilty taking up her time like that, but Kate held up her hand to silence me.

'No, I'm not taking your money. I'm doing this as a favour to Beau. He's never asked this of me before, so I know it's important to him. You're important to him.' Her smile lit up her eyes and I blushed.

'He's important to me too. He's about the only person that gets me at the moment. He really understands what I'm going through.'

Kate smiled sadly, 'he really does.' Her face was reflective as she studied me. 'Has he spoken much about himself?'

'He's told me about his mum and sister, what his dad did and how he ended up here, if that's what you mean.'

She nodded thoughtfully. 'He had a tough time, and it took him a long time to open up to me. But I'll tell you one thing; if he has told you even a fraction of his experience, it means he trusts you implicitly. He's very careful whom he allows into his world and if he's let you in, I guarantee he will always have your back.' She smiled proudly, then added, 'he's a good guy.'

'I never even knew he was friends with Tom. Tom never mentioned him, but I guess that's not the only secret he was keeping from me.' I was mad at myself for being snarky towards Tom, but I was so pissed at him for keeping me out of something that was obviously difficult for him.

'Lottie, I know you're upset about possible secrets but it's not my place to talk to you about what was concerning Tom. I will, however, help you in any way I can, and I think delving into these dreams you've been having will bring you some clarity and help you deal with your feelings towards Tom in a more productive way.'

I felt embarrassed for trying to get her to spill Tom's secret. 'I know, I'm sorry. I shouldn't have mentioned Tom. It's just so frustrating you know?'

'I know.' She nodded her head towards the glass door behind me and I turned to see Beau in the kitchen. I stood and thanked Kate.

'Give it a few days to process and then call me, okay?' She hugged me warmly and I turned towards the kitchen, my only focus in that moment was on the guy standing there.

'Hey,' he smiled and stepped towards me. 'I thought that was your car, are you okay?' His eyes were full of concern for me, and I completely believed what Kate had said about him.

'Yeah, I just felt ready to talk. How was your exam?'

'It's hard to say.' He shrugged and acknowledged his foster mum as she came in from her office.

'Lunch anyone?' Beau asked us both as he studied the contents of the fridge.

'I thought you'd moved out,' Kate said, laughing as she pulled him out of the way and gathered some ingredients together.

'Yeah, but you have better food than I do,' Beau threw an arm around her shoulder and kissed her on the head, 'and you love me.'

She shook her head playfully and started to prepare lunch for the three of us. I watched their easy banter and felt warmth in my heart, but at the same time, a huge gaping hole.

'Well, I'll leave you two to it, I'm going to quickly eat this and go pick up Connor for his orthodontist appointment,' Kate said as she handed us both a plate. 'Lock up when you leave,' she told Beau.

'Thanks Kate, I really appreciate today.'

She smiled and I followed Beau into the lounge room where we dropped onto the couch and tucked into our sandwiches.

'Who's Connor?' I asked.

'Oh, sorry, he's Kate's other foster kid, the one I carry the spare helmet for,' Beau said with a grin, reminding me of my outburst when I thought he was using his bike as a pick up line.

'Sorry I haven't called,' he said. 'I've been so focused on my exam. How have things been?'

'Not great, things with my friend Rosie aren't good. Her mum told me to just concentrate on myself and Rosie will be fine.' I sighed, 'I don't know, I guess I feel guilty but also don't have the energy to deal with it.'

I finished my lunch and Beau reached for my hand. We sat silently holding hands for what seemed like forever. I loved the feeling of simplicity between us, the stillness, the silence. It was effortless yet it felt immense at the same time. I tilted my head to the side as I contemplated my thoughts silently, our eyes locked on each other.

'What are you thinking about?' he asked, his words startling in the silence.

'You're so beautiful,' I replied without a second thought. His eyes darkened rapidly, and his mouth was on mine in a split second. He gently eased me backwards, straddling my hips as his lips brushed mine, gliding down my throat to my neck. Our hands were still locked, and he pushed my arms above my head holding them in place as he explored me, looking up at me to get my green light. I nodded in encouragement, feeling the pleasure flutter through me like a thousand butterflies. His mouth travelled up to my ear and a gratified groan escaped my lips. He released his hand from my grip and wound it through my hair, his thumb brushing my temple before moving his lips back to mine and easing my head towards him gently. His tongue probed mine and I was losing myself in him. I needed more of him. I pushed my hips towards him desperate for contact. He jerked back quickly and rolled to the side, leaving me feeling exposed beside him. I closed my eyes to the tears that were threatening to emerge. He let out a breath and turned onto his side. I could feel his breath on my cheek, but I couldn't open my eyes for fear of giving myself away.

'Lottie, I'm sorry, I had to stop.' His voice was raspy, his breathing shallow. 'I don't want to take advantage of you. You're in a vulnerable place.'

Never more sure of how I felt in that moment, I opened my eyes and turned to him. 'You wouldn't be taking advantage of me Beau, I've never wanted anything more than I want you right now.' I didn't want to beg but I felt so frustrated.

His eyes were full of lust as his thumb ran smoothly across my lower lip. 'Not here Lottie, not like this,' Beau whispered. 'I really care about you, and I know you're hurting right now. I'd never forgive myself if I took it too far and caused you more pain.' He looked so sincere, and I couldn't help thinking how lucky I was that he cared so damn much. My head knew he was right, I just wished my heart would catch up.

'Thanks for caring.' I smiled at him in defeat. 'I care about you too.'

He leaned in and kissed me affectionately, lingering long enough that I understood how much he wanted it too.

Beau's bike rumbled into the driveway, and I quickly grabbed Tom's old leather jacket, figuring it would give me better protection than my denim one. His scent lingered, mixed with the smell of the leather and I breathed him in, stirring my emotions. I wondered what his secret was. My mind wandered into all kinds of scenarios that he may have found himself alone in and I couldn't come up with a single thing that he would have been too afraid to talk to me about. I paused for a moment, anxious. The knock on the door broke through my trance and brought me back to the fact that Beau was outside waiting for me. I held one finger up through the glass letting him know I'd just be a minute.

Mum shouted from her room, 'who's at the door?' I stopped a moment; I'd forgotten she was even there; it'd been days since we'd spoken. Her words sounded slurred, probably from the sleeping tablets.

'No-one,' I shouted, slipping out the door. I refused to get into an argument with her and I knew that was where it would lead if I answered her question. I opened the front door and Beau's proximity provided immediate stillness. Without hesitation, he pulled me in tight for a hug, which left me considerably less anxious than I was only moments ago.

'Hey,' he whispered. His lips brushed the top of my ear. A shiver ran through me as his voice resonated through my chest.

'Let's get out of here,' I told him as he released me from his grip. I climbed on the bike behind him, shuffling as close as I could, grasping his waist for both security and self-gratification. He hadn't told me where we were going, and to be honest I didn't care. Just being with him transported me into my new reality, the place where I was starting to feel at home, the place I felt safe. Heading west, Beau guided the bike through the rush hour traffic, eventually taking us north over the road bridge crossing the river. The sun began to set over the ocean casting a tangerine glow across the darkening sky. It was so beautiful to watch I squeezed Beau a little tighter wanting to share my joy. He took one hand off the handlebars and rested it briefly on my knee to let me know he was right there with me. The traffic began to diminish as we headed further north up the coast road and as we left the hustle of the city behind us, I felt a freedom like never before. The sky darkened quickly, and I caught a glimpse of the moon as it began its ascent.

I had no clue how long we'd been riding, but my back was starting to feel stiff. It was difficult to think about my problems nestled so close to Beau. He was like a dreamcatcher. Although my dreams were often front and centre in my mind, his presence helped me to look at them with a much calmer perspective. They were so vivid; I was certain they were trying to express some kind of subconscious thoughts. I just had no idea how to interpret what they were trying to tell me, and I was looking forward to hashing it all out with Kate.

The stiffness in my back snapped me back to the present and I began to fidget on my seat. Beau slowed the bike and I saw a twinkling of lights ahead, illuminating the way after a long stretch of darkness. I gripped him tight as he guided the bike around a tight corner into a car park next to the brightly lit building. Beau pulled into a small space, shut off the engine and kicked the stand down. He motioned for me to climb off and I pulled off my helmet and shook my curls loose.

'I hope you like seafood,' he said, nodding towards the old rundown shack at the edge of the beach. I smiled as I took the hand he offered and followed him into the building. Wooden tables with bench seats were scattered randomly, and sliding doors opened out onto a deck overlooking the beach. A small counter in front of a hatch, which opened up to the kitchen was occupied by an old man. He appeared to be of Aboriginal heritage and his broad grin upon seeing Beau was engaging. They obviously knew each other well and he stepped from behind the counter to greet us. Shaking Beau's hand, he patted him on the shoulder firmly, and then pulled him in for a hug.

'How are you holding up?' he asked. 'It's a bloody tragedy.'

Beau puffed out a long breath, followed by a faint nod of the head.

I was a little confused by this interaction. What tragedy did he mean?

'Clinton, I'd like you to meet Tom's sister, Charlotte,' Beau said. 'Lottie, this is Clinton, the owner of the best seafood restaurant in town.'

'You knew my brother?' I asked by way of greeting.

Clinton nodded. 'My sympathies to you Charlotte, Tom meant a lot to many people,' he said, shaking my hand. He turned to Beau, 'two specials?'

Beau looked at me and I shrugged. 'Yeah, two specials please Clint.'

'On the house tonight mate, in memory of Tom.' He bowed his head towards us, and I felt a rush of gratitude that my brother had been surrounded by so much love.

Beau draped his arm around my shoulder, ushering me towards the deck. 'Are you good to sit outside?' he asked.

'Sure,' I said. We sat close to each other on a bench seat, staring out towards the darkness of the ocean. The waves crashed on the shoreline, calm spreading over me.

'How do you know Clinton?' I asked, intrigued by the obvious close relationship between the three men.

'I've known Clint forever,' he said. 'When I was younger my dad brought me here to camp on the beach. We'd fish and build campfires. Clint was always around, and he'd come and join us after he closed the cafe. He used to live in a caravan in the parking lot. I didn't see him for a few years after dad went to prison, but Kate brought me straight here once I opened up to her about him. He'd obviously heard about dad but had no way of contacting me. He was devastated; couldn't believe his friend could turn like that. I brought Tom here when he was looking for a subject for an assignment. Clint was taken from his family as a small child and raised by a white family. His story was just what Tom had been looking for and they hit it off immediately. We'd often come here on the bike and play cards together.'

As much as Beau's speech conjured up a real sad story, one I was interested to know more about, I laughed at the image he evoked in my mind.

'So, all those nights I thought Tom was out partying and living the student life, you're telling me he was really here playing poker with an old man?'

Beau smiled, 'I love to hear you laugh Lottie.' His forehead wrinkled as he said my name and he paused in deep thought.

'Can I ask you something?' he asked cautiously.

'Of course,' I replied, uncertain of where he was going to go.

'It seems weird to me calling you Lottie.'

That was definitely not what I was expecting to come out of his mouth, and I was unsure how to respond. I frowned as I stumbled over my words.

'That's my name, why would it seem weird?'

'Tom always referred to you as Charlie or Charlotte, never Lottie. I was confused when Ben introduced you as Lottie, it took me a second to realise you were the same sister. I've just always thought of you as Charlie.'

I was shocked by his words. That seemed odd, I'd always been Lottie.

'Really? I wondered why you introduced me to Kate and Clinton as Charlotte. I'm not sure why Tom would've done that. He did call me Charlie sometimes when we were younger, but it was usually when he was mad at Mum. She never liked him calling me that. I don't know why, I quite like it,' I pondered.

'I do too, it suits you.' Beau smiled as the doors opened and Clint arrived with huge baskets of seafood.

'Wow! This looks amazing,' I told him as he put a basket down in front of me.

'Thanks Clint,' Beau said, and Clint responded with a questioning look. Clint's eyes quickly darted to me and then back to Beau as if wondering why I was there. Beau shook his head and laughed. 'You always were nosey Clint, mind your own business.'

Clint winked at me and headed back inside. Beau and I ate our food in silence, devouring every mouthful. It tasted so good; I couldn't believe I'd never been here before. When we'd both finished, Beau took the trays inside to Clint and grabbed a couple of bottles of water from the fridge. Watching him through the glass, I saw him get his wallet out to pay but was waved away by Clint. They launched into what appeared to be an intense discussion, and then Beau looked my way and smiled. Clint clapped him on the back as if praising him.

Beau returned a few minutes later, sitting close to me and handing me a bottle. 'Are you warm enough?' he asked. I nodded, my focus on the emerging stars.

'It's so beautiful here, I've never been before.' I turned to Beau. 'I feel like the more time I spend with you, the closer I feel to my brother.'

Beau studied me carefully. 'Is that why you're here? I mean with me— to feel closer to Tom?'

I was shocked that he'd even think that, and I knew from the look on his face that he regretted asking me.

'Is that why you've been spending time with me? Because of Tom?' I asked.

He kissed my forehead, leaving his lips lingering on my skin. When he pulled away, he looked into my eyes, his face close to mine.

'No, I mean, maybe at first. The way he talked about you was like he had you on the highest pedestal. He thought the world of you Charlie.' He faltered over the slip in my name. 'I'm sorry, Lottie.'

'It's okay, I like the name Charlie. It kind of fits in with this version of myself that no-one knows but you,' I tell him, beginning to accept my new reality.

His relief showed on his face, and he took a deep breath.

'When I first saw you that night in the bar, you took my breath away. I had no idea who you were, and I know it sounds crazy, but you made me feel something, as though I knew you already. Then when you got in Ben's car later that night, I couldn't believe you were Tom's sister. I knew he would want me to make sure you were okay, but it's become way more than that for me. I hope you feel that. I've got some really strong feelings going on and I'm not quite sure what to do with them.' Somewhere during his little speech, his eyes had closed. They opened quickly and locked on mine, studying me closely as if to assess the impact of his words. I didn't say a word; I wasn't sure I'd be able to even if I wanted to. Beau was so switched on to his emotions, and secure in his own vulnerability. It was such an attractive feature in a man.

He continued, 'I don't want to overwhelm you, I know things are all over the place for you right now. And I don't want you to confuse my feelings for you. I'm here to help you, but I also care about you.' He paused, 'a lot.'

I nodded, taking him all in. His eyes were brimming with emotion and honesty. I knew his feelings for me ran deep, even in the short time we'd known each other, and I did respect him for not wanting to rush me. I loved the depth of his character, but God sometimes he was infuriating, and all I wanted was to rip his damn clothes off.

'It's more than that though.' He straddled the bench to face me properly and held both of my hands in his. His breathing became heavy and his face impassioned. 'Lottie, Charlie, both versions of you are so fucking beautiful, it takes all the strength I have to keep this slow. I want you in ways I never even knew were possible, so don't ever think I'm only here for Tom, or that I'm only after one thing. It's everything, you're everything.'

I was physically shaking after his speech. He squeezed my hands tight to try and still me, constantly rubbing his thumbs in soft circles.

'I think that's the most you've ever said to me in one go,' I said, and he laughed, easing the sexual tension rising between us.

'I didn't think my message was coming across strongly enough with my usual silent charm.' He'd broken the intensity with his light-hearted response, but I still needed him to understand my position too.

'Beau...' His laughter stopped at the sound of my voice and his forehead furrowed as I brought the tone back to a serious note. 'The same goes for me. I'm not here to feel close to Tom. I'm here because you make me feel things I've never felt before. You make me think differently, you understand how I feel, and you seem to know me more than I know myself. You bring me peace. Just being near you calms me and gives me clarity. Yes, I'm doing it tough right now; I feel like I've lost a hell of a lot more than my dad and brother, but I also feel like I've gained so much with you. I respect you so much for the way you care about my feelings, but honestly my feelings for you are so strong, I'm beginning to fall for you.'

There was a stillness in the air surrounding us, and the last words I spoke lingered on the breeze. Beau's eyes twinkled in the moonlight.

'I feel the same.' His hands released mine, sliding up my arms and into my hair at lightning speed. His kiss was the most powerful drug. His warm breath mingled with mine, intoxicating me as his tongue feverishly explored my mouth leaving every tiny nerve-ending ablaze. I couldn't get enough of him. I pushed my hands inside his jacket to get closer to his chest, igniting sparks at the close contact. The kiss ended leaving me breathless and dizzy, craving more of him. There were no words to express the energy I felt when I was with him. He made me feel so alive and liberated, as though I was exactly who I wanted to be.

Eva 1962

After what seemed like an endless bus ride, Eva knocked on the door of Charles's bedsit. As she waited, she began to question herself. Had Charles meant what he'd said or had he had the chance to change his mind. Eva turned away, suddenly feeling silly for turning up out of the blue.

'Eva?' She heard her name and turned to see Charles in the open doorway, his hair wet and a towel in his hand. Fresh from the bath, Charles was clean shaven, his shirt undone.

'Eva! Are you okay?' Charles reached his hand out and took hold of Eva's, gently pulling her inside. Kicking the door closed behind him, Charles took Eva's face in his hands.

'Did your father change his mind?' he asked. 'You look beautiful by the way.'

Eva smiled. 'Thank you, but no, my father would never back down. I came anyway,' Eva shrugged like it was no big deal.

'Eva, as much as I'm overjoyed that you're here, I don't want you to make things worse for yourself.' She could hear the concern in his voice and was overwhelmed by the intensity of his feelings for her.

'My dad had gone out, but I told my mum I was seeing you. She didn't try and stop me.'

'What if they throw you out Eva? I mean, would they do that?' Charles wasn't sure but from what he'd seen of her father, it seemed like something he was capable of.

'I don't think so. But what if they did? It wouldn't be the worst thing, would it? I could move in here.' Eva's face lit up.

'Before we're married?' Charles questioned. 'Wouldn't that bother you?'

Eva laughed. 'Why would it bother me? It's not like I'm a virgin!'

Charles laughed along with Eva, his serious tone finally lifting.

'Well, no, but the neighbours don't know that.'

'Listen, Charles, I love you. I don't care what anyone else thinks. I am going to marry you just as soon as you propose to me properly,' Eva told him forcefully. 'I want a ring too,' she added, winking at him.

Charles pulled her to him and hugged her fiercely. 'I love you too,' he whispered, 'and don't you worry, I have plans.' He kissed her cheek. 'Right, I'd better get dressed properly so I can take you dancing.'

Eva mooched around the tiny kitchen while Charles fastened his shirt and combed his hair. He splashed cologne on his face and turned to Eva.

'How do I look?'

'Very handsome,' she said moving towards him slowly, 'maybe a little too handsome.' She brushed her fingers lazily across his jawline, biting down gently on her lip trying on a new seductive side. 'Maybe I don't want to go dancing after all.' Eva stood on her tiptoes and trailed her lips where her fingers had just been.

Charles groaned, 'Eva, you're killing me.'

Eva smirked, her confidence rising. Charles made no effort to stop her as her hands began to explore him further, slowly untucking his shirt. Eva's senses heightened and she became dizzy, leaning against him to regain balance.

Her pause gave Charles the opportunity to break the moment. 'Come on, let's go out. I promised you a night you would never forget.'

Eva took a deep breath as Charles picked up his jacket, discreetly patting its pocket before putting it on.

'Can we come back here afterwards?' Eva asked shyly, a departure from her previous boldness. Charles was intrigued by the two sides to her character.

'Of course,' he whispered back.

'Where are we going?' Eva asked Charles as they settled into their seats on the bus.

'I don't want to spoil the surprise,' Charles replied lifting their entwined hands and kissing her fingertips.

Eva had guessed as soon as she saw the destination on the front of the bus. A new dance hall had opened in town; some friends from work had gone the previous week. She'd been enthralled by their stories and had relished in all the details. It sounded just wonderful. She'd hoped Charles would take her there and now she was all but sure. Eva couldn't wait to see the lights on the ceiling; her friends had described it like a million stars lighting up the sky. She couldn't wait to dance with Charles, being close to him made her feel so loved. He was very tactile, touching her or brushing his fingers against her every chance he got. She looked at him now only to see him watching her intensely.

'What are you thinking?' he asked, quietly.

'I'm thinking about where we're going, and the night we're going to have.' Her face beamed and Charles was captivated.

From the bus it was a short walk to the dancehall, and Eva's face lit up when she saw the line and all the excited people eager to get inside.

When it was finally their turn, they handed their jackets to the cloakroom attendant and Eva waited impatiently wondering what problem Charles was having with his jacket. Eventually he joined her, and they walked into the illuminated hall hand in hand. Eva gasped at the starlit sky and pulled Charles eagerly towards the dance floor.

Charles laughed. 'Don't you want to get a drink first?'

Eva looked torn. 'Just one dance and then a drink,' she pleaded.

Charles shook his head and smiled at her enthusiasm, following her through the crowded room.

After several dances a song began to play that they hadn't heard before, so they made their way to the bar. Eva suddenly felt shy and immature, not knowing what drink to order. She didn't want to seem like a child and order lemonade but had no clue what else to order in a place like this. Charles immediately sensed her discomfort and took over.

'Babycham?' he asked her casually as though that was her drink of choice.

She nodded and managed a half smile, feeling stupid.

The young couple found some seats in a dark corner, and Charles poured her drink from the miniature bottle.

'Hey, what's wrong?' he asked Eva as she ran her finger aimlessly around the base of the glass.

'I felt like a child. I didn't even know what to order. What are we even doing?' Eva was questioning everything. Did she even belong with Charles? He seemed so mature and wise, even though the age difference was only a few years.

'Eva, don't talk that way.' Charles rested his thumb on the side of her jaw, lifting her chin so he could look in her eyes. 'I love you. You are beautiful and intelligent and fun and have so much energy and enthusiasm for life. That's why we're here, that's why we're together. You don't have to be embarrassed about the things you haven't done before; I want to experience all the new things with you.'

'I'm sorry, I love you too. I just don't want you to think I'm a baby, I feel like one sometimes. My parents have kept me so sheltered.'

'Eva, it's not a bad thing to be a little naive, in fact I love that innocence about you. I love when you're impulsive and fearless, but when you're feeling vulnerable, you look at me in a way that just makes my heart melt.'

Tears glistened in Eva's eyes, and Charles knew this was the moment he'd been waiting for. Pushing his chair back, he reached into the pocket of his trousers and removed the little box he'd anxiously transferred from his jacket, causing delay at the cloakroom. Falling to one knee, he held out the velvet box in front of him, opening it for Eva to see.

Her hands flew to her face as she gasped at the sight.

'Yes, yes! A million times yes!' She squealed the answer before he'd even asked her the question.

Charles laughed at her enthusiasm. 'I'm loving the answer, but can you give me a second to ask the question first?'

'Oh, I'm sorry, go ahead,' Eva blushed at her eagerness.

Charles cleared his throat, 'Eva, my love. In the short time we've known each other you've completely turned my world upside down. I can't even remember a world without you in it. I want to spend my life with you, having adventures and creating memories. Will you marry me?' Eva's tears spilled over and trickled down her cheek. She was speechless.

Charles took her hand and pushed the ring on her finger. 'You already said yes so I don't need you to answer again,' he said, chuckling at the overwhelm on her face.

'Of course, yes!' Eva admired the stunning ring which now took pride of place on her left hand. She'd never in her life owned anything so beautiful. The ring was made of silver with a sapphire set amongst diamonds. It was stunning, and perfect for her. 'How did you afford this Charles?'

Charles looked sheepish. 'It was my grandmother's, I hope you don't mind. She passed a few years ago but gave this to me when she became ill. We were very close; she was the only member of my family that understood my love of literature. We would spend hours reading books together when I was young.' Charles smiled at the memory. 'She was such a romantic and she wanted more than anything for me to marry someone who would light me up whenever she walked in the room.'

'Charles…' Eva began.

Charles was kneeling now on both knees, still holding Eva's hand in his. His voice was shaky and breathless, but he continued, 'I wish you could've met her Eva. She would have loved you as much as I do. She would be very proud to know that you're the one wearing her ring.'

Eva released her hand from Charles's grip and took his face in both her hands. 'I love the ring, I love you, and now I love your grandmother.' She smiled and then brought her lips to his.

'Eva, wake up.' Charles shook her gently as the sunrise began to gleam through the gap in the curtains.

Eva stirred, rubbing her eyes before opening them and seeing Charles laid before her. Surprise lit up her face and she glanced at the clock on the nightstand.

'Oh gosh, we fell asleep. I've been here all night, my parents will kill me.' She jumped out of bed and went into full panic mode. 'They'll throw me out for sure.'

'I'm so sorry, it's my fault. We shouldn't have come back here; I should've just taken you straight home.' Charles looked regretful.

Eva's panic evaporated as she took in what he'd said.

'No, Charles please don't say that. I had the best night of my life. I wanted to come here.' Her engagement ring caught the sunlight, glistening in her eyes and she grinned. 'We're engaged! You're my fiancé! Do you know what? Let them say what they want because we're getting married and there's nothing they can do to stop us.' Eva smiled a seductive smile and climbed back onto the bed, pushing Charles backwards from his sitting position. Situating herself carefully on top of him, Eva began to kiss the smattering of hair on his chest. She felt bold and shameless as her mouth ventured lower. Charles gasped and Eva drew her eyes up towards him, silently questioning his reaction. Barely moving his head, he gave a nod, encouraging her to continue. His body tensed as her mouth moved further still, her tongue exploring every inch of him until he felt every hair on his body stand on end. The sensation was electrifying; sharp pulses turned into a resounding tremor as his entire body began to convulse. Eva watched him, delighting in his pleasure, before collapsing in a heap on his slick body.

Charles ran his fingers, lazily tracing the gentle curve of her behind as he allowed her body to relax into his. He inhaled her scent, a heady mix of last night's perfume and a night in his bed. She was intoxicating. He nuzzled her neck until she turned her mouth to his and he breathed her in like he was taking his last breath.

It wasn't until the bus stopped at the end of the lane that led to Eva's kitchen door that she began to slip back into the panicked state she'd been in earlier. Charles could feel his nerves rising but he was determined to hold himself together to support Eva through whatever was about to happen. They reached the back lane and Charles stopped, turning Eva towards him.

'Whatever happens, I want you to know that I'll be right by your side.'

Eva nodded, the uncertainty of her immediate future playing on her mind. Charles grasped her hand as though his life depended on it, and they walked boldly down the lane towards her back door.

Through the window, they could see Eva's mother at the kitchen table, her head in her hands. She looked up as she was disturbed by their footsteps on the gravel path. Her face was blotchy, her eyes bloodshot. There was a half empty bottle of Scotch on the table. Eva turned to Charles, now even more worried about what they were about to walk into.

Eva's mother was up out of her seat by the time they opened the door. She rushed at Eva, in a display of affection Eva had never experienced from her before.

'Where have you been? I've been so worried,' she asked.

'We went out and then it got late, and we accidentally fell asleep. I'm sorry, Charles doesn't have a phone.' Eva was matter of fact. After seeing her mother's display, the nerves had lifted. She looked around the kitchen and then realised her mother was dressed the same as she was last night. 'Have you not been to bed?'

Her mother nervously glanced at the whisky bottle on the table and flushed red. 'No, Eva, I was beside myself with worry about you. You've never behaved like this before. I'm beginning to think your father was right about this courtship.' Her mother glanced at Charles and pursed her lips.

'Where is Dad?' Eva asked, suddenly curious about her father's absence so early on a Sunday morning.

'He didn't come home from the pub.' Her mother sat back down again, and all inhibitions now gone, she poured herself another shot.

'Mum! It's eight o'clock in the morning! What are you doing?' Eva shouted at her mother, wondering what on earth had happened to her in the few hours she'd been away.

Her mother looked suddenly sheepish and pushed the glass away, shaking her head as if that would clear away her poor choices. Eva and Charles looked on in astonishment.

'Have you called the police? What if he's been hurt?' Eva asked, in an unusual showing of concern for her father.

'Oh, I know where he is, and who's bed he's keeping warm. He thinks

I'm stupid.' Mrs Thompson was slurring her words and Eva was dumbfounded at what she had just heard drip from her mother's lips.

Eva felt a surge of pity for her mother.

'Mum, why don't you go upstairs and clean yourself up. I'll make you a strong cup of tea and some toast.'

Eva's mother nodded, feeling chastised by her own daughter. Maybe Eva was old enough to get married after all, she thought.

While her mother was upstairs, Eva and Charles busied themselves tidying the kitchen and making several rounds of toast.

'What the heck just happened Charles? I feel like I'm in an alternate universe,' Eva said, half laughing.

Charles folded her into his arms to comfort her. 'I have no idea, she certainly wasn't the same woman I was talking to yesterday, that's for sure.' He paused, then continued, 'and what's that about your dad? Did you know about that?'

'No! I'm just as shocked as you are. I mean, they have a miserable marriage so I can't say that I'm surprised but I had no idea. I wonder whose bed she could've meant?' Eva mused.

Eva's mother reappeared looking only slightly better than before, but at least she was wearing clean clothes and no longer smelled like a distillery.

'Sit down Mum,' Eva said, passing her a cup of tea and a plate of buttered toast.

Her mother did as she was told and began to pull at her toast, breaking small pieces off and letting them melt in her mouth like a small child would.

A look passed between Charles and Eva, and Eva nodded, glancing at the sparkling ring on her finger, a complacent smile shadowing her lips.

'Mum, I have something to tell you.' Eva spoke cautiously.

'What's that?' her mother asked, dismissively.

'Charles asked me to marry him last night.' Eva paused, waiting for a reply but her mother continued to suck on her tiny pieces of toast.

'I said yes, if you're interested.' Again, Eva waited for a reply.

'Well, we'll be getting married just as soon as we can get things organised.' Eva heard a noise at the door into the living room and looked up to see her father standing there with a thunderous look on his face.

'Dad!' Eva's voice faltered and her demeanour changed immediately.

'What is he doing here?' her father demanded. 'I told you yesterday you wouldn't be seeing him again.'

Charles squeezed Eva's hand to let her know he would back her whichever way she wanted to play this. Charles's presence emboldened her.

'And I told you we would be getting married.'

Eva's father leaped through the doorway towards her, and Charles immediately moved in front of her in protection mode.

'Step aside son, this doesn't concern you.'

'With all due respect sir, it does concern me. I won't let you hurt Eva.'

Eva's father was taken aback but soon gathered himself.

'You will not speak to me like that in my house. Now, get out.' Charles stood his ground.

Eva moved from behind Charles's back to confront her father.

'Dad, Charles and I are getting married. You can accept it or not, but it is happening.' Eva flashed her ring for her father to see. 'And to be perfectly honest, after learning where you've been all night, you have no right to make judgements on my choices.'

Her father stared at her mother, a look of horror tormenting his face. Her mother visibly squirmed in her seat at Eva's words.

Not knowing what else to say to his daughter, he turned to her and said, 'Eva, Charles is obviously the reason for your recent insolence, and I will not tolerate it. If you continue to disobey me then you will not be welcome in this house.' Eva was shocked. She hadn't really expected him to throw her out.

Looking her father in the eye she said simply, 'I'll go pack.'

Lottie 2019

My throat constricts from the compression around my neck. My fingers claw at my chest, trying to loosen the pressure but there's too much force. I'm helpless. Pressure builds in my head, and I no longer have the strength to fight. My body goes limp. My vision goes black.

Sweat pooled on my body, and my heart raced as I strived to catch my breath. I stared at the ceiling until my breathing slowed, then picked up my phone to check the time. It was 4am. Beau would be asleep, but I checked messenger just in case. He hadn't been active for over three hours. Feelings of disappointment crept into my head. Firstly, because he wasn't there when I needed him and secondly, and more importantly I was disappointed in myself for relying on him to fix me. I hated that feeling of needing someone, but he was the only person I could talk to.

I tossed and turned and couldn't get back to sleep, the dream playing continuously in my head. Who was trying to hurt me? Were the dreams trying to tell me something? I had no idea what was going on in my head, but I was starting to feel crazy. I noticed my phone light up on my nightstand. It was Beau.

I noticed you were online, are you okay?

Yeah, I had a dream, and I can't get back to sleep. Why are you awake?

There was a long pause with no reply, and I wondered if he'd gone back to sleep. Then my phone rang.

'Hey,' I whispered. 'Are you okay?'

'Yeah, I've just been lying here thinking about you. Since we're both awake, I know a great spot to watch the sunrise if you're interested?' he asked.

'What, now?' The anticipation of seeing him found its way into my voice and took it a notch higher.

'Well, neither of us can sleep, we may as well make use of our insomnia.'

'Okay,' I said, trying to control my voice, 'if you're serious, I'll come and pick you up. I don't think I'll be able to balance a coffee on your bike!'

He laughed at my addiction, 'see you soon.'

I hopped out of bed and pulled on some old jeans and a hoodie. I brushed my teeth and quickly ran a make-up wipe over my face. Grabbing the fleece blanket off my couch, I picked up my car keys and crept out of the front door, hoping mum wouldn't hear me. I didn't want my suddenly happy mood crushing. I pulled up outside Beau's apartment in less than ten minutes and saw him waiting in the shadows.

'Hey,' I said as he climbed in the passenger seat and leaned over for a kiss. It all seemed so natural, like I'd known him my whole life. A shiver of excitement ran down my spine when I thought of how normal I felt in that moment, and I felt myself falling a little bit deeper.

'You'll have to direct me,' I told him as we pulled away along his street, 'I've no idea where we're going.'

'First to Macca's, I don't think anywhere else will be serving coffee at this hour.'

I drove towards the nearest twenty-four-hour McDonalds and picked up two coffees from the drive through. Beau then gave me directions to where we were headed. He cranked up the music and we drove in silence. When his directions brought me off the freeway at the city exit, I looked at him confused.

'Oh, we're going to Kings Park,' he said smugly. 'Best view of the sunrise.'

'Well, you could've just told me that instead of directing me every two minutes. I am capable of getting to Kings Park.'

He shrugged as I continued to navigate my way into the park. Coffee and blanket in hand, we wandered near the war memorial and sat on the grass. Beau huddled close to me as we wrapped the blanket around us in the dark. The sun wouldn't be up for a while yet, so we sipped on our coffee until Beau broke the silence.

'Tell me about your dream. Was it like the others?'

'Yeah, it was so vivid, I felt like I was dying. I couldn't catch my breath, it's hard to explain.' I felt so frustrated because I really couldn't get my head around it.

'I don't think there's always an explanation. Sometimes dreams are just your subconscious mind's way of helping you process things. I do think they're probably connected to your grieving process. I'm sure Kate will help.'

The arm that was hugging me under the blanket pulled me closer and I snuggled my head onto his shoulder. We finished our coffee as the first light broke beyond the hills, and I felt confident that the new day brought with it a new spark, a flame to light the way through this new chapter in my life. In that moment I felt positive that I would get through this and come out the other side. Not as the same Lottie though; I'd seen a huge shift in my perspective over the last few weeks and I knew I would never be the same again. The more time I spent with Beau, the more I began to think about the name Charlie and the way it made me feel. I wondered about Tom's reasoning for using that name when he spoke about me to the people I didn't know, and I wondered why it felt more in keeping with my current self.

The sunlight burned through the darkness and Beau took his phone out of his pocket, capturing my silhouette against the brightening sky.

'You're so beautiful,' Beau nuzzled his lips against my hair and murmured in my ear. I turned to face him, ignoring the radiant glow of the sunrise behind me, and stroked my fingers softly in the morning shadow on his face.

'I love you.' Those three words were the most natural words in the world for me to say right then, and I couldn't have said anything more true and honest. Beau remained silent but I could feel his breath become heavy, and the intensity with which he was looking at me left me exposed. The silence between us was charged; the energy was electric, and I could feel the cool air begin to sizzle. Beau closed the space between us, and his lips met mine, consuming me breath by breath. The bitter taste of coffee lingered on his tongue, and the warmth spread through my mouth as Beau's passionate assault captured every cell in my body. I lay back on the grass, pulling Beau with me, not wanting to detach from him for a single second. One hand travelled down my body, stopping at my hips, while the other gently brushed my ear, his fingers twirling my hair. My hand held the back of his neck, keeping him close to me, craving his affection.

By the time the sun had risen, the park began to slowly fill with early morning joggers. We were both breathless and dazed from our intense make-out session and were met with a few knowing glances as we brushed the grass from our clothes and shook the blanket. I felt light as a feather and glimpsed a twinkle in Beau's eyes. We smiled shyly at each other before heading back to the car. My body temperature had lowered by the time I started the engine, and I turned the heater on full. The music was loud, and Beau and I both reached for the dial at the same time, brushing our fingers and creating another rush of heat. He turned the music off completely, taking my hand before I had the chance to move it.

'Charlie, look at me,' he said. His voice brimmed with emotion, and as I looked into his eyes the midnight shimmer softened into a beautiful, melted chocolate. I was fascinated by the way his eyes changed with his emotions, like they were the embodiment of his deepest thoughts.

'What you said back there,' his words were soft and heartfelt, his eyes never leaving mine, 'it kind of took me by surprise. I mean we've only known each other a few weeks.'

'It feels like a lifetime Beau,' I interrupted him.

'I'm not trying to get you to justify yourself Charlie, I'm trying to tell you that it made me realise I feel the same.' He paused to see if I'd caught up with what he was saying. I kept watching him intently, waiting for him to finish.

'I love you too, so damn much.' My head whirled from his statement. My mouth was dry, and I was rendered speechless. He leaned in, pressing his cheek to mine and it was the best damn feeling. All I could do was close my eyes and breath it all in. Breaking the moment, Beau suggested we drive back before my mum started wondering why I'm not there.

'I don't think I'll be missed,' I told him. I wasn't sure whether I felt angry or sad. 'Mum won't notice or care.'

'I'm sure she cares; she's just not coping with it all. She needs some help,' Beau reassured me.

'She won't take any help. I've tried, Gina's tried, she's just given up.' I'd had enough of talking about her. I was sick of being the grown up.

'Hang in there,' Beau squeezed my shoulder to let me know he was on my side as I put the car in drive.

I spent the next few days finishing up my final paper. I struggled to find the motivation, not sure I even wanted to be a teacher anymore. It was the distraction I needed though, from the intensity of my life. I'd asked Beau to give me some space while I tied everything up with uni and it was killing me that he'd taken me seriously. I tried to push him out of my mind and managed to wrap it all up before my appointment with Kate. Just as I was about to leave the house, I thought about what Beau had said to me about mum. Maybe I should've made more of an effort, so I took her a cup of tea before I left. I set it on her nightstand and turn her blind, opening her window to let in some fresh air. The room smelt stale; I dreaded to think how long it was since she last showered. Her eyes were open, but she made no attempt to speak or acknowledge the tea I'd brought her.

'Mum, you need some help,' I told her.

'Go away Lottie.'

I didn't have the energy to argue with her, so I just shook my head and closed the door on my way out.

Kate opened the door with a bright smile and ushered me through to the back.

'Grab a seat, Lottie. Coffee?'

'Sure, thanks Kate.'

Settled in Kate's oversized chair I talked in depth about my dreams; I recalled every last detail, desperately hoping something would make some sense.

Kate carefully looked over her notes as I drained my coffee cup. Her brow was furrowed, deep in thought. She paused for a long time before she spoke.

'I'll be honest with you Lottie, there's a lot of controversy around repressed memories showing up in dreams but I'm inclined to believe that we might be dealing with something along those lines.'

'What do you mean? Like I've been abused in my past or something?' I was extremely dubious about the direction Kate was going. I'd had an ideal childhood. As much as mum and I had been having problems since the accident, up to that point both her and my dad had been wonderful parents.

'Goodness, no Lottie, I'm not saying that at all. I'm saying you might have experienced some kind of trauma in the past that you've forgotten about, and your recent trauma has triggered a memory. It doesn't necessarily mean that what's happening in your dreams has happened to you in the past, just that there could be something you've buried, and this is your subconscious way of digging it up. Am I making any sense?'

'So, you're saying I've had some kind of experience in my past that I've forgotten about and the dreams are my mind's way of dealing with the grief of losing Dad and Tom?' I clarified.

'I'm saying it's possible that your grief has triggered something in your memory that you've detached yourself from. I'm not saying this definitively. Our minds are very complex and often work to protect us from something or to help us heal.'

I let everything sink in before going to the next obvious question.

'So, how do I figure out what's going on and stop the dreams?' I asked her.

'That's the difficult part,' she laughed, 'but there are methods we can try. I'm thinking maybe we could try hypnosis. How would you feel about that?'

I wasn't sure how to respond, I felt a little self-conscious about exposing myself in that way.

'I can see you might be uncomfortable with that,' Kate said while I was still thinking it over.

'I don't know. I guess I'll try it if you think it might help. I just want the dreams to stop.'

'I honestly think it might help Lottie, but only if you're willing to give it a try. I'm not here to pressure you into anything. The dreams you're having appear to be a type of recurring dream that I would call serial dreams. Each one has the same theme, and they evolve from dream to dream. In my experience these types of dreams tend to stop once you've processed the dream and the message it's presenting to you.'

I tried to take it all in, wondering what the dreams were saying. Did I really have memories in my subconscious that I'd forgotten about? I had an underlying feeling that perhaps Kate knew more than she was letting on, because of her sessions with Tom. Whatever his issues were, I was beginning to wonder if they somehow related to me too. But if that was the case, Tom would have told me.

Kate stood to signal the end of our session. 'You've done well today Lottie, it's a lot to take in.'

I nodded, overwhelmed by how draining talking about everything was. As we reached the kitchen she asked if I had plans to see Beau later.

'Yeah, I'm on my way there now.'

'Great, I've got leftover lasagne for him. Would you mind taking it with you?'

'Sure, no problem,' I said. Kate handed it to me, and I leaned in to smell it.

'It looks enough for two, maybe I'll call and pick up a salad and invite myself for dinner!' I joked.

Kate quickly returned to the fridge and grabbed a container. 'Here, take this one.'

'You're sure?' I asked, feeling a little guilty.

'Absolutely, have fun.' She winked at me, and I blushed. I got the feeling she was happy if not a little surprised by my relationship with Beau. I wondered if he'd ever introduced his girlfriends to her before.

Balancing the two containers in one hand, I fumbled in my bag for my keys. I carefully set them down in the foot well before plugging my phone in and choosing a playlist. It wasn't far to Beau's apartment, and I was only half way through the second song by the time I pulled up outside.

The front door opened and a freshly showered Beau with wet hair was standing before me in dark grey sweatpants and a fitted t-shirt. He was wearing dark rimmed glasses and I was struck by his presence.

'I brought dinner,' I motioned to the container, smiling at him, hoping he wouldn't object to me staying. He reached for the food and gave me a grin, standing back so I could step into the hallway.

I followed him down the corridor to the kitchen where he put the food in the fridge and turned the oven on.

He reached up to the cupboard above the fridge for a glass, then turned to me. 'Wine?' he asked.

'Oh, I can't I'm driving.' I felt a little disappointed, wine would've gone down so well after that session with Kate.

He stilled and I could almost hear his mind whirring. He put the glass on the bench top and moved towards me. Brushing my hair behind my ear, he leaned in, his lips millimetres from my ear.

'Stay,' he whispered. Holy shit, my face burned from his closeness, and I couldn't seem to form any words in my mouth, so I just nodded. He returned to the cupboard to retrieve another glass and I felt his absence immediately. After pouring the wine, he pulled me down onto his couch and quickly found my mouth with his.

'I've missed you,' he said when we eventually came up for air. His voice was croaky, his eyes black as the midnight sky. His hunger was tangible, the heat of his desire burning me. I knew we both wanted to give in, but I just wasn't sure it was the right time. This was not just a flirtatious hook up; this was intense, and I knew that I needed to get my head around my situation before I lost myself in him.

I rolled to the side and sat up, nestling into him. He leaned forward, grabbing both glasses from the coffee table and handed me one. I swallowed a mouthful and turned to position myself so I could see his face.

'What was your mum like?' I finally felt like we'd reached a point that he might open up to me a little more. I felt him stiffen as I watched his jaw clench, his eyes unable to meet mine. Maybe I'd got it wrong. He blew out a breath and leaned forward to put his wine back on the table. I mentally chastised myself for ruining the mood but as I went to touch his arm to let him know it was okay, he removed his wallet and slipped out a photo. He stared at it for a few seconds before a sad smile appeared on his face, his eyes glistened with repressed emotion.

'That's the last photo taken of them,' he said sadly, handing me the photo. I stared at it; his mum, his sister and Beau all with big smiles on their faces.

'She was beautiful,' I told him. 'You look a lot like her.'

'People always used to say that. My sister Liv looked like dad. I struggled with that when I first saw him afterwards. I hated him, but I could see her in him, and it hurt so much.'

I reached for his face and gently brushed my fingers along his jawbone, turning his face towards me. Once his eyes were on mine, I lowered my hand to his chest, holding the physical connection to let him know how much I cared.

'Mum had a difficult life. Dad had turned to his addictions a good few years before he killed them. I guess I'd known something was wrong, but I didn't really understand until not long before they died. She hid it from us well, we always came first, and I think she suffered a few beatings because of it. She should have left him, but I guess she felt trapped, or she still loved him, I don't know. It's difficult to get your head around how someone can hurt someone they love. And how could she still love him after all he did to her?' Beau rubbed a hand over his face and scratched the three-day growth on his chin. He looked so vulnerable in that moment, sitting there sharing his feelings. I pressed a kiss to his lips gently.

'I don't know. I guess no one knows until they're in that situation. And the alcohol, it changes people. Maybe she loved the person he was when he wasn't drinking. Maybe she lived in hope.' He'd told me a lot and I didn't want to push him but was intrigued to know how his relationship with his dad was, if he even had one.

'Do you see him? Your dad?' I asked, not sure how he'd react.

Beau closed his eyes and a single tear trickled down towards his ear. I caught it with my lips, kissing it away.

'I'm sorry Beau, you don't have to answer that.'

'He passed away. In prison.' His voice was barely audible. 'I never forgave him.'

A lump was growing in my throat, restricting my voice, and a torrent was threatening to surge from my eyes. I was heartbroken for Beau. I wrapped my arms around him, and we snuggled together in complete silence because there was nothing left to say.

Our conversation had become so unexpectedly deep, it was difficult to pull back from and we ended up snuggled on the couch reading for much of the evening. It wasn't quite how I'd anticipated my first time staying at Beau's apartment, but it wasn't the right time to explore our relationship further.

I arrived home after coffee and toast to find mum's bedroom door open and her passed out sideways across the bed. As I moved towards her, the smell of alcohol fumes almost knocked me out. I started to panic, not wanting to go any closer, fearing the worst.

'Mum? Can you hear me?' I cried. A small grunt expelled from her lips and the breath I didn't know I was holding rushed from my mouth. I lifted one shoulder so I could see her face and I recoiled at the smell of vomit.

'Oh, Mum. What the hell?' I foraged through my brain trying to think of what to do. I thought about calling Beau but worried this might be too triggering after what he'd told me about his dad. I decided to call Gina, she'd know what to do. Besides, mum and her had always been friends so it might be less embarrassing for her than calling a complete stranger.

'Lottie? Are you okay?' Gina asked as I sobbed into the phone. I couldn't catch enough of a breath to answer.

'Are you at home Lottie?' She asked me and I could just about manage a 'yes' in reply. 'I'm on my way. Stay right there.'

The phone went dead, and I sank to the floor wondering if I should call an ambulance. Within minutes Gina was at the front door. She knocked and walked straight in, finding us both in mum's bedroom. She glanced at mum on the bed, passed out but breathing, and while never taking her eyes off me she dialled triple zero. She rattled off a string of questions to me, relaying what the emergency operator was asking and after giving her as many answers as I could she hung up the phone and told me an ambulance was on its way.

I noticed an empty vodka bottle next to the bed and wondered how full it was last night. We left mum face down on the bed with her head slightly tilted and figured it was the best we could do for her until the ambulance arrived. Gina started to tidy up a little, and I joined in to try and keep myself busy. We came across several more empty bottles lying on the floor beside her bed, partially covered by blankets and pillows. I felt ashamed for not seeing what was going on before. I just thought she wasn't eating.

The ambulance arrived and I let the paramedics in. One of them checked mum out while the other spoke to me, asking questions. I nodded in response, feeling numb.

'Lottie, you go with her in the ambulance; I'll be right behind you, okay?' I nodded at Gina, unable to formulate words.

The ride to hospital didn't take long and as soon as I reached the waiting area, the night of the accident came flooding back. I slumped into a hard plastic chair waiting for news. Gina rushed in minutes later, and taking the seat next to me, she folded me into a hug.

'So many empty bottles,' I murmured.

'We'll get her some help Lottie, try not to worry.'

'I should've been there Gina; I was so angry at her I just let her get like this. I've been too wrapped up in myself to notice.'

'Lottie, listen to me, this is not your fault. You've tried to help her. I've tried to help her. Maybe we didn't try hard enough, maybe we should've intervened sooner and got her some help. But it is not your fault.' Gina's stern voice shocked me, and I knew she was right even if I couldn't admit it.

We sat in the waiting room for what seemed like hours before the nurse came and told us she'd been taken to a ward.

'We'll keep her in for a few days. She'll have a mental health assessment and you might need to think about getting her checked into a facility. She's in a bad way but she'll pull through. You can see her now if you like,' the nurse said kindly.

We didn't stay long with mum; she was completely out of it. Gina tried to get me to go home with her, but I told her I just wanted to be alone.

'Call me if you need me Lottie,' Gina said as she dropped me home. 'I mean it, any time, day or night.'

I thanked Gina and unlocked the front door, letting myself into the house. It was eerily quiet, like it had been for weeks; no life, no laughter, no music. It felt empty and I just felt tired. I was sick of being stuck in this place. Stuck in my own head, going round in circles. The worry I was feeling over mum had turned to anger again. I couldn't believe she could do this to me. I knew in some part of my subconscious that I shouldn't blame her, but I couldn't help myself. I needed to blame her, I needed to blame someone. I sat on the edge of mum's bed, staring at the wall, wondering where to start cleaning up the mess.

I feel like a prisoner in my own head with nowhere to go to break free. I'm stuck in this place with no way of escape. This confinement begins to stir my memory and I start to remember who I once was. I was carefree and spirited. I had grit and determination, full of piss and vinegar for anyone standing in my way. I need to fight for that, for Charlie.

My chest was tight, and I struggled to catch my breath. The air around me felt stagnant and I recoiled from the stench of vomit and alcohol soaked into the bed sheets. As I staggered to my feet, I noticed the light outside was dim and I wondered how long I'd been out of it. I checked my phone and saw countless missed calls and messages. I knew I'd have to clean mum's room at some point but right then I closed the door behind me and left it how it was.

Lottie 2019

The last dream replayed in my head as I made myself some mac and cheese for dinner. I'd not eaten since the toast I'd had at Beau's that morning and my stomach was turning. My dreams had all been emotive and very real but this one was even more so. It felt so personal. As I looked in the mirror at myself, I tried to evoke an image of the person in the dreams. Was it me? I couldn't picture a face, but the thoughts felt intimate, like I was intruding somehow. My mind worked overtime trying to piece together this puzzle that was slowly driving me crazy. My mind was trying to tell me something that I wasn't quite ready to hear. I knew I was stopping myself from listening, but I didn't know how to open myself up to it.

I sat on the leather couch, tucking one foot underneath me and curled up with my bowl of macaroni, silently obsessing over my dreams. Thoughts of my mum alone in a hospital bed pulled me from my self-absorption and I picked up my phone to call the hospital. I saw all the missed calls from Beau and decided I should probably call him first to let him know what had happened.

Beau answered on the first ring.

'Hey, is everything okay? I've been ringing all day.' He sounded worried and my chest tightened at his concern.

'It's been a day, I'm sorry if you've been worried.' I told him what had happened with Mum, and I could hear his movements on the other end of the line.

'I'm on my way, I'll be there in five,' he said hurriedly, before hanging up abruptly.

I sat and looked at the phone for a moment trying to get my head around how quickly I'd allowed this guy into my heart. I questioned myself for the first time since I met him, wondering if it was what I wanted or needed right now. I'd never felt this way before and never imagined I would ever feel so completely connected to a guy. The second I opened the door and saw the depth of concern in his eyes, my question was answered. My feelings were so strong I couldn't even understand where they were coming from.

Without a word he gently folded me into his arms and held me so firmly that all my thoughts were squeezed from my head, and all I could do was breathe him in. When we eventually broke apart, he kissed the top of my head.

'You should've called me; I'd have been here for you. You didn't have to go through that alone.'

'I wasn't alone. My friend's mum Gina came with me. I wasn't sure whether it might be triggering for you, which is why I didn't call you,' I told him.

He nodded slowly, understanding my reasons.

'That's really thoughtful,' he said quietly, 'but I would've been here for you.'

'I know you would, but I also don't want my weakness to define our relationship. I don't need to be constantly saved by you, that's not who I want to be.'

'Lottie…'

'I think I prefer it when you call me Charlie,' I whisper.

'Charlie,' he smiled. 'Don't ever think of yourself as weak, you're one of the strongest people I know. You've had a lot of shit to deal with and asking for help is not a sign of weakness. I care about you; I want you to get through this and be happy. I want us to be happy together.'

I didn't reply, I just took comfort in his words and rested my head on his chest.

We eventually moved further into the house, and I realised I'd never finished my mac and cheese. Beau picked up the bowl and reheated it in the microwave for me before sitting down on the couch next to me. He had a quick forkful before handing the bowl to me.

'That's so good, I've not had mac and cheese in years,' he said.

'I can make more if you want some?' I suggested.

'No, no I'm good. I've already eaten but I'll take a rain check.'

'Deal.' I grinned at him.

'So, how's your mum doing? Have you heard anything from the hospital?' he asked, his eyes darkening as the conversation turned serious again.

'I don't know,' I told him. 'I was just about to call when I noticed all the missed calls from you. I'll call soon.'

We chatted easily while I finished my dinner. He asked about my friends, and I told him about Rosie, how she'd always been so loyal to me and the guilt I felt for the way I'd been treating her lately.

'It just feels so weird,' I explained. 'I feel like I've changed so much since everything happened and I'm not sure she'll understand me anymore.'

'Give her a chance Charlie.' I smiled at the name he used. It made me feel stronger, and the more time I spent with him, the more I felt I was becoming Charlie. I still didn't understand why Tom had referred to me as Charlie, but after my latest dream I couldn't help but think the two were connected somehow.

'From the way Tom spoke about you, you don't seem that different to me. Maybe it's just how you see yourself that's changed and to Rosie you're just the same best friend she's known and loved for all those years,' Beau said.

I chewed my bottom lip as I thought about what he was saying.

'You didn't know me before though. I've always been the people pleaser, never questioning, just getting on with my life. Now I'm questioning everything.'

Beau took my hand in his and shifted his position on the couch, his face so close his breath tickled my cheek.

'I'm not saying you haven't changed Charlie, because there's no way you can experience what you have and come through it unscathed. Everything you experience changes the way you are, the way you think, the way you love. But that's mostly internal, the shift will be so subtle to your friends, and Rosie will understand. Don't look at the change as a bad thing; look at it as growth. I promise I will help you through this every step of the way, like Kate did for me.'

I tilted my face up slightly so my mouth was level with his, and there was a split second when heat began to rise up between us before our lips touched and I felt the charge in the pit of my stomach. His hands left mine and moved up to my hair as he gripped the sides of my head in a way that was so intense it felt like he was branding my scalp. His tongue explored my mouth with a feverish passion, and I never wanted it to end. I relinquished myself completely to him as he gently pushed me back against the cushions, adjusting himself to make me comfortable. His hands softly explored my body, while I gripped one bicep and rubbed my other hand under his t-shirt, tracing lazy circles with my fingertips.

His lips pulled away leaving me feeling suddenly empty, and he dipped his mouth towards my ear and gently whispered,

'Come home with me tonight.'

I didn't trust myself to speak so I squeezed my arms around him tighter in response; my heart wrapped up in a giant-sized grin.

After hastily packing a few things in an overnight bag, I followed Beau in my car back to his apartment. I was both excited and nervous. This was all new to me. Not the sex, it wasn't like I hadn't been there before, just not with someone I was in love with. Just that thought in my head felt strange to me. I knew it would be intense; everything with Beau was intense, but I wanted to feel relaxed too. I didn't think I'd ever wanted something so much in all my life. As I pulled into his driveway, Beau hopped off his bike and waited for me. He was so beautiful standing there in the twilight, his hair catching the glimmer of the late sun. I stopped overthinking and climbed out of my car to join him, more excited now than nervous at what lay ahead.

Beau greeted me with a quick kiss and then pulled me back in for a deeper one as if he'd not just seen me a few minutes before. His breath was unsteady, and I could sense his nerves. I pulled back and questioned him with my eyes.

'I love you, Charlie; I want tonight to be special.' His voice was wobbly but his eyes had never been more sure.

'I love you too and whatever happens, it will be perfect,' I replied with a surety in my voice. I flipped my bag on to my shoulder and took his hand in mine, pulling him towards the door.

It was obvious when we got inside that he wasn't going to just rip my clothes off and take me over the kitchen bench. Not that I had ever imagined for a second that would be Beau's style. This was going to be a slow build and I was looking forward to savouring every single moment. Beau grabbed two glasses from the overhead cupboard and half-filled them from a bottle of Pinot. Drinking wine, just the two of us, with the promise of what lay ahead felt strangely comfortable. My nerves had all but gone and I was right where I was meant to be.

We sat on the couch together, our feet entwined, relaxing and sipping our wine. We chatted with ease about anything and everything. No subject was left uncovered, and as I learnt more about him, the deeper I could feel myself falling in love with him. He told me stories of his sister Liv, and I talked about Tom and the fun we had as kids, and how we'd always been so close. Beau and I had so much in common, from our love of books and quiet nights in, to our traumatic experiences losing a parent and a sibling in tragic circumstances. The connection I felt with him went so deep, way beyond how I expected to feel when I fell in love for the first time. I decided to ask Beau the one thing we hadn't yet talked about.

'Have you been in love before?' I asked.

He studied my face for a while, and I wondered what was going through his mind. I suddenly felt nervous about his answer and began to regret my question.

'I thought I was once,' he replied. 'Her name was Zoe. We were together for just over a year and I thought it was love. I didn't know any different. I was sad when we broke up, but I wasn't heartbroken.'

He looked me right in the eyes, his intense gaze seared through me.

'I know now it wasn't love. It was an entire galaxy away from the way I feel when I'm with you.'

Neither one of us moved. We just allowed the intense burning feeling to sit between us, like molten lava bubbling feverishly before it overflows. Beau dampened the heat slightly by asking me the same question.

'How about you? Have you ever been in love?' he asked quietly.

I laughed at the question that seemed so futile after the answer he'd given me.

'I've never even had a boyfriend before.'

Beau was visibly surprised by my answer.

'What, never?' he asked incredulously. 'But you've…?'

'Oh yeah, of course,' I jumped in quickly, heat rising up my neck, 'just not with anyone special.'

The way he was looking at me told me it was time. This was the moment we'd been building up to. Beau gulped down the last mouthful of wine and taking my glass from my hand put both glasses on the coffee table. Without a word, and with his eyes never leaving mine, he took my hand and led me silently towards his bed, flicking off the light in the living area as we went. The only source of light was coming from the streetlight outside his window, casting a dusky glow through the blinds.

As Beau eased me backwards onto his bed, my heart rate increased rapidly, and I was captivated by the intensity of the situation. As I laid on my back feeling more alive than I'd ever felt in my life, Beau's brow creased, silently asking for permission to touch me. I twined my fingers in the curls at the nape of his neck and gently pulled his lips to mine in answer. My consent fired him up in a way I'd never seen before. His usual controlled demeanour had been taken over by a frenzy of passion that had me longing for him. His mouth crashed into mine, his tongue sweeping my mouth. It was warm and tasted of Pinot. His breath was erratic as his body pressed into mine, our limbs entwined.

I felt a sense of loss as his body released mine from its intimacy.

'Slower Charlie, we have to slow down,' Beau said breathless, his body hovering above me. The glow from the streetlight shimmered on the sweat beading on his forehead. He slowed his breathing down and pulled his t-shirt over his head, revealing his strong abs and sun kissed skin. I was unsure how he expected that to slow me down, it just made me want more. I reached my fingers and gently stroked his chest, rubbing his nipple with my thumb. He knelt backwards, resting on his feet and pulled me up to a sitting position, my legs straddled around his knees. He pulled the bottom of my shirt swiftly over my head and released my bra strap.

Gently pushing me back down, his lips gently brushed my skin in a lazy pattern down my stomach, all the way to the top of my jeans. With one hand he quickly unfastened the buttons and I lifted up off the bed to give him access to remove them. He pulled them off complete with my underwear, and sat back admiring my naked body. As a swimmer, I grew up with people looking at me in next to nothing and have always been confident in my own skin. Being an athletic type, I'd never had any body image issues but lying there naked for the first time in front of Beau, I felt a vulnerability I hadn't experienced.

Never taking his eyes off my face, Beau unbuckled his belt and slid his jeans and jocks to the floor. Reaching to his nightstand for protection, we quickly escalated things to the next level and what seemed like hours later, we laid side by side as Beau's breathing settled back into a steady rhythm, and my own contentment brought me my first dreamless sleep in weeks.

Eva 1967

'Eva!' Charles was breathless as he ran up the stairs to Eva's tiny office. They'd bought the end terrace house two years earlier after Eva had published her first book. It was a book of poetry that had gone on to sell better than even the publishers had predicted. Eva was making a name for herself in literary circles. Her first novel had been published just a few weeks previously and Eva was currently working on her next work of fiction. Charles was incredibly proud of his wife; from the way she had stood up to her parents all those years before, to the way she had worked hard to establish her own career, while being a constant source of joy in his life. She was as beautiful as the day they met, and her intelligence overwhelmed him. Their life together up to that point had been everything they could have wished for, except one thing. Eva longed for a child and ever since their wedding night, their lovemaking had been completely without protection. It had been almost six years and Charles could see the heartbreak in Eva's eyes every month.

Eva was sitting at her desk in the third bedroom that Charles had lovingly converted into an office for her. Her desk sat underneath the window, overlooking the moors they both loved so much. She turned to him when he burst through the door, newspaper in hand, a furtive grin spread across his face.

'What's going on?' Eva asked, smiling at his enthusiasm for what, she was unsure.

'You'll never guess.' Charles was bursting at the seams.

Eva laughed, 'well just tell me then!'

'Baby, you've been shortlisted for the John Llewellyn Rhys Prize!' Charles picked her off her chair and spun her around, immensely proud and excited.

'What? No way!' Charles set her down on the floor and she grabbed him to steady herself. Her head was still spinning, and a sense of nausea rushed through her. Eva quickly grabbed the wastepaper bin and emptied the entire contents of her stomach.

Charles rushed to the bathroom to get her a glass of water and returned with tissues to wipe her face. He frowned at her, 'I'm sorry, did I make you do that?'

Eva shook her head. 'No, I've been feeling a little off for a few days.'

'What? Why didn't you say anything?' Charles was saddened to think she'd kept it from him, she usually shared all her feelings with him.

'I didn't want to get your hopes up in case I'm wrong,' Eva replied sheepishly.

Charles stared at her in confusion. 'Wrong about what?'

'I'm two weeks late,' Eva told him.

Charles was about to open his mouth to ask what she was late for when Eva witnessed the reality dawn on him.

'You really think you could be?' he asked, trying to keep his voice level.

'I don't know. I probably should get tested.' Eva allowed herself a hopeful smile.

'Oh, my darling, let's get an appointment straight away.' Charles knelt in front of her and held her hands in his. 'I love you so much and whatever happens, I am always here for you. You know that don't you?'

'Of course I do. And Charles? You are enough for me, don't ever think that you're not. I see how you look at me every month and I know it hurts you to think I'm not happy with just the two of us.'

'No, my sweet…' Charles interrupted but Eva put a finger to his lips.

'Shh, please don't say anything, I know it hurts you. I want you to know I am happy as we are, but I would love to bring a child into our little family. We have so much love to share.'

Charles kissed her and stood up. 'I'll go and make that appointment, shall I?'

Eva knew without the appointment that she was pregnant. She'd been feeling not quite herself for a few days. For the first time in years, she hadn't kept track of her period. She'd been so busy with the publishers getting her book out while working on her new one that she hadn't paid any attention to her body. But the first sign of nausea sent her head into a spin, questioning her dates. She was never this late, and paired with the nausea and vomiting, she was sure, but she hadn't wanted to vocalise her thoughts in case she was wrong.

Eva brushed her teeth to rid her mouth of the bad taste, then went downstairs to find Charles. She remembered his reason for bursting into her office earlier before they were side-tracked by her sickness. Charles was just finishing his conversation on the phone when Eva reached the bottom of the stairs. Charles hung up the phone and turned to Eva.

'You have an appointment in the morning,' he said, his face beaming.

Eva nodded, biting her lip. Charles held his arms out for her to step into, folding her up, blanketing her from the stress he could feel in her body.

'It'll be okay my love, whatever happens.' He kissed her forehead, then held her out at arm's length, taking in the moment.

Eva tilted her head to one side, questioning Charles about his earlier statement.

'Did I really just get shortlisted for a literary award?' she asked, not quite believing it.

'You did!' Charles said, his face beaming with pride, eyes glistening with the emotion of the morning. 'You deserve it. You work so hard and I'm so proud of you.'

'Thank you, your support always means the world to me. You know I would never have been in this position without you. I can't bear to think what my life would have been without you in it.' Eva didn't often talk of the past, or her parents. Neither of them had attended their wedding, which had been a quiet affair in the registry office with only a couple of witnesses. It seemed fitting their witnesses should be their newfound friends from the book club where they'd first met. They were the people who had supported their relationship from the beginning. Eva had been disappointed but not surprised by her parents' reaction to her relationship with Charles. Granted, it had been a whirlwind romance but even Charles's offer to have a long engagement hadn't been enough to win them over. Eva had come to realise over the years that it had all been about control. They wanted her to 'marry up,' be respectable and not bring any kind of disgrace to them with her fanciful ideas and romantic notions. Although Eva had reconciled herself with the situation, she'd felt comforted by the pearl hair comb she'd worn to her wedding, a little piece of family history. She often wondered if her parents were following her success, or whether they'd washed their hands of anything to do with her the night her father threw her out.

She had seen her mother from afar only once in the years since she got married and had contemplated saying hello but, in the end, she decided against it. Her mother looked much the same, looking down her nose at those around her, speaking down to the cashier. Ironically, the success Eva was having with her writing career was the kind of success her parents would have liked to brag about.

'Do you ever regret the way you walked out that night?' Charles could see the way Eva's mind was working and he knew she was thinking about her parents.

'I have no regrets, only that my parents didn't support us.' Eva paused before adding, 'but I do sometimes wonder whether things would've been different had we slowed things down.'

Charles had worried about this from the start. He hadn't wanted to cause a rift between Eva and her parents, but his head and his heart had different ideas. Eva had spent years waiting to get out from her parents' control and Charles had been eager to help provide her with the wings to fly. As much as he didn't want to come between Eva and her parents, he equally didn't want her parents to come between Eva and her dreams.

'I honestly believe they wouldn't have, or if they had been, we wouldn't have been where we are today.' Charles held her face in his hands. 'And I wouldn't change that for the world.'

It was an excruciating week waiting for the results, but luckily Eva had all the awards buzz to keep her mind occupied. Her agent had called the previous week with all the details and although Eva didn't expect to win, she was over the moon that her debut novel was getting so much hype. The award nomination meant her sales had increased substantially. She even had her own display in the doorway of the local bookshop, local critics comparing her to the Brontë sisters. In her own estimation that was the highest honour she could ever receive.

The boys Charles taught at the Grammar School were impressed with their teacher's wife. Charles was becoming increasingly popular among both teachers and students at the school with his forward thinking and progressive views, and Eva's recent success had only added to his popularity. He was overjoyed to see how many of his students were engaging with literature. His move away from only teaching the classics towards a more modern syllabus had really encouraged their curiosity and the school's headmaster was thrilled with the results coming out of Charles's classes.

'Maybe I could add, "Before Her Time," to the student reading list for next year,' Charles mused as he flicked through the newspaper in the doctor's waiting room.

Eva laughed at his suggestion. 'I'm not sure that would be appropriate.'

'Why not? Because the content's not suitable for boys or because it was written by my wife?' Charles asked. 'Both of which are nonsense by the way, and you know it.'

Eva blushed at his compliment, 'I don't know, it just feels a little indulgent.'

'Oh, but you know how much I love to indulge you my darling.' Charles leaned over and kissed her cheek.

'Eva Hartley,' the doctor appeared in the doorway to her office and called her in. Eva stood, nervously smoothing her skirt with her hands.

'I'd like my husband to come in with me, if that's all right,' Eva said to the doctor.

'Of course, please.' The doctor directed them into his office.

The couple sat side by side, Charles reached for Eva's hand. He wasn't sure whether it was to support Eva or to ease himself.

The doctor pulled a brown envelope out of Eva's file and unfolded the flimsy sheet of paper inside. His eyes ran over it quickly before he passed it across the desk to Eva and Charles. Before they'd even had the chance to read any of it the doctor beamed.

'Congratulations!'

Charles was speechless. Eva's emotions were all over the place. A single tear traced a path down her cheek and as she felt it drip off her chin, she laughed before a floodgate opened and a cascade of tears poured down her face. Charles and Eva hugged each other in their moment of pure joy, while the doctor watched on happily.

He gave Eva a few instructions before telling her to make an appointment with the midwife to begin her care. Eva nodded gratefully and stood to leave. Once the formalities were out of the way, and Eva and Charles were alone in the car, they grinned at each other, quietly basking in their wonderful news.

'We're going to be parents Charles, I can't believe it,' Eva whispered.

'It's been a long time coming. I know how much this means to you,' Charles's voice cracked.

'And you?' Eva asked, not entirely convinced he wanted this as much as she did.

'It means the world Eva. I've longed for this as much as you have, but

I wanted to be strong for you and not let myself get wrapped up in it all.'

She smiled at him, moved by the heart-warming glint in his eyes.

The early months went by in a blur, with Eva doing publicity for "Before Her Time," whilst also making progress with her current novel. Her sickness alleviated after a couple of months, and she was feeling well, just in time for the big awards ceremony. Eva's pregnancy was just beginning to show, and she was struggling to find a suitable dress to hide it.

'Don't hide it my love. This is our baby; you should show off your bump to everyone. Be proud of it, you have never looked more beautiful.' Charles kissed the tip of her nose and smiled down at her flushed cheeks.

'I just don't look very pregnant; I look more like I've eaten too many cakes.' Eva patted her swollen belly.

'I think you should get the red one,' Charles decided. 'It complements your figure beautifully, and when you're standing on that stage collecting your award, everyone will think you are exquisite, and I'll be the proudest man in the room.'

'Flattery will get you everywhere Mr Hartley, I'll take it.'

Eva disappeared back into the fitting room to change back into her own clothes. The awards were only a week away in London. She'd left it as late as possible to buy a dress to lessen the chance of her growing out of it before the ceremony.

She'd created quite a buzz about her novel, both good and bad, and some critics had even tipped her to win. The novel, set in a future where women had equal rights had seen the second-wave feminists jump on the back of its glory, and adopt it as a catalyst for the movement. Eva was excited to be involved and had been interviewed by leading members of the Women's Lib movement. She felt a bit of a fraud, having got married at just eighteen but knowing if she hadn't, she would be stuck in a situation that these women were fighting to end. That didn't bear thinking about for her. She knew her life was privileged, having a husband who supported all her dreams, and saw her as his equal. She also knew it was rare to have a husband who valued her intelligence above her beauty, and her opinions over her ability to cook. Eva would be eternally grateful for the day they both walked into that meeting.

Charles and Eva took their seats at a round table in the ballroom of the Imperial Hotel along with Eva's agent, her editor and a representative from the publishing house. They toasted Eva with expensive champagne and Eva felt giddy after just one sip. She felt a little overwhelmed by the company they were keeping. There were some big names in the literary world there, many of them knowing her by name and introducing themselves to her and Charles. By the time they had finished supper and settled in for the announcements, Eva was shrinking in her seat, humbled by her competition.

When Eva's category was announced, Charles sat upright, taking Eva's hand in his. He leaned in and whispered, 'whatever the result, you will always be my number one.'

That was all Eva had needed to rid her of her apprehension about the evening. When the winner was announced, she breathed a sigh of relief and joined the applause for her fellow writer. As much as she would have loved to win, she felt relief that it was over and couldn't imagine the extra publicity in her current condition. It was time for her to concentrate on her new book and get ready for the baby to arrive.

Lottie 2019

I woke to the smell of fresh coffee and the sun's first rays peeking through the blinds. I sat up and looked around, remembering blissfully the previous night. Pulling the covers up, I brought my knees up and hugged them tight, grinning to myself.

I could just see Beau in the kitchen pottering about, busying himself making breakfast. He put two coffee mugs on a tray and added a stack of food. As he picked it up, he caught me watching him. He smiled tentatively at first, his face bursting into a broad smile as soon as he saw my grin. There was a lightness about him that I didn't recognise, or was that just me? Maybe I was seeing things from a different perspective, having had such a good sleep.

'Good morning sleepyhead,' he said handing me a coffee mug.

I took a slurp and allowed the caffeine to seep through me before replying.

'Good morning,' I said softly. 'I slept so well, I forgot where I was.'

Beau put the tray on the bed and sat down opposite me. He leaned over for a quick peck, and I pulled away quickly, thinking of my morning coffee breath. He laughed at me and shook his head handing me a plate of warm freshly baked croissants. I took one, biting into it, the buttery flakes melting in my mouth.

'Oh my God,' I mumbled with my mouth full. 'If this is what's for breakfast every morning, I'm moving in.'

Beau's face suddenly turned serious, and I baulked at what I'd just said.

'Do it. Move in.' He was deadly serious.

I laughed, trying to lighten the mood.

'Don't be crazy, I've only known you a few weeks. I was only kidding.'

'I'm not kidding,' Beau grinned at me. 'Charlie, I love you. This is it for me; I don't ever want to be without you.'

I squeezed his hand. 'I love you too but let's just enjoy this and not get ahead of ourselves.' I brought his hand to my lips and kissed his knuckles, then turned my attention back to the buttery goodness in front of me.

The mood lightened as we both devoured our breakfast and relaxed back into an easy chat, sipping our coffee.

'What are your plans for today?' Beau asked me. 'Do you need to study or are you going to see your mum?'

'No, I finished my last assignment, but I will go and see Mum at some point. How about you?'

'I've got a few errands to run this morning, but I have time to take you to the hospital later if you don't want to go alone.'

I knew he wouldn't say it if he didn't mean it, but I was also aware I'd been taking up a lot of his time lately.

'Maybe, I'll let you know,' I told him as I moved to get out of bed and realised I was naked underneath the covers. Beau picked up on my dilemma quickly and to prevent any awkwardness, leaned in for a quick kiss and told me he needed the bathroom. I smiled at his consideration and quickly dressed myself while he was gone.

As I was leaving, Beau grabbed my hand and spun me around to face him. Those expressive eyes turned dark again, and I sensed he was about to go all serious on me again.

'Last night...' he began.

We'd kind of skirted around the topic of the previous night, which I was surprised at. He was usually so forthright when it came to talking deep. I wondered what he was going to say, and I was hoping there were no regrets.

'I'm blown away Charlie. You've kind of got me speechless.'

I breathed a sigh of relief and reached my arms around his neck for a hug, then planted a kiss firmly on his cheek.

I grinned at him as I walked through the door, and he yelled after me. 'Call me.'

I was on a high when I got home, which was a good thing when I walked into the chaos that mum had left behind. I opened all the windows and blasted out my music as I got to work cleaning up. I couldn't believe Mum had ended up in that state without me having noticed. I tried not to blame myself, I knew it wasn't my fault, but it was difficult. The satisfaction I felt once I'd finished cleaning her room gave me the motivation to get stuck into the rest of the house. I was pretty sure neither of us had lifted a finger since the accident. After throwing out most of the food in the fridge and giving it a good clean, I showered and called Beau to see if he was still up for coming to the hospital with me.

Of course he was, and we arrived at the hospital a little over an hour later. I was feeling a little nervous about seeing Mum, and tried hard not to be angry with her, but I still couldn't help feeling a little disappointed.

'You go on in Charlie, I'll just be out here if you need me.' Beau squeezed my hand before releasing me and grabbed a chair in the waiting area.

I pushed the door gently and walked in, but I didn't approach the bed. I hung back trying to assess the situation. Mum looked awful; she was thin, and her eyes were dark and sunken. I gasped when her hollow eyes met mine. She was hooked up to a drip and her body looked so frail.

We stared at each other in awkward silence, and I couldn't work out whether she was remorseful or wallowing in self-pity. I started to fidget, running my fingers along the zip of Tom's leather jacket.

'That's Tom's jacket,' Mum said, barely loud enough for me to hear. Her voice was thick and heavy, probably from the tube she'd had down her throat last night.

I nodded. 'I came on Beau's motorbike. Protection,' I told her, patting the front of the jacket.

Mum's eyes closed and I could see a tear slide from under her closed lid. She blinked it away but didn't have the energy to wipe it from her face.

'How could you ride on a motorbike after what happened?' Her voice was quiet, but disapproving. 'And who's Beau?'

I tried to keep calm, but I was visibly shaking. 'Dad and Tom were driving a car, and their accident had nothing to do with a motorbike, and Beau is a friend of Tom's and the only reason I'm not lying in a hospital bed next to you. So don't you dare lecture me.' I turned away but as I reached the door I stopped. Turning back towards her I let her know exactly how she'd made me feel.

'I know you're grieving mum, and I know you have problems, but you need to take responsibility for yourself. You have no right to criticise my choices when you almost killed yourself. I'll see you again when you're ready to apologise.' I retreated from the room and leaned against the wall opposite the nurses station. I tried to steady myself with deep breaths, but I could feel myself sliding down the wall into nothingness.

A sharp blow to the back of my head causes my legs to crumple with the pain. I can't stop the falling sensation and I hit the ground hard. There's a kick to my guts. It strikes repeatedly and I know this is it. I find myself struggling to stay awake and in this moment everything becomes clear. It's time. It's time to go...
Charlie!

I woke to a faint humming sound and a mask covering my nose and mouth. I looked around, confused at what was happening. Someone squeezed my hand and I saw Beau sitting at my bedside, his head hung low.

'Beau...' I tried to speak but my mouth was parched. Beau looked up at the sound of my voice and called for a nurse.

'Charlie, what happened? Are you okay?'

I remembered the dream, and a stream of thoughts rushed my mind. Why did it feel so important to me? Was it because I'd heard the name

Charlie again? Aware of what Kate had said about them possibly being serial dreams, they did seem to be evolving, but there was still something missing, and I just couldn't join the dots. A nurse appeared above me and lifted the mask off my face.

'Charlotte? How are you feeling? You had us all worried there for a while,' she said, 'especially this one.' She nodded towards Beau and smiled.

'What happened?' I asked, trying to remember.

'You collapsed outside your mum's room. Did something happen in there?'

I remembered back to the conversation we had and shook my head. 'We just had a disagreement.'

The nurse checked me over and told me I was okay to go home but preferably not on the back of a motorbike just to be sure.

'It's okay,' Beau interjected. 'I've called Kate, she's on her way.'

The nurse left the room and I sat myself up on the edge of the bed. Beau was concentrating on my face, looking for a sign that I wasn't okay.

'I'm fine Beau, I promise. I just need to get out of here.'

He helped me stand just as his phone beeped.

'It's Kate, she's waiting outside,' he explained.

We made our way out and I stopped at the nurses' station to find out what was happening with mum. The nurse from before explained that she would be assessed later that afternoon and then a decision would be made as to what would happen from there.

'I'll see you back at my flat?' Beau asked hopefully as I opened the passenger door of Kate's car when we got outside.

I stopped a moment before turning to him. 'I'd rather just go home to be honest. I just want to be on my own for a while, I have some thinking to do.'

Beau nodded thoughtfully but didn't say a word. He seemed a little hurt by my decision, but it wasn't something I had the capacity to deal with, I just needed to get home. Kate's intuition immediately sensed I had no desire to talk, and she turned up the music, for which I was grateful.

'Call me when you're ready,' she told me as she dropped me at home.

I smiled and thanked her. I breathed a sigh of relief when I closed the front door behind me and focused on trying to understand my dreams.

The first place I went was Tom's room. It was pretty much as he had left it when he moved out, apart from the two big packing boxes on the floor full of stuff that Ben had packed up from their apartment after the accident.

I had no idea what I was searching for, but I delved into the boxes looking for anything that might give me a clue as to what was going on in Tom's life before he died. Beau hadn't mentioned what was troubling Tom, but he had mentioned Tom visiting his friend Clint at the fish shack and chatting to him about research for a paper. I began to wonder if there was more to Tom's visits than even Beau knew about. Maybe

Clint knew more than he'd let on. My phone beeped and a message popped up from Beau.

Take all the space you need to make sense of everything. I'm here whenever you're ready. I love you xxx

I replied with three kisses.

The following morning, I woke to the glimpse of early morning light through my blinds. I thought back to my sleep and tried to remember any dreams I'd had. I startled at a picture of Tom and I, huddled together on a bunk bed, and couldn't be sure whether I'd dreamed it or if it was real. My palms began to sweat, prickles danced on my skin, my body filled with a sense of déjà vu, and I had a sudden need to escape the house. I dressed quickly in warm track pants and Ugg boots; the weather was still unpredictable at this time in the morning. Calling at the drive-through for coffee, I drove down to the river. Despite my warm clothes, there was a chill in the air that made me shiver. I sat on the edge of the jetty, my feet dangling over the water, slowly sipping my coffee as pelicans flew overhead, making their descent onto the glasslike water. A dolphin broke through the surface, gliding elegantly before dipping back underneath out of sight. The sun rising over the hills took me back to the morning in the park and I suddenly found myself missing Beau. I sent him a selfie with the hashtag, *#wishyouwerehere* and then tried to lose myself in my surroundings.

It felt good to be out of the house, but I couldn't seem to escape the thoughts that had been troubling me since my episode at the hospital yesterday. Swallowing down the last dregs of my coffee, I stood to leave. As I turned, I saw Beau walking towards me carrying two coffees, and I grinned.

'You got my message then?'

'Of course.' He cocked his head to one side and smiled at me, squinting into the morning sun. 'It took me a while to work out your location though.'

I laughed. 'Glad to keep you on your toes.'

He passed me a coffee, and then glanced towards the empty cup in my other hand. 'You'll be buzzing by breakfast.'

We walked back down the jetty to the riverside path, and he asked how I was feeling after my episode at the hospital. I talked about the dreams that I'd had since I saw mum and told Beau about the confusion over my name cropping up. Beau was quiet and I couldn't work out whether he was just being himself and processing things internally or if I could sense an awkwardness about him when I mentioned Tom. I didn't press the matter. Beau switched hands with his coffee cup and weaved the fingers of his free hand into mine. We wandered along slowly, dodging all the runners and cyclists that seemed to have appeared from nowhere.

'I think I need to see Kate today. Do you know if she'll be free?' I asked, breaking the silence.

'Give her a call, I'm sure she'll make time for you.'

He stopped in his tracks and turned me around to face him.

'You'll get through this Charlie, I promise. I know it all seems heavy right now, but it will get easier.' He paused, not sure whether to continue. He opened his mouth and then quickly snapped it shut. I watched him, expectantly waiting for him to reveal a little bit more of himself to me. He blew out a long breath.

'You know, when my dad died, I struggled to accept the fact that I hadn't forgiven him. I beat myself up over it for weeks. Then you came along, and you helped me realise that I didn't need to forgive him. He was a killer and didn't deserve my forgiveness. I accept that now.'

I was confused by his words.

'What do you mean I helped you? We've barely spoken about your dad. I feel like our entire relationship has been based on me. I'm feeling pretty needy to be honest.'

'You have no idea how much just having you in my life has changed me, Charlie. I've never spoken about my family to anyone other than Kate before. I know I might not talk much but knowing that I can without you judging me is a huge deal to me. Watching your strength grow, and seeing you face your demons head on, you inspire me.' His final few words were sheathed in husky tones, and the intensity left me reeling. I reached my hands around his neck and clung to him, never wanting to come up for air.

Beau broke away first and walked me to my car.

'How long ago did he die?' I asked, curious after what he'd said. I'd assumed it had been a few years but something Beau said didn't sit right.

'A couple of months ago.'

'Months?' I asked, raising my voice an octave higher than necessary. 'So, you were dealing with that guilt over not forgiving him, along with the grief of losing him when we first met?' I was shocked, and Beau looked uncomfortable.

'Yeah, like I said, you helped me deal with it.'

'Why didn't you say something? I feel so selfish now.' I didn't know why I was shouting at him; I was so angry with myself for not realising he was suffering too.

'Hey,' Beau said, his hands firm on my shoulders. 'You are the least selfish person I know. You've lived your entire life living up to everyone else's expectations, without question. How could you know how I felt if I didn't tell you? This is all on me Charlie.'

I refused to make eye contact, feeling a little dramatic after my outburst. I felt his fingers under my chin, and he lifted it gently, forcing our eyes to meet.

'Helping you to heal has helped me to heal. Maybe I'm the selfish one.'

I shook my head gently in response to his question. His breath skimmed my lips and we edged closer until our lips were just touching. Sparks danced between us until I felt his mouth on mine, his tongue lighting fireworks in my belly.

Pulling up at Kate's later, I was both nervous and a little excited to share my thoughts with her. My hands were sweaty when I knocked on the door and I quickly wiped them on my jeans when she answered the door.

'Hello love, come on in.' She stood back as I walked past her. I smiled nervously and she touched a hand to my shoulder. 'Don't worry, we won't go anywhere you're not ready to go.'

When we reached her room at the back of the house, the blinds were closed, and the lights dim. There were candles burning, and a pile of snuggly looking blankets on the couch. She could obviously see the questions running through my head and pointed to a chair for me to sit.

'Now, you can say no if you want, it's entirely your decision, but I thought we could maybe try some hypnosis if you're up for it. It might help bring some clarity to the dreams and explore them in a little more detail,' she explained.

I was a little dubious about hypnotherapy when she'd first suggested it, but I was resolute that I wanted to resolve whatever issues my grief had exposed.

'It's really dependent on how open your mind is to it. I've had great results with some clients, others not so much.'

'Tom?' I asked, curious.

Kate shook her head no.

'Okay, let's try it. What have I got to lose apart from more sleepless nights?' I consented.

I laid on the couch with the blankets and concentrated on listening to Kate's voice. It took a while before I forgot the strangeness of it all and became immersed. She was talking about my dad a little but mostly she concentrated on Tom. She talked about Tom and me together, our childhood, our relationship, my earliest memories. I felt quite spaced out and I reached a point where I wasn't really hearing what Kate was saying anymore but I was conscious of the fact that she was still talking. Images came to me of Tom and I as small children. We were in a house I didn't recognise. I only remembered living in the house I lived in now; I thought I'd lived there since I was a baby. There was a set of bunk beds against one wall. Tom had the top bunk; I could see stickers of rocket ships on the wall. We were both sitting up there together doing a jigsaw puzzle. It was a picture of The Wiggles. I smiled to myself; I had loved The Wiggles. I could hear shouting and Tom covered my ears with his hands, pulling my head to his chest. I could feel him shaking against me and the shouting seemed to be getting louder. Glass shattered, and a high-pitched scream sounded. I couldn't understand why we were just sitting there on the bed and not going to find out what was happening.

I could hear sirens in the distance, and I tried to concentrate on them to shut out the noise of the shouting and screaming. There were tears rolling down my face, but I didn't make a sound. There was such a familiarity about the situation, I felt like I'd lived it over and over. The sirens got closer until all the images I could see disappeared and I became aware of Kate's voice again.

'Focus on your breathing, I'm going to bring you out now.'

I opened my eyes, and I could see her watching me closely.

'Get up when you're ready and come and sit down. There's a glass of water on the table for you, I'll just go and make some coffee while you process the experience.'

She left the room and I hopped off the couch, taking a blanket with me. I felt so thirsty. I gulped the water and began to reflect on what had just happened. The vision was crystal clear, I remembered being there in that room with Tom. There was a smell that I couldn't quite place but I was sure it was linked with the images I saw.

'How are you feeling?' Kate asked as she set two coffees down on the table.

'I'm okay.' I spoke slowly, not sure if I really meant it. 'That was so weird. I felt like I was really there.' I laughed awkwardly, not quite sure what to make of it all.

'Tell me about what you saw.' Her voice was calm and reassuring, giving me the confidence to talk about my experience. I described the room to her, how I was sitting with Tom on the bunk.

'I remember that room, it's so clear to me now but I haven't seen it for such a long time. Tom and I shared it. I've always thought I lived in my house from being a baby, but I remember this other house. It was small and had a green front door. There was a wooden letter "C" over my bunk, which was pink with fairies on it.'

'Did you see anyone other than Tom?' Kate guided my thoughts.

'No, there was no one else in the room, but there was shouting and screaming. We were terrified.'

I paused as I tried to bring my mind back to what I could hear. I gasped. Fragmented memories began to appear in my thoughts.

'The dreams I've been having, I've been thinking they were about me, but I know now, it was my mum. It was her pain, her screams. She lived that.' I clamped my hand over my mouth as memories and images started slotting together like a puzzle, and the full realisation hit me.

Kate kept quiet and nodded along as she watched me process it all in my head. She passed the box of tissues from her desk, and then leaned over and took hold of my hand. She still didn't say anything; she just waited for me to collect myself.

'That's why Tom came to see you isn't it? He remembered we had another mum before, that we were adopted.' I was taken aback. Not only by the realisation, but by the fact that I could have forgotten something so monumental in my life.

Kate contemplated my question and nodded.

'Why didn't he tell me?'

'He wanted to, but he needed to get it all straight in his own mind first. He'd always retained some memory; he just didn't understand it. I guess he struggled to fit the pieces together in his head. He confronted your mum and she begged him not to tell you. He promised he would keep the secret providing she would speak to you herself. He struggled with it, both keeping it a secret and not knowing what had happened for you to end up being adopted. I don't know much more than that, just that he wanted to make contact with your birth mother, or at least find out what happened to her, but he wanted you on that journey with him. He came to me to try and process things in his head, but I only saw him a few times,' Kate explained. 'I didn't feel it was my place to tell you, I hope you understand that Lottie, but I hoped with a little assistance, you'd eventually remember yourself.'

I contemplated Kate's words, and I was struck by Tom suddenly reverting to calling me Charlie, and the name appearing in my dreams.

'I think my mum must've changed my name to Lottie. I wonder why?'

'I'm not sure,' Kate pondered. 'Tom never actually mentioned that you were called Lottie, he only ever referred to you as Charlie. Maybe it was his way of holding on to the past,' Kate suggested.

'It's a lot to take in, I don't even know where to begin.' There was a heavy feeling in my heart, knowing Tom was waiting for me to catch up and he never got the chance to find our birth mum. 'Do you know any more details?' I was suddenly curious.

'I'm sorry, I don't. Like I said, I only saw him a few times professionally.' Kate shook her head and a glint emerged in her eyes, like she had recalled something relevant. 'Has Beau ever told you about Clint? He's a friend of Beau's dad, he has a fish shack up the coast.'

'Yes,' I told her, 'Beau took me to meet him. He was really upset about Tom.' I was hoping this was leading somewhere.

'Tom spent a lot of time with him. Beau mentioned they'd become quite close. Maybe that's somewhere you could start if you do want to take this further, he might know more.'

I heard what she was saying but I was way ahead of her. I needed to take this further, I couldn't believe something so important had been kept from me all my life. I wish Tom had spoken to me and I wanted more than anything for him to be here right now. I brushed away the tears that were beginning to sting my face and took a big slug of coffee before I stood.

'I need to go.' My words came out abruptly. I didn't mean to be rude, but I needed to get out of there.

'Are you sure you're okay? I can call Beau for you.'

'No, honestly, I just need to be alone.'

Eva 1968

Eva had just finished re-typing her last line. Her novel was finished and ready to be posted to her editor. It had been touch and go whether she would meet her deadline after the scare she'd had the previous week. She was convinced the baby was coming but the pains had stopped after just a few hours and she'd felt nothing since. As she pushed her manuscript into an envelope, she balked at the taste of the glue. Her tastebuds were off today. Even food was tasting funny to her. She waddled her way across the landing to the stairs and carefully descended, gripping the rail as she went. She was uncomfortably large. Reaching the bottom, she placed the envelope on the hall table ready to post when they went out later, but as she turned towards the kitchen door, she doubled over at the excruciating pain thundering through her belly. She panted to get her breath and tried to call for Charles. A warm sensation between her legs spread rapidly towards her knees and she crouched slowly, feeling for the ground with her knees. Once Eva was on all fours, she managed to call out Charles's name. He appeared in the doorway within seconds and started at the sight of his wife before him, the anguish on her face belying her calm tone.

After a few seconds delay, Charles rushed to action, collecting her bag from the under stairs cupboard. He carefully guided his wife to the car and got her settled and then took care of a few last-minute details. Sliding into the driving seat, he turned to Eva, 'are you ready for this?'

'Well, it's a bit late now if I'm not.' Her voice was jovial until another wave crashed through her, and she screamed out in pain.

Charles turned the key and the engine spluttered to life. He began to reverse down the driveway and braked suddenly at Eva's roar.

'Are you okay?' he asked, fumbling over the question that he knew to be stupid.

'We need to post my manuscript,' Eva cried.

'Eva, it can wait. We need to get you to the hospital,' Charles insisted.

'No, it can't. I've worked my backside off to get it finished before this baby comes and that means it must go in today's post.'

Charles was not about to argue with his wife's persistence, especially in the midst of labour. He shifted the gear stick into first and pulled back up the driveway, quickly retrieving the manuscript from the hall table. He pulled into a parking space right outside the post office whilst Eva contended with another round of contractions. When he saw the queue inside the Post Office, Charles did something that was so out of character he shocked himself.

'Please, my wife is outside in the car in advanced labour. Is there any way I can jump the queue? She is insisting I post this before we get to the hospital. I'm so sorry.'

Every single person before him stepped aside and he was deeply grateful for their kindness.

He left the post office to calls of 'congratulations' and 'good luck,' and when he returned to the car, Eva was doubled over, panting to try and keep the pain at bay.

Charles broke every single speed limit on the drive to the hospital and pulled up outside as Eva was ready to push.

He dumped the car and ran inside to get help. A doctor and a midwife walked calmly to the car and spoke to Eva, asking her several questions whilst Charles hopped around impatiently from one foot to the other. A nurse appeared with a wheelchair and the three of them lifted Eva into it, wheeling her inside the building as she screamed in pain.

As the midwife changed Eva into a hospital gown and settled her into the bed in a delivery room, Charles paced anxiously.

'Mr Hartley, you may wait in the waiting room if you wish,' the nurse suggested.

Charles was offended by her suggestion, taking it as a slight on his character.

'Not a chance, I will be right by my wife's side, every step of the way. I got her into this mess so I will sure as hell help her get out of it.'

The nurse laughed at his candid statement and showed him where to sit to be of most use.

The labour didn't last long at all after the initial checks. Eva was fully dilated and began to push almost immediately. Elizabeth was born within the hour and Charles and Eva were smitten. Charles was immensely proud of his wife, as he always had been, but the overwhelming feeling of love for both Eva and his new daughter floored him. He hadn't realised his love could grow so much and he watched with wonder as Eva gently positioned the baby on her breast intuitively as though she had done this a thousand times. The moment Elizabeth began to suckle was the most serene moment he had ever experienced. Eva watched her daughter with such tenderness, her eyes gleaming, and Charles broke down in a torrent of happy tears.

The midwife had offered to make up a bottle for Elizabeth, but Eva was adamant she wanted to feed the baby herself, even though it wasn't the fashionable thing to do. She was also reluctant to allow the nurse to take the baby away to the nursery, but she'd promised to come and wake Eva when Elizabeth needed feeding. Charles had also been reluctant to leave Eva and his daughter but had been ushered out of the room to let Eva get some rest.

It was the first night they had spent apart since the day Eva was thrown out of her home, and Charles felt hollow as he let himself into their house alone. The jumble of emotions in the space of just a few hours had left him depleted. He settled himself in his armchair with a beer and swiftly drifted off into a deep sleep.

He awoke at three o'clock in the morning to a stiff neck and a loud rumbling in his belly. He made himself a corned beef sandwich and cup of tea and took them upstairs into the nursery where he sat on the rocking chair he'd bought Eva from an antique store. He had lovingly restored it so she would have somewhere to sit and feed the baby. He smiled to himself now; he was a daddy. He had a daughter and he vowed right there that she would be the most loved child in the world. Her opinions would be valued, and she would be encouraged to try new things. She would be curious, strong, and independent, and encouraged to follow her dreams. He would make sure of that. There would always be a home for her, and he would never allow her to be treated like Eva was by her parents. He thought about Eva's parents now, and his own for that matter. His own situation had been slightly different to Eva's. There had never been an argument or a big fall out, there was just a disinterest from both parties. His parents had never really cared what he did, they were always out at business events and dinner parties, rubbing shoulders with the important people. He had nothing in common with them and once he'd left home to become a teacher, he'd rarely heard from them. He wondered whether Eva would contact her parents now they had a granddaughter. He couldn't imagine that she would, she'd made peace with their estrangement many years ago, but he couldn't be sure.

Now he was wide awake and satiated he used his spare time to mark some of his students' papers, eagerly watching the clock until visiting time. He grinned at the prospect of seeing them again soon.

Lottie 2019

Without thinking, I headed straight to mum's wardrobe where she kept all the old photos. The ones in albums were all labelled, and skimming through them I quickly realised they weren't early enough for what I was looking for. There was an old shoe box filled with random photos, so I took the lid off and emptied them all out on the floor. I found baby photos of me, of Tom, ones of us together, but none of them were with our parents. Not my mum and dad, or my birth mother, the woman from my dreams. How had I never noticed there were no baby photos with my mum before? I stared at the pile on the floor, my mind whirring through what to do next. I decided to head straight up the coast to see if Clint could throw some light on things.

There were only two other cars in the car park when I pulled up near the door to the Fish Shack. As I stepped inside, I took a quick look around. A couple with a baby were sitting near the back doors just finishing up. I spotted Clint stocking up the fridge and he turned, sensing me as I got closer.

'Charlie! Good to see you. Where's Beau?' He welcomed me like an old friend, using the name he knew me by.

'Oh, he's busy. I've actually come to see you. Do you have a few minutes spare?' He looked at me curiously then nodded his head towards the door.

'Follow the path with the lights, there're some steps at the end leading to the beach. Grab a seat down there and I'll bring you some supper. Me and Tom had our best talks down there, and it sounds like that's what you might need.' He turned to the counter and shouted for a seafood basket as I disappeared through the door.

It was a stunning view from the steps; the sun was just beginning to dip and an orange haze floated over the ocean, sending a shimmer of light across the water. There was a chill in the air, but I felt warm in Tom's jacket. I pulled it tightly around me, my nose pressing into the crook of my arm taking in the smell of leather and Tom.

Clint appeared and sat beside me handing me the basket.

'Thank you, you didn't have to feed me,' I said gratefully.

'So, what's this all about Charlie?' he asked.

I took a deep breath before I spoke. 'I just found out I was adopted when I was little.'

Clint nodded. 'Your mum told you then?'

'No, we're not exactly on good terms at the moment.' I was saddened by my acknowledgement.

Clint looked surprised, 'Beau told you?'

That rocked me harder than the actual discovery about the adoption.

'Beau knew?' My voice was weak, I felt strangled.

Clint bowed his head at the realisation he'd just dropped Beau in the shit.

'I'm sorry, Charlie, please don't be mad at him. Tom was waiting for your mum to tell you; I'm sure Beau would've just been respecting his wishes.' I was floored by Clint's revelation, but my brain went into autopilot and I continued the conversation.

'I had hypnosis. It brought up memories that I'd forgotten, so I kind of worked it out myself. Mum and Beau aren't even aware that I know.'

We sat in silence while I picked at my food and tried to process the fact that Beau knew what my dreams were all about and watched me suffer when he could've put me out of my misery. I tried to push my thoughts to the back of my mind and focus on the reason I sought Clint out.

'Do you know anything?' I blurted out. 'About why we were adopted, I mean. Did Tom say anything to you about it?' I was so desperate for details.

'He didn't know much love; his memories were pretty vague and your mum didn't know many details. He wanted to look into it further but had concerns and decided the two of you should do it together. He mostly just talked to me about how he felt, I think he felt I'd understand, with me being adopted too. I know mine's a different story, but he needed someone to talk to.'

I nodded, encouraging him to continue.

'He was angry that your past had been kept secret from you both. Like I said, he had vague memories but didn't understand where they fit in to his life. He remembered it wasn't always happy Charlie, he thought your birth father was violent. I think maybe that's why he was a bit hesitant about moving forward.'

I nodded slowly. 'I remembered sitting on our bunk bed, Tom's hands covering my ears to protect me from the shouting.'

Clint shook his head and patted my hand with his.

'I think you should go talk to Beau. He's a good man Charlie, don't blame him for keeping this from you, he was put in a difficult position.'

I sat by myself for a while, thinking about what Clint had said. I got it; Beau felt indebted to Tom. But surely our relationship had gone way beyond that level. I'd been suffering, trying to come to terms with everything. He knew how much I'd struggled with my dreams and that

I was desperate to get to the bottom of what was going on in my head. There was no excuse for him not telling me. I left quickly, driving back down the ocean road, straight to Beau's unit.

I banged on the door with my fist and didn't stop until it flew open. Beau was standing in front of me, a worried look on his face. My heart began to soften at the sight of him, but my head convinced me I was still angry.

'What the hell Beau?' I shouted at him, slapping his chest with both hands. He gripped my elbow and led me inside, kicking the door shut behind me. He loosened his grip but continued to lead me through to his lounge area. Slowly turning me around to face him, his eyes zoned in on mine.

'Charlie, what the hell is going on?' he asked calmly.

'All this time you knew,' I spat at him. 'I'm adopted and you knew. How the fuck do you think that makes me feel?'

Beau's head dropped. I could hear the crack in his heart and I almost crumbled.

'I'm sorry Charlie, I didn't want to let Tom down. He promised your mum.'

'You didn't want to let Tom down? He's dead Beau, but I'm very much alive. Do you not think it might've helped me to understand what my dreams were about? You know how many sleepless nights I've had over this. I thought you cared. You told me you loved me.' I was shaking uncontrollably.

Beau's voice was broken. He was broken. 'I wanted to tell you, I thought about it so many times, but he promised your mum and I didn't think it was my place. But I do love you Charlie, please know that. I'm so sorry,' he pleaded with me to forgive him.

'That just says it all. You betrayed me, you care more about my dead brother while I'm the one still alive, suffering. I can't forgive you for that.'

Beau slumped down on to the couch; his head bowed in defeat. I almost felt sorry for him, and my heart shattered as I turned and left the room. In the hall, I noticed the keys for his bike on a hook near the door. I glanced back to see if he could see me then made the most impulsive decision I'd ever made. I grabbed the spare helmet from the box on the back of the bike and swung my leg over the seat. I'd never ridden a motorbike by myself, but I'd watched Beau enough times, it couldn't be that hard.

Eva 1986

The years were kind to Charles and Eva; they felt blessed to have had the opportunity to raise their beautiful daughter. Elizabeth was a free spirit with dreams of becoming a photographer for National Geographic. She wanted to travel the world, experience different cultures, climb Machu Picchu, and hike the Milford Track. Charles and Eva had encouraged her dreams, while emphasising the importance of education. She had blown their minds with her hard work and dedication to her studies and had accepted a place at London's Royal College of Art, which she had deferred for a year to enable her to travel and experience some of what the world had to offer first. She thought it would mature her outlook as an artist and provide her with a stronger foundation to begin her degree.

Eva stood at Lizzie's bedroom door, watching her daughter throw random clothing into her backpack. She was an eclectic mix of both of her parents, with her father's kind and gentle nature and her mother's determined spirit. She had been a delightful girl growing up and Eva couldn't be more proud of the tenacious and charismatic woman she had become.

'I'm going to miss you so much my little treasure,' Eva sighed wistfully.

Lizzie looked up from the array of belongings scattered around her room. 'I'm going to miss you too Mum, both of you. But I'll write every chance I get and send photos of my travels.'

Eva smiled at her only child. 'Have I ever told you how proud I am of you?'

Lizzie laughed. 'Only every day of my life, Mum.'

Eva's tone grew serious. 'I never wanted you to feel like I felt my whole childhood. My opinions were never valued, my intelligence was dampened, I had no freedom to choose. I fought against my parents constantly trying to keep my spirit alive. If I hadn't met your dad, who knows where I'd be now,' she mused.

'You'd still have got there Mum, it's who you are. Meeting Dad just propelled you forward. Like, super fast! I still can't believe he proposed to you after only knowing you a week! And you were younger than I am now! Can you imagine if I came home and told you I was getting married to a guy I met a week ago?' Lizzie was incredulous.

'Well, I would be shocked, but you know I would always sit down and hear you out.'

'You would, I know,' Lizzie admitted, 'but you also know that would never happen! I certainly don't want to be tied down to a man at my age. I want to see the world and meet lots of men.' Lizzie giggled unashamedly.

Eva reached out and pulled her daughter towards her, squeezing her tight and breathing in her scent. 'You meet as many men as you want my love but promise me you'll be careful.'

'Of course I will, I don't want to get stuck with a baby either,' Lizzie said, horrified at the thought.

'Mum? Can I ask you something?' Lizzie was quiet now, pensive.

'Anything, you know that.' Eva confirmed.

'Do you ever regret not getting back in touch with your parents? Did you ever think about it?'

Eva stilled. She'd thought about it several times over the years, wondering if they'd be different with their granddaughter than they had with her. She wanted them to experience the joys of this wonderful child, but she also didn't want any of their influence rubbing off on Lizzie.

'I wonder about it sometimes, question my decision to deprive you of grandparents.' Eva watched her daughter's reaction. 'But no, I don't regret it. I've had the most fantastic life without them in it. And I don't think for one minute that you've missed out on anything. But I'm not sure that was my decision to make. Maybe you should have been able to make that choice for yourself.'

Lizzie looked deep in thought and Eva was curious to know her feelings on the subject. She waited for her to speak.

'Mum, I know you wouldn't have made that decision without good reason, you've never deprived me of anything in my life. In fact, if anything you've probably been a little over-indulgent.' Lizzie paused. 'I do think about them though. I mean, not often, but sometimes I think it would've been nice to have grandparents to spoil me like my friends had. I guess they wouldn't have been that kind of grandparents though.' She looked at Eva now. 'I don't know how you've done it, living all these years without your parents, knowing they're living not far away. I can't imagine not having you and dad in my life.'

'Don't you worry, I'll never let that happen darling.' Eva kissed the top of Lizzie's head.

The following morning, Charles and Eva stood in line with Lizzie at the British Airways desk. The day had finally arrived, and all three of them were quiet as they waited to check Lizzie on to her flight to Singapore. There she would begin her trip around southeast Asia before heading on to New Zealand and Australia.

Once Lizzie was checked in, they sat together drinking coffee in the cafe near security. It was a tense time, not because Charles and Eva didn't want her to go, they absolutely did. And not because they were worried either. They had every faith that Lizzie could look after herself, but they would miss her terribly.

Lizzie would miss them too, but she had so much to look forward to.

'Hey, I'll call, and I'll write, and I'll be home before you know it,' Lizzie said trying to break the tension in the air, 'and Mum, just think how many books you'll be able to write without me under your feet all the time.'

Eva laughed; although her writing career had gone from strength to strength, Lizzie had always come first, and Eva had declined a very lucrative offer for a five book deal. Her name was well known in literary circles, her books were on high school and university syllabuses the world over, and she had even made the New York Times bestseller list with her last novel. Her writing had become a little more mainstream in the last few years.

'I might even find the time to write a book,' Charles chimed in on the conversation.

Eva looked at him with admiration. She had always known he had his own aspirations to write, but with his work as a teacher and now headmaster, as well as being the champion and support network for his wife's career and an equal share in the upbringing of their daughter, he just hadn't had the time.

'Dad, that's amazing. You should do it.' Lizzie leaned in and hugged him. Eva popped her camera out of her bag and quickly snapped the moment. She smiled at the beautiful relationship they shared. She knew Charles would be a mess later, as would she.

Lizzie looked at her watch solemnly and took a deep breath.

'It's time to go,' she whispered, her voice catching at the finality of the moment.

'Let's just get one last family photo,' Eva said, trying to hold herself together.

A gentleman at the next table offered to snap it for them. With Lizzie in the middle, the three of them smiled through their tears as the flash went off. The man passed the camera back to Eva and she hugged it to her chest, already treasuring the photo.

The little family hugged and cried at the security gate, and Charles and Eva looked on until Lizzie had disappeared from view. They stood forlornly, not wanting to leave and go home to an empty house.

'Come on, let's go out for lunch somewhere nice,' Charles said, trying to lift his own spirits as well as Eva's.

They drove to an old country pub where they sat together quietly, eating the meat and potato pie from the specials board. They'd both felt the need for comfort food.

'I can't believe she's gone,' Eva told Charles. 'If this is what my mother felt when I left home then I'll spend the rest of my life with remorse.'

'Eva, this is an entirely different situation. Your parents threw you out and never contacted you again. They could've sought you out, they could've apologised. You would go to the ends of the earth for Lizzie, there is no way your mother felt a smidgen of what you're feeling right now. We haven't lost her, she's going on an adventure, which is what we raised her to do. This is a good thing, we must keep telling ourselves that,' Charles said with pride.

Dear Mum and Dad,

I'm having such an amazing time here; I've decided to extend my stay by another twelve months. I know, I'm sorry, but you guys could fly out to see me - I know you'll love it here too. I've arrived in Queensland where I'll be staying a while. I know it's not the National Geographic, but I've got a job with a cruise company on the Great Barrier Reef as their photographer! I get to sail out to the reef every day and take photos - life is pretty good!

I've found an apartment to rent in Palm Cove, which is just north of Cairns. It even has a spare room so there's no excuse for you not to come.

Please say yes!

I miss you guys.

Love Lizzie xxx

Eva finished reading the letter out to Charles. They were disappointed that Lizzie wouldn't be arriving home next month as planned. It had been a long year for them both without their daughter, but Charles had been true to his word and had written a book of his own. It was a far cry from his wife's literary work, but he had sent his crime thriller out to several publishers and was awaiting their replies. Eva's agent had passed his manuscript on to one of her colleagues who had a big interest in crime novels, for which Charles had been extremely grateful.

'Why don't we go?' Charles asked Eva. 'Another year is a long time and I'd love to see where she is, it sounds like she's having a fabulous time. What do you think?'

Eva put the letter down on the table and sipped her tea, pondering over Charles's question.

'I guess we could, I would love to see her. Can you get time off work?'

Charles was already deep in thought about the best time for them to travel.

'Maybe we could go at Easter? I'm sure I could tag an extra week on the end of the school holidays, and we could go for three weeks.'

Eva's face lit up, the prospect of seeing her daughter now becoming feasible.

'Do you really think so?' she asked, excitedly.

'I'll find out on Monday,' Charles said, decisively.

The plan came together, and Charles and Eva booked their flights. Lizzie was so excited to see her parents again and show off her idyllic life to them. She already knew she wanted to stay there permanently but hadn't broached that subject with them yet. She knew how important education was to them.

Eva told her agent she would be unavailable for three weeks and was looking forward to a relaxing holiday. She had worked tirelessly over the last year, filling up her time working on two new novels. She'd felt lost when Lizzie had first left and often wandered around the house aimlessly searching for something, usually ending up in Lizzie's bedroom, if only to feel her presence.

It was a strange time for both Charles and Eva, adjusting to life on their own again, finding new activities to fill up the space that Lizzie had left. They'd been very hands on parents and had always had a lot in common, it was just a matter of re-establishing their relationship as a couple. It had taken time, but they reached a new balance, as they both knew they would. With both of them now writing, they'd had an extension built on the back of their house, which incorporated a new office for the pair of them and a sunroom. They had contemplated moving house, but they loved their cottage, the location was perfect, and it had been home to them for a long time. They had happy memories there.

On the morning of the flight to Brisbane, they travelled to Manchester to get their first flight to Singapore. They'd thought about having a few days there to break up the long flight but in the end decided they just wanted to get to Cairns as soon as possible.

By the time they arrived in Singapore, Eva was glad Charles had talked her into paying the extra money for business class seats.

'We can afford it Eva, our house is paid for, you're an internationally bestselling author, not to mention your recent venture into the film world. Let's enjoy the extra comfort.'

'You're right, why not?' Eva had agreed. Her agent had been dealing with film companies, and one had finally optioned one of her novels. It would be made into a film very soon. She was excited but a little worried at the same time as there were countless films produced that turned out nothing like the book they'd been adapted from. She didn't want that, she loved her books and what they had to say, and so her lawyers had been meticulous with the details.

Charles and Eva were awed by Changi airport. They couldn't believe the size of it, and after a little exploration were grateful for the business lounge where they showered and refuelled ready for the next leg of the journey. They'd booked an overnight stay in Brisbane before flying into Cairns the next day, and by the time they arrived at their hotel, they were both beat and ready for bed.

They slept late and almost missed breakfast but just managed to sneak into the buffet for a quick bite and some English Breakfast tea. They had a few hours before their flight and ventured out to have a quick look at the city before leaving for the airport. Grateful for the short flight they landed in Cairns filled with excitement at finally seeing their daughter.

With no immigration to go through, and their bags one of the first off the carousel, it was a matter of minutes before they walked through the doors in anticipation. Eva spotted her daughter immediately, and tears flooded her face. Lizzie was grinning as her mother swept her into her arms. Charles gathered them both and joined in the hug.

The three of them held each other close, breathing in the familiar scents. It was Lizzie that let go first.

'Come on, let's go get you in the car and I'll take you to my apartment. You'll love Palm Cove.'

Lizzie had bought herself an old open top jeep. Charles squeezed in the back and let his wife sit up front with Lizzie on the trip up the coast.

Eva was floored by how much Lizzie had changed in a year. She was tanned and her hair had bleached in the sun. She looked every bit an Australian now. She had a glow about her that Eva hadn't noticed before.

'I think the sunshine agrees with you my darling,' Eva said. 'You look well.'

'Thanks Mum, it's a great life. Everything is so laid back here and I've met so many new people. There are backpackers from all over the world, it's been the best experience.' Lizzie smiled and turned to her mum. 'I've missed you guys though. I'm so glad you came.'

Lizzie pulled the jeep up outside a three-storey apartment block. 'I'm on the top floor,' she told her parents. 'And there's a balcony overlooking the beach.' She was excited to show her parents her little apartment, she'd been looking forward to this new grown-up relationship with them.

Lizzie showed them to their room, which she had made up lovingly for them. The apartment had come furnished with basic modern furniture, but she'd added bedding and bedside lamps to make it more homely for them. She knew her mum would love the little touches.

'I'm so proud of you Lizzie,' Eva said wandering into the kitchen where her daughter was fixing some lunch. 'You're so grown up, where's my little girl gone?' Tears stung her eyes as she hugged her daughter.

'Go out to the balcony, I'll bring lunch out,' she told her mum.

Eva found Charles at the bookshelf. It was tiny and only had a small collection of novels and a few photography books. She'd not lived there long and couldn't buy too much but when Eva recognised the book in Charles's hand, she felt a sudden rush of emotion. Charles held up her own book, proud that his daughter had bought a copy for her new home.

Lizzie came in with a tray of sandwiches and a jug of lemonade. She noticed the book Charles clutched in his hand and grinned.

'A house is not a home until there's an Eva Hartley on the bookshelf.'

Eva laughed, proud of her daughter once again.

The three of them enjoyed an afternoon on the balcony, catching up and wallowing in the heat.

'It's humid, do you ever get used to it?' Charles asked Lizzie.

'I guess so, but it's not that bad today Dad, you should've been here in the height of summer, your clothes are just constantly wet. That's why no one dresses up much, it's just shorts and t-shirts and flip-flops. Or thongs as they're known here.'

'I brought champagne,' Eva exclaimed, clapping her hands together. 'It should be cold now, I put it in the fridge when we arrived. I think us all being here together is cause for celebration. Shall we have some?'

Lizzie laughed. 'Absolutely! It'll have to be in wine glasses though, I don't have any flutes.'

'You know me, Lizzie, I'm not precious about that kind of thing,' Eva said, surprised that Lizzie would have even thought that an issue.

Lizzie shook her head, 'I know Mum, I forgot myself for a second there. Some of the people we get on the cruises don't adapt to the Aussie lifestyle too well.'

Eva cleared the little table of their lunch things and went to the kitchen to grab the champagne. As she busied herself washing up and finding glasses, she watched her husband and daughter deep in conversation. They'd always had a close relationship and from an early age, Charles had engaged her in important conversations regarding everything from politics and religion to science and the arts. Eva loved watching them debate and discuss, sometimes heated, but always empathetic towards each other's views. She smiled now as she gathered the glasses and champagne bottle.

Eva handed the bottle to Charles to open. It went with a pop, and he expertly poured the fizz into the glasses without spilling a drop.

'To family,' Charles toasted, raising his glass.

'To the best family,' Lizzie clinked their glasses and took a sip, sighing at the taste. 'It's not often I get to drink champagne, it's not usually in the budget of a backpacker.'

Charles laughed then turned serious, his fatherly protective head taking over.

'Are you okay for money Lizzie? Are they paying you enough to get by?'

'I'm fine Dad. It's not great pay but I don't need much. I can pay my rent and put petrol in my car. I get fed when I'm working so don't need much food at home. I don't go out much, my friends and I tend to hang out on the beach in the evenings with a few beers.'

'It sounds like a wonderful life Liz,' Charles sighed, reading Lizzie's thoughts easily. She obviously loved it here and she was so alive. He knew right then in that moment that she wouldn't be coming home or taking up her place at the Royal College of Art.

Charles and Eva's time spent in Queensland with their daughter was the most blissful time of their lives. Lizzie had managed to book a week off work and the three of them toured around in her little Jeep, taking in all the tourist spots. Once Lizzie was back at work, she invited her parents on the Great Barrier Reef cruise that she worked on. They were treated like VIP's and enjoyed every minute of the experience. They snorkelled on the reef and Lizzie took some beautiful underwater photos of them together. They loved watching Lizzie work, she was a natural with the guests onboard and she lit up whenever she had a camera in hand. Although the time she spent out and about taking candid photos on the reef was her favourite part of the job, it was the staged souvenir photos that paid most of the bills. Families standing in front of a life buoy in their wetsuits were the photos that most people bought, but Lizzie's real creativity happened in the natural world.

The rest of their holiday was spent relaxing at the beach, wandering aimlessly, sharing long lunches with a bottle of wine. They shopped every day and cooked for Lizzie when she arrived home in the evenings, or the three of them would go out to expensive restaurants and fill themselves with delicious seafood. They loved spoiling their daughter after such a long time apart.

One afternoon towards the end of their holiday, Charles and Eva sat on the beach together, talking intimately about their life together.

'I've never seen you so peaceful Eva,' Charles whispered.

'I am peaceful my love. I love the pace of life here, just being here with you and Lizzie is extraordinarily tranquil. I know it has to come to an end, but I'll treasure these memories forever.'

'You know she's not coming home, don't you?' Charles hadn't had any confirmation from Lizzie about her future plans, but he knew his daughter and he could sense that Eva knew it too.

Eva closed her eyes and sighed, 'I do.' Charles reached for Eva's hand and squeezed. 'I'm at peace with it. She's so happy here and I know she's not here to get away from us; I feel closer to her than ever. She's living her life in her own way and that's what we always wanted for her. So yes, I'll miss her terribly, but I'm happy.'

Charles leaned close to Eva until his shoulder was resting against hers. 'I'm happy too.'

On their last night in Palm Cove, they went to Lizzie's favourite restaurant. It wasn't fancy but the food was excellent, and the tables overlooked the beach. They drank cocktails and chatted easily about life. The conversation turned sombre for a while when Charles questioned Lizzie about her plans.

'You're not coming home, are you Liz?' Charles asked.

Lizzie stuttered and blushed at his question, but she was honest. She knew her parents could read her like a book.

'Are you mad?' she asked sadly.

'No sweetheart, we're not mad. A little sad maybe, but not mad. We can see how much you love it here.'

'I'm sorry. I wanted to tell you, but I didn't want to spoil your holiday,' Lizzie told her parents.

'We just want you to be happy Lizzie, that's all that's ever mattered to us,' Eva added.

'I know. I miss you guys so much, but I can't imagine living through another British winter. Or being stuck inside a classroom when I can be out here photographing one of the seven natural wonders of the world every day. You can come and visit any time you like. Maybe next time you come you can explore other parts of Australia too.'

Eva looked at Charles across the table and he nodded. 'We'd like that.' Eva said.

As much as everyone was happy, the next morning at the airport was heartbreaking for all three of them. Charles and Eva hated leaving their little girl behind, and Lizzie had loved having her parents there to spoil her again. Their faces were awash, but they were all insistent that time would pass quickly until they could be together again.

Charles and Eva boarded their flight to Singapore a couple of hours after their arrival in Brisbane and flew to their destination with their hands firmly grasped together, not speaking a word to each other. Their arrival in Singapore awoke them from their melancholy and soon after checking into their hotel they were ready to begin the next part of their adventure.

Charles had surprised Eva by booking three nights at The Raffles Hotel. He knew it would inspire her love of literature, having been frequented by some of the literary greats such as Rudyard Kipling and Somerset Maugham. They began their adventure with a classic Singapore Sling in the Long Bar, savouring every second of their time together. They wandered the streets like teenagers in love, rekindling the passion of their younger days. They strolled through the vibrant maze of Chinatown hand in hand, stopping to try the delicacies the food stalls had to offer. The aromas drawing them in were exquisite and the taste exceeded all expectations.

They drank cocktails and champagne, swam in the tranquil pool and dined in elegant restaurants. Their three days were filled with love, and a closeness that had Eva craving Charles in a way she hadn't felt in years. Their love had continued to grow over the years but family life, publishing deadlines and school marking had got in the way of their intimacy. They hadn't had the time or space to properly enjoy each other like those early days when nothing mattered to them but lazy Sundays spent in bed.

On their last night, they had dinner in the hotel followed by drinks in the bar. Charles had bought Eva a beautiful dress with a low cut back, which showed off her curves and set his pulse racing. Sitting in the bar as the evening was drawing to a close, Charles ran his hand along Eva's thigh, which peeked out seductively from the lengthy slit in her dress. Eva shivered at his touch, and heat immediately rushed to Charles's face. As controlled as he was, he needed to get Eva alone. Slipping off the stool, he took her hand and led her to their room. Luckily there were people in the lift when they stepped in, otherwise Charles felt he wouldn't have been able to wait.

Charles had removed his shirt by the time Eva had closed the door. She watched as he fumbled with the buttons on his fly, pulling his shoes and socks off and standing before her in only his underwear. Eva's face slipped into a grin, and she felt young and beautiful as Charles's eyes took her in. He moved towards her and in painstakingly slow motion, unzipped her leaving her dress to fall to the floor.

He laid her gently on the bed and cherished every moment of their night together. In the early hours of the morning, Charles wrapped his arm around his wife as she snuggled into his side, drifting together into a blissful sleep.

Beau 2019

I contemplated going after her, but I knew she needed time. Today had been huge, and I was so pissed off at myself for screwing it up. I should've just told her; I knew how much she was struggling with it all.

'Fuck. Fuck. Fuck.'

There was a knock on the door and my heart soared, hopeful that she'd forgiven me. I bolted to the door only to find Kate letting herself in.

'Beau, what's wrong? Is Charlie okay?' she asked concerned.

'She left me.' My chest was heavy as I spoke the reality of those words.

She looked past me into the lounge, her brow knitted together in confusion.

'Where is she?' Kate asked.

'She's gone, she won't forgive me. I should've told her Kate.' A sob ruptured my chest and I fell apart in Kate's arms. She was the closest thing to a mum I'd had in a long time and I knew she'd always be there for me but in that moment, it was Charlie I needed. I pulled away and Kate still looked confused.

'Her car is still outside Beau, I assumed she was here.'

I pushed past her to the door and didn't even really notice her car. The only thing that registered with me was that my bike had gone.

'No! Fuck!' Fear like I'd never felt hit me, robbing me of all my breath. I squatted down, trying to bring my breathing under control whilst trying to think where she would've gone.

'Beau, what?'

'She's taken my bike.'

Kate immediately took over, grabbing my jacket and pushing me out of the door. We got into her Toyota, and I sank down in the passenger seat, unable to bring myself to think about Charlie riding my motorbike without a licence.

Kate broke the silence. 'She might've just gone home; we'll try there first.'

As the car swung into Charlie's driveway, I jumped out before it even came to a stop. There was no sign of my bike, but I banged on the door anyway. I couldn't see any lights on inside, or any sign of her so I hurried back to the car.

'Do you think she might've gone to see Clint?' Kate suggested. 'I mentioned him to her today, told her Tom might've confided in him.'

'Let's go.' I fastened my seat belt and tried calling Charlie, but it just rang out. My eyes searched everywhere in the dark, looking for a single headlight. Driving up the ocean road, I made Kate pull into every car park on the way, just in case. There was no sign of Charlie or my bike by the time we pulled into the Fish Shack, where Clint was just closing up for the night. I ran to the door and rattled it, waiting for him to turn around. Recognition dawned on him, and he came back to let me in.

'Has Charlie been here?' I asked, skipping the pleasantries.

'Yeah, she was here earlier, is everything okay?' Clint asked.

'Was she on my bike?'

'Your bike?' Clint was confused, and I didn't have time to waste.

'My fucking motorbike Clint, was she on it?'

'No son, she was in her car.'

I turned, and without a goodbye I got back in the car and slammed the door. My head in my hands, I didn't know what to do. My shoulders heaved and I just managed to get the door open in time to empty the contents of my stomach on the car park floor.

By that time, Clint had walked over to Kate's window. I had no idea what they were saying but their faces looked grim, and they were speaking in hushed voices. Clint's eyes washed over me, and he gave me a half-hearted smile. As Kate's window rose, Clint tapped the roof of the car before making his way back to the shack.

'You okay?' Kate asked quietly before setting off. I closed my eyes, shaking my head.

'Can you think of anywhere else she might've gone Beau?' Again, I shook my head. She pulled out of the car park, heading for home and I felt defeated.

Racking my brains, a thought came to me. 'I've taken her to the lookout in the hills, she might've gone there.' I hoped to God she hadn't. Those winding roads were difficult enough to handle for an experienced rider in the dark, never mind someone who'd never ridden and was already in an incredibly fragile emotional state. Kate nodded and turned left at the next intersection to head east. There was silence in the car, but not a comfortable one. We were both terrified of speaking. My phone buzzed in my pocket, and my heart leapt. My face screwed up at the unknown number, but I answered anyway.

'Hello?'

'Hello. Am I speaking to Beau Cipriani?' It was a stranger's voice, a woman.

'Yes, this is Beau.' My voice trembled.

'There's been an accident involving a motorbike which is registered in your name.' A high-pitched squeal sounded in my ears, and I wondered where it was coming from until I realised it was me. The car had stopped, and Kate grabbed the phone from my hand. White noise assaulted my ears. Kate's mouth was opening and closing but I couldn't hear what she was saying. She passed the phone back to me and set off driving in the direction of the city. When she pulled up outside the emergency department, Kate abandoned the car and jumped out. I couldn't move. I didn't know what had happened and I was too scared to ask. Kate ran round to my door and opened it.

'Beau, get out.' I didn't move.

'Beau, get out of the car. Your girlfriend is lying in that hospital fighting for her life. She needs you to fight for her, not fall apart.' I'd never in my life heard Kate raise her voice so I knew she meant business. I tried to process what she was saying to me. Fighting for her life? That meant she was alive. Oh my God, she was alive. I looked at Kate's face, fierce and determined. She spurred me into action, and I got out of the car. We ran inside to the admissions desk, where Kate took charge, providing all the details they asked for. They asked for her next of kin, but Kate explained the situation and told the nurse which ward her mum was on.

We were shown to a waiting room. The clinical smell made me want to heave. I tried to hold it together, but it was difficult with all the images and scenarios racing through my head. I didn't know how long we'd been waiting but Kate was dozing in the chair while I paced the floor.

It felt like we'd been there a lifetime when a nurse came in and introduced herself.

'Charlotte's in surgery, she's pretty knocked up,' she explained. My breathing shallowed as she continued. 'She has a broken leg and ribs, and some internal bleeding. The doctor will come and see you when she's finished in surgery. She'll be a while yet though, why don't you go down to the cafe and get something to eat, it'll help with the shock.' She smiled sympathetically and turned to leave.

'What if she doesn't pull through this Kate?' The sound of my own voice breaking ripped me apart and I dropped to the floor, heavy sobs racking my body. I hunched over, pulling my knees to my chest trying to strangle the pain. Kate's arms circled my body, and I slumped into her in the middle of the hospital corridor. I thought about Charlie and all the shit she'd had to deal with in the weeks that I'd known her. I thought about our relationship and how far it had come in such a short time. She meant everything to me.

'I love her Kate; I can't lose her.'

'She's tough Beau, she'll fight. You've both lost so much but you have each other now. She'll fight for that; she loves you too.'

'She hates me. She said it was over.'

'She didn't mean it, she was hurting. She'll come around,' Kate said. 'Come on, let's go get something to eat.'

The minutes turned to hours and the dawn pierced through the skylights above the waiting room. It felt like the longest night of my life, waiting and pacing. I eventually talked Kate into going home to get some sleep with a promise to call as soon as I had news. It was a little after 6.00am when the doctor finally appeared.

'Beau?' she asked, her eyes quickly scanning the room.

'Yes, that's me, is she okay?' I questioned her eagerly.

'Charlotte is out of surgery. She has a broken femur and tibia. Her left leg was a mess, she has screws and plates holding the bones together. She has several broken ribs and there was a lot of internal bleeding. We've managed to stem that bleeding, but she will remain in critical condition. Any questions?' She was very matter of fact, a little blunt even but I appreciated her honesty.

'Can I see her?'

'Just for a while, follow me.' She led me to the ICU and stopped as we reached the door. 'Just to warn you, she has a lot of surface wounds. Her skin was pretty torn up by the road. Lucky she was wearing a helmet.'

'Thank you, Doc,' I told her appreciatively as I walked through the door she was holding open for me. My heart raced as I got closer to her, then time stilled and all I could hear was the monotonous beeping of Charlie's monitors. My throat constricted and pain stabbed at my chest. I gasped for air and reached out to a chair for balance. My heart was shattered at the thought of losing her.

I needed to pull myself together, for Charlie. I reached for her hand resting on top of the covers. It was covered in tape, holding a cannula in place. The other one was fully bandaged. I stroked her palm, circling her fingertips with mine then gently rested my forehead on the bed.

I must've fallen asleep because I was suddenly woken with a start. Nurses were milling around Charlie's bed.

'What's going on?' I asked groggily, wiping sleep from my eyes.

'It's okay, we're just checking on her.' I glanced at my watch, surprised to see I'd been asleep for a couple of hours. The nurses hadn't asked me to leave. One of them looked at me kindly and suggested I go grab some coffee and food.

'If you leave your number at the desk, we can call if there's any change,' she assured me.

'Thanks,' I told her, 'I'm not going far though.'

I decided to call Kate to let her know what was going on. I was just hanging up as I reached the nurses station and noticed two police officers chatting to the nurse. She looked up and smiled at me in recognition.

'Ah, here he is now,' she told the officers. The policewoman turned to face me, and I stared at her, waiting for her to speak.

'Mr Cipriani?' she asked.

'Yes.'

'We've retrieved your motorbike. It was in an accident involving Charlotte Flowers. Is that right?' she asked for confirmation.

'Yes, she's my girlfriend.'

'Are you aware she doesn't have a motorcycle licence, and therefore no insurance?' I didn't like her tone and I had to fight with myself to remain calm.

'Yes, I know that. We had a fight, and she took it. I didn't know until later.' I worried I was incriminating her just by speaking.

'So, she stole it?'

'No, she didn't steal it. She's my girlfriend, she just borrowed it.'

'Without your permission?' Geez, this woman was relentless.

'Was there another vehicle involved? Or anyone else injured?' I asked, trying to steer her away from her persistent line of fire.

'No,' she said, a little less abruptly. 'It would appear that Miss Flowers lost control on a bend. She slid into a traffic signal.' I breathed a sigh of relief that no one else was involved.

'Can I go now?' I asked. The police officer nodded before taking my number, in case she needed me further. I also left my number at the nurses' station and made my way to the cafe, ordering a bacon and egg roll and a cup of coffee. I sat in the cafe wondering if Charlie would even want to see me when she woke up. What if she still hated me? Picking at the roll I thought about how different things would be if I'd just told her. Why did I think it was more important to honour Tom's promise than to help Charlie? No wonder she hated me, that was such a dick move.

I threw the uneaten roll in the bin and took my coffee back to the ICU. A nurse was in the room when I returned, looking over Charlie's charts.

'Hello love,' she looked up from the charts. 'She's doing okay, there's no sign of bleeding.'

I rubbed my hand over my face and tried to stifle a yawn I could feel coming.

'Why don't you go home and get some rest? We'll call you the minute there's any change.' I knew she was only trying to help but there was no way I was leaving Charlie there alone.

'I'm fine, I'd rather stay.' I settled back into the chair as she finished her rounds. Sleep overpowered me and I found myself drifting off only to be woken several hours later by a scraping sound. I looked up to see Kate pulling a spare chair up beside me. She leaned over to hug me, holding on a little longer than she normally would. When she released me, she kissed the top of my head, and I was so grateful for this woman. My life could've gone in so many different directions after my mum and Liv died but this completely selfless woman saved me from my demons.

'How are you?' she asked quietly, as she sat down.

'Not great,' I shrugged. 'There's no change,' I said motioning towards Charlie. 'The nurse said that's good because it means there's no signs of internal bleeding. We just have to wait for her to wake up.'

'Look, I know you won't leave so I've brought you some stuff,' she said handing me a small bag. 'Just a toothbrush and some clean clothes. Oh, and your phone charger and a book.'

'Thanks,' I told her.

Kate stayed for a while. It was nice to have some company even though I didn't have much to say. She tried to take my mind off the situation, but I really wasn't interested in talking. I just wanted Charlie to wake up so I could apologise for being a dick and hoped she forgave me. And even if she wouldn't forgive me, at least she'd be awake.

Eva 1990

'Hello, Mum?' Lizzie was breathless on the other end of the phone.
'Lizzie? Is everything okay?' Eva asked her daughter.
'Everything's great, Mum. I'm ringing with some news.'
'What is it darling?' Eva was curious as to what had Lizzie so excited. She wondered if she had a new job. She'd been with the cruise company for three years now and Eva had thought the last time they'd visited that she seemed a little tired of it.
'I'm getting married.' Lizzie couldn't wait any longer to share her news.
Eva was taken aback. 'What do you mean you're getting married? Who to?' Charles and Eva hadn't even been aware she had a boyfriend.
'His name is Mick. I met him on one of the cruises and we just hit it off. He lives in Sydney, but he's been coming up to see me every few weeks. I love him Mum, I can't wait for you to meet him.'
Eva felt like she'd been kicked in the gut. She was worried that Lizzie hadn't know him long enough and wondered why she'd never mentioned him before. She didn't want to project her fears onto Lizzie, she knew her daughter had a good head on her shoulders. She was wildly independent and knew she wouldn't get tied down to a relationship with someone who wasn't special.
'Congratulations darling, I can't wait to meet him,' she told her, all the while feeling sick to her stomach.
'We're going to organise the wedding to coincide with your next visit. I couldn't get married without you there.'
'That's great, I'll pass you on to Dad so you can tell him your news yourself.' Eva couldn't speak any longer and held the phone out to Charles.
She could hear the conversation as she walked away and could tell by Charles's voice that he was as shocked and disappointed as she was.
When Charles hung up the phone, he found Eva in the sunroom rocking gently in her old rocking chair staring out of the window. Charles was pained to see his wife so sad, and he shared in her sorrow.

143

He knelt in front of the rocking chair and placed his hand on the arm to stop her rocking. Eva leaned forward and wrapped her arms around his neck.

'Oh Charles, what is she doing? I've always been happy for her, but I can't get my head around this,' Eva sobbed on Charles's shoulder.

'I don't know Eva; it seems so out of character. I didn't think she'd get married until she was at least thirty, if at all.'

'I want to be happy for her, I really do, but I can't help thinking she's got herself into something. What do we know about this guy? Did you ask her anything?' Worry lines creased Eva's face.

'I didn't ask much; I was in shock. She told me his name is Mick and he's a bit older than her,' Charles sighed.

'Older? How much older?' Eva's ears had pricked up at that, Lizzie hadn't mentioned that to her at all.

'I'm not sure, she didn't say.'

'I bet that's it, he's manipulating her,' Eva hissed.

'Now let's not jump to any conclusions. We need to try and find out what's going on without making her think we're criticising her choices.' Charles had always been the diplomatic one in their relationship.

Eva was distracted and barely wrote a sentence over the next few weeks. She tried everything to try and clear her head, from walking on the moors to drinking wine, but nothing would take away the worry she felt. Luckily, she didn't have any pressing deadlines looming, which she was grateful for. She was only in the early stages of her next book and wasn't currently under contract with her publisher. Maybe that wasn't a good thing for her state of mind; she usually worked well under pressure, but then she hadn't had to worry about her daughter marrying a complete stranger on the other side of the world before.

It was only a couple of months until their next trip. They'd planned it for during the long school holidays in July and August to give them the opportunity to travel a little further. They had booked two weeks in New Zealand in a camper van to finish off their trip, but now Eva was dreading leaving Australia with their daughter married to an older man. She had spoken to Lizzie only once since she'd told them her news and casually mentioned age in the conversation. Mick was thirteen years older than Lizzie, which worried Eva more than she had been. She couldn't help thinking that was a big difference to a twenty-two-year-old girl with an adventurous spirit. Lizzie had been excited about the wedding plans, and Eva had tried her hardest to be happy for her. The wedding would be taking place on the beach in Palm Cove, a few days before Charles and Eva were due to leave for New Zealand. Lizzie hadn't wanted to miss out on any time with her parents by going away on honeymoon during their stay.

Charles had offered to send money to help with the costs, but Lizzie said Mick was covering it all; it sounded like the man was quite wealthy. Charles hoped that wasn't the reason she was marrying him. He was sure she wasn't motivated by money; she never had been previously, but things changed. He never thought she'd get married so young, but here she was.

'Eva?' Charles shouted as he came in from work. He walked straight through to their shared office space, expecting her to be at her desk working.

'I'm in here,' she called from the sunroom next door.

Charles popped his head through the doorway to find Eva sitting in her rocking chair nursing a glass of red wine. He frowned then looked at his watch. It was four o'clock and this was out of character for Eva.

'What's going on love?' he asked, taking a seat next to her.

'I don't know Charles. I can't write, I can't stop thinking about Lizzie. Am I not allowed to drink wine when I want to?' Her tone was snarky, which was also out of character.

'My darling, I'm not criticising you for drinking wine. It's just unusual that's all, I'm concerned about you,' Charles breathed. 'What can I do?'

Eva stared at him and shrugged. 'Other than telling our daughter not to marry this man you mean?' she laughed without humour.

'I know it's hard Eva, but it's her life and we have to accept it. We haven't even met the man and we're judging him. He might be genuine. I can't imagine Lizzie falling for someone who isn't.' Charles tried to talk Eva round but knew he wasn't having much success.

'I'm not judging him, I'm judging her. We didn't raise her to get herself tied down at twenty-two,' Eva snapped.

'I really don't think we're in any position to judge her for that Eva. You were eighteen when you accepted my proposal and we were married within two months of meeting,' Charles reminded her calmly.

'That was different Charles, and you know it.' Eva was angry now.

'Why was it different? We met and fell in love. How do you know Lizzie doesn't feel exactly the way we did? You know how strong our feelings were for each other right from day one.'

'But I didn't have any other option, my parents wouldn't have let me see you otherwise,' Eva spat.

Charles was floored by her cruel revelation. His mouth hung open, not sure what words would come out next. He didn't want to exacerbate the situation, so he just walked away.

Eva was immediately regretful. She hadn't meant that, she had loved him fiercely and wanted nothing more than to spend her life with him. She had to make amends. In all the years they'd been married, they'd never fought like this.

She found him in the kitchen preparing dinner.

'Charles,' she whispered.

He turned to face her, leaning against the kitchen bench looking broken.

'I'm so sorry,' she apologised, moving towards him, she took his hands in hers. 'I didn't mean it; you know that's not what happened. I was just angry.' Charles's silence distressed her. 'Please forgive me,' she choked.

'I know you didn't mean it Eva but to hear you say something like that after all these years,' Charles blinked away tears. 'It hurt.'

Eva closed her eyes and hung her head low. A single tear squeezed from the corner of her eye and steadily made its way down her cheek. Her shoulders shuddered, heaving with the sobs that were now flowing freely from her body. Charles wrapped her in his arms and hugged her tight.

'It's okay,' he whispered into her hair. 'I know you're hurting. We'll get through it, I promise.'

Charles and Eva were nervous as they disembarked the A320 at Cairns Airport. Eva's fingers twirled her necklace as they waited for their luggage at the carousel. Her emotions were mixed but the excitement at seeing Lizzie was significantly drowned by the worry. They'd spoken a lot over the last couple of months and the more they spoke, the more anxious Eva became. Lizzie seemed to be concealing her feelings, covering every conversation relating to Mick in a rose-coloured tint, and Eva wondered if she was beginning to have second thoughts. She'd hopefully have a chance to speak to her alone before the wedding. She wasn't sure when Mick would be arriving in Cairns.

Eva's worry dissipated the second she saw Lizzie waiting at the barrier, looking just as happy as always, her face beaming. There were hugs all round before Lizzie looked at the older man standing next to her.

'Mum, Dad, this is Mick,' she said casually.

Eva and Charles were both taken aback, not realising he'd be at the airport to collect them.

Eva held out her hand to shake Mick's and was shocked when he dismissed it and hugged her instead.

'We don't need to be so formal, we'll be family soon,' Mick said, his Australian drawl already grating on her nerves.

Mick hugged Charles too and then picked up both their cases and led the way outside to the car.

Charles hurried to keep up, a little annoyed that this man had swooped in and left him feeling incapable. Eva and Lizzie hung back slightly.

'I've missed you Mum,' she said.

'I've missed you too darling.' Eva stopped walking and turned to Lizzie. 'Are you happy?' she asked, unable to wait any longer.

'Yes, I am. Why do you ask?' Lizzie replied, curious.

'I just want to make sure you're not having second thoughts. It's quite all right if you are. You never have to do anything you don't want to,' Eva assured her.

'I knew you weren't happy about this wedding,' Lizzie accused her mother. 'You think I'm too young, or I haven't known him long enough, but you cannot stand in judgement of me with your history.' Eva had never heard Lizzie so angry at her. Well, not since she was fourteen years old, and Eva refused to allow her to go to the pub. 'I love him Mum, he's good to me and he gives me whatever I want.'

Eva was gobsmacked. 'He gives you whatever you want? That's a good reason to marry him?'

Lizzie shook her head and rolled her eyes, looking every bit that teenager having a tantrum. 'That's not what I meant. I meant that he's kind and will do anything for me.'

Eva hated this conversation. She hadn't seen her daughter for almost a year, and this wasn't how she wanted the visit to play out.

'Lizzie, I'm sorry. I'm tired from the journey and I just want to make sure you're happy, that's all.'

Lizzie nodded but didn't speak. When they arrived at her Jeep, which was an upgrade from the old one she'd had on their previous trips, Mick got straight into the driving seat, and Lizzie climbed in beside him, clearly brooding. Charles glanced at Eva and shrugged. It looked like they were both in the back. It was a sting in the tail for Eva, Lizzie had always insisted her Mum sit up front with her so they could catch up on the drive to Palm Cove.

When they arrived at Lizzie's apartment, Charles and Eva freshened up while Lizzie prepared lunch for them all. In their bedroom, Charles and Eva hugged tightly, both torn over their feelings about the situation. Mick's overbearing presence hadn't done anything to resolve their concerns about him. He spoke the entire drive up the coast, pointing things out as though he was an expert tour guide, and this was their first visit. Lizzie had fawned all over him, and his hand had rested on her thigh the entire journey, which made Charles want to punch him.

'Come on, let's put on a brave face, for Lizzie's sake,' Charles whispered to Eva.

'There you are,' Mick called from the balcony. 'We were about to send out a search party. Come sit down and have some lunch.'

Charles and Eva made their way to join them. There was now an outdoor setting that seated six that had replaced the two-seater table and chairs Lizzie had before. Eva tried not to be affronted by all the changes that Mick had seemingly made to Lizzie's life, but he rankled her more than she'd been prepared for.

The four of them sat and Mick served them steak with potato salad. He cracked open a beer for Charles without asking him and poured red wine for Lizzie and Eva. Eva wanted to tell him she didn't want it but remembered Charles's words. They needed to give him a chance.

'So, what do you do Mick?' Charles asked, sticking to a generic topic.

'I'm a motor mechanic, I run my own business. I inherited it when my dad died.'

Eva could have sworn she glimpsed a frown on Lizzie's face when he said that, but she didn't question it.

'So, if that's in Sydney, what's the plan after the wedding?' Charles turned to Lizzie, 'will you be moving?'

Lizzie blushed. 'Yes, the lease is up on the flat in another month anyway so it's perfect timing.' She hadn't brought this up with her parents yet and had wanted to talk to them in private.

'So, you're leaving your job too?' Eva questioned.

'Yes, I was going to tell you, but I've only really made the decision in the last few weeks.' Lizzie was quiet, and if Eva knew her daughter at all, she would've said she was embarrassed by her choice.

'So, a new start in Sydney? What will you do for work?' Charles was trying to be upbeat and positive, as though he was excited by the new prospects his daughter had.

Mick butted in and answered for Lizzie. 'She doesn't need to work; I earn enough money for the both of us.'

Lizzie didn't make a sound, but she was clearly horrified that Mick had said this in front of her parents. She didn't say anything to refute what he was saying, and that silence validated every worry that Eva had. She felt in her heart that things weren't right, but she was careful not to air her concerns until she could get a better read on the situation.

Mick filled the silences talking about himself. He talked about his family, which again, Lizzie looked surprised at. His stories didn't quite sit right with Eva, she feared he was either lying or he hadn't shared many details with Lizzie before.

'So, when do you finish work Lizzie?' Charles asked, in an attempt to steer the conversation away from Mick.

'My last day is at the end of this week, Friday. Then after the wedding when you guys leave, we'll pack up here and drive down to Sydney before going on our honeymoon. Mick hasn't told me where we're going yet.' Lizzie smiled and looked comfortable for the first time since they'd hugged at the airport.

'Do you think you'll be able to get us on the cruise one day? I'd love to see the reef again,' Charles said.

'That's a great idea,' Mick interrupted. 'The three of us can go.'

Lizzie looked uncomfortable again. 'Of course, I'll see when the best day is.'

Charles reached out with his foot and gently stroked it on Eva's leg under the table in a subtle attempt to comfort her, knowing she was seething at Mick's interference.

That evening, Charles and Eva retired to their room early, feigning jet lag, but they just couldn't bear the company of Mick for a second longer.

They sat together in bed, silently reflecting on the day's developments. They hardly dared speak in case their conversation could be overheard, and for the first time they felt like strangers in their daughter's home.

Charles held Eva's hand, and Eva rested her head on his shoulder. They needed to let Lizzie deal with this. She was grown up and they had instilled in her good values. She was not the kind of girl that would allow herself to be walked over by a man. This must be what she wanted otherwise she wouldn't be letting it happen. It was time they put their faith in their daughter's good sense and sit back and enjoy their visit. Eva couldn't help but think that if they carried on with their judgement, then history would repeat itself. That was something Eva would never allow to happen.

Beau 2019

Day merged into night and back into day. I was living on a diet of coffee and the occasional power nap. The longer Charlie didn't wake up, the more anxious I became. Nurses came and went with a smile and a few kind words. They'd mostly given up on trying to get me to go home; there was no way that would happen until I knew Charlie was out of danger. Kate had brought more clean clothes and one of the nurses let me use a patient shower on the ward next door. Kate also brought decent coffee; the stuff in the hospital tasted like sludge. Sipping on it slowly, I asked Kate about Charlie's session with her.

'You know I can't discuss that with you Beau,' she looked at me sympathetically.

'I know, I know, I just thought I'd try.'

She laughed and then her face turned serious. 'I'm sure Charlie will talk to you about it when she's better. She'll need you, and if her mum doesn't come out of the rehab centre in time, she's going to need somewhere to stay.'

'I don't even know if she'll want to see me Kate, never mind stay with me. The last time we spoke she told me she'd never forgive me.'

'I'm not going to lie Beau; it was a huge shock to her and finding out you already knew would've hurt her. She will feel extremely vulnerable, and she'll probably take time to work out who she can trust, but she'll come around. Just be there for her. Don't rush her or expect too much. Just be her friend.' Kate got up to leave and I stood to give her a hug.

'Thanks for everything,' I told her, and her eyes glistened with unshed tears, I knew she was staying strong for me, but I was aware of how much she cared about me, and I knew in that moment she was sick with worry.

I settled back into my chair, my hand on Charlie's. It was comforting to feel her; the physical contact gave me a connection. I listened to the sounds of the machines, the monotony of the night, of the nurses going about their duties. Heaviness descended on my eyelids, forcing them closed and I leaned forward to rest my head on the hospital bed, close to Charlie, drifting off to sleep. I dreamed of a future filled with adventure. I dreamed of Charlie in far off places, the two of us traveling the world together. I dreamed of a house, a family, and helping kids like us; kids with nowhere to go. I was roused from my sleep by a firm hand on my back and a voice calling my name. I sat up and rubbed my eyes, there was a nurse standing over me.

'Look who's back.' Her eyes were shining, and she had a big grin on her face. I followed her eyes and saw Charlie, awake but looking groggy. Her eyes searched mine warily, as if she was judging what my reaction would be. I took everything in, and then leaned over and kissed her, full on the mouth. I lingered long enough that she would feel the love I had for her. I turned to thank the nurse, but she'd already gone.

'It's so good to see you.' I squeezed her hand and she flinched. My eyes went straight to hers, worried she was rejecting me again.

'Hurts.' Her voice was thick and croaky, and as though that one word had drained all her energy, she closed her eyes and sighed.

'You scared me babe, taking off like that.' I kept my voice low, I wasn't trying to blame her, I just needed her to know how worried I'd been and that I was not accepting what she'd said to me. 'I should've told you; I know that now. I'm so sorry Charlie, I'm here for you. We'll get through this together, whatever you need.'

There was no visible reaction on her face, and I wasn't even sure she'd heard me, until a single tear leaked from the corner of one eye and slowly slid down her face. My heart weighed heavy in my chest as I leaned over to catch it with my lips.

'I'm so sorry Charlie,' I whispered again, trailing my lips across her cheek to her ear. 'Please forgive me.' Her head turned slightly, and her cheek rested against mine.

'Sorry too,' her voice was raspy and flushed with emotion, she was too exhausted to speak much.

'Ssh,' I murmured.

'Your bike?' she asked.

'I don't know, I never asked. But don't worry, it's not important.'

The nurse came back in to check on Charlie and asked her a few questions. Charlie fought to keep her eyes open as I gently stroked her arm, not sure whether I was comforting her or myself.

'This one's a keeper Charlie,' the nurse said, tipping her head towards me. 'He never left your side from the moment you came out of surgery. Maybe now you're awake you can persuade him to go home and get some proper rest.' She patted Charlie on the shoulder and winked at me.

'Surgery?' Charlie's eyes knit together in confusion. My eyes rapidly shifted to the nurse, and she nodded in response to my silent question.

'I'll leave you to it,' she said, and left the room.

I explained to Charlie what happened to her leg and ribs and about the complications of her internal bleeding.

'You really messed yourself up. Had us worried there for a while.' She seemed to awaken a little more, shifting in the bed to get comfortable.

'Does my mum know? About why I'm here?' She was concerned her mum knew what she'd found out. I didn't know how to tell her I didn't even know if her mum knew about the accident. I shook my head no and tried to leave it at that.

'Does she blame you then?' she asked. 'For my accident?'

I sighed heavily, blowing out more air than I knew I had in me.

'I'm not sure if she's even been told you're here Charlie. She's been checked into a rehab centre so I'm unsure what she knows.'

She looked relieved. I guessed she wasn't ready to confront her mum head on.

'Was the nurse being serious when she said you haven't left?' Her voice was still croaky, but her words were becoming clearer. I felt guilty at her question, like she was going to call me out on it.

'Yeah, there was no way I was leaving your side Charlie, so deal with it,' I said firmly so she didn't have any comeback. She burst out laughing and it was the most magical sound, until her face contorted from the pain she had caused her ribs. She started to cough, which put her in worse pain. I ran to the door and shouted for a nurse. The nurse was right behind me when I got back to Charlie, and she quickly slipped an oxygen mask over her face to help her breathe again.

'Enough exertion for one night Missy, it's time for you to rest. Beau will be back to see you in the morning.' Then turning to me she added, 'please go home, get at least six hours sleep and I'm sure Charlie will be feeling a little stronger tomorrow.' Her eyes pleaded with me, and I finally decided to take her advice. I nodded in submission, and she smiled at me. I kissed Charlie's forehead, careful not to dislodge the oxygen mask now that her coughing had died down.

'I'll be back in the morning. Get some sleep, I love you.' Her eyes slow blinked in response. I picked up the bag that Kate had brought in for me and headed out of the hospital for the first time in almost a week. The cool air hit me as I left the building. It was 2.00am, I had no transport and no key to get into my apartment. I was tempted to just turn around and go back inside but I knew I needed to leave Charlie to rest. I ordered an Uber to take me to Kate's house. I thought about wandering around the house to check for open windows or doors, but then I thought about how freaked out Kate would be if she heard me trying to break in, so I decided to call her. She said she'd leave her phone switched on in case I needed her, and she answered quickly.

'Beau? Are you okay?' she sounded frantic, no one enjoys a middle of the night phone call.

'I'm at the front door, can you let me in?' I spoke quietly. Within a minute I heard keys jangling on the other side of the door, quickly unlocking it. Kate pulled me inside and hugged me as she kicked the door closed. She stepped back to look at my face, figuring out my mood. I smiled.

'She's awake.'

Kate burst into tears and buried her face in my chest. I drew my arms around her and held her until she calmed.

'Oh Beau, I'm so happy. Is she talking?'

'Yeah, a little, she remembers taking the bike,' I yawned.

'Come on, let's get you to bed, you can fill me in tomorrow.' She ushered me towards my old room, picking up on my exhaustion.

'I didn't have a key for my apartment, did you take it?' I asked.

'Yes, I did. But stay here tonight, you're exhausted. I'll drive you home in the morning.'

'I will, but I'm still wired. I might just make myself a drink first,' I said.

'Come on then, I'll make some hot chocolate,' Kate suggested, leading the way to the kitchen. I followed blindly, wondering how I managed to luck out with such a great foster mum.

Eva 1990

The morning of the wedding, Eva and Lizzie were up bright and early. Charles had paid for them both to have a morning of pampering in a local hotel spa. It was the only way he could manage to find a way to give mother and daughter some alone time without Mick hovering. They'd enjoyed their stay, and once they let their guard down, Mick seemed pleasant enough, but he did seem a little too intense when it came to Lizzie, a little too possessive. Eva and Lizzie enjoyed a lovely morning together having massages, a manicure and pedicure. They sipped champagne and enjoyed a light lunch before heading back to the apartment to finish getting ready. Eva had subtly tried to get Lizzie to open up a little but with no luck. She seemed to think the sun rose and set with Mick, and Eva had come to the conclusion that all she could do was to be there to pick up the pieces if it all went wrong.

The ceremony wasn't until early evening and just a few friends of Lizzie's had been invited. There was no one on Mick's side attending, he'd mentioned that his father had passed but he'd brushed off Charles's questions about other family members.

It was a beautifully simple ceremony; everyone was barefoot and dressed in simple summer clothing. The bride wore a white linen dress with spaghetti straps and a low cut back, finishing off her natural style with her mother's pearl hair comb. Eva had been surprised when her daughter had asked if she could wear it, she thought it would be too old fashioned for her taste, but she had to admit, it finished off the outfit beautifully. She looked stunning, and Eva felt emotional watching Charles walk her down a makeshift aisle in the soft golden sand. She was equally impressed by her husband, dressed in chinos and a linen shirt, as handsome in her eyes as the day they met.

The vows were quick and personal, and the wedding guests and onlookers applauded as Mick dipped Lizzie and kissed her. Eva watched Lizzie's face light up and finally felt at peace. The backdrop for the photos was stunning, the sunset cast a dazzling hue and after several photographs had been taken, the photographer, a close friend of

Lizzie's, ushered the party over to the restaurant for a celebratory meal.

There were only ten guests altogether and so the dinner was quite intimate. One of Lizzie's friends from the cruise line was sitting next to Charles. He took an instant liking to her and could see why she and his daughter were friends. She spoke with intelligence and curiosity, and blushed when she told him she was a big fan of his crime novels. He'd had two published by now, and Ellen couldn't believe it when she'd first found out her favourite author was her friend's dad. They'd been at the beach together and Ellen had tried to introduce Lizzie to this new author. Lizzie had wound her up a little at first before taking out her phone and showing her a photo of her and her dad.

'You know him?' Ellen had asked. Lizzie stayed quiet and watched the cogs turn in her brain. 'Hartley! Oh my god, he's your dad! Why didn't you tell me? Will he sign a book for me?'

Lizzie laughed at her friend. 'I'm sure he will, you can ask him when you come to my wedding.'

'I'm going to meet him?' Ellen was fangirling hard.

'You know my Mum's Eva Hartley, right?' Lizzie asked.

'Who?' Ellen hadn't heard of her.

'Never mind. She's way more famous than Dad.' Lizzie rolled her eyes at her friend's ignorance.

Ellen used the opportunity of sitting with Charles to ask his opinion on something that had been worrying her.

'Can I ask you something Charles? Please tell me to mind my own business if you think I'm crossing a line here,' she said.

Charles's forehead furrowed, concerned about what line she could be crossing.

'Are you happy with this wedding?' She spoke in hushed tones.

Charles bit his lip, straightening his thoughts before speaking.

'Why do you ask?' Charles said tactfully.

Ellen sighed. 'I don't know, I don't have anything concrete, but there's just something about him I'm not sure about. I obviously haven't known her for that long, but I'd say we're pretty close and it just seems so out of character for Lizzie. It all seems so rushed. I did ask her if she was pregnant but that didn't go down well.'

'To be honest Ellen we're not thrilled, and you're right, it's extremely out of character. We don't know what we can do; Eva hasn't spoken to her parents since they threw her out of their house when she was eighteen for agreeing to marry me without their consent. We're not exactly in a position to judge.'

'I'm sorry, I didn't know.' Ellen was regretful.

'Nothing to be sorry for Ellen, you're a good friend, Lizzie's lucky to have you looking out for her.' Charles patted Ellen's hand on the table. 'If you wouldn't mind keeping an eye on her though, I'd appreciate it. I can give you my home address and telephone number and you can contact me if you're worried about anything.'

'Of course,' Ellen said, grateful she hadn't spoken out of turn.

As the evening wore on and more drinks were had, Charles felt the atmosphere relax, and Eva and himself enjoyed chatting with the young people, listening to stories of their travels. Charles regaled them with the story of how he and Eva had met, and they were all enamoured with their love story. He got the impression they all relaxed a little when they realised Lizzie had taken things slowly in comparison to her parents. As the end of the night drew near, Charles settled the bill and Lizzie and Mick headed off first to the hotel where Charles and Eva had paid for the honeymoon suite, an excuse to give themselves a little space in Lizzie's apartment to come to terms with the day.

Charles and Ellen swapped contact details as promised, and Lizzie's friends thanked them both for a lovely day. Charles and Eva wandered back to the apartment hand in hand, making the most of the sultry evening. Eva collapsed on the couch and Charles poured them both a nightcap. Snuggling into his side, tasting the sweetness of the brandy on her tongue, Eva relaxed.

'She looked happy today,' Eva mused.

'She did, I must admit,' replied Charles. 'I'm scared though Eva, to leave her with him. I can't say that I completely trust him.' He was going to tell her what Ellen had said but thought it best not to stir up the hornet's nest. He would do the worrying for the both of them.

'No, I don't either, but there's nothing we can do. We have to trust her judgement. She knows if she needs us, we'll be on a flight at the drop of a hat.'

Charles nodded in reply, his eyes had begun to feel sleepy, and they sat quietly until they both drifted off to sleep.

After helping Lizzie pack up her apartment the following day, they arrived at the airport a little early for their flight to New Zealand. The family said their emotional goodbyes after sitting together in the cafe until the last moment. With hindsight, Eva and Charles would have hugged their daughter a little bit harder and a little bit longer.

Charlie 2019

My throat felt like it had been slashed with razor blades, and breathing was a struggle, which was probably from the broken ribs. There wasn't much sensation in my leg, and I didn't know how bad the damage was there. It was difficult to come to terms with the amount of damage I'd caused all round. I felt guilty for what I'd done to Beau's bike, but he'd been so calm about it. I said some shitty things to him too, it wouldn't have surprised me if he'd never spoken to me again.

I thought back to the memories that had become clear to me in my session with Kate. I could remember that day so well; I didn't understand how Tom and I could have both repressed it. Why didn't we talk about it together? Tom must have remembered more than me, but I wondered why he waited till he was twenty-four before he figured out what was going on. The times he called me Charlie when we were younger must've been times when he was remembering, maybe certain things triggered him. I wish I could've talked to him to find out what he knew. That day in our bedroom was the last time we saw our birth mum and dad. We were taken away that day, but I had no recollection of where we went. I'd started to remember sirens and flashing lights. And people, crowded in the street. Tom and I huddled together in the back of a car, clinging on to each other with fear in our eyes.

I tried hard to remember my birth parents, but they were just blank faces that I wouldn't have been able to pick out of a crowd. Did I look like them? Was I like them in any way? I had so many questions but no one to provide any answers. I was mostly sad that mum and dad had felt they had to hide our past from us. How had they made us forget? My whole life felt like one big lie. I'd been so lost since Dad and Tom died; I had no idea who I was anymore. Lying on the hospital bed, I was unsure of myself, of my life, of everything. I didn't know who I could trust.

My throat constricted and my breathing became more painful as I fought for air. Panic set in and my eyes searched frenziedly for help. I tried to scream but no noise came out. A passing nurse sensed my anxiety and reached for the oxygen mask. She sat quietly on the bed stroking my arm to calm me.

'Feeling better?' the nurse asked as my breathing began to return to normal. I nodded, leaning back on my pillow, my eyes closed.

'It's normal Charlotte. To panic after the kind of trauma you've suffered. You're not alone.'

She thought this was about my accident and I wanted to tell her it wasn't, but I wouldn't even know where to start so I just lifted the mask and smiled weakly.

'We can arrange for you to talk to someone, help you deal with your experience,' she offered.

'Thanks, but my boyfriend's mum is a psychologist. She's been helping me deal with some stuff,' I explained. I didn't want to have to start again with someone I didn't know.

'Ah, Beau and his mum, such lovely people. They've been very worried about you, you're a lucky girl.' She patted my arm and continued, 'I think you'll be moving to your own room today.'

I hadn't been aware I wasn't in my own room. The curtain was always pulled across so I could only see the wall next to me or straight ahead through the doors. I was left alone again, or maybe someone was next to me on the other side of the curtain.

It seemed weird to me how you could live your whole life without really thinking for yourself. You're just this person that the people around you have moulded and trained to think what they want you to think. The last few years I'd been studying English and Teaching. I wasn't even sure I wanted to be a teacher anymore, or if I ever did. Why had I never questioned that before? Now that I understood I'd had a whole other life that my parents had kept from me, I began to question everything I'd ever thought. What if my whole life had been manipulated and none of my thoughts and ideas had been my own?

As much as I hadn't had the energy to deal with Rosie's upbeat nature after the accident, I'd developed a strong need to be with someone who'd known me before. I needed to get perspective from someone who knew me well and I couldn't get that from Beau. He only knew me as Charlie—tragic, broken and lost.

I didn't even know if Rosie knew I was in the hospital. I couldn't imagine Beau would've reached out to find her, he had enough going on. I needed my phone, but I wasn't sure what had happened to my stuff when I was brought in. I wasn't even wearing my own clothes, just a hospital gown. I looked around, panic suddenly rising in my throat. Realisation dawned on me how alone I was. I pressed the call button and waited for a nurse.

'You okay love?' The nurse from earlier stood in the doorway.

'Yeah, I was just wondering what happened to my stuff after I was brought in. What would've happened to my clothes? And my phone and house keys?'

'I'm not too sure love, although your clothes were probably cut off to get you into surgery. I don't know about your personal belongings, let me try and find out.' She smiled and asked if I needed anything else. I shook my head sadly, remembering it had been Tom's jacket I'd been wearing. I rubbed my hand across my face to wipe the tears away and jumped at the pain it caused. I switched hands to the one not covered in bandages and gently ran my fingers across my cheek. It felt swollen at the top of my cheek and around my eye. I wondered what other injuries I had, apart from the obvious ones.

I drifted in and out of sleep, probably something to do with all the drugs being pumped into me. Or it could just be boredom. Lying there with nothing to do and no one to talk to drove me crazy. My eyes felt heavy and began to flutter into yet another nap when a bunch of flowers appeared in front of my face. Beau's face appeared from behind them. He was smiling but his eyes looked tired. My eyes, still heavy, closed the last little bit, shutting out the picture of Beau and the flowers. I wasn't pretending to be asleep; I just didn't have the energy to talk. I could hear him moving things around on my cupboard to make space for the flowers. The chair scraped across the floor, and he sighed heavily as he sat down. I imagined his worried face concentrating on mine. His forehead would be crinkled, his thoughts deep. He'd be leaning forward, elbows on his knees, maybe pulling on his bottom lip with his thumb and forefinger. I'd watched his intense thought process so often in the short weeks I'd known him. I knew he was worried, and I knew he was deeply sorry for keeping my past from me. I loved him with all my heart, but I felt so betrayed by everyone in my life that I didn't know how to even think about moving forward. I knew that I needed to find out the details of my adoption, but beyond that, I had no idea.

My eyelids fluttered and I could make out his shape through the small slit in my eyes. He wasn't looking at my face, so I raised my lids a little more. I felt like a fly on the wall, watching a scene play out that I was the centre of, but also not a part of at all. As though I was looking in on a life that wasn't really mine.

I watched him closely until his eyes locked on mine. He didn't speak but his eyes told me everything he was thinking. He was worried about my injuries, but mostly about what was going on in my head. He was concerned how I felt towards him. He shouldn't have doubted the fact that I loved him, but I could see he questioned the strength of our relationship. He was wondering if we could get past it, if I could forgive him for choosing his loyalty to my dead brother over me. The intensity in his eyes implored me not to go there. But I knew I had to.

'Charlie, please forgive me.' He sounded desperate and my heart shattered for him, but I needed to stay strong. 'I'm so sorry I hurt you.' His head dropped and I noticed his shoulders shake as he wiped tears from his eyes. My own eyes filled as I watched him. He lifted his head, and his eyes came back to mine.

'I love you Charlie, so damn much. Please don't let me lose you.'

I stifled a sob. 'I love you too Beau.' His face brightened until I continued. 'But I need some space. I need time to process all this, it's just too much.' His face clouded over again as he processed what I was saying.

'I'll help you Charlie, we'll get through this together, I promise. And Kate, she'll help too.'

I shook my head before he had chance to break my resolve.

'I can't Beau, I need to do this alone. Every single person in my life has lied to me. I need to figure things out for myself.'

He stood, his shoulders slumped, his head hanging in defeat. He leaned in, bringing his face to mine.

'However long it takes, I will be here for you whenever you're ready. I will not stop loving you, Charlie. Always remember that and come back to me.' His lips brushed mine and I desperately wanted to pull him closer and breathe him in. But I couldn't. I had to let him go so I could figure myself out. Beau gently cupped my cheek and pressed his forehead to mine. He blew out a soft breath and it was all I could do not to devour him. I pulled my head away sharply and he left, not looking back. I could tell he was trying to keep it together.

As soon as he was gone, my resolve shattered, and my heart was in a million little pieces. I allowed the tears to flood down my face as I broke apart. A nurse came in and sat with me, pulling me towards her, making shushing noises in my ear. She handed me tissues to dry my eyes and blow my nose, then looked at me questioningly.

'We just broke up,' I blurted out. She looked shocked but refrained from asking questions. She just held my hand until my breathing calmed.

'Do you want to talk about it?' she asked, but I shook my head.

'Did you find out what happened to my phone?' I asked hopefully.

'No, there's no record of it anywhere. Do you need me to call someone?'

'I want to call my friend Rosie. I know her home number. I just want to tell her where I am.' She handed me a pen and asked me to write down the number, then she left me alone.

Sleep once again consumed me. It wasn't like there was anything else to do with the endless amount of free time I'd found myself with and the painkillers were keeping me drowsy.

Comforting arms envelop my tiny body. Trying to control my sobs and the snot running from my nose, I bury my face in her chest. She smells of soap. My pyjama shorts are wet, and I shift uncomfortably on my bed sheets. Gripping my head with her soft hands, she lifts my face to look directly in my eyes. She's so beautiful.

'Let's get you cleaned up,' she whispers. She brings her finger to her lips, urging me to be quiet. I can hear cupboard doors banging and crashing in the other room. Bad words being shouted as he searches the house for something.

Mummy straightens the covers on my bed and quickly tucks my wet pyjamas under my pillow.

'We'll deal with them later,' her soft tone barely audible. She grabs a pack of baby wipes and cleans me up, dressing me quickly for the day. Tom is watching on, a worried look on his face. Mummy waves him over and he joins us for a big hug.

'Don't worry my darlings, everything will be okay. We'll sort this out when he's gone. There's no need for him to know anything. Keep quiet, okay?'

We're always scared of him. I don't mean to wet the bed and I try not to, but sometimes I can't help it. He hurts mummy when I'm bad. Sometimes he hurts Tom too. He hasn't hurt me yet, but I'm scared he will.

I woke abruptly from my slumber. I remembered her face. My mind whirled, trying to remember more details. Tom had been right, our father had been violent, I was sure of it. My hands were shaking, and I tried to still them. My eyes darted across the room towards the door to see if anyone had seen the way I was acting. Rosie was standing there in the doorway, watching me silently with a frown on her face. I froze when I realised she'd seen me wake from my dream.

'Hey,' my voice was drowsy from sleep or drugs, I wasn't sure which.

'Hey Lots, you look like shit,' she greeted in typical Rosie fashion. A smile broke out across my face, and I laughed at her honesty. She took that as a cue to come closer. She edged towards me, hovering next to the bed, not knowing whether to touch me or sit down. I held out my arms for her and she leaned over to hug me.

'I've missed you so much Lots.' She stepped back and sat in the chair beside the bed. 'I've been so worried about you, then I got this phone call saying you're in hospital. What the hell happened?'

'I'm sorry Rose, I just couldn't handle everything. Mum's a mess, she's in rehab having treatment for alcohol and grief.' Before I could continue, Rosie interrupted.

'What? Anna? She's an alcoholic?' She laughed but quickly corrected herself. 'I'm sorry, I didn't mean...'

'It's okay, I was shocked too. I found her in a pool of her own vomit. Did your mum not tell you? She came to the hospital with me.'

Rosie frowned and shook her head.

'No wonder she'd barely been speaking to me,' I told her. 'She was obviously wasted. I found empty bottles in her room. I had no idea.'

'Shit Lottie, I wish you'd called me. I can't believe Mum didn't tell me. I was trying to give you space, but it was a struggle not being there for you,' Rosie said.

'I know Rose, I'm sorry. I just felt so different. I feel like my entire life has been a fraud. I needed space to discover who I really am. Being with Beau was kind of a relief because he didn't know me before...' My voice trailed off when I saw the look of confusion on Rosie's face. She had no idea what had been going on in my life.

'Sorry, you have no idea who I'm talking about do you? Beau, he's the guy from the bar the night of your birthday. We've kind of being seeing each other but...'

'But what?' Rosie asked. 'He's hot, there are no buts!'

'Well, I found out he'd kept something from me, and I was angry, so I stole his motorbike and trashed it. And here I am. So yeah, that's kind of a big but!'

'Wow! You don't do things by halves do you?' Rosie couldn't believe this was her quiet, hardworking, never done anything wrong in her life friend. 'I'm sorry. Is it something you can fix or is it over?'

I sighed, 'I don't know. I love him, I do, but I'm not sure I can get past the fact he kept something so important from me. I feel like everyone I've ever known has been lying to me.'

'Wow. I don't know what to say. I mean, I'm pretty sure I've always been honest with you, probably too honest at times.' I laughed at her reaction. She had always been honest with me, even if the truth hurt my feelings.

'I know, that's why I got the nurse to call you. I just hoped you would forgive me for the way I treated you.'

'There's nothing to forgive, you were grieving. I'm so glad you called me Lottie.'

'I'm calling myself Charlie now. It's the nick name I had when I was little.' I bit my lip and readied myself for Rosie's reaction to what I was about to tell her. 'When I lived with my birth parents.'

There was a long silence as I watched the cogs turning as she processed the information in her mind. As soon as the penny dropped, her face was priceless. I didn't think I'd ever known Rosie speechless but there she was opening and closing her mouth, unable to produce words. I decided to put her out of her misery and tell her my story. I told her everything I'd recently found out, including the full reason for ending up in the hospital.

'Wow, that's some story. I guess I can understand you slowly forgetting your past, over time. You would've been so young, but Tom? Surely he would've remembered stuff.'

'That's the thing,' I told her. 'I think he did remember; he just didn't understand it when he was younger. He obviously started questioning things that didn't add up, which is why he started looking into it. He saw Beau's foster mum, Kate to help him deal with stuff. I guess he was pretty confused by it all. According to Kate, he confronted my mum and she made him promise not to say anything to me until she got the chance to talk to me about it. That's why Beau didn't tell me, he said he was honouring Tom's promise to my mum,' I explained.

'I get that too. I guess he would've felt like he was betraying Tom's memory,' Rosie said quietly.

'But Tom's dead, and I was hurting and confused. Telling me what he knew would have saved so much time and worry.'

'So, what happens now? I mean, when do you get out of here? Where will you go? Do you want to try and find your birth parents?' Rosie was excited. I guessed I would've been too under different circumstances. If I hadn't been lied to. If I hadn't just broken up with my boyfriend because of it.

'I have no idea where I'm gonna go.' The realisation hit me that the hospital wouldn't release me unless there was someone to look after me. I sighed at the thought of spending much longer in there.

'You can some stay with us Lottie…Charlie,' Rosie corrected herself. 'That's gonna take some getting used to! You know how much mum would love to fuss over you,' she laughed. 'Although she'll probably drive you insane.'

Rosie turned serious, which was not something I'd seen too often. 'You know me and mum will be here for you, whatever you want to do. Please don't shut me out again and try not to blame Beau. It's hard to know what's best when someone's grieving.' She winked at me and stood up. 'Besides, I kinda want to experience what it's like for my best friend to date a hot guy!'

I blushed at the thought of him. I did hope I could get past it all but in that moment, the hurt was too raw.

Rosie leaned over and hugged me. 'I'll speak to mum, and I'll come visit soon okay?'

I smiled as she left the room. I hadn't realised how much I'd missed her; it was so good to have her back.

Eva 1991

Eva had been stewing over her emotions for weeks. She knew Charles was pushing it to meet his deadline on his third novel, and with his headship at school, he was spread very thin. She didn't want to put any pressure on him, but she was more than a little worried now. She hadn't heard from Lizzie in weeks. She phoned every day, at different times in the hope that she'd catch her, but the telephone just rang out. The answering machine didn't even kick in. She'd been distant for a few months now, when they had spoken Lizzie was always distracted or on her way out.

She tossed and turned in bed, struggling to get comfortable. Her mind was playing out different scenarios and they all involved with one thing - Mick. She was positive something was going on, this behaviour was so unlike Lizzie and she'd seen for herself the possessive, almost creepy behaviours Mick had displayed when they were in Australia for the wedding. Eva looked at the clock. It was 1.00am and she hadn't had a wink of sleep yet. She looked across at the empty space in the bed beside her. Charles must still be up writing. She was worried he would burn out if he kept this up. He couldn't expect to run a school on so little sleep. She'd be glad when this book was finished.

Pulling on her dressing gown and nudging her feet into her slippers, she made her way downstairs. She could see the glow from the desk lamp in their shared office space, Charles hunched over his word processor, fingers tapping at the keys. The word processor had been a wonderful replacement to the typewriter and both of them had embraced the new technology. Eva couldn't imagine how Charles would have managed both jobs working on his old typewriter.

Charles heard Eva in the doorway and turned.

'What's got you up at this hour?' he asked.

'I can't sleep. I'm going to make a hot chocolate; can I get you one?'

'I'd love one, thank you.' Charles smiled at his wife and thought how beautiful she still looked after all these years and with tousled hair to boot. 'I'm nearly done actually. A couple more lines and I'm ready to print.'

'That's great, you need a rest. You're working too hard my love.' Eva's eyes softened and her demeanour changed. Charles could always pull her back from her thoughts.

She stirred the milk in the saucepan and poured it into two mugs, mixing it with the chocolate powder. Charles liked to have sugar in his, but Eva had hers with a sprinkle of cinnamon. She heard the printer wake up as Charles's manuscript began its transformation into a hard copy. He appeared behind her, his arms wrapping around her, his chin resting on her shoulder. He breathed her in as he nuzzled his nose into her neck.

'I love you Eva,' Charles murmured. 'I don't feel like I've seen you lately. I'm sorry for that.'

Eva leaned her head back on Charles's chest and smiled at his words. She loved him too.

She picked up both mugs and handed one to Charles who was reluctant to let go of her. They settled in the sun room on the little love seat and admired the starlit sky. It was a clear night, and the Milky Way was visible. They loved living on the edge of the moor with little light pollution. They couldn't see the Milky Way in all its splendour too often but when they could it was a spectacle. Looking at it now made Eva think of Lizzie. It was a common sight in Australia and so much brighter than it was here. Eva sighed.

'What's on your mind my darling? You're preoccupied.' Charles knew her so well.

'I'm worried about Lizzie.' Eva decided to just come right out and say it. 'I haven't been able to get hold of her in weeks. She never answers the phone. I've tried all different times of day; I don't know what's going on.'

Charles was shocked. 'I know I've been in my own bubble lately but why haven't you said anything?'

Eva shrugged. 'I didn't want to worry you and I thought maybe they'd made last minute plans to go away. I'm really worried though Charles. This is not like her, something's going on, I'm sure of it.'

Charles's forehead furrowed as he let Eva's words sink in.

'I've got her friend's phone number, the one we met at the wedding. Why don't I call her? See if she knows anything.'

'Ellen? Yes, can you ring now? I don't want to leave things any longer and it will be morning there.'

Charles flicked through some papers until he found the number and dialled carefully.

'Hello?' An Australian accent said.

'Is this Ellen?' Charles asked.

'Yes, who's this?'

'Hello Ellen, it's Charles Hartley, Lizzie's dad. We met at Lizzie's wedding.'

'Of course, of course. Is everything okay? Is Lizzie okay?' Ellen's voice turned to panic.

'We were kind of hoping you'd be able to answer that. My wife has been trying to get in touch with her for weeks but hasn't had any luck. We're a little worried,' Charles explained.

Ellen was quiet. 'Charles, I don't know what's going on. After she moved away to Sydney, she barely kept in contact. She cancelled our plans for a weekend away and she hardly ever returns my calls. I just thought it was one of those things but now you mention it, it does sound a little concerning. Let me ring around, see if I can find anything out.

Can I get back to you?'

'Of course, thank you so much Ellen. Eva and I really appreciate it.'

'No worries, I'll call as soon as I find anything out. What time is it there?'

'It's one in the morning but don't worry, I'll answer any time,' Charles told her.

Eva was pacing waiting to find out what Ellen had said. Charles put the phone down and relayed Ellen's words to her.

'I knew something was up. Why would Lizzie cancel on her like that with no explanation? Oh Charles, I'm really worried now. What if he's brainwashed her? You hear of it don't you? Men who are psychologically abusive. They slowly take everything away from their wife until she has no independence or support network. Oh gosh Charles! That's what it is, it started when we were there when he mentioned her not having to work when she moved to Sydney.' Eva was becoming hysterical. 'Why didn't we do something? We should've put a stop to the wedding.'

'Eva, darling, let's not jump to conclusions. That's not going to do us any good. We'll wait to hear from Ellen and if that doesn't bring us any news, we'll book a flight to Sydney and we'll go find her ourselves.'

'But what about work? You can't just take time off.' Eva knew how important his work was to him.

Charles laughed. 'Eva, this is our only daughter we're talking about. I would do anything for her.'

Eva squeezed his hand. 'I know, I'm sorry. I don't know what I was thinking.'

'Come on, let's get to bed and hopefully we'll know more in the morning. Let's not get ahead of ourselves, there's more than likely a straightforward explanation.'

Charles's level-headedness soothed her a little, enough to get a few hours' sleep at least.

The shrill ring of the telephone startled Charles and Eva from their slumber. Charles reached for his glasses from the nightstand and glanced at his alarm clock quickly before jumping out of bed. It was a little past five in the morning which meant the only person calling would be Ellen. Charles prayed silently to himself as he raced down the stairs to pick up the phone.

He picked up the receiver and sat down on the stairs.

'Ellen?' he breathed heavily.

'Charles, yes it's me. Did I wake you?' Ellen asked.

'Don't worry, it's fine. Have you found anything?' Charles listened desperately to what Ellen had to say.

'Nothing as to Lizzie's whereabouts, but enough to be worried.' Charles glanced up at Eva who was tip toeing slowly down the stairs. Ellen continued, 'I called all our friends, and no one has heard from her in weeks. A couple of them had plans with her but she's either cancelled or just not turned up.'

'That doesn't sound good Ellen.' Charles's heart began to race, and he began to make plans in his head.

'I'm sorry Charles, I know. I wish I'd done something sooner, I promised I'd let you know if I had any concerns.'

'Don't blame yourself Ellen, this is not your fault.'

'I did manage to find out something, but I'm not sure how it can help us, other than confirm our worst thoughts,' Ellen's voice quavered. 'My cousin lives in Sydney, and he recognised Mick's surname when I told him he was a mechanic. He looked it up and found the shop, but it turns out Mick hasn't worked there in over ten years. The owner is Mick's dad.'

'What? That doesn't make sense. He told us his dad was dead and that he'd inherited the business.' Charles looked at Eva who was silently questioning him from the next step.

'It gets worse. My cousin asked him if he knew where Mick was, and he told him he hadn't seen him since he went to prison ten years ago which was when he left the job.'

'What?' Charles shouted causing Eva to jump. 'What the hell was he in prison for?'

'Charles, I don't know how to tell you this.' Charles turned cold as Ellen's voice trembled.

'Just say it Ellen, please.' He reached to his shoulder where Eva's hand lay, and gripped her, needing her touch to get him through the next few seconds.

'He got two years for assault.' Charles could barely hear Ellen's whispered tone, but he heard enough. He was numb. He didn't know what to say.

'Charles, tell me what to do,' Ellen pleaded. She would help in any way she could.

'Do you have Lizzie's address?' Charles's adrenalin kicked in and he somehow detached himself from his emotions.

'No, she never gave it to me. We just phoned.'

'Okay, do you have a pen?' Charles waited for Ellen to grab a pen, then continued. 'Write this down, this is her address. If your cousin would be kind enough to call at the house and see if they are there, we would be very grateful. As soon as the travel agent opens, I'll be booking flights to Sydney. If you can speak to your cousin and get back to me with anything, I would appreciate that Ellen.'

'Of course Charles, I'll get onto it now. Let me know when you will arrive in Sydney and I'll arrange to meet you there,' Ellen said.

'Thank you, Ellen, but there's really no need, we can take care of things from there.' Charles didn't want her to put herself out.

'Honestly, I want to help. Lizzie's my friend, and it sounds like she may need us all. I'll speak to you soon. Take care.'

The call ended and Charles relayed the new information to a terrified

Eva.

'Oh Charles, I should've spoken up sooner. What if we're too late?'

As much as he wanted to be there for Eva right now, Charles was more focused on getting things done.

'We need to stay positive Eva. I'm going to go shower and then get organised so we can be first in line when the travel agent opens. I'll phone Derek soon to let him know what's going on.' Derek was Charles's deputy. He would need him to step up and take charge until this mess was sorted out.

Eva sat alone on the stairs, listening to the rush of water in the shower upstairs. She went over and over everything Charles had said, picking apart every conversation she'd had with Mick, trying to pick up on something. Why had Mick said his dad was dead? Had his father disowned him, or had it been the other way round? Did Ellen's cousin have any more details? Who was the victim of the assault that got him put away? Was it his girlfriend or wife even? Had Lizzie known he'd been in prison for assault, or had he kept that from her? Eva couldn't imagine Lizzie would be with someone violent. But then Eva had felt all along that there was something not quite right. She should've spoken out, been honest with Lizzie from the beginning. Hindsight was a wonderful thing.

She heard the shower turn off and made her way upstairs to get ready herself. When she was showered and dressed for the day, Eva found Charles in the kitchen making breakfast for the two of them. Eva felt nauseous and wasn't sure she could eat but Charles had gone to the effort of making bacon sandwiches and she knew it would only be the cause of more tension if she didn't eat it.

She thanked him and picked up her plate and mug of tea. They barely spoke as they sat in separate chairs in the sunroom. Eva picked at her sandwich until Charles took it off her, frustrated. She knew he'd calm down; this was always his go to reaction when something set him off guard. He was matter of fact, focused and driven to work through the problem. Once he took back some control, he would calm down and manage to breathe.

Eva and Charles were stood outside the travel agents in Main Street at ten to nine, watching the staff busily prepare their desks for the day and fire up their computers.

'Good morning, you two are eager for a holiday this morning.' The agent said as she held the door open for them. 'Come on in and take a seat.'

'Thank you,' Charles nodded.

Charles explained a very brief outline of the situation and insisted on the first available flights to Sydney. He didn't care how much the tickets cost, he just wanted two seats on the next flights that landed in Sydney the earliest, as directly as possible.

'There's a flight via Singapore heading out this evening. I can get you both on that,' the agent smiled.

'Perfect, book it please.' Charles was business-like in his tone. 'Preferably in business class.'

The agent nodded and Eva sat in silence, contemplating all she would need to organise to enable them to be at the airport in time. It was doable but it would be a rush. She'd need to call her agent. She had become a very close friend over the years and Eva could trust her to look after things at home while she was gone.

It took time to take all the details and secure the flights. They were to pick up the tickets at the airport desk. Charles paid on his credit card before thanking the agent. He stood to leave, and Eva followed, dazed.

'Good luck,' the agent said, and Eva forced her mouth into a smile.

The tension between them was fractious. They'd barely spoken all day as they'd busied themselves organising last minute details. Charles had spoken to Ellen but had no further news other than that she was going to meet them at the airport.

Eva settled herself into her business class seat, feeling completely helpless at the situation. She wanted to talk to Charles but didn't know how to approach him in this mood. He'd only ever been this way for a couple of hours at most and never to this extent. Not only was she worried about her daughter, but she was also becoming increasingly worried about her husband. She fastened her seatbelt, and when the flight attendant served champagne before take-off, Eva polished it off in one mouthful. It went straight to her head and released her emotions. As the plane taxied down the runway, tears pricked Eva's eyes and the pent-up grief of the day spilled down her face.

As soon as the seatbelt signs were turned off, Eva reclined her seat and closed her eyes. She slept soundly for ten hours and by the time she woke, lunch was just being served before landing in Singapore. She looked across at Charles who was reading.

'Charles,' she whispered.

He looked across at her now for the first time in the last twenty-four hours, and she saw utter devastation in his eyes.

'Have you slept at all?' she asked, leaning over and taking his hand.

He put his book down on the tray table and rubbed his eyes. He shook his head.

'Not really, I dozed a little. You've had a good sleep though,' he said as he squeezed her hand. The tension between them lifted slightly.

'Probably catching up, I haven't slept in weeks.' A dark cloud rose around them again, sucking out the air and Eva silently chastised herself for mentioning it.

'I'm sorry.' Eva had never felt this way with Charles before. She'd never felt like she couldn't talk to him. This was a whole new concept.

Charles didn't reply, he just smiled at the flight attendant as she put their meals in front of them.

The layover in Singapore was much the same, they went straight into the business lounge for a shower and a drink. Charles helped himself to the food at the buffet table and Eva ordered herself a brandy. She didn't usually drink much but she needed something to numb this pain. Charles sat in the seat opposite her and watched her as she gulped the brandy and went and ordered another.

By the time she had drunk the second one, her emotions had gone from sad to mad. She was angry now at Charles for treating her this way. She knew he was dealing with the situation in his own way, just as she was but that didn't give him an excuse to behave so unpleasantly towards her.

'Charles, I'm done with your behaviour, snap out of it now. You can blame me all you like, but where have you been for the last few weeks? Did you make time to call our daughter and find out how she was? No! It's not my fault Charles. We were both concerned about Lizzie at the wedding and neither of us said anything to her about it, so stop putting this all on me.'

Eva slammed her glass down on the table and glared at her husband, waiting for a response.

Charles took a deep breath and sighed.

'Eva,' he scooted forward on his chair and took her hands. 'I don't blame you at all. I don't blame anyone. I'm just completely shattered, and I don't know what to say to you. I look at the devastation on your face and the sorrow in your eyes, and it just breaks my heart that I can't fix it. I've never felt so utterly out of control in my whole life as I do right now. My mind is going to the worst possible scenario every time and I'm just fighting not to fall apart.'

A tear bubbled in the corner of Charles's eye, and Eva quickly swished it away with her thumb, her fingers lingering on his jaw.

'Oh, my darling, don't push me away. I'm not expecting you to fix this, don't be so hard on yourself. We need to stick together like we always have done, that's the only way we're going to deal with this. I'm here for you just as you are for me. I love you with all my heart, please don't ever forget that.' Eva took his face in both hands and kissed him gently, feeling relieved that the tension had finally broken.

They sat in an embrace for several minutes, broken only by the call-to-gate announcement over the tannoy.

The next leg of the journey was much more pleasant as Charles and Eva went over their plans for the next few days. Ellen had flown down from Queensland earlier in the day and would be meeting them at the airport with her aunt's car. Her cousin had explained the situation to his parents and Ellen's aunt had offered to put Ellen, Charles and Eva up during their stay. Charles had graciously accepted the offer.

Eva spotted Ellen right away when they made their way through the doors into arrivals. She held her arms out for a hug, and tears stung Eva's eyes at the lovely welcome from her daughter's friend. Ellen looked like she hadn't slept in days. She spoke quietly, concern in her voice as she caught Charles and Eva up to date on the progress she'd made since she arrived.

'So, Brett, that's my cousin, he went back to the address you gave me this morning and there was someone home,' Ellen told them as she began to drive out of the carpark.

Eva's face lit up but quickly dimmed again as Ellen continued.

'Unfortunately, the lady he spoke to said she'd bought the house from the previous owner over two months ago.'

Eva gasped. 'So, they moved out two months ago and never told us?'

Ellen shrugged. 'I'm not sure Eva, the name of the owner she bought it from wasn't Mick, and she didn't think it was being rented out. She said it looked like a family were living in it, there were kids bedrooms with toys.'

'That just doesn't make any sense,' Charles spoke up from the back seat. 'Did they ever live there? Why would Lizzie give us a fake address?'

'Lizzie never gave it to me, it was Mick. I never confirmed it with Lizzie once she'd moved. The only thing we know was definitely theirs is the phone number. I wonder if we can trace that to an address through the telephone company?' Eva directed her question at Ellen, for no other reason than she lived in the country and might know where to start.

Eva 1991

The car pulled up at a beautiful traditional looking home outside of the city. Ellen explained they owned ten acres and she'd spent a lot of time there when she was growing up. Her parents were both busy doctors in Brisbane and Ellen and her brother often flew down here to spend their school holidays with their aunt and uncle and cousins.

Her aunt was waiting on the front porch to meet them, and Ellen did the introductions as Brett came bounding round from the back to help with the suitcases.

'It's lovely to meet you, Jennifer. Thank you so much for putting us up, we won't be any trouble,' Eva promised.

Jennifer brushed off the thanks. 'No worries, we don't get many visitors these days, it's nice to fill the house a little. It's a bit big for the two of us now the kids have all grown.'

'Hey, I'm still here,' Brett chirped in, mock offended.

Jennifer laughed. 'Sometimes you are. You're like a whirlwind, I never know when you're gonna blow in.'

Brett moved past the group into the house with the luggage, and Ellen invited Charles and Eva to follow. They all congregated in the kitchen, which was the centre of the home. It was a relaxed open plan living environment which led out onto a large deck at the back which then led out onto a small paddock with a couple of horses. There was a large swimming pool to one side and a shed to the other.

'Why don't I show you to the guest room and you can freshen up? My husband will be home soon, and we can sit down to dinner and make a plan of action.' Jennifer made it clear she wanted to help with their search.

'Thank you,' Charles said, 'we appreciate your kindness.'

An hour later, Charles and Eva had showered and changed into more weather appropriate attire. When they appeared back downstairs, Jennifer was busy in the kitchen making a salad and taking a potato bake from the oven.

'Can I help?' Eva asked.

'You can take the plates out to the table for me,' Jennifer said smiling.

'Bill is cooking steaks on the barbecue.' She handed the oven gloves to Charles, 'would you do the honours and carry this out for me?' she asked, pointing at the baking dish.

'Absolutely,' Charles replied, grateful to be of help.

'Hello,' Bill shouted as Charles and Eva made their way on to the deck. 'Welcome.'

Charles put the hot dish down on a pot stand and extended his hand to Bill.

'Charles,' he introduced himself, shaking Bill's hand. 'Thank you for having us, we're very grateful.'

'No worries. Whatever we can do to help, you let us know. I can't imagine what you must be going through.'

Charles nodded in appreciation.

Over dinner, Charles and Eva relayed the full story, explaining how they'd been very wary of Mick from day one. Ellen agreed that she'd also been dubious about the relationship and believed Lizzie was acting out of character. Brett repeated what Ellen had told them about his visit to the address they'd had for Lizzie, and Ellen mentioned Eva's idea about contacting Telstra about the phone number.

Jennifer believed they should get the police involved immediately as it had now been over three weeks since anyone had had any contact with Lizzie.

'I'll take you down to the station first thing in the morning,' Bill said. 'I know a couple of the officers down there, I'm sure they'll do whatever they can to help.'

Eva looked worried at the thought of getting the police involved, and Jennifer picked up on her concern straight away. She leaned across the table and gripped Eva's hand.

'It's just a precaution Eva, I'm sure nothing untoward has happened. We just want to help find Lizzie as soon as we can and the police will have better resources to do that,' Jennifer explained gently.

Eva smiled at her thoughtfulness, but the smile didn't reach her eyes. She was beginning to feel exhausted. The recent lack of sleep on top of the travel had knocked her for six.

'If you'll excuse me, I think I'm going to turn in for the evening,' Eva told the table as she began to clear plates.

'Leave those Eva, honestly I'll clear up, you look exhausted,' Jennifer said kindly.

Eva was about to argue and then thought better of it. She really was tired and needed to sleep. She nodded her thanks and left the table.

The group was silent for a few minutes before Bill ran through a plan of action for the next day. He had booked a few days leave so he could be available to assist in the search. Charles was floored by the generosity of these complete strangers.

'Do you have a recent photo of Lizzie and Mick Charles?' Jennifer asked. 'It would probably be handy to give to the police.'

'Yes, I packed their wedding photo as a last-minute thought before we left home. That's the most recent picture we have.' Charles felt desolate at the memory. He felt Eva's guilt every bit as much as she did, even though he knew in his heart they had to let Lizzie make her own decision. He was sure that she'd see sense eventually, he just hoped it wouldn't be too late.

Charles turned to Brett now and asked him if he would be able to take him back to the mechanic shop that Mick's dad owned. He was hoping he might be able to shine some light on the situation.

'Absolutely Charles, whatever you want mate,' Brett told him. 'He didn't seem to know anything about his whereabouts though. I gave my number to the lady at the house, and she said she'd call if she found anything out. She said she would look through all her details from the house purchase to see what information she could find.'

'We could also check with the airlines, see if we can find out if they've flown anywhere,' Jennifer mused. 'Although I don't know how much people will tell us, that's why I think it's good to involve the police; at least they have the authority.'

'Well, I might go join Eva. I'm starting to feel rather sleepy myself.' Charles stifled a yawn. 'Thank you again for your hospitality, we wouldn't have known where to begin without you.'

'Like I said Charles, we can't imagine what you're going through but we're more than happy to help out. Ellen's like a daughter to us and any friend of hers is a friend of ours. Now you go get some sleep and we'll regroup in the morning.'

Charles nodded his thanks. His emotions were all over the place at the moment and he no longer trusted himself to speak.

Charles and Eva were nervous when Bill pulled up outside the police station the next morning. It made the situation even more real. Once inside, Bill asked for an officer by name, and they waited several minutes before he came out to meet them.

'Bill, how are you mate? Long time, no see.'

Bill stood and after a moment of small talk, he introduced Charles and Eva and asked if there was somewhere they could speak privately.

'Absolutely, follow me. I think interview room two is free.' The officer's name was Jim.

Once they were all seated, Bill explained the situation to him, and Charles chipped in with extra information every now and then.

'So, you're saying your daughter's never lived at the address they gave you, but you've spoken to her several times since she's supposedly lived there?' Jim asked, a little confused.

'Yes, that's right officer,' Charles answered.

'And at no time did she give you an updated address or inform you the address you had was incorrect?'

'No.'

'Then, I'm not really sure what I can do. It sounds like she's acting out of her own free will. She could've told you at any time during any one of the many phone calls her new address, couldn't she?' Jim was not angry as such, but his tone seemed a little off, as though they were wasting his time.

Bill could sense the heightened tension and felt the need to interrupt. 'Jim, this guy has a previous conviction for assault. He's served time in prison, which he's kept to himself. He told Charles and Eva that his father was dead and that he'd taken over his business when he died. My son went to the business and the father is still very much alive. He just hasn't seen his son for ten years since he went to prison. Surely that's dodgy and justifies you doing a little background check.'

Jim sighed, 'I'll see what I can do, but I'm not promising anything, okay?'

'Thank you,' Eva said, 'we appreciate anything, no matter how small.'

Charles and Eva left the room while Bill stayed behind to have a chat with his friend.

The next stop was the mechanic shop owned by Mick's dad. He couldn't tell them much more than he'd told Brett, but he seemed like a genuine guy and was happy to help in any way he could. He gave them the name of the victim, who was a young woman by the name of Michelle. She'd been engaged to Mick at the time.

'I don't know what happened to her after he was sent down, we didn't keep in touch. I think she probably wanted to break all ties with the family, can't say as I blame her. Nice girl she was, never knew what she saw in my son.'

He wrote down the last address he'd had for her and told Charles and Eva the names of her parents to give them a bit of help in tracking her down. Charles promised to let him know the outcome of their search.

They returned home for lunch and when they arrived, Jennifer had received a message from the police station and had been waiting anxiously for them to get back.

'There you are, how was your morning?' she asked as they all settled at the kitchen bench.

'Didn't really get anywhere to be honest. I'm not sure what we can do next.' Charles looked disheartened.

'Jim called,' Jennifer said, trying to lift their spirits a little. 'He said he traced a car to Mick, an old Holden.'

Charles and Eva exchanged a glance. They'd been driving the new Jeep when they'd left Queensland.

'The car was registered at the address you gave him. Had been for several years. He also pulled up some details of his conviction. I've written it all down here.' She passed them a piece of paper with all the information on.

Brett appeared then. 'Hi, I've just been talking to the lady at the address you had. She said she'd contacted the previous owners via the real estate agent, they're a Mr and Mrs O'Sullivan. They'd owned the house for twelve years and Mick had crashed at their place from time to time whenever he was in town. Him and Mr O'Sullivan were apparently old school friends. Him and Lizzie had stayed with them for a few weeks but had obviously left when he sold the house. He'd not heard from them since. He said everything seemed fine between Mick and Lizzie though, he didn't see anything that would be of concern.'

'Thank you, Brett,' Eva said kindly. 'At least we know now that they did live there, and it wasn't a total lie. Did you ask about the phone number at all?'

'The lady transferred her own number so I'm not sure whether the O'Sullivans took that one with them. You said there's been no answer for a while?'

'No, thinking about it, that probably dates back a few months - Lizzie has been the one to call me and she's never picked up when I've phoned her.'

'Why don't I try it now? Do you have the number?' Brett asked.

Eva went to her room and brought out her address book, reading the number out to Brett as he dialled. Brett listened as the number rang out. He hung up and shrugged.

'I'm not sure if we'll have any luck with Telstra, it's probably all confidential,' Bill chipped in.

'Well, lunch is ready,' Jennifer told them. 'Let's sit and eat before we plan what's next.'

They enjoyed homemade pumpkin soup and fresh rolls out on the deck. The weather was warm, and the sun was high in the sky. Eva strolled down towards the fence and the horses trotted over to meet her. She held her hand out to the chestnut one and gently stroked his neck. It reminded her of back home, the fields and wildlife. Everything, but the weather. They didn't get many days like these back home. As she thought about home, her mind went straight back to Lizzie and all the plans she'd had for her future. She hadn't been too concerned at the time when Lizzie had decided to defer her place at uni to go travelling. She was sure in her mind that Lizzie would get to it eventually. She was a very talented photographer and she hated to see her talents wasted. Now, standing here she wasn't so sure. She thought they'd all been duped by this man and all she could hope was that they would find her before he did something unthinkable.

The next few weeks went slowly for Eva and Charles. Their avenues of hope had begun to dry up. As far as the police were concerned, nothing untoward had happened other than Mick was driving a car that was registered to an address he no longer lived at. That didn't give them any cause to investigate the disappearance any further.

'So, what now?' Charles yelled at the police officer. 'We just wait until she turns up in hospital with a black eye and broken bones? Or worse, in a morgue somewhere?'

The police officer was taken aback by Charles's sudden outburst, but he understood his frustration.

'Look, Mr Hartley, I know you're frustrated but there really is no evidence to suggest foul play. Your daughter was still speaking to you long after she'd left the address she gave you. She could've easily updated you of her whereabouts or informed you of her plans. But the reality is that she didn't, that's not a crime. I'm sorry but there's nothing else I can do.'

Charles's anger levels began to escalate further but before he had chance to open his mouth, Eva took his arm and led him away. She looked back at the officer with heavy eyes, understanding his predicament but devastated at the outcome.

Because the police were not prepared to investigate, they were also unable to find anything out from the telephone company. Everything was confidential and they'd come to a dead end.

They left their contact details with everyone they'd come across, both at home back in England, and Jennifer and Bill's number. They hated to leave with the situation unknown, but it was all they could do. They couldn't stay on indefinitely waiting for Lizzie to turn up, and if she did need them, they were better off at home so she could contact them. Ellen had flown home to Cairns the week before and promised to let them know if Lizzie contacted her or any of their friends. Brett also promised to keep his eyes and ears open for any news that might be relevant. His contacts were expansive throughout Sydney and if anyone knew of Mick, he'd find them.

Charles and Eva took Jennifer and Bill out for dinner on their last night to thank them for their kind hospitality. They were so grateful to them and felt blessed to have met such wonderful people. It was unfortunate that it was under such difficult circumstances, but they were sure they'd be friends for life. They genuinely felt like they'd gone through it together.

'We're so sorry to see you leaving without any answers but believe me, we will continue to do what we can from this end. If you ever need anything doing, please ask, you won't be putting on us,' Jennifer told Eva.

'Jen's right,' said Bill. 'It's been a pleasure to get to know you both. Anytime you want to come back, our door is always open.'

'Thank you both, you've done so much for us, we can't thank you enough. It works both ways though, if you ever fancy a trip to the UK, you must come and stay with us.' Eva said with mixed emotions. It was difficult to amalgamate her feelings of something so good coming from something so bad.

'We'll hold you to that,' Jennifer said, her eyes lighting up at the prospect of an overseas trip.

Charles and Eva were in low spirits when they boarded the plane to Singapore the following day. They'd decided not to break up the journey on the way home like they usually did, they didn't feel much like sightseeing. They just wanted to get home and back to work, although Eva didn't feel much like writing either, she just felt so sad. She prayed her answering machine would be full of messages from Lizzie when they got home but she knew in her heart that it wouldn't be. She wondered if she'd ever hear from her again. A tear trickled down her cheek as the plane began to taxi, and Charles reached across and held her hand.

Neither of them spoke much throughout the journey; there was no tension, they were just both so sad. The thought of their only daughter being seduced by this man to the point that she would disappear from their lives was incomprehensible. What hold did he have over her? What had he said to her to make her feel she couldn't ring them? Eva couldn't wrap her head round how this had happened. Lizzie would've been the last person she thought would get played by a man. She usually saw through that type of behaviour. Eva made a mental note to contact Lizzie's best friend from school when she got home. She didn't expect that Sally would've heard from her, but she thought she should inform her of the situation anyway.

As they approached the moors in the taxi, Eva felt relief to be home to normal life. She knew life was far from normal and would take time to get used to, but it was as normal as it was going to get until Lizzie came home.

Charles grabbed the luggage from the boot while Eva unlocked the front door. The first thing she did was press play on the answering machine. She listened carefully, deleting each trivial message as she went. There was one message she listened to twice and pressed save. No one spoke but she thought she could hear the soft sound of someone breathing.

'Is that her Charles? Is that Lizzie?' she cried.

'It isn't anyone Eva, no one's said a word.' Charles was tired and wasn't in the mood to deal with phantom phone calls. He didn't want Eva to start clutching at straws. What they needed was some cold hard evidence of some kind. A sighting or contact with Mick's friend that they'd lived with. Anything that would point them in the right direction. Charles didn't hold out much hope, but the thoughts were on constant replay in the back of his mind.

Eva busied herself unpacking while Charles sat down with the mountain of mail. She finished putting the last of the clothes away before joining Charles in the sunroom with a cup of tea for each of them.

'Thanks love, how are you feeling?' he asked.

'I'm okay, tired. How are you?'

'To be honest I feel numb. I don't know where we go from here.' Charles said.

'Me neither, but we'll have to find a way,' Eva muttered.

They sat in silence with their own thoughts for a few moments before Charles passed Eva a brown envelope.

'What's this?' she asked curiously, before peeking inside.

'The education department is offering early retirement packages for those over fifty,' Charles told her.

Surprised, Eva questioned him. 'Are you considering taking it?'

'I don't know, it looks like a pretty decent package, it might be worth considering.' Charles looked more animated than he had in weeks. He sighed, 'I'm honestly not looking forward to going back to work on Monday, I don't feel like I've got the energy for it anymore. I think maybe it's come at the right time.'

'If you're sure that's what you want, but don't make that decision based on what's happening with Liz...' Eva choked on her daughter's name. Charles took his wife's hand.

'I'm always here darling, we'll get through this together. But no, I was having second thoughts about teaching when I was struggling to get the last book finished. Since taking the headship, I've lost my passion for teaching. I love the whole writing process and I think that's the direction I'd rather take,' Charles explained.

'Then you should do it, take early retirement and write full time. You deserve it. Maybe we can even travel a little more,' Eva suggested.

'I'd like that,' Charles smiled warmly.

Charlie 2019

Over the next few days, I started to feel much better, and the nurses gradually reduced my pain meds, which stopped me feeling so sleepy. It meant I was functioning enough to start thinking more about my future and make a plan to begin looking into my adoption. I was a little disappointed that I'd heard nothing from Beau. I knew that made me sound like a hypocrite but somewhere deep inside me I wished he'd have fought harder. I knew that was wrong, he was only doing what I'd asked him to do but I missed him. He'd become such a huge part of my life and his absence weighed heavy on me. I'd been feeling quite upbeat since seeing Rosie again but thinking about Beau tore at my heart.

My eyes filled with tears and were fully threatening to spill over when Kate appeared in the doorway. The sight of her tipped me over the edge and I tumbled into full on melt down mode. She rushed to my bedside and folded me into her arms, and I had never in my life needed my mum more than I did right then. I didn't even know how she was doing, if she'd improved or even if she'd been told about my accident yet. Kate held me firmly until my sobs began to subside and then silently handed me a tissue to wipe the accumulated snot from my face.

'Sorry,' I sniffed, 'you walked in at the wrong time.'

She smiled sympathetically. 'I'd say I walked in at exactly the right time. Want to talk about it?'

I shook my head but after a few seconds of silence, I spilled all my random thoughts, firing them at her like a machine gun. She watched and listened intently like she does in a therapy session, nodding occasionally to prompt me to continue.

'Charlie, it's okay to feel like this. You feel let down by the people who love you, that's perfectly understandable. It's okay to be angry but what you don't want to do is let that anger control you. We need to find a way to channel it into strength so it can help you. I'm not saying your family or Beau were right to keep things from you, but what I'm saying is try and look at it from their point of view. Generally, when people keep secrets it's to protect you, not hurt you; they all had your best interests at heart.'

My breath faltered when she mentioned him, and I had to look away. My eyes began to fill again as Kate's hand clasped around mine.

'He'll be okay Charlie. Don't ever feel guilty for doing what you had to do. You're still figuring all this out and you have to do it in whatever way you need to. You have so much life ahead of you, and if you and Beau are meant to be together, then you'll find a way to get past this. If you're not, then look at it as a life experience.'

I was surprised that Kate wasn't fighting Beau's corner, knowing the hell he'd already been through in his life. But I guess being a single foster parent and running her own business, she was a champion of women, even if that did mean her own son was hurting.

'Thank you, I wasn't sure how you would feel. I know you love Beau, and he's been through a lot. I am so sorry that he's hurting, but I am too.' She nodded her understanding.

'Any news on when you'll be able to leave here?' she asked.

'I'm not sure but I'm going to stay with my friend Rosie when I get out. I guess I'll need help with stuff for a while.'

'That's good, but please don't hesitate to reach out to me, I'm here for you Charlie, separate to Beau. How have the dreams been since your accident?' she asked, changing the subject.

'I had one, more like a memory though. I was with Tom and our birth mum. I'd wet the bed and she was helping me hide it, I think so my dad wouldn't find out. We were terrified of him.'

Goosebumps prickled my flesh at the reminder. 'I'm nervous about finding out what happened.'

'You know you don't have to, but if you do want to, I'll be here to help you through it, Beau too.' She looked at me pointedly. 'He's dealt with some traumatic experiences in his life Charlie, but he has learnt how to deal with his memories. I'm not trying to push things but he's probably the one person who will truly understand.'

I knew she was right. I had no idea how I would have dealt with the last month or so without him, but that can't be the basis of our relationship.

A nurse popped her head round the door. 'Time for your physio Missy.'

I groaned, and Kate and the nurse both laughed.

'That's my cue to leave then,' Kate said standing up. 'Think about what I said Charlie, and take care.' She hugged me and I watched her leave, dreading my physio.

A porter arrived with a wheelchair. The nurse helped me into it, and covered with a scratchy blanket, I was wheeled off into the room of torture and suffering, otherwise known as the physiotherapy department. I knew it was for my own good but that didn't mean I wanted to do it. The exercises were hard work, and it wasn't long before I was exhausted. The physiotherapist had a weird sense of humour that was way over my head, and he really wasn't getting the responses he was after. He eventually gave up trying and focused on getting my exercises finished. By the time the porter arrived to take me back to my room, I was in a bad mood. The nurse sensed my low spirits and put it down to the session. She helped me into bed and reclined it for me so I could take a nap.

Clutching Tom's hand tightly, holding my blanket to my nose, I huddle behind the lady in the flower dress. She's nice but I just want my mummy back. The yellow door in front of us reminds me of sunshine, and when it opens the lady standing in the doorway has a big smile that lights up her whole face. I peek a little further from behind the flower dress to get a better look. The sunshine lady crouches down in front of Tom and tells him that her name is Anna. Tom's eyes dart to mine, urging me out of my hiding place so he's not all alone. Slowly creeping forwards, I stand beside Tom in full view of the lady with the smile.
   'Hello Charlotte, I've been so excited to meet you both. Do you like cupcakes? I've made some chocolate ones for you.' She straightens up and we all follow her inside. There's a man in the kitchen making tea and I stop dead as he turns and sees us.
   'Hi guys, I'm Rob. It's good to meet you.' He comes closer and I flinch; a whimper sounds from my lips. He takes a step backwards looking sad, and I feel bad for being scared of him. The lady in the flower dress steps forward and tells us that we are going to live with Anna and Rob now, and that there's no need to be scared. Anna asks if we'd like to see our new bedrooms and I really want to go but Tom's grip on my hand tightens, and his eyes grow dark. I look up at Anna and shake my head sadly. She looks to Tom and frowns before quickly covering it with a beaming smile.
   'Let's go eat some cupcakes,' she says in a happy sing song voice. She takes my hand and reaches for Tom with her free hand, leading us to a little round table with two low down chairs. She throws a cushion on the floor and drops onto it, sitting with her legs crossed. Tom and I sit at the chairs and Rob brings over a plate of cupcakes and cookies. Tom stares at me as though he's trying to tell me not to have one, but my mouth is watering at the smell of chocolate. I reach for one and greedily suck the shiny glaze off the top, licking my lips before taking a big bite out of it.

I woke, startled. My breathing was rapid, and I felt lightheaded. I remembered meeting mum and dad.

Each day merged into the next and I began to get stronger. I didn't have many visitors, only Kate, and Rosie and Gina. Each time Rosie visited we talked more and more about what had happened. I described my dreams and the little snapshots of my life that I'd been remembering, I talked about Dad and Tom, about Beau, and Mum. She listened and not once did she judge me or blame me for my actions. It felt so good to have her back in my life.
   'I missed you Rose. I'm so sorry,' I told her again after we'd had a long chat about Beau.

'Yeah, you should be, dumping me for a guy. A hot guy, but still a guy.' She grinned at me, and I shook my head at her.
'As if that would ever happen. And stop treating him like an object. He's more than a pretty face with abs!'
'So...' Rosie paused and looked at me questioningly, 'you still have feelings for him?' She was testing me.
'Of course.' My voice was quiet. 'I love him.'
Her smile brightened up her whole face, excited for me.
'It doesn't mean anything. I've got a lot on my mind, a lot of shit I need to process. I've got a whole relationship I need to rebuild with my mum, and I might have other relationships to build with my birth mum. I need to find out what happened to make her give us up for adoption. I know she loved us; I can feel it.'
'I know Lots, sorry, Charlie. Not sure I'll ever get used to that one.'
I smiled at her to let her know it was okay. 'I can't expect everyone to suddenly call me a different name without slipping up from time to time. It's just that I feel so different from Lottie after everything that's happened. I feel like Charlie, like I need a new identity.'
'So, what are your plans now then?' Rosie asked excitedly. She'd always been overly enthusiastic about everything, and I loved her for it.
'Plans for what?' My face was blank as I feigned ignorance.
'For your life! What's next? What are we gonna do first when you get the hell out of this place?'
I laughed at her excitement about my life, and then felt subdued as I thought about how normal I thought my life was just a few months ago.
'I guess speaking to Mum is my first job. I need to know everything she knows about my past before I can go any further.'
'And Beau?' I knew Rosie wouldn't let this drop, but I couldn't think about him, I needed to focus on myself.
'What about Beau?' I pondered the question aloud. 'I love the guy, but he hurt me.'
'You hurt me, Charlie. I'm not saying that to be mean, but you did, and I forgive you for it. Beau was only trying to do what he thought was best. Don't let him get away. He sounds like a keeper.'
'What century are you living in Rose? It's not just about that. I need to focus on me right now, I'm not putting my needs on hold just so I don't lose a guy. If he's worth anything at all to me, he'll be around when I've sorted through everything. And if he's not, then he's not the guy I think he is.'
Rosie stared at me without saying a word. Then a huge smile cracked her face and she hugged me tightly.
'You know, you have changed through all this but that's something that's remained the same. You always do the right thing.'

I was starting to move around the ward by myself and I finally got the news I'd been waiting for; I could finally leave. I called Gina and Rosie to ask if they could pick me up and waited excitedly for them to arrive. When they finally walked through the door I burst into tears.

'Hey, what's wrong?' Gina asked.

'I don't know,' I told her honestly. 'I can't wait to get out of here.'

'You've been through a lot Charlie, I guess it's overwhelming for you with everything still up in the air. Your mum will be home soon, and you'll be able to talk to her and get things out in the open. I'm sure you'll start to feel better.'

'I know, it's scary though.' I brushed the tears from my cheeks and took a deep breath. 'Let's go then.'

It felt good to have some fresh air, but the car ride was a little uncomfortable. Gina and Rosie helped me inside and I got settled on one of the leather recliners.

My eyelids grew heavy, and Gina and Rosie's voices became distant.

'I called her Mummy today,' I tell him even though I know he'll be mad.

'Charlie, no, she's not your mummy.'

'I'm called Lottie now, that's what new mummy calls me, so stop calling me Charlie.'

Tom gets off my bed and stomps into his own room and slams the door. Mummy comes rushing in to see if we're okay.

'He's mad that I called you mummy, he's just stupid,' I tell her. She sits beside me on my bed and holds my hand. She's warm and she smells like cookies.

'Lottie, you can call me whatever you like but don't call your brother stupid, he'll come around eventually. Some people just need more time.' She hugs me and whispers in my ear, 'the cookies are ready.'

I grin at her. She makes the best cookies. Mummy stands up and holds out her hand for me. I take it and follow her to the kitchen.

The smile on my face felt foreign. I hadn't thought about my mum in a positive way in a while. She really did make the best cookies, I thought to myself. The way mum dealt with Dad and Tom's deaths had really clouded my memories of her. I needed to remember all the good times, just like Rosie had been doing with me. She hadn't let the way I treated her, or the changes in me ruin our friendship.

I spent a couple of weeks at Rosie's mending, both physically and mentally. Kate had been to visit a few times and we'd talked about lots of things; what to expect when I saw mum again and I even asked her how Beau was. She told me he loved me but was determined to give me the space I needed. She also told me that if I changed my mind and wanted to talk, he would be by my side in a heartbeat.

Gina had a call from Mum to say she was home. She'd apparently been kept up to date with my progress as she'd grown stronger and was ready to deal with it. She wanted me to go home but told Gina that she would understand if I wasn't ready. I felt it was time.

So, there I was, sitting in Gina's car outside my house.

'Come on Charlie, I'll grab your crutches.' Gina smiled at me, encouraging me to take the next step.

I arranged my crutches so I could hop out of the car, and as I was getting them in the right position, Mum opened the front door. She looked like her old self, pre-tragedy, and I let out the breath I'd been holding. The relief was palpable. The mum that was carted away in an ambulance, swimming in her own vomit wasn't the mum I wanted welcoming me home.

'Lottie,' she said tentatively, 'it's good to see you.' She smiled but I could see the concern in her eyes. I didn't mention my name, there was plenty of time to go there later and I didn't want things to start off badly.

'Hey Mum, I'm so glad you're home.' I hobbled up the drive towards the door and she hesitated before coming out to meet me. I stood still and she wrapped her arms around me. It felt so good to see her again.

'I'm so sorry Lots. I let you down and I'll never forgive myself for not being there for you when you needed me.' Her tears wet my face as she pressed her cheek to mine.

'Hello Anna,' Gina said gently as she stood behind us with my bags. Mum released me and pulled Gina towards her.

'Thank you so much for looking after my girl Gina, I don't know how I can ever repay you.'

'No need Anna, you'd have done the same for me. Shall we get this stuff inside and get the kettle on?' Gina handed a bag to Mum, and I followed them into the house.

The two of them were being polite and making small talk and I just wanted to get started on a real conversation. Gina sensed me fidgeting and made her excuse to leave.

'Well, I'll be off then, I'm sure you and your mum have got lots to talk about Charlie.'

Mum frowned at the name Gina used, but remained silent as she walked her to the door.

My hands became clammy, and I nervously chewed the skin around my thumbnail as I waited for Mum to come back. She sat down next to me and finally we were alone, the tension rising between us.

'Since when did Gina call you Charlie?' Her voice quivered as she forced a smile.

'Mum, a lot's happened, so many things have changed in such a short space of time. Tom used to call me Charlie, didn't he? Before we came to live with you, I mean.' I got straight to the point. I needed to get to the truth.

Mum sighed heavily, resigned to the fact that I'd found out about my adoption. 'He did, yes. I'm sorry you didn't hear it from me. I had promised Tom I would talk to you; I was just waiting for the right time.' She paused while she chose her next words carefully.

'We never meant to keep it secret, it was just so difficult for you in the beginning, we thought it would be easier for you both if you could just move on.' Mum looked at me like she used to, as though the past few months had never happened.

'I'm proud of you honey, for getting through all this by yourself. I'm so sorry I let you down, I hope you can forgive me one day.'

'I'm trying Mum, but I really need you to be honest with me from now on. How much do you know about my past?' I asked hopeful.

'I honestly don't know that much. We were told you came from a violent home, and we were given counselling on how to manage your needs but to be honest Lottie, at the time your Dad and I kept our heads in the sand. We wanted a new start for you both in a loving home and we wanted you to forget what you'd been through. We waited a long time for a child, we never expected two of you to come along at once.' She smiled and her eyes brimmed with tears. 'We were so happy, but it was tough in the beginning. You settled much more quickly than Tom; I guess he remembered more, being older, and he was quite jealous in the beginning. You began to forget your parents and started calling us Mummy and Daddy, but Tom tried to hold on to the past for much longer. I guess his memories stayed with him, but he wasn't sure where they came from. When he confronted me before he died, he was so angry with me and told me I had to talk to you, or he would tell you himself.'

'Were you going to tell me?' I asked quietly.

'I wanted to. I asked him to give me time. I planned to tell you after your graduation, and he promised he would give me that.' She shook her head slowly. 'Of course, I regret that now. We never fully made up Lottie and I have to live with that for the rest of my life.'

Her breath was uneven, and I could hear her stifled sobs. I guess that's why she'd hit the bottle so hard. Not only did she lose her son; he was angry with her when he died. Mum couldn't hold back any longer and she broke down. I rested my hand on her arm tentatively and she pulled me in for a hug. It felt so good to have her back on side.

She eventually calmed down and sat back on the couch, curling her legs beneath her.

'So, are you going to tell me how the hell you ended up in hospital?'

I smiled and told her about Beau and his motorbike. I told her about my dreams, and the therapy with Kate, and how Beau knew I was adopted but kept it from me because of Tom's promise to her.

'He sounds like a decent guy, I'm sure he was doing what he thought best,' Mum said. 'I can understand where he was coming from.'

'I know, but it still hurt. I felt so betrayed. My dreams started to feel more like memories, and I was struggling to understand them. I just felt like he could've saved me so much heartache and suffering.'

'So you stole his motorbike to get back at him?' Mum asked. 'That doesn't sound like you.'

'Getting wasted and hiding vodka bottles doesn't sound like you Mum.' I didn't mean to throw that back at her, but I really didn't need to feel judged.

'Touché,' Mum said.

'I honestly wasn't thinking when I took the bike; it wasn't a deliberate thing, I was just mad.'

'And how are things now?' she asked. I shrugged in reply because I really didn't know how to answer her.

'So, you never did tell me about the sudden name change,' Mum said, but she didn't sound as bitter this time.

'It started when I met Beau. He was good friends with Tom, and he said Tom had only ever called me Charlie when he spoke to him about me. The same with Beau's foster mum. When I started processing the dreams, I began to recall some memories of Tom calling me Charlie. Then the name started to appear in the dreams. I think that's when I started to connect the two, and after the hypnotherapy the memories began to come back. My mum,' I paused at the use of the name, 'my birth mum I mean, she called me Charlie and she was nice to us. I remember how she would cuddle me when I wet the bed and keep it quiet from my dad so he wouldn't get mad. I feel like my name connects me to her somehow and I've discovered such a lot about myself over the last few weeks, I feel like I've outgrown Lottie and become Charlie.' I kept my head down, my eyes focused on the fingers picking at my shorts. I had no idea how Mum would react.

Her hand pressed on mine, stopping my nervous picking and I lifted my eyes to meet hers.

'Charlie, that's a beautiful way to honour her. If you want to find out what happened, I can help you.'

I sighed. 'I do, but I'm scared Mum. I know I was only little, and I don't remember much but I know my dad was a bad man. I know he hit her, and Tom too.'

Mum's eyes closed and I could see her willing herself not to lose any more tears.

'Did he hit you too?' her voice trembled.

'I don't think so,' I told her shakily. 'I have vague memories of having to be quiet when he was home but having so much fun when he went to work. We baked cupcakes and danced and sang. I remember being happy, which is why I'm scared. I know deep down she wouldn't have given me up willingly, so that can only mean one thing.'

'I'm glad you have some happy memories of her, I was afraid it was all bad,' Mum smiled. 'I'm here for you, whatever you want to do. Sometimes confirmation of what you already know can bring you peace. You just let me know when you're ready.'

I felt so much happier after our talk. It had been good for both of us. There was only one thing that worried me, so I decided to come straight out and ask.

'Mum, there's one more thing.'

'Yes, honey?'

'How are you feeling? About the drinking I mean.'

Guilt and shame blanketed mum's face and she shook her head. 'I promise that will never happen again.'

Eva 1993

Charles and Eva never lost hope that Lizzie would contact them one day, but something was lost between the two of them. Neither would ever have believed their marriage would hit rock bottom but losing Lizzie had taken its toll on both of them and subsequently, their marriage. What they experienced over the years following Lizzie's disappearance was tantamount to grief. Sadness turned into depression for Eva, and she suffered for a long time. She couldn't bring herself to write and found herself in breach of contract with her publisher. She jumped every time the phone rang. Occasionally she would answer and there would be no one on the other end, and she was convinced it was Lizzie attempting to make contact.

'Lizzie is that you?' she asked. Eva was positive she could hear someone breathing. 'Please Lizzie, just one word to let me know you're okay. I'm not mad at you, I just need to know you're safe.' There was silence before the line went dead.

Eva spent her days walking, sleeping or staring at the wall. Charles tried everything he could to bring her back to him, but the stress was taking its toll on him too. It wasn't until he had a health scare that Eva began to take back more control over her life. She couldn't bear the thought of losing him too, and she felt deep regret for the way they had handled their marriage over the last couple of years.

Eva walked cautiously into the ward right on visiting time. She'd phoned the hospital that morning to find out how Charles was doing, and they'd told her he was up and about. She breathed a sigh of relief. Charles was sitting up in bed, reading the paper when she approached the bay of four beds. His face lit up when he saw her, the same way it had a thousand times before, but she hadn't seen it in a while, or she'd been blind to it. Eva sat on the edge of the bed and took his hand.

'How are you feeling?' she asked, quietly.

'I'm okay love. It wasn't a heart attack, a bit of stress they think.'

Eva looked away, guilt eating her up on the inside.

'Eva, this is not your fault, so don't you go blaming yourself.' Charles knew his wife so well.

Eva blushed. 'I've been a terrible wife to you Charles,' she wept.

'Eva, please stop this. I am drawing a line here; it's gone on long enough. You have been a wonderful wife to me, and the most loving mother. What has happened is not your fault, it's not my fault, and it's not Lizzie's fault either. The one person who takes the blame in all of this is Mick. He's the one that has manipulated and lied and brainwashed our daughter into believing he loved her. I have faith in Lizzie, she will come to her senses eventually. She's strong, she'll be back in our lives one day but until then we must move forward with our own lives. We've lost ourselves in this mess, but we still love each other. We need to fix it.' Charles had teared up by this point and Eva was moved by how much he still loved her after all this time and the misery of the last few years.

'I love you, Charles. It hurts me so much that we've let this happen to us,' Eva sobbed.

'I love you too my darling, that will never change. We can fix this, I promise. We can go to therapy if we need to. I'm all in, whatever it takes,' Charles promised.

Eva hugged her husband as though she hadn't seen him in years. She felt immediate relief and knew in her heart that this was the beginning of their future. They would move forward and live their life together like they were always meant to. They would never forget their daughter and they would always hope to be reunited but they wouldn't allow her disappearance to take any more away from them than what had already been taken. They would always keep a line of enquiry open; they would continue to reach out to their friends in Australia, and follow any leads that might come up, but in the meantime, they would enjoy each other and their work.

Eva drew inspiration from their chat, and when she returned to visit Charles that evening, she told him the idea she'd been pondering over all afternoon.

'I need to write about it,' she told him.

'You want to write?' Charles was taken aback. It had been so long since he'd seen Eva in the process of writing a novel or even a poem. 'Eva, that's fantastic news.'

'I need to write our story,' she emphasised.

'Our story? Like an autobiography you mean, a memoir?'

'No, I don't think so. I want it to be fiction, but I want to write a story about what happened to us, to Lizzie, as a kind of warning to others about how easily these types of behaviours can be missed. People need to know about these men Charles. If our own daughter could be sucked in by this, there are millions of other vulnerable women out there at risk. I want to draw attention to it Charles. People think abuse is all about black eyes and broken ribs. So many women suffer every day from emotional and mental abuse. It breaks my heart to think of Lizzie being manipulated in this way. I know we're only speculating about the circumstances she's living in, but we saw his behaviours first-hand, his subtle controlling habits that he disguised as caring. People need to be aware of these subtleties.'

'Eva, that's a great idea, have you contacted Seb yet?' Charles enquired. Seb had been Eva's editor for years; he'd been the one to champion her novel, "Before Her Time" all those years ago, which had given her a literary award nomination.

'I haven't. Things didn't end well with me breaking my contract. I'm sure he won't hold a grudge though. I'll give him a call tomorrow. Put some feelers out.'

'I'm so proud of you Eva. This is a big deal. It's been difficult to watch your creative passion fade away. That's what drew me to you that first day at our book club. When you talked of that poem, Life, your optimism and passion leapt from your face and I knew that was it for me,' Charles grinned.

'It's time,' Eva nodded. 'You know that poem gave me hope through my teenage years that life for me would be so much more than it was for my parents. And it was, for many years, until it wasn't anymore. I need to remember that poem and keep it in my heart. "Yet hope again elastic springs." I'm not going to allow this to keep me down, I am going to use it for good.'

Charlie 2019

The weeks passed quickly, my results came out and I officially graduated. But instead of applying for jobs like I'd planned, I put my efforts into looking after myself and fixing my broken relationship with Mum. She drove us all over, to the beach, up into the hills, to the country and the wineries. We had long lunches by the river and coffee in vintage coffee shops. We talked constantly about everything. I explained the guilt I felt for the way I treated Rosie, and how she hadn't let it affect our friendship. We talked about the future, about hers and mine, and I told her I wasn't sure if I still wanted to be a teacher. I had a lot of decisions to make.

Mum took me to all my hospital appointments, and I'd even attended some counselling appointments with her at the rehab centre. We were trawling through our grief together, and I was so grateful that we'd managed to get back on track. Our relationship had changed too, not just been fixed. I felt much more open as I didn't feel that I had anything to prove. I grappled with a thought in the back of my mind suggesting I did everything I thought Mum and Dad had wanted because I feared being taken away again. That's a lot of pressure to put on yourself as a young child. Mum encouraged me to make all my future decisions for myself, not anyone else.

As we were leaving an appointment at the hospital, Mum asked if there was anywhere I'd like to go. I thought for a minute and then gave her directions to Clint's Fish Shack. Her face was full of questions.

'There's someone I'd like you to meet Mum. He was a good friend of Tom's.'

On the journey up the coast, I told her about Clint's history and his friendship with Beau's dad and then Beau. We talked about how Tom met him and how they developed a friendship. When we arrived in the car park, mum hesitated before getting out of the car.

'It's okay Mum, he's a good man, you'll like him,' I reassured her.

'He probably doesn't think very highly of me though.'

I'd never seen her come across so insecure.

'It'll be fine, I promise.'

Mum held the door open for me while I hopped through on my crutches. Clint looked up from behind the counter and immediately came over to say hello.

'Charlie, I heard what happened, how are you?' he asked, with genuine concern.

'Hi Clint, I'm good thanks.' I wiggled my crutch and laughed. 'Well,

I've been better!'

Clint nodded at me and looked at mum, his eyebrow raised.

'Clint, this is my mum, Anna. Mum, this is Clint,' I introduced them, and they shook hands politely.

Clint turned to me with concern. 'Did you get everything worked out?'

Mum interrupted, 'I'll go grab a table, you order Charlie.' I smiled at her, she hardly ever called me Lottie anymore.

She wandered off to find a table and Clint shouted our order to the kitchen staff. He turned back to me and waited for me to answer his question.

'Things with Mum are working out. We've talked a lot and I understand so much more about what happened. She's carrying a lot of guilt about how things were between Tom and her before he died though.'

Clint nodded thoughtfully. 'That's understandable, these things take time.' He paused as he contemplated his next words. I waited, knowing exactly where the conversation was going. 'What about Beau? He loves you, Charlie. I've never seen him look so lost.'

'I know, I love him too. It's just hard you know.' I realised how much I missed him and how much I wished he was still in my life. 'Maybe we've been through too much,' I said sadly.

'It's never too late to fix things Charlie, you of all people should know that,' he said. 'Listen, I don't want to butt in your business, at the end of the day it's your decision, but I will say this. I've known Beau since he was just a kid and the only time I've ever seen light in his eyes was when he was here with you. He drove here the night of your accident looking for you and he was distraught at the thought of losing you. I'm not telling you what to do Charlie, but I think you should see him, if only to get some closure for the both of you.'

I nodded sadly and walked over to the table where Mum was sitting. As I adjusted my crutches to sit down, she saw the heartache on my face.

'Baby what's wrong? What did he say to you?' She jumped straight into defensive mum mode.

'Nothing, we just talked about Beau, and he made me realise how much I miss him,' I told her honestly.

'Then call him. You've got nothing to lose.'

Clint came over with our seafood baskets and put them down in front of us. He nodded then turned away, pausing before turning back to Mum.

'Mrs Flowers, Anna, I...' He blew out a breath and started again. 'I've had the pleasure of getting to know both of your children and I want to say what a credit they both are to you.' Heat flushed my face as I listened to Clint praise me. He cleared his throat and continued. 'I don't wish to speak out of turn, but I spoke with Tom on quite a personal level before he passed, and he talked of his memories of his birth parents. He remembered being physically abused and he watched his mother suffer abuse on a much larger scale.' Mum's eyes widened as this stranger told her personal things about her own son. I wasn't entirely sure how she'd take it, so I reached across the table and squeezed her hand.

Clint continued, 'I know you and he were having some struggles, but you need to know how grateful he was for the wonderful and safe life you gave him and Charlie. Make peace with it.' He touched Mum's shoulder gently and walked away as a single tear escaped down her face.

'He's right Mum, you do need to make peace with it. Tom loved you, he was a good guy, and you would've worked things out given time. The same way we have. You have to focus on that because you can't change the past.'

Mum smiled and nodded her head in agreement. 'And you need to take your own advice and go sort things out with Beau. And when you do, I'd love to meet him.'

Eva 1995

It had taken Eva some time to get back into the routine of writing, and now with Charles at home and sharing an office space, it was difficult not to get distracted. Charles had poured all his sorrow into his writing since taking early retirement from teaching. His series of crime thrillers had hit the stratosphere; each book becoming a New York Times bestseller. Eva was extremely proud of him. It wasn't a genre she ever thought he'd write but after his first two books, he'd really fallen in love with the protagonist and couldn't bear to leave him behind and write something different. He felt like he was being disloyal somehow. He'd published six in the series now and each one was dedicated to the two loves in his life - Eva and Elizabeth. He always wrote a cryptic message in the acknowledgements, reaching out to Lizzie, never losing hope that she would read it and remember the love her parents would always hold for her.

Seb had welcomed Eva back into his life with open arms and couldn't wait to read what she had for him. He was enthralled by her ideas for her new book and knew she had it in her capabilities to smash this and take the literary world by storm.

Eva looked over at Charles now, as she added the finishing touches to her manuscript. He was engrossed in his work, his brow furrowed as his mind tried to understand the psychological aspects of his protagonist. He'd taken a few short psychology courses over the last few years in order to do his character some justice. He was fascinated by the workings of the human mind and each novel in the series went that little bit deeper than the last. Eva watched him for several minutes before he sensed her, and she smiled at him when his eyes flashed to hers. They still had some difficult moments but the last couple of years had returned their marriage to a happy state. They'd begun counselling, both together and individually and it had helped them to deal with their loss, but what they'd discovered to be the biggest strength in keeping their marriage alive was their 'debrief' every evening. Working together wasn't necessarily the best thing for communication so they made sure they spent a good thirty minutes at the end of their workday discussing any issues they'd had that day, whether it be a work problem, creative or otherwise, or something they just needed to get off their chest. Those thirty-minute sessions often spilled over into their dinner time, and long after.

'What are you smiling at?' Charles asked, his eyes gleaming.

'Oh, you know, I just love you,' Eva murmured.

'I love you too, always.' Charles felt a lump in his throat, as he thought about how close he'd come to losing the love of his life. He still admonished himself at how he got so wrapped up in his own grief that he just let Eva go through hers alone. It was something that he couldn't believe he had let happen and he vowed he would never put himself first again at the risk of losing his wife.

'I'm finished,' Eva said simply.

'The book?' Charles asked excitedly, and Eva nodded.

'I can't wait to read it, Eva. I just know it will be fabulous,' Charles boasted, standing from his desk and walking the few short steps to his wife. He held out his hand to her and she took it as she stood to join him. He held her in his arms as they swayed to the classical music they always played in the background. Charles's nose nuzzled Eva's ear and she could hear his breathing rapidly quickening. Eva ran her hands from where they'd rested on his hips, up his back to his neck. Her fingers twisted gently in the curls at his nape; even at fifty-six he still had a full head of thick curls. Charles turned his face to find Eva's lips and gently prising them apart, he explored her mouth with his tongue. Eva's senses were immediately heightened, and she found herself responding with a zest she'd not experienced in a while. Charles held her face in his hands as he trailed his lips across her cheek back towards her ear.

'Come upstairs,' he whispered.

Eva was excited and followed quickly. Their love making had been the last thing to return to their marriage, and although it was more of a regular thing than it had been in several years, Eva had felt they'd lost the fire that had blazed in their bedroom. She felt that heat now though, as Charles led her into the bedroom and gently turned her to face him. He worked slowly and deliberately, removing her clothing gently, never once unlocking his eyes from hers. His touch sparked every nerve in her body and by the time they were naked, she couldn't hold back any longer. They made love with a fervour that illuminated her from within. She hadn't felt so light in such a long time and her body glowed in the aftermath. Eva laid wrapped in Charles's arms, her head gently resting on his chest. Her fingers entwined with his on his stomach as she admired his form. It wasn't his looks that had drawn her to him that day in the village hall, it was the way he'd spoken so passionately about what he believed in. But that night in his bedsit when they'd made love for the first time, his physical form had been very much at the forefront of her desires.

'Are you okay?' Charles muttered, listening to Eva's even breathing.

'I'm wonderful Charles,' she murmured back, happy and exhausted.

Charles grinned at her answer. 'You are wonderful, you're right,' he told her. 'I can't begin to tell you how wonderful that was. As much as I love you for your mind, I've missed this.'

Eva shifted her position so she could look at Charles.

'Me too, more than I'd realised. The way you can still make me feel after all these years is so special Charles. I love you so very much.' Eva kissed him then, reigniting the sparks between them.

Charlie 2019

'Mum,' I said tentatively on the drive home.

'Yes?'

'I think it's time,' I said cautiously. I knew she said she'd help but I wasn't sure how she would feel when it came to the crunch.

'Time for what?' she asked absently. 'To see Beau?'

'To find out what happened to my birth parents,' I stammered.

Mum turned her head to look at me. She was silent for what felt like forever, then she nodded.

Once we arrived home, Mum went straight into her wardrobe and brought out a cardboard box. On closer inspection, I noticed it was an old beer carton and I wondered what was going on. She took a knife and sliced through the tape holding it together, pulling out an old wooden box from inside.

Fighting back tears, Mum looked at me with regret.

'This was dropped off by the social worker a few days after you came to live with us.' She pushed the box across the kitchen bench top towards me. 'I think it belonged to your birth mum; I've never opened it.'

We looked at each other and I was torn, not sure what to do with it.

'Go on, it's yours,' Mum encouraged me to open it. I realised this must be difficult for her, but I was so eager to find out more about my past. My hands were shaking as I turned the little key in the lock on the front. I lifted the lid slowly, unsure what to expect.

The first thing I pulled out was an old-fashioned hair comb covered in pearls.

'Wow, that's beautiful,' Mum said, and I nodded in agreement.

The box was full of photographs of Tom and I as babies and toddlers. There was one of us at a beach I didn't recognise. I was just a baby and Tom must be about two or three. A solid lump formed in my throat and my eyes swam with tears. Mum watched me closely. I closed my eyes and took a deep breath. I wanted to carry on and see what else was in the box.

There was a professional photo taken on board a boat at the Great Barrier Reef. It was of my birth mum with two older people, I guessed were her parents. I turned it over to find writing on the back.

It read, "Charles and Eva with Lizzie - 1988"

'My mum's name was Lizzie?' I wasn't really asking; I was just wondering aloud. 'They must be her parents; don't you think Mum?' I turned to Mum feeling like I needed some clarification.

'I guess so honey,' Mum choked. I could see her eyes turn glossy and I balked.

'Mum, you don't have to do this, I know it must be difficult,' I reminded her.

'It is difficult, I won't deny that. But honey, this is your history, and you deserve to know. I'll be with you every step of the way.' She grasped my shoulder and pulled me towards her for a hug.

I continued my search through the box and found an envelope containing various documents. There was a birth certificate with my birth mum's name on it which confirmed the identity of the people on the photograph. Charles and Eva Hartley were her parents, and she was born in Bradford, England. I turned to Mum with wide eyes.

'Are you thinking what I'm thinking?' I asked incredulously.

Mum stared at me, completely unaware of the reason for my disbelief.

'Charles and Eva Hartley are both famous writers,' I explained. 'Do you think it could be them?'

Mum pondered on my question for a moment before joining in with my anticipation. 'Are the writers married to each other or do they just share a surname?'

'I have no idea. Let me go grab a book and see if there's an author bio.' My enthusiasm was bursting now, the thought of being the granddaughter of literary royalty was like a dream. My eyes scanned my broken bookshelves searching for one of Eva Hartley's books and then I remembered I'd lent her most famous novel, "Controlled" to Beau before my accident. My heart deflated for a moment, both at the disappointment and the hurt. My heart rate quickened, and I tried to slow my breathing. Mum appeared at the door wondering what was taking so long and I caught her frown.

'I'm okay,' I told her quickly, trying to quell the rising panic. Once I'd calmed down, I looked at her concerned expression.

'What's wrong Charlie?'

'I couldn't find the book, I thought it was here, but I remembered I lent it to Beau. It hurts to think of him that's all.' I suddenly felt Mum's arms wrap around me and she brought a feeling of safety. Despite the difficulties we'd had lately, she could always make me feel secure and loved.

'Let's just google them,' she suggested, once she released me from her grasp.

I grabbed my laptop and took it to the kitchen bench. I nervously typed Eva Hartley into the search engine and looked for a Wiki page. I scrolled down to the heading, "Personal Life" and found what I was looking for. Married to crime author Charles Hartley they have one daughter, Elizabeth.

Mum and I stared at the screen in shock. Our mouths hanging open, unable to speak. There was no other mention of Elizabeth, so I tried different pages to see if she came up anywhere but only drew a blank.

'We could try their Facebook pages,' Mum suggested.

I turned my head and her demeanour had changed. She was excited now, like we were going on an adventure. I felt like I needed to put the brakes on slightly, I was beginning to feel overwhelmed by this newfound knowledge.

'I think I need to find out what happened to Lizzie before I try and contact them.'

'Good idea,' Mum agreed. 'We're probably getting a little ahead of ourselves.'

Mum searched through her files to try and find the adoption details. The documents she had were a little hazy. There appeared to be a lot of confidentiality around our adoption and many details had been undisclosed. Mum had kept letters from the Department of Child Protection so we decided that would be the best place to start.

It was difficult finding any information over the phone, so we were advised to make an appointment and bring as much identification as possible. When I hung up the phone Mum and I were suddenly lost for words. We'd spent the afternoon digging up so much information and now we'd come to a pause.

'I have an appointment on Wednesday,' I finally broke our silence. 'Will you come?'

'Of course I'll come sweetheart. Whatever you want, I'm here for you.'

Eva 1997

Eva's book was released to a remarkable reception. Not only had the literary world been without any new work from Eva for several years, the third wave of feminism had ignited and Eva, a respected author in the feminist movement, was expected to have something important to say. "Controlled" was highly anticipated by many, and Eva felt the pressure strongly.

'I've never felt this pressure before,' she told Charles on the eve of publication. 'What if it fails?'

Charles looked at his wife in astonishment. 'You've read the reviews from the pre-release copies Eva; everyone has raved about it. You have absolutely nothing to worry about. This book is winning prizes, I have no doubt about that.'

Eva was still unsure how to tackle the press interviews when people asked about the birth of the story. She knew she didn't want to tell her story about Lizzie. On one hand, they'd wondered whether telling their story could be a good thing, it might bring attention to Lizzie and shed light on her situation. But what concerned them more was that highlighting the situation might put Lizzie in danger. Eva knew she would never live with herself if her actions led to Lizzie being hurt.

In the end, Eva and Charles had decided that it was an issue that seemed to be on the rise and needed addressing. That's what would become her go to line when asked where her idea came from.

On the morning of publication, Charles bought Eva a huge bouquet of flowers and a bottle of Moet to celebrate.

'I'm so proud of you my darling,' he said as he handed them over.

'Thank you,' Eva whispered. She'd always been shy of praise.

By teatime the phone was ringing off the hook, anyone who was anyone in literary circles had called to congratulate Eva on her long-awaited novel.

By the end of the week, it had broken records for the fastest selling novel. She was invited on talk shows the world over, and TIME Magazine offered her the cover. Eva was overwhelmed by all the attention and asked her agent to sift out the most important events for her to do.

It was a whirlwind, and Eva and Charles barely saw each other for several weeks following the publication as Eva was whisked around the country doing press. She agreed to a book tour of North America and one of Australia and New Zealand, which were her biggest markets, and highly recommended by her agent. Charles decided to put his own book on hold for a couple of months so he could travel with Eva. They hadn't been back to Australia since Lizzie's disappearance but had kept in touch with Jennifer and Bill regularly. Ellen wrote to them from time to time too, asking how they were. Sydney was scheduled as the last stop on the tour and Eva and Charles planned to visit their friends for a holiday; they'd need to relax after the number of dates planned. Eva was secretly hoping some news about Lizzie would turn up, or that she'd see her mother on a TV show or attend one of the book signings.

Charles and Eva didn't get much chance for sightseeing throughout the US and Canada. They were whisked between cities and moved from hotel rooms to book shops to the occasional restaurant, and vowed to return one day to see the sights they'd missed out on. Touching down in Sydney after a whistle-stop tour of Australia, Charles held Eva's hand, a little concerned about how they would both react to being in Sydney again

'Are you okay?' he wondered, as much about himself as Eva.

'I think so,' Eva replied. 'I'm tired though, glad we're coming to the end.'

Melbourne had been particularly busy with the TV shows, but the end was in sight. There were only two more functions to attend, and they could begin to enjoy their holiday with their friends. Eva had remained positive throughout the trip and although she had hopes, she wasn't going to let them take over and control her holiday.

After the final book signing, Charles and Eva were happy to spend time alone and returned to their hotel room to order room service. They enjoyed an expensive bottle of wine, sitting on the bed mindlessly watching TV.

'I watched you as you were speaking today,' Charles mused. Eva looked at him, wondering how he had noticed. She'd thought she was being discreet.

'I should have known I couldn't get anything past you,' she sighed.

'I only noticed because I was doing the same thing. You were looking for her weren't you, in the crowd?'

'I was. I kept on seeing her too, in my head.' Eva's underlying sadness radiated through as she fought to hide her feelings.

'Eva, please don't do that, don't hide from me. We promised we wouldn't go back to that.' Charles reached his fingers to her chin and gently turned her face to look at him. 'You're not alone in this, okay? We'll get through it together.'

Eva nodded. 'I thought being back here would be good for me but...' her breath caught as she felt a lump growing in her throat and her eyes began to leak. 'I just keep seeing ghosts.'

Charles wrapped her in his arms and they both let their sorrow spill out. It was going to be harder than expected but they had each other. They would get through it, as Charles had said.

The following morning after checking out of the hotel, Bill picked them up and drove them to their house where Jennifer was busily preparing lunch.

'Charles, Eva, it's so good to see you both,' Jennifer cried as she flung the door open to greet them. 'Come in, come in,' she told them, ushering them through the doorway. 'We saw you on TV, didn't we Bill? We had no idea you were so famous, we thought Charles here was the famous one. Turns out you're both bigwigs in the book world.'

Eva smiled at her friend. They'd exchanged many letters over the years and had developed a very close relationship, discussing things very personal to themselves. It was wonderful to see Jennifer again.

'I'm so happy to see you Jen, it's been a long time.' Eva hugged her friend. 'How are you?'

'I'm really well. I've been looking forward to seeing you again, under different circumstances. I know life will never be the same without Lizzie in it, but I'm so glad the two of you managed to sort things out. You deserve happiness.' Jen knew a lot of what had gone on between Eva and Charles over the last few years and was thrilled when they got back on track.

'Thank you, Jen. Your letters meant so much to me during those difficult times; I'm not sure I would've got through it without you.' Eva welled up. 'But we're good now, writing the book helped me work through a lot of things too. I just hope Lizzie gets to read it, or at least has seen me on TV. That's the main reason I agreed to the tour, for her. To reach out and give her some hope.'

Jen grasped Eva's hand. 'I hope so too Eva.'

Jen and Bill had an action-packed schedule planned for Charles and Eva's visit. They took them to all the tourist sights they didn't get chance to visit on their previous trip. Some days were better than others for Eva. She'd never forgotten Lizzie but being in Australia heightened her memories of their daughter, some places more than others. Lizzie had always loved the natural world so their trip to the Blue Mountains was particularly poignant. Eva tried to see it how Lizzie would have, through the lens of her camera, trying to choose an angle to get the best shot. As they rode the scenic railway down to view the Three Sisters, Charles watched Eva retreat into herself. He knew her so well; he could always feel her pain and he knew she was suffering right now.

'Hey, my love, what's going on?' he breathed discreetly in her ear.

Eva broke her stare and turned to him, smiling sadly. 'Just thinking how much she would love this. I wonder if she's ever been here.'

Charles squeezed her hand. 'She would love it and her photos would be spectacular.'

The railway car reached the bottom, and the guests all vacated the ride. They followed the walkway down towards the vantage point with the best view of the Three Sisters. Bill told them the Aboriginal dreamtime story of how the rock formations came to be and Charles was fascinated by the ancient legend. He watched Eva admiring the view and caught a smile on her face, a look of serenity. Charles reached his arm around her shoulder and pulled her towards him, kissing her temple.

'What are you thinking?'

Eva snuggled her head into the crook of his neck, 'I was just thinking of another family of three sisters very close to our hearts.'

Charles laughed. 'Of course! How could I forget our very own three sisters? We have a lot to thank them for.'

'We sure do, without our beloved Brontë sisters, we never would have met.' Eva remembered that first meeting fondly.

Charles tipped her chin with his finger and kissed her. 'I love you so much.'

'I love you too my darling.'

'Come on you two lovebirds, time to move.' Jen smiled at their tender moment, warmed by the fact that their love was still so solid. She'd worried for a long time that their marriage wouldn't survive their loss. Some of the letters she'd received from Eva had just about broken her heart, but here they were, solid as the rocks before them and Jen was thrilled. She could only hope their daughter would be encouraged by Eva's book, or her television appearances to come forward and reach out to complete their circle of happiness.

'Sorry, we're coming,' Eva blushed. Charles still gave her butterflies even after all these years. It had been difficult for her not feeling his touch for those years, but she was so grateful they hadn't completely given up on each other and had found their way back together.

Eva and Charles had a wonderful time with their friends, who were the most gracious hosts. They'd taken them everywhere they could possibly think of and finished their trip with lunch at a famous harbour side fish and chip restaurant. Sipping on a crisp Sauvignon blanc, they enjoyed a long, leisurely lunch overlooking the ocean. It was a perfect way to finish their holiday, and the long book tour.

It had been good for Charles and Eva to get away, and they both agreed they needed to travel more often. The two couples chatted happily between themselves, reminiscing about their adventures over the last few weeks and planning future trips together.

'I know we met under terrible circumstances, but I am so grateful that Ellen brought you into our lives,' Jen began. 'I really do value our friendship.' She reached across the table and squeezed Eva's hand.

'Me too,' Eva replied. 'You're both very special to us.'

Eva suddenly tensed as she caught a glimpse out of the corner of her eye. A young woman was pushing a pram, a toddler skipping along by her side. She felt her heart begin to race, and her breathing quickened. Charles watched, startled by her sudden agitation. He followed her eyes to see what she had seen, and there in the distance he saw what had made her stop.

'Oh God, Eva is that her?' Charles choked.

Their faces were both ashen and neither could move from their seat. Jen and Bill looked on, concerned.

'What is it? Have you seen her?' Jen asked.

Charles suddenly scraped his chair back as the young woman disappeared around the corner. He ran from the restaurant, heading in the direction the woman had gone. His eyes darted in all directions trying to spot her, but she'd vanished. He slowed down, taking more time to look properly and as he slowly made his way towards the road, his heart sank. He began to berate himself for sitting for so long before making a move, he should've acted faster. Leaning against a lamppost to catch his breath, he saw a car pull away from the kerb. Emerald green eyes stared out of the window of the passenger seat and locked with his for a second. Her face jarred by shock, and then brimming with shame at seeing her father, she turned her head. Charles ran after the car, dodging vehicles on the road until he could no longer keep up. Hands on his knees, his heavy breathing broke into sobs, and he slid to the ground.

'Charles!' Bill's voice shouted through the busy street as he saw his friend bereft on the floor, clutching his knees to his chest. Eva followed closely behind, tears shedding for her husband.

'Charles, are you hurt? Was it Lizzie?' Eva panted.

Charles nodded, unable to speak.

'You're hurt?'

He shook his head and managed a few words, 'it was her.'

Bill helped Charles to his feet and led him to a nearby bench to catch his breath. Charles's sobs slowly eased as Eva's voice gently calmed him.

'I couldn't see where she'd gone at first and then just as I'd given up and thought maybe we'd been mistaken, I saw her. She was in the passenger seat of a car; I couldn't see the driver.'

'Did she see you?' Eva asked.

Charles nodded. 'She saw me, she looked so sad, so ashamed. Eva, why didn't she stop? Am I such a bad father?'

Eva's tears welled up in her eyes. 'This isn't about us Charles. And it isn't about Lizzie. This is him, it's his doing. We were right about him, he's controlling her.'

Jen arrived to join them after staying behind to pay the bill in the restaurant. Bill took her hand and led her away to explain what she'd missed.

Charles and Eva sat together in silence on the bench, the pair shedding more tears over their loss. Seeing her there stabbed them both through the heart like a knife.

'Eva,' Charles sniffed, a sudden wave of realisation sweeping over him. 'We're grandparents.'

Charlie 2019

I was nervous as we pulled into the car park for our 9.30am appointment. I'd brought all the documents we could find; my birth certificates, both my amended one, and my original one that we'd found in the box, my adoption certificate, my passport, driving licence and all the correspondence Mum could find from the time we first went to live with her and my dad.

The waiting room was grey and uninviting. We sat on hard plastic seats, and I twiddled my finger through my hair, twisting it until it was knotted. Mum brushed my hand away and gave me a knowing smile.

'You've done that your whole life whenever you've been nervous,' she reminded me. 'When you first came to us you had this big, matted clump above your right ear. It took a while before you'd let me tease it out.' Mum smiled at the memory, and I grasped her hand, grateful that she was there with me.

'Charlotte Flowers,' a tall lady with a mass of black curls and bright green glasses called my name.

Mum and I stood and followed her into a small room. There was a table and four chairs, a ceramic vase with plastic flowers sat in the centre. It was only slightly more inviting than the waiting room.

'So, Charlotte, you're trying to find records from when you were adopted, is that right?' She introduced herself as Erica.

We discussed the details and what we already knew, and Mum explained how she'd known I'd come from a violent home, and they'd decided they didn't need to know the details.

After checking all my documents to confirm I was who I was claiming to be, the case worker opened the file sitting on the table in front of her. She scanned the documents and took an audible breath.

'I'm sorry to inform you that your birth parents, Michael and Elizabeth Marsh, are both deceased.'

It really didn't come as a shock. The limited memories I had of my mother told me she would never have given us up unless something tragic had happened, but the confirmation still hit me hard. Mum took my hand and gave me a squeeze.

'Are you able to tell me the circumstances?' I asked, not sure if I really wanted to know.

Erica's face looked ashen, and I saw her hesitate. Her voice quaked as she delivered the news.

'It was a domestic violence situation. Elizabeth had been strangled, and Michael died from knife wounds. She was pronounced dead at the scene, and he died on the way to hospital. The triple zero call was from a young boy.' Compassion poured from her voice as she choked on her words. 'I'm so sorry Charlotte, this must be extremely difficult to hear. I assume the boy was your brother?'

Mum and I exchanged a look, and I nodded sadly.

'He passed away a few months ago, car accident.'

'I'm so very sorry for your loss.' Her voice was kind, and she gave us a few moments to gather ourselves before I remembered to ask about Elizabeth's parents.

'Do you know if Elizabeth had any family? I guess I'm wondering why my brother and I were put up for adoption and didn't go to live with grandparents or aunts and uncles.'

Erica scanned through the file, her eyes skimming backwards and forwards across the pages. She frowned and looked up. 'There's no details about Elizabeth's family. It does say here that Michael's parents were deceased though.'

I glanced at Mum, and she frowned.

'Thank you for all the information Erica,' I said, standing up. 'You've been a great help.' Mum stood beside me, and we both shook Erica's hand.

'It's my pleasure. Please let me know if I can be of any further assistance.' She turned as she opened the door for us. 'Once again, I'm very sorry for your loss.'

Mum and I both smiled our thanks.

I opened the passenger door of Mum's car and sighed as I collapsed down into the seat. Mum started the engine quickly and turned the air con on full.

'Are you okay honey?' Her voice was quietly concerned.

'I'm fine Mum. Like you said, I was confirming what I knew. I am confused about the grandparents though; I wonder why they didn't take us. Surely if your daughter had been murdered, taking in her kids would be something you would do.'

Mum mulled over her thoughts before voicing them to me. She obviously didn't want to say anything to upset me, she was still treading on eggshells around me.

'We don't know the situation, it's difficult to judge,' she said.

'I guess so. Maybe they can answer that themselves. I think I'll do what you said and check out their Facebook pages if they have them.' I quickly calculated that they'd be in their seventies by now.

'They're famous authors, they'll have them,' Mum reassured me. 'Come on, let's get home and we can have a look.'

Mum started the engine and pulled out of the car park as I sat back and closed my eyes, thinking about the crazy direction in which my life had turned. I wanted to share it all with Beau and I was starting to come around to the idea that he had only done what he thought was right.

I must've fallen asleep on the way home, and I jolted awake when Mum switched off the engine in our driveway.

'Come on sleepy head,' Mum teased.

I scrubbed at my face with my hands trying to wake myself up and yawned as I manoeuvred my crutches and navigated my way out of the car.

Inside, I grabbed my laptop and opened it on the kitchen bench top as Mum busied herself in the kitchen making coffee.

I logged into my Facebook page and carefully typed Eva Hartley in the search bar. There were several listed so I clicked on the top entry. It was a verified author page not a personal account. I scrolled through to see if I could find any information or a way to contact her. There was nothing. I tried searching again to see if I could find a personal page but none of the entries were the correct Eva Hartley. I searched Charles, and again his was an author page but it did have a link to send messages.

'Mum, what should I write?' I wasn't sure how I should word it. What do you say to your long-lost grandparents?

'You're the writer in the family Charlie, not me.' Mum realised what she'd just said, and her face fell. 'I guess it's obvious where you got your writing gene from,' she mused.

'You're still my mum, and always will be. This doesn't change anything for us,' I reassured her.

'I know honey, it's just all a little confronting. I knew we should've spoken to you about it when you were younger, I guess I was putting off the inevitable. I knew you'd be curious, and I also knew Tom would have some memories. I regret that he suffered because your dad and I were too scared to face it, and I regret that the two of you never had a chance to go on this journey together. I'm so sorry sweetheart.' Tears pricked Mum's eyes as her apology spilled out.

'I know Mum, I forgive you. We have to move on.' She nodded as I thought about the other person I needed to find forgiveness for.

I began to type.

Dear Charles…

It sounded too informal.

Dear Mr Hartley,

I apologise for the directness of this message, but I was wondering if you had a daughter named Elizabeth who lived in Perth, Australia? My name is Charlotte Flowers, and I was adopted at the age of three along with my five-year-old brother, Tom. Due to difficult circumstances, I have only recently found this out and after a little research I now understand the reason for my adoption. My birth mother was Elizabeth Marsh, and I found this photo in a box of her belongings that my adoptive mother had saved for me. The photo has the names Charles, Eva and Lizzie written on the back, and I think you may be my grandfather. I'm not sure if you're aware of the circumstances or if you even know I exist, but if there's any possibility that I am your granddaughter I would love to get to know you.

I took a quick snap of the photo and added it to the message.

My hands were shaking by the time I'd finished, and Mum handed me a much needed coffee.

Eva 2019

Eva sat in the sunroom in her old rocking chair looking out over the moors. The chair had seen many repairs over the years, but she had never had the heart to let it go, it seemed to have its own soul. It was the source of so many memories, both happy and sad, and she smiled wistfully now as she thought back on her life with Charles. They'd had a good life together, although marred with tragedy. They'd been back to Australia several times over the years, spending time with their dear friends Bill and Jennifer but had never heard any news about the whereabouts of Lizzie. It still pained them to this day, but they had found a way to live with their sadness in a way that it didn't consume their life. They'd both found huge success as writers in their own genres; Eva had won the coveted Booker Prize for her novel "Controlled," and she'd gone on to write several more novels before finally retiring several years before.

Charles had continued his writing and had recently published the twentieth book in his crime series. He had told Eva that would be his last, although she'd been dubious until he'd killed off his protagonist. He did have one more book up his sleeve he'd told her; he wanted to write their memoir, together. Eva was touched by his suggestion but the thought of reliving those difficult years scared her. She'd told him she would think about it.

She watched him now as he sat in his favourite chair, playing word games on his iPad. Her lips curled as she reflected on the wonderful conversations they'd had over the years, discussing everything from literature to art to politics. They didn't agree on everything, but they had learnt to disagree harmoniously, most of the time anyway. She'd felt disappointment in the beginning when her father had thrown her out, but she'd known deep in her heart that she was making the right decision in marrying Charles. She couldn't imagine what her life would have been had she not made the stand against her parents. Her thoughts drifted to Lizzie, and she wondered how her life had turned out. Her stomach soured thinking about her daughter, Eva had been sure Lizzie would get in touch eventually. Knowing she had two children had made the situation so much harder. They would've loved to have grandchildren to spoil.

Charles's voice broke her reverie.

'Eva.'

Charles looked like he'd seen a ghost and Eva began to panic, thinking he was having a heart attack.

'Charles, what's wrong? Are you okay?' Eva sat forward on her chair, her full attention on her husband.

'I'm fine, but you should read this,' Charles gestured towards his iPad.

'What is it?' Eva questioned.

'I've got a message from a young lady by the name of Charlotte Flowers. She says she's our granddaughter.'

Eva gawked at him tying to comprehend what he'd just said.

'Our granddaughter? Did she mention Lizzie?' Eva's face brightened.

Charles scanned the message again.

'Only that she's her daughter, but it says here that she was adopted when she was young.'

'What does that mean? Why was she adopted?' Eva was stricken. 'Charles, Lizzie wouldn't give up her daughter.'

Charles sank to the floor and knelt before her, holding her hands in his. They stared at each other for a long moment as the undeniable reality of the situation knocked the wind out of them, and their hearts broke into a million tiny pieces. They grasped each other sobbing, knowing that their worst fear had come true.

Charles and Eva sat in silence; their hearts heavy. Eva's thoughts were ticking over.

'Charles, did this young lady say anything else? I mean, is there proof that she's definitely our granddaughter? And why now?'

Charles leaned over to reach his iPad, reading the message out loud to Eva.

'She says here she's only just found out she was adopted. And she's attached this photo, Eva.' He turned the iPad around to show her the picture of them from years before when they'd first visited their daughter.

Eva clapped her hands to her face, the proof right there before her own eyes.

'There's an email address and a phone number here Eva,' Charles croaked, his voice thick with emotion.

Eva contemplated Charles's comment, her eyes swollen and glazed as they fixed on him, trying to process the roller coaster of emotions. She willed herself to say something but nothing that came to mind felt right. How could she find harmony between the joy of having a granddaughter and the likely death of her daughter?

'Eva, my love, we've waited for news for over twenty years, this is our chance to find out the truth. As things stand right now, we have nothing to lose. We have a granddaughter out there who wants to know us and other than Lizzie coming home, I don't see what could be better than that.' Charles was gentle with his wife, he knew she wanted this as much as he did, he just needed her to know that too.

Charles could see the fear in Eva's eyes, and he took her face gently in his hands. 'We don't know how much time we have left Eva, please, we need this.'

'I'm scared Charles. As much as I would love to know our grandchild, I'm not sure I'm ready to know the truth about Lizzie. The only reason

I've managed to keep going all these years is the hope I've held in my heart. What if I don't have that anymore?'

'Eva, you have me, and you have a granddaughter. This young girl has grown up without knowing her mother, she deserves to know her family. We failed our daughter; we are not going to do the same to our granddaughter.' Charles kissed Eva's lips gently, his thumbs tenderly wiping away her tears.

'What time is it in Australia now?' Eva asked. 'Did you say Perth?'

Charles smiled at his wife affectionately and checked the world clock on his iPad.

'It's six o'clock in Perth. Should we message first or just call?'

'Let's call. Like you said we have nothing to lose,' Eva said.

'Okay,' Charles said. 'Here goes.'

The two of them moved over to the settee so they could sit together. Charles pressed the video call icon on the screen, and they waited.

Butterflies thrashed around in Eva's stomach while they waited for the connection.

'Hello.' They heard a familiar Australian accent before the picture appeared. When Charlie finally appeared on the screen, Eva and Charles both gasped. It was like seeing Lizzie again. They both stared at the screen speechless.

'Hello,' her voice was hesitant, wary. 'I'm so glad you called.'

'Charlotte, hello,' Charles stuttered. 'I'm sorry, we're both lost for words, you look so much like your mum.'

Charlie smiled sadly. 'She was very pretty; you must miss her. And please, call me Charlie.'

Eva eventually found her voice. 'Charlie, do you know what happened? Why you were adopted?' she asked in barely a whisper.

Charlie looked shocked and cast her eyes to Anna for support. Anna grasped her hand, nodding for her to tell her story.

'I'm so sorry, I had no idea you didn't know. I've been wondering why my brother and I were adopted and not sent to live with relatives.' Charlie took a breath as Charles and Eva braced themselves.

'My parents both died when I was three.'

Charles and Eva took some time to console each other. Charles hugged his wife tight, and Charlie felt immediate affection for her grandparents, giving them time to grieve.

'Was it an accident?' Charles asked once he'd regained some composure.

Charlie's eyes brimmed with tears, fearful that the next part of the story would destroy them. She hesitated.

'It's okay sweetheart, you can tell us. Was it him? Was it your father?' Eva encouraged gently.

Charlie blew out a puff of air, collecting herself. 'I only learnt this today so it's all very raw for me. My father killed my mother, and then he died from injuries on the way to hospital.' There was an audible gasp from both Charles and Eva.

Eva wiped at the tears that had spilled down her cheeks and Charles shook his head mournfully.

'I'm so sorry.' Charlie was heartbroken by their reactions, and they all needed a moment to collect their thoughts before they continued their conversation.

Charles explained to Charlie the concerns they'd had when Lizzie had married Mick so quickly and then had disappeared and stopped calling them. They told her about his stint in prison for assaulting his ex-girlfriend and their numerous trips to Australia to search for them.

'We suspected abuse for a long time, but no one would help us,' Eva sighed. 'I think, deep down, we knew this outcome was inevitable but we never stopped hoping she'd manage to escape him one day. I'm sorry Charlie, this is your father we're talking about, it must be difficult for you to reconcile.'

Charlie shook her head vehemently. 'No, I don't have many memories from before I was adopted, but I do remember being terrified of my father. And knowing that he murdered my mother... well, I have absolutely no feelings for him whatsoever,' Charlie confirmed, and Eva nodded in sympathy.

'Can I ask you something?' Charlie ventured.

'You can ask us anything sweetheart,' Eva encouraged.

'Your book, "Controlled," it's about them, isn't it? My mum and dad?' Charlie was a little embarrassed asking such a question to her famous grandparents.

'You've read my book?' Eva asked, flattered that her granddaughter would have read her book that had been written before she was even born.

'I've read all your books, I'm a big fan,' Charlie replied sheepishly. 'Of both of you,' she added, not wanting to offend her grandfather.

'Yes, it was about Lizzie and Mick,' Eva said, sadly. 'Even though we didn't know for sure what was going on, we couldn't think of any other reason that our beloved daughter would cut off contact with us. We knew in our hearts that he was controlling her, abusing her. I thought it was something people needed to be aware of.'

Charlie nodded, unsure what to say next. She was just so happy to have found them.

'Charlie?' Charles asked. 'Can I ask you something in return?'

'Of course, anything,' she replied.

'Have you been happy? Have you had a good life so far?' Charles wanted desperately for that to be the case, but he worried when a cloud fell across Charlie's face. She looked deep in thought before she replied.

'I've had a wonderful life; my adoptive parents have been amazing.' She glanced above the camera and smiled, and Charles assumed she was looking at them now. 'Unfortunately, this year has been difficult. We've suffered a huge tragedy.'

Charlie told them about her dad and Tom, and then the situation with her mum and Beau. Her mum had nodded her approval from across the table before she shared her story.

'Oh, Charlie sweetheart, I'm so sorry. I want to give you a big hug,' Eva cried.

Charlie laughed through newly spilled tears. 'That would be amazing. I'd love to meet you both.'

Charlie 2019

My leg was finally out of its cast, and I was beginning to get my strength back thanks to the physical therapy. I was desperate to get in the ocean now the weather had warmed up, but I wasn't sure I was at that stage yet. I could finally get around by myself and as much as I'd enjoyed connecting with Mum again over the last few weeks, it felt good to get my freedom back.

I'd decided not to contact Beau until I was feeling stronger. If there was any chance of our relationship working out, it had to be as equals and not because I needed him. I wanted to be healthy, both physically and mentally and I felt like I'd finally got there. I'd come to terms with some difficult information, but Mum and I had worked through it together and I felt ready to move forward. It was time.

Hey Beau, I typed.

I saw that he'd read my message straight away and I held my breath waiting for the three little dots to tell me he was replying.
There was nothing.
I felt sick.
Then I saw them and started to panic.

Hey.
It's good to hear from you.
How are you?

The relief was clear on my face. A grin appeared and I continued to type.

I'm good. How are you?
Better now I've heard from you x

The grin on my face couldn't possibly get any bigger.

I was wondering if you'd like to meet up. I feel we have unfinished business. I was thinking about our look out in the hills.

This was the tester.

I can be there in an hour. I'll bring the coffee xx

I sent him a smiley face in reply and rushed around getting ready to go. Mum was sitting on the deck with her Kindle, catching the sun. She looked up as I slid the screen door open.
'I'm going out to meet Beau.'
She smiled, 'drive safely.'
"I will.'

Driving up the winding road, nerves began to catch up with me and I turned up the radio to try and drown them out. As I pulled into the gravel parking area I looked around for Beau's motorbike and felt a sudden onset of guilt when I remembered I'd trashed it. I wondered what had happened to it and if he'd got a replacement.

I noticed a small car parked up and caught sight of him leaning on the rail, two paper coffee cups in his hands. My heart raced at that first glimpse, giving me pause before I stepped out of my car. My muscles were a little stiff after the drive, so I quickly stretched out before I walked carefully and slowly towards him. He took a deep breath when he felt my presence beside him and handed me a cup without saying a word. I immediately felt the electricity between us.

'Thanks,' I told him, and looked away quickly.

I leaned on the rail next to him and sipped my coffee. I turned my head to peek at him and discovered he was blatantly staring at me.

'You look good.' His voice was croaky. 'I've missed you so much.'

I smiled at him. 'I've missed you too.' My free hand rested on top of his on the railing and he turned it over to lace our fingers together. His touch felt explosive, and I felt an inexplicable need to make small talk otherwise I was going to get way ahead of myself.

'Thanks for getting my phone back to me. And Tom's jacket,' I added. Kate had dropped them off when they'd been released by the police. Apparently, they'd been kept with Beau's bike as evidence.

Beau looked at me, seemingly amused by the small talk, aware that neither of us were good at it.

'I'm so sorry about your bike, I'll make it up to you, I promise,' I told him.

'No need, I'm just glad you're okay.' His deep concern for me, and his complete dismissal of what I'd done shattered me. I felt tears brim my eyes and he pulled me in for a hug. My face buried in his chest, I breathed him in for the first time in what felt like forever. His head rested on the top of mine, and I could feel him breathe in the scent of my hair. My nerve endings had woken up and I felt alive again, desperate for his touch. I pulled back and reached my fingers to his face, pulling him in for a kiss. It was soft at first, a gentle brushing of our lips, until we both lost our composure, and our tongues fought for control. His hands ran over my body firmly, then skimming the waistband of my shorts with his fingers, he stilled, and his body relaxed into me, his mouth moving more slowly, his tongue gently stroking mine. He drew away slightly, his eyes fixed on mine, an unspoken declaration of love swimming in his gaze.

We caught our breath and I smiled shyly at him before turning back to the view and picking up my coffee. We stood together, a comfortable silence taking over for a while. His body shifted slightly to the right so that his front was up against my side, and his right hand draped around my back, resting on my hip. I tipped my head to the left, resting in the crook of his arm. I was right where I needed to be, I felt home.

'How's your mum?' Beau broke the silence, his voice quietly concerned.

'She's good, we've spent a long time talking things over, coming to terms with our loss, and the adoption.' I felt him tense at the mention of my adoption. It was time to address that elephant in the room.

'It's okay Beau, I know you were doing what you thought was best. It hurt me, I'm not gonna lie, but I forgive you.' He squeezed me with his arm to show his appreciation.

'I know it was wrong Charlie, I see that now. You should've been my priority and I let you down. I promise I will never do that again. I thought I'd lost you and it broke my heart. I've been so grateful for the little snippets Kate has told me about your recovery, and I've never stopped hoping that this wasn't over.' His sincerity made my heart burst, and I had no idea how I'd gone so long without him in my life.

'I never wanted it to be over Beau. I just needed to get through all my shit by myself. I didn't want to be reliant on you to fix me. I want our relationship to be based on love, not trauma. There's been way too much of that in both our lives. I think we both deserve more than that.'

His face beamed, his eyes brighter than I'd ever seen them, as he leaned down to drop a kiss on the top of my head.

'God, I love you,' he murmured into my hair.

We headed down the hill to a little cafe for lunch. I was grateful for the few minutes alone in my car to gather my thoughts together, it had been an emotional morning and I felt drained by the depth of our conversation. But at the same time, I was on a high like I'd never felt before. I had so much to tell Beau, and so many plans for my immediate future. I was excited, but also a little nervous as to what his reaction would be.

After we'd ordered, we passed our menus to the waitress and Beau began to fill two glasses from the water jug on the table.

'So, I've got something to tell you,' I ventured.

Beau was silent, a little nervous perhaps.

'Mum helped me find out about my birth parents,' I said. Beau looked at me warily, knowing what I was about to say couldn't be good. He reached across the table and took my hand.

'Go on,' he encouraged me to continue.

I took a deep breath and then blurted it out. 'He killed her Beau, the day we were taken away.'

A single tear trickled down Beau's cheek and rested precariously on his chin, his heart breaking for the both of us. I reached over and wiped the tear, leaving my hand on his cheek for a moment.

He let out a slow breath, steadying himself. 'I'm so sorry Charlie.'

'Tom dialled triple zero, the records show the transcript. He told them his daddy was hurting his mummy. Beau, he must've lived with that memory his whole life. He was five years old; it breaks my heart that he never got the chance to share it with me.'

'I know,' Beau said, and I was profoundly aware just how much he understood.

I could see in his eyes that he had questions, but he wasn't sure what to ask.

'My father died of stab wounds, he bled out on the way to hospital. I'm not sure whether they were self-inflicted or if my mum fought back.' My statement was matter of fact. I had no emotions for him or his memory. From what I knew, he was a monster, and I was glad I didn't have to deal with the guilt that Beau did over his own father's death.

'Have you processed it all Charlie?' Beau asked, obviously worried.

'I think so, Kate has been a great help,' I paused before telling him the good news. 'It's not all bad Beau, some good has come of all this.' I smiled at the thought of what I was about to tell him.

'I have grandparents, and they're alive. They live in England and I'm going to go visit them.'

Beau's surprise was written all over his face and his smile lit him up. 'That's amazing Charlie, I'm so happy for you. When will you go?' His smile faltered a little, and I could see his mind turning to the thought that he was about to lose me again.

'Soon I hope, it depends.'

'On what?' he asked.

'On whether you'd like to come with me.' I said hopefully.

'You want me to come and meet your grandparents in England?' Beau asked incredulously.

'You don't want to?' I asked, disappointed.

'No, it's not that, I would love to. I'm just shocked, I guess. This morning I didn't even know if I'd ever see you again, now you're planning an overseas trip with me.' I realised he needed time to process all this new information. I'd been planning all this without his knowledge, and it was unfair to just expect him to catch up.

'I'm sorry, I've jumped the gun a little. I guess I had it all planned out in my head and just expected you to fall in line. I was wrong, I'm sorry. I know you have your own life.' I'd been so thoughtless, and I felt a little foolish.

'Charlie, I'm not saying no. I honestly would love to come if we can time it right, you just caught me off guard, that's all. I mean, I've not even met your mum yet. Well, not properly anyway.'

'Well, we can fix that right now if you like,' I said eagerly.

Beau laughed at my childlike excitement, and I suddenly felt like Rosie with her enthusiasm about everything.

'I'd love that,' Beau smiled.

I grabbed his hand as we left the cafe and he walked with me to my car.

'Oh, and Beau?' I added, as I climbed in my car.

'Yes?'

'My grandparents are Charles and Eva Hartley,' I taunted him. I closed my door and drove off, leaving him staring after me open-mouthed.

I reached my house a little before Beau, so I let myself inside to tell mum he was on his way.

'I'm glad you sorted things out Charlie, I'm looking forward to meeting him.'

The doorbell rang on cue, and I ran to answer it to find Beau standing there with flowers. That was obviously why he took longer than me to get here. I smiled at his thoughtfulness and stood back to let him in. He didn't even wait for introductions; he just walked right up to my mum and handed her the bouquet.

'Mrs Flowers, it's good to finally meet you,' he said formally, and I squirmed a little inside, but knew Mum would love him immediately.

'Thank you, and please call me Anna. I'd like to say thank you for being there for Charlie,' she paused at my name, knowing Beau had been a big catalyst behind the reason I changed it. 'You were there for her when I wasn't, so I'm grateful to you.'

'And I'd like to apologise for being the reason she almost lost her life; I will never again own a motorbike.' Mum nodded, grateful for his honesty and I looked at Beau questioningly. I knew how much he'd loved his bike, how much I loved riding it with him.

'Beau, no,' I told him. 'Don't say that, you love riding. Don't stop that because of me.'

'Charlie, I'm not even having this conversation. My decision is made. You are way more important.' His voice was firm, and I wasn't about to challenge him on it.

'Come and have some coffee, I was just about to make some,' Mum said smiling at both of us. We wandered through to the lounge room and Beau whispered to me, 'Charles and Eva Hartley?'

I nodded and grinned at his disbelief.

The three of us sat and chatted over coffee, about the future, our plans and the next steps we would take to begin to rebuild our lives. There had been so much trauma and loss for all three of us, but it was time to move forward. It was time, not to forget, but to learn to live in peace with the past and grasp the future with both hands.

Epilogue

The taxi leaves the motorway and descends into the lush green countryside of Yorkshire. The twists and turns take a little getting used to after spending my life on the long, straight roads of Perth. Only the roads snaking their way up to our lookout resemble anything like these winding roads.

I look across the back seat of the car at Beau. I'm so excited to be here but even more so that he came with me. I smile at him watching every new moment pass him by. He's like a kid at Christmas and I love that I'm getting to share his excitement with him. He's such a deep thinker, and he's had his fair share of difficulties, this isn't a side of him I get to see often. He catches me watching him and reaches his hand across to hold mine.

'I love you.' He mouths the words to me, and I do the same in return.

I spot a road sign directing us to Haworth and butterflies begin to flap wildly in my stomach.

'I don't know why I feel so nervous,' I tell Beau. 'We've spoken so many times on video calls.'

'It's different, you get to hug them. They're a part of you Charlie. I'm sure they're even more nervous, I can't imagine how they're going to feel seeing you in the flesh. You must remind them so much of their daughter, you're so alike.'

I hadn't thought of that. We sit in silence for a while and enjoy the rest of the journey. My excitement starts to build again as we begin to see the moors, the backdrop for the Brontës novels. I know a little of my grandparents' love of the Brontë Sisters. Once I found out they lived in Haworth, the home of my favourite authors, I couldn't wait to ask them questions. Charles told me I'd have to wait to hear the story of how they met until I saw them in person. Eva told me it would be worth the wait. It seems crazy to me to have so much in common with an elderly couple I've never met, but we connected immediately. I can only hope it feels the same in person.

The taxi pulls up outside an idyllic looking stone cottage and the butterflies return with a vengeance. I look at Beau and he smiles reassuringly.

'Here we are, I'll get your bags.' The driver announces our arrival and jumps out of the car.

As we're stood at the rear of the car getting our bags, a tall figure appears behind us with a wad of cash. He speaks to the driver and hands over some money to pay for our ride.

227

Dumbfounded by the speed of the transaction, Beau and I stand and stare as the driver jumps back in his car and drives off.

Gathering myself together, I turn to my grandfather and before I know it, I'm swept up into the warmest hug.

'I'm so glad you're here sweetheart, you don't know what this means to us,' he whispers in my ear. I can feel his tears as he kisses my cheek and I'm overwhelmed by a huge surge of love for this man that I've never met before. He feels like family. He feels like home. When he finally lets me go and goes to shake Beau's hand, I hear Beau introduce himself as I lock eyes for the first time with my grandmother. She's standing nervously at the garden gate, her eyes glassy as she takes me in. I walk over to her and hold my arms out. She feels so tiny in my embrace as I hold her tight and we cry together for all that we've lost, and all that we've now found.

Beau brings our luggage as Charles and Eva usher us inside. I take in my surroundings, awed by the number of books cluttering every imaginable space. I glance at Beau knowing he'll be just as awestruck as I am.

'Can I get you both a drink and something to eat? Are you hungry? Do you need to use the bathroom?' Eva falls over herself to make us feel comfortable.

'I'd love a coffee if you have it,' I tell her.

'Of course love, I bought one of those pod machines especially for my favourite granddaughter.'

'You didn't have to do that.' I was touched by her thoughtfulness.

'Nonsense, I'll spoil you as much as I like. Beau?' she asks him the same question.

'Black coffee for me too. Thank you, Mrs Hartley.'

'Oh, stop that, I'm Eva and this is Charles. You'll make me feel like an old lady if you call me Mrs Hartley, and I know Charles has had enough of being called Mr Hartley after thirty years teaching.'

Charles laughs and shows us through to a large airy room at the back of the house. It looks like it's been added on after the original build, with large windows overlooking the moors.

'It seems so familiar to me,' I say to no one in particular as I stand close to the window and look out at the view.

Eva comes in the room carrying a tray of mugs and a plate of cookies. She puts it on the coffee table and responds to my statement.

'It's Cathy and Heathcliff,' she says knowingly. My heart surges and I feel tears prick my eyes. Beau's arm wraps around me and he draws me in to his side.

'So, first things first,' he says. 'We're dying to hear the story of how you two met.'

The coffee hits the spot, and Beau and I settle on the couch and listen to Charles and Eva tell their story. They take it in turns to tell different parts and like a well-oiled machine they take us smoothly through to their wedding. At that point I jump up, remembering the pearl hair comb in my hand luggage. I take the box carefully from the bag and hand it to Eva.

'I think this belongs to you,' I tell her.

She carefully unwraps it from the tissue paper and gasps when she sees it again.

Charles picks up a double photo frame and hands it to me. The photographs are both black and white. The one on the left is of Eva aged just eighteen wearing a simple white ballerina style dress and the pearl comb. The one on the right is my birth mum, Lizzie, wearing a simple white linen dress with spaghetti straps, also with the pearl comb in her hair. I smile at the photo and then at my grandmother.

She carefully wraps the comb back up and returns it to the box.

'Thank you for bringing it for me,' she says, and then leans over and hands me the box. 'I'd like you to have it Charlie, something old for your own wedding day.' She glances at Beau and then back to me. I'm touched by the sentiment.

Beau kisses my head gently just above my ear and whispers, 'I can't wait.'

Acknowledgements

I've always wondered about the acknowledgement section in books. Have all those people mentioned really had an influence on the book getting published? When I began to think back to what got me to this point, I was surprised by the number of people who have had an effect on my lifelong dream to become a writer.

Firstly, I must thank the most important people in my life—my family. I love you all.

Bruce, who constantly supports and encourages my dreams, even if his main objective is for me to get rich so he can retire.

Lily, my reader child, who proofread the very early (and terrible) draft of this book, chapter by chapter, and told me she loved it. She inspired me to pick it back up years later and actually develop it into something I love too.

Izzy, my writer child, who could knock out a romance novel in her sleep, although going by all her past English essays, there's bound to be something deep and dark in there too! Thanks for all the inspiration!

Mum, who read (and kept) all my stories, and educated me that there were other ways to end a story than, 'and then they died.' I promise my endings have improved.

Craig, who helped me to develop my writing skills at a young age, when he nominated me as 'chief writer' on our Sunday morning 'Land and Sea Warfare' projects. I miss you.

My niece, Lauren, who may or may not be the inspiration for the Justin Bieber comment!

My Mother-in-law, Pat. The first time I went to her house I noticed there was a half-read book in each room, and I immediately felt at home. Thanks for all the book chats, and also the deep and meaningful, putting the world to rights chats!

My adorable kitties, Aspen and Blizzard, who walk across my keyboard and delete entire scenes at critical moments — who needs an editor?

And to my friends who are like family...

My dear friend Kate, our shared love of reading and writing cemented our long-distance friendship with our one-hundred-page letters throughout our teenage years. Thank you for staying the course for nearly thirty-five years, and always being there when I need you, you are truly special. I'm looking forward to drinking cocktails with you soon!

Rachel, Penny, Lorraine and Lee, my sounding board on our group chat whenever I'm stuck! Thank you for all the food, cocktails and laughs we share, and the numerous author talks and book signings we've been to over the years. I look forward to many more years of friendship.

Lisa and Darryl, who had absolutely nothing to do with me writing a book, but my life wouldn't be the same without them in it. I love you and miss you every day and I can't wait for the day the world is back to normal and I can hug you again.

Jo Fowler, for helping me get out of my own head so I could make my dream become a reality. I appreciate you.

The Facebook Ladybirds, an amazing space to learn, grow, and ask the stupid questions. I thank you for your valuable experience, knowledge and support.

Every author I have ever read, you have all inspired me in one way or another. My life wouldn't be the same without books.

About the Author

Lyndsey Jeminson grew up in Bingley, West Yorkshire, a stone's throw from Brontë Country. She moved to Perth, Western Australia where she lives with her husband and two daughters, along with their British Short Hair Silver Tabbies, Aspen and Blizzard. She has a Bachelor of Arts degree in History and Australian Indigenous Studies and loves nothing more than a walk on the beach and an almond latte.

Printed in Great Britain
by Amazon